THE MIND OF THE RADIANT

D. S. KOGLER

Chapter 1

Clouds like inky tendrils stretched across the sky as the ground shook from the dark forces awakening beneath it. Atop a hill overlooking the ruins of the Forgotten Temple hovered a transparent glowing beast in the shape of a fish. Atop the fish-like zodiac sat Birdie — the now de facto protector of Doxla. Five years had passed since she'd last faced the Great Destroyer Apollyon. The scars of her former battle still stained the land, and now it was time to put the terrible fiend down again.

An older man's voice behind her called out, though not to her. "Are we sure this is safe? We're awful close to that temple place."

Jax Ruthoree, the young captain of Birdie's most loyal soldiers known as the Shadow Guard, answered the man. "Relax, Waylen. Birdie's beaten this thing before. We don't have anything to worry about."

Jax maneuvered his horse closer to Birdie.

"Do we?" he asked her quietly. "Syrus still hasn't joined us."

"We knew he might not come," Birdie answered, not much for conversation at the moment.

She was confident she could win, but her last battle with Apollyon had very nearly been a loss. Thoughts of who was and wasn't present would only serve to distract her as she mentally went through Apollyon's weaknesses and abilities, acting out different scenarios in her head. The process was always unsettling yet strangely natural. It was as if another part of her that, at the same time wasn't part of her, existed for that exact purpose. She'd never told anyone else about that part of her, but she'd named said part her "othermind."

"What should we do, then?" Jax asked. "He's the only other one strong enough to do any good here."

"You came because you wanted to see the battle," Birdie finally turned her head towards Jax. "You and everyone else wait here and don't approach until I've put Apollyon back in the ground. If its darkness gets too close, retreat. Those are your orders."

Jax nodded, finally taking the hint, and brought his horse back closer to the rest of the group as the rumbling of the ground intensified. A horse on Birdie's left whinnied at the sudden change, nearly throwing its rider.

Birdie addressed Jax's sister as she worked to calm her horse. "You okay, Ev?"

Ev stroked her horse gently and looked up at Birdie sheepishly. "Yeah, sorry about that. Buck isn't exactly used to apocalypses."

Birdie couldn't help but smile, but she needed to get away from these distractions. Apollyon would be awakening in less than thirty minutes now, and she also needed to get into position. She slipped from her mount and handed its reigns to Ev. "Please try to keep Big-Eyes from running off. Last time it took me over an hour to get it back."

"Is it time already?" Ev asked.

Birdie nodded. "I know you won't want to, but if Jax says you need to leave, then you need to leave, understand?"

Ev looked like she wanted to protest, but she didn't. They both knew very well that arguing about it was just wasting time.

Birdie looked back at Jax and the handful of soldiers who'd all insisted on seeing her in action. Without a word, she melted into a dark puddle that slid rapidly along the ground until it reached the edge of the enormous pit at the center of the ruins. When she emerged from the puddle, the dark-haired woman was gone. In its place was a being of pure shadow with glowing white eyes. Her human disguise took minimal effort to maintain, but against Apollyon she would need all of her focus on the singular task of surviving long enough to bring it down. A bow would be very useful in this fight, but she'd learned last time that mobility was far more important, and she couldn't slide around as a puddle while holding onto physical equipment.

Minutes passed, and a cold wind began to blow from the abyss before her. The tremors continued to grow in intensity until suddenly everything stopped.

Birdie closed her eyes and held out her arms, creating seven doppelgangers of herself and casting the Radiant-class enchantments — the highest level that a Divine could reach — of magic-cloaking and invisibility upon herself. With those enchantments, Apollyon would be unable to sense her magic or see her. She maneuvered her doppelgangers away from the hole and near large piles of rubble before opening her eyes once again, the familiar yet still unnerving feeling of her othermind returning as she did so. Once they were in position, she was ready.

A massive shock shot through the ground, nearly knocking Birdie over as a pillar of darkness erupted from the abyss mere feet in front of her. In an instant, every last remaining bit of light from the sun vanished from the land. An icy wind blasted outward in all directions as purple streaks of lightning began arcing from the ground to the sky — the only source of illumination in the otherwise pitch blackness.

This suited Birdie just fine. As a being of darkness, she was at her most powerful in this environment. The minuscule light was more than enough for her to make out the monster in front of her — a hulking tower of black and purple flesh twisting in on itself as it stretched from the pit to over a hundred yards above her, ten crablike appendages jutting out from its sides forming a sort of ribcage near its top, with red globular eyes protruding from between the knots of flesh all the way up. That was just the portion of it above ground. She could sense its incredible magic all around her, coursing through tentacles now spreading rapidly across the world through the ground below. The center of its "ribcage" was her target, marked by a prominent circle of eyes, but before she could reach that she would need to cripple Apollyon to bring it down to her level.

Apollyon immediately noticed Birdie's doppelgangers. Birdie in turn sensed powerful curses being lobbed at them as Apollyon slammed its torso downward, stabbing with its limbs at her alter egos.

Her othermind took control of her mirror selves, making them feign the effects of the curses it knew Apollyon would cast as they darted for cover. In the midst of the chaos, Birdie formed a large blade from the shadow of her arm and sliced deep into the base of her opponent, ready to melt and slide away from what she knew would come next.

Sure enough, massive tentacles erupted from the ground where she had been. The red eyes were now aware of her presence and would try to see through her illusions, but she was no longer where they'd be searching.

Birdie emerged from shadow once again, now behind Apollyon, the eyes on its back still blissfully unaware that they should also be searching for illusions. As she prepared a second strike at its base, her doppelgangers attacked its legs. They wouldn't do much damage, but it would keep Apollyon's attention as she slashed once more deep into its flesh.

Apollyon erupted in a gurgling roar, its eyes lighting up as it prepared to bathe the battlefield with explosive balls of energy.

Birdie was pleased with herself. She was doing much better than last time — already a quarter of the way through the first phase of the fight. She melted into shadow again and darted for cover when something strange caught her senses. It felt similar to a curse her creator Syrus had mastered, but... different. The curse flew past her and struck Apollyon just before it unleashed its onslaught.

Safely behind the largest standing structure she could find, she waited for the cacophony of explosions to ring out, but it never came. Instead of explosions, the balls of energy burst with loud pops, barely even marking the ground. The land then shook as Apollyon crashed down upon it, barely able to hold itself up on its shaking limbs.

Birdie stepped out from her cover dumbstruck. Not at what she was seeing, but at what she felt. Apollyon's energy had almost completely vanished — not just aboveground, but in the tentacles below as well. She took a brief glance in the direction the strange curse had come from but saw nothing. Whatever that had been, she couldn't waste this opportunity.

She and her doppelgangers rushed towards the fallen Apollyon, Birdie slicing deep into its base while her other selves cut through its limbs without effort.

Apollyon struggled to fight back, but it was pointless. It wasn't able to move, and the only spells it could cast were so weak that any of her companions back on the hill would have shrugged them off.

She maneuvered one of her doppelgangers towards the ring of eyes that was her target and with a single half-hearted strike, ended the battle.

The Great Destroyer Apollyon ceased its struggle and melted down into a sludge that slowly poured back into the hole from which it had emerged. The tremors and lighting disappeared, and the sky lit up once again. In another five years, Apollyon would again return, but that wasn't Birdie's concern at the moment. Turning her attention back to where she was sure the curse had come from — a dead forest in the valley of two small hills — her disbelief of what had happened gave way to concern. There was no sign of Syrus or anyone else, which meant whoever had cast the spell didn't want to be spotted. That meant it couldn't have been Syrus who was responsible, and *that* left a feeling of unease deep in her soul.

Out of the corner of her eye, Birdie spotted Ev and the others riding towards her. As much as she wanted to investigate, she didn't want to risk antagonizing whatever force had struck down Apollyon while the few people she cared about sat in the line of fire. That, and she needed to make sure Syrus knew about this. Dying would make that a tad difficult.

Jax was the first to arrive on the scene, his jubilant grin a clear sign that he had no inkling of what had actually transpired. His soldiers were right behind him, all with expressions of awe, while Ev trailed further back due to having to pull Big-Eyes along with her.

Birdie phased her weapon back into her body as she dispelled her doppelgangers and put her preferred human guise back on. She turned to face her comrades but kept an eye on the forest in the distance.

"That was incredible!" Jax shouted. "I can't believe how fast you beat that thing."

"That *was* incredible," repeated one of the younger soldiers. "I've never heard of Apollyon being defeated so quickly, let alone by a single Divine — Radiant or otherwise. That shouldn't have even been possible."

Jax turned on his steed in response, grin still wide. "I told you, Tallis, Birdie's unbeatable. She's the most powerful Radiant to ever exist!"

"I didn't do this," Birdie stated flatly as Ev joined the rest of the group. Her announcement was met with nearly uniform stares.

Jax chuckled nervously. "What are you talking about? We saw you…." His expression dimmed as he noticed Birdie's.

Jax, Tallis, and even Waylen all appeared to want to question her further, but ultimately the only one who did was Ev. "So, if you didn't kill Apollyon, what did?"

Birdie turned her attention back to the forest once again. "I technically killed it, but something from the forest brought it down for me."

"Something from the forest?" asked Jax, now scrutinizing the dead trees in the distance. "Was it another Radiant?"

"No," replied Birdie, still looking at the forest. "I would have sensed a Radiant."

"Well, what was it, then?" he asked, but a glance from Birdie told him she didn't know. "Do you want us to check it out?"

Birdie whipped her head around. "Absolutely not. I can recognize every spell the Masters ever created, and whatever hit Apollyon was none of those."

Jax didn't seem to process the immensity of what she was saying, but Ev clearly did. "But that would mean someone's figured out how to make new spells."

"Impossible," stated Tallis. "Scholars have spent centuries trying to create new spells. Only the Masters have that ability."

"Exactly," was Birdie's somber response.

Shock washed over the faces of everyone in front of her. Ev barely managed to get out, "You don't think they've actually returned, do you?"

Birdie subtly shook her head. "No. If they had, they would have already erased me because of what I am, but whoever did this could well prove just as dangerous."

Still keeping her senses trained for any abnormality, Birdie walked over to her mount and climbed aboard. "We need to get back to Roehelm. Syrus is the only one who might be able to fight that kind of power. If whatever happened here turns out to be a threat, he's our only hope of stopping it."

* * * *

Back at the citadel of Roehelm, while people celebrated the defeat of Apollyon late into the night, Birdie went upstairs to discover Syrus's chambers still empty. The only sign of his presence was a tiny yellow crystal, known as a marker, hovering above a chair in the corner of the room. He would reform from that crystal when he returned to the world, but until he did so, there was no way for her to contact him from here.

Birdie cursed to herself. It had been three weeks now since Syrus had gone off to whatever realm true Divine such as he called home. She was absolutely sick of him leaving her in charge of everything. Admittedly, it was probably her fault he'd disappeared. Their last conversation hadn't exactly ended on a pleasant note. Still, that was no excuse for him to be gone for this long, especially on the one day he *knew* she actually could have used his help.

Not content with simply waiting for him to return, Birdie ambled over to his bookshelf to see if there was anything that might explain how a new spell could have come into existence. After scanning his library, however, she was disappointed to find that he didn't own any books she hadn't already perused.

There was nothing on nor in his desk, either — no notes that he'd left behind or clues to his research. Birdie couldn't say she was all that surprised. If he'd been studying how to make new spells, Ev would have already told her. Ev had taken up a position as his apprentice, after all. This meant that Birdie's only options were to either wait for his return or to travel to Ars Summis. The City of the Divine was the only place she'd be able to send him a message. Considering the implications of what she'd witnessed, she doubted waiting would be the wisest of ideas.

A familiar magic caught her senses, letting Birdie know that Ev was approaching. With no reason to remain in Syrus's room any longer, she exited into the hall to meet her friend.

"Any luck?" Ev asked as soon as she saw Birdie.

"Of course not," Birdie answered cynically, crossing her arms. "Honestly, I'm starting to think I should rent out his room at this point. People would pay good money to live in the home of a Radiant."

Ev smiled sympathetically as she drew closer. "He's trying to repair our world and figure out how to break the rules of the Masters all at once. It's not exactly an easy task. I'm sure he's still working on it wherever he is."

Birdie sighed, or at least gave the illusion of it. At this point her mimicry of human mannerisms was habit. She gave a slight smile as she remarked, "And you'd know, wouldn't you? I still think it's a tad ironic that a cleric has devoted herself to unraveling everything that the Masters created."

Ev frowned as she stood up tall. "The Masters betrayed us. They created our world for the Divine to play with and then left us to die. You and Syrus are the only ones who actually care about us."

Birdie cocked her head and placed her hand on her hip. "Yeah, well, to be fair, I am also the only Divine who isn't really a Divine. I'm kind of stuck here with you."

Ev mirrored Birdie's stance. "You know, you might be able to tell other people that, but I know better. I also know that as much as you won't want to, you'll come with me to the celebration downstairs because it would mean a lot to everyone if you did."

Of course that was the reason Ev had come up here. Birdie looked up at the ceiling and closed her eyes. "You do know how important it is that I contact Syrus as soon as possible, don't you?"

"Of course I do," Ev replied, hands now behind her back, "but if he's not here, that means you need to travel to Ars Summis. Come on. You don't need to stay for long. Just come for a couple of hours. You don't even need to go to the big one. Jax and I set up a special celebration just for you away from everyone else. I promise there aren't a lot of people there."

Birdie groaned. Of all the responsibilities she'd inherited five years ago when she defeated Lord Grandis, the constant social interaction was easily the worst. She was fine dealing with a few people when it suited her, but now it was always mandatory. Giving people orders, attending festivities, managing treaties — it was never ending. Still, she supposed the trip to Ars Summis would give her a few days' break from all of it. She might as well go to this thing. It wasn't often people held parties for her, after all.

"Fine," she agreed at last.

Ev clapped her hands together. "See? I knew you'd agree. The party's this way. We made sure it was away from the main celebration for you."

Birdie walked alongside Ev down hallways lined with suits of armor, ornate tapestries, and thick carpets. The walk was admittedly nice. No one else, save for Syrus and Jax's friend Gare, was as comfortable around her as Ev was, though Birdie hadn't seen Gare in over three months. Jax, for his part, tried his best to act comfortable around her, but there was an unmistakable tension between them that Birdie chalked up to her status as a Radiant. Still, she appreciated his presence and was glad that he and Ev had both moved to Roehelm after their battle with Grandis. It would have been nice if Gare had joined them, too, but she understood his desire to stay with his family in Marisol. Besides, Gare's family was somewhat influential, which meant his vouching for her helped keep stability in that area. That was much appreciated, as Birdie had enough trouble from Grandis loyalists as it was.

After a few minutes of walking and conversation about Ev's experiments on behalf of Syrus, the two of them arrived at a small banquet hall on the northern side of the citadel. As Ev had promised, the number of attendees was low, consisting of Jax, Ev, their grandmother, a few members of the citadel staff, and the soldiers who'd followed Birdie to watch her battle Apollyon. She could have done without most of the soldiers, seeing as the only one she knew well was Waylen, but she supposed she could put up with them for a time.

Jax was the first to notice their arrival. "Glad you decided to join us!" he shouted, raising a goblet into the air. "To Eclipse, and to another defeat of Apollyon!"

Birdie was glad she'd never made blushing a habitual reaction. After everyone had concluded their toast she walked over to him. "Did you have to call me 'Eclipse'? There's no one here who doesn't know I prefer 'Birdie.'"

Jax did blush. "Sorry, I just got done giving a speech to the public. 'Eclipse' just… you know."

Birdie rolled her eyes.

"Here," Jax said, grabbing a glowing flask of dark liquid from off the table. "A gift from Dezeroth, allegedly."

"So from Zun-Roven, then," Birdie remarked, knowing full well Dezeroth would never give anyone a gift. She almost felt sorry for his chancellor, working so hard to maintain an image for that brute of a king.

Taking the flask, Birdie had to admit it was a nice gift. There weren't many types of dark magic she didn't have easy access to, but necromancy was one of those exceptions. After being surrounded by the darkness of Apollyon she'd be overflowing with energy for some time yet, but once that wore off, the bottle of concentrated necromantic energy would make for a nice exotic treat.

Birdie called one of the party's attendants over and asked him to take the flask to her room before turning back to Jax. "I guess I'll have to remember to send Zun-Roven a 'thank you' sometime tomorrow."

Jax rubbed the back of his head. "Please don't antagonize Dezeroth. As much as I hate him, we kind of need him to keep the peace right now. We *don't* need him getting offended and pushing his borders closer to us."

Birdie rolled her eyes a second time and put her hand on her hip. "Fine. I'll send a second letter thanking Dezeroth. Happy?"

Jax looked concerned, but quickly hid it with a shrug. "I guess so. Mind if I go grab a bite to eat?"

Birdie dismissed Jax with a motion of her hand. She turned to head back to Ev, but the young soldier named Tallis accosted her before she could take a single step.

"Um, excuse me," he began, "but do you think that, since this is a party, you could tell me more about the Divine?"

Birdie raised an eyebrow. "What does being at a party have to do with anything?"

"Oh, no, you're right," Tallis stumbled. "It's just that we've never really gotten a chance to talk. Captain Ruthoree told me not to bother you on our trip to battle Apollyon, and you're always busy or off somewhere else at other times."

Birdie cocked her head. "Yeah, well, I hate to disappoint you, kid, but I'm not exactly an expert myself. If you want to know about the Divine, talk to Ev or Syrus. The only things I know about them are things they told me."

"W-wait," the kid stuttered as Birdie started to turn away. "Aren't you a Divine?"

"Technically," Birdie answered, trying not to be rude but not exactly keen on continuing this conversation, "but unlike every other Divine, I'm a part of this world. I have so little interest in the real ones that your captain could tell you just as much about them as I could."

"I knew it!" exclaimed Tallis happily, almost startling Birdie. "The Divine are eternal beings from beyond our world, but you were created. I knew there was no way you could be a true Divine!"

Birdie felt like she should feel insulted, but the kid seemed overcome with genuine excitement — as if he'd made the discovery of the century. There really wasn't any tone of intentional disrespect in his voice.

Jax must have overheard Tallis, however, as he was now heading over with a stern expression on his face. Birdie subtly lifted her hand, signaling to him that she was fine.

"You know, if that's all you wanted to know, you could have just asked," Birdie said, crossing her arms. "For the record, though, I'm glad I'm not a true Divine. If literally only one in a million of them stayed behind to actually care for our world, that's not exactly a group of people I want to be associated with."

Tallis opened his eyes wide, as if he'd been scolded. "Oh, no, I didn't mean — of course I know that—"

"Lady Eclipse," a voice from behind her called out.

Annoyed at the use of her true name, Birdie turned to see a guard saluting her.

"Excuse me," she began, "but I'm in the middle of a conversation."

The guard, whose name she seemed to recall was Edgar, put his arm down. "Forgive me, my lady, but a visitor has requested your immediate presence. He claims that another Radiant has returned to Doxla."

That got Birdie's attention. She'd set up a guard around both the Throne of Ascendance and the Altar of Restoration to ensure that the handful of Divine still in Doxla couldn't ascend to Radiance and cause her more trouble. If a Radiant was here now, then either one of those groups had been overpowered or a Radiant had been lying dormant for years. Either way, if this visitor was telling the truth, that was a problem she would have to deal with immediately.

"Take me to this visitor," she demanded, and Edgar escorted her from the party down to a small room near the front of the citadel.

Edgar opened the door for her. "Sir Orwick had us bring him to this room so as not to disturb the other guests."

Birdie gave a quick glance toward Edgar and entered the room. Edgar then closed the door behind her.

A well-dressed man sat behind the desk in the middle of the room, having made himself comfortable prior to Birdie's arrival. Birdie sensed a strange enchantment on the man but couldn't quite place it, immediately putting her on guard. On seeing Birdie, the man stood and raised his arms in greeting.

"Esteemed Lady Eclipse," the man began, "I am truly humbled that you'd take the time to meet with me in the midst of such celebration."

"Did you tell my guards that another Radiant has returned to Doxla?" Birdie asked, not in the mood for the man's brown-nosing.

"Why, yes, I did," the visitor replied, bowing. "Allow me to introduce myself. I am Cray Richman, a servant of Exalted Lady Lux Rosa."

Birdie struggled to suppress her surprise. She hadn't expected her visitor's mere introduction to tell her so much information. The title of Exalted Lady was enough to tell Birdie that this Lux Rosa had risen to the second highest class of Radiant. Birdie had never heard the name Lux Rosa before, so this Lux would need to have been in hiding for at least ten years if this Cray was telling the truth.

"I see," said Birdie, crossing her arms. "In that case I have to ask why you're here. I somehow doubt it's just to tell me your master has returned."

Cray spread his hands wide. "Of course, of course. I think you'll be quite pleased with my reasoning actually. Lady Rosa would like to make a deal with you, you see."

Birdie raised an eyebrow. "Is that so? What sort of deal?"

Cray clasped his hands together and smiled a smile that seemed a tad too genuine for Birdie's taste. "Well, you see, Lady Rosa is actually quite a big fan of yours, which makes sense, seeing as she is one of the Divine who helped create you."

A twinge ran down Birdie's neck. She'd known Syrus hadn't created her on his own, but there was no way this Lux Rosa could have helped him, was there? If so, then Cray had better have some answers for her.

She cocked her head. "Let's say what you claim is true. Where has your Lady Rosa been these last five plus years? Where was she when Grandis tried to end the entire world?"

Cray waved his hand dismissively. "Now, now, Lady Eclipse, you have to understand. When Grandis defeated your first incarnation, he also split all of the Divine who supported you. He took everything from them, and worse, your reincarnation was nowhere to be found. You were their only hope, and you were gone."

"That doesn't answer my question," Birdie replied, though the fact that this man knew she reincarnated rather than revived like true Divine was unsettling.

Cray sighed. "Listen, the truth is Lady Rosa fled. She made a mistake. She knows that now. She knew the moment you defeated Apollyon five years ago, and ever since that day she's been working to find a way to make it up to you.

Now, she thinks she has one."

A frown on her face, Birdie waited for Cray to continue.

"Lady Rosa knows you don't want to be a leader to these nepacs. She knows you just want the world to be safe and would rather spend your days not worrying about all the details of maintaining peace or running armies. She'd like to take that all away from you."

Birdie's frown turned into a scowl. "So, let me get this straight. You think I hate being in charge so much that I'll just hand the job over to any Radiant who comes asking."

Cray waved his hands wildly. "Oh, no-no-no-no, not at all, my dear. Lady Rosa doesn't want the responsibility of managing this world, either. She wants to make it so that all the problems the Masters caused — the problems of Apollyon, monsters, Dezeroth, all the other immortals they created — she wants to make those problems disappear."

Birdie's scowl softened. "I'm not sure I like the idea of getting rid of immortals, but if she wants to erase monsters and Apollyon, she's more than welcome to try. Syrus has been working on that for years with little to show for it. That still leaves me with one very big question, though."

"You want to know what she wants from you, yes?" Cray smiled.

"You did say you wanted to make a deal."

Cray tapped his fingers together gently. "Oh, it's nothing much. Lady Rosa just doesn't want your friend Syrus getting in the way of her work, so she asks that you not tell him about her return… or about what you saw when you fought Apollyon."

Another twinge ran down Birdie's neck. "That spell… that was Lux Rosa's doing?"

"Indeed," Cray smiled as a wave of unease made its way through Birdie, "and just as a token of agreement, she would also like it if you could share with her Lord Syrus's true name."

Birdie willed her appearance to remain stoic but began focusing magic into her arms and legs. "Why do you need me to tell you his name? Shouldn't someone who worked with him already know it?"

"It's been a very long time since they last talked," answered Cray. "It can be hard to remember such trivial details."

"Is that so? Well, that's a shame, because he never told me he had any name other than 'Syrus.'"

"Oh, dear," remarked Cray, excessive disappointment on his face, though his eyes told her his expression was a lie. "I do hope that isn't actually the case."

Birdie shrugged. "Sorry. Looks like I can't help you."

"Well, how about we change the offer then?" Cray cooed, his expression once again pleasant. "How about either you tell me his name, or I kill every single soul in this worthless town of yours."

Without a moment's hesitation Birdie's shadow stretched across the floor and wrapped Cray in a sheet of darkness.

"I say 'no deal,'" she growled as she squeezed tightly, crushing him.

Her attack was immediately retracted, however, as the horrifying sensation of the spell from before coursed through her shadow and into her main body.

Birdie stumbled backwards as every ounce of strength left her, then watched in horror as Cray lifted up his shirt to reveal the nub of a dagger's hilt grafted into his skin. Cray casually removed the blade from his stomach, seemingly oblivious to the pain as blood poured out of the wound he created.

"What? What are you?" Birdie panted, surprising herself with the wheezy voice that left her body. Looking down, she saw she was no longer maintaining the guise of a woman.

Blood running down his legs, Cray stepped around the desk with that same pleasant smile on his face. "I will give you one last chance. Tell me Syrus's name, and the only life I take today will be yours, or does a machine like you not know how to care about the lives of others?"

Fear unlike anything Birdie had felt in years welled up within her. Not just for herself, but for everyone she cared about. There was no way she could fight this guy in her current state, and there was no telling how much damage he would do if he wasn't stopped.

Dropping down into a puddle, she slid towards the crack of the doorway when she was pulled back into solid form by a blinding light emitted from Cray's dagger.

"Wrong decision," he muttered, firing a massive ray of light from his free hand.

Birdie instinctively let her othermind take over the moment she sensed the attack coming, distorting her figure to avoid most of the blast that tore a gaping hole in the wall.

She shouted in pain as she lunged through the hole, dark smoke and ink briefly spewing from her side before the missing chunk of her torso reformed. Edgar jumped backwards in surprise as Birdie dashed toward the nearest tapestry. A bright light filling the hallway warned her that Cray was in position to attack again, so she dove behind a suit of armor with just enough time to melt into a puddle before another ray of light blasted apart her cover.

The sound of Edgar shouting was followed quickly by a short scuffle as her pursuer dealt with the soldier. Her othermind told her to take advantage of the distraction, as selfish as that action may have been.

With no other chance at survival, she did.

Birdie rushed to the nearby tapestry and pulled at it with all her might, dislodging its rod from its brackets just as she saw Edgar fall to the ground. Placing the tapestry over her, she darted straight down the hallway, pacing herself so she'd be near the next door at the right moment. As soon as she felt Cray preparing to attack again, she threw the tapestry upward and jumped toward the door from behind it. The light tore through the tapestry as she slipped into the dark room, locking the door behind her.

The room was more or less identical to the one she'd just been in, but now she had a clear shot towards the window. Knowing that even another glancing hit from Cray would be the end of her, she started toward it, but a thought entered her head.

Dropping into a puddle once again, Birdie slid up the wall over the doorway. Perhaps her foe was oblivious to pain, but it was clear he could still be injured. Between the wound he'd given himself and the damage her shadow must have done earlier, he had to be in critical condition.

Cray burst into the room, his light forcing her back into solid form, but that was what she needed anyway. As she fell above him, she pulled shadowy blades from her arms and drove them deep into his eye sockets with all of her might.

To her shock, Cray spun around with such force that she lost her grip and slammed into a bookshelf. Cray slashed wildly in the air and fired magical blasts in every direction as Birdie scrambled to avoid his attacks, eventually taking cover behind the large desk in the room. She might have somehow failed to kill him, but at least she'd blinded him.

After a moment his attacks slowed, and he began to stagger. A few seconds later, the light from his dagger faded as he fell to his hands and knees. He then started laughing.

"Oh-ho-ho, very impressive, Eclipse, but make no mistake. This is far from over. The moment you fled, I flashed a signal through the window, and soon your town will burn. Even if you somehow stop it you are only delaying the inevitable. If you care at all for the people of this world, you and Syrus will stay out of my way. You will soon enough see what I am truly capable of, and I will not hesitate to use that power to erase anyone who tries to stop me."

The strange enchantment Birdie had sensed on Cray disappeared as his body fell limp. Birdie felt a small portion of her former strength return, but it was nothing like she'd had before. She fell back against the wall, utterly exhausted, in severe pain, and in shock at the realization of what that enchantment she'd been sensing was. The man she'd just killed may have been named Cray, but the person she'd just fought and spoken to had been none other than Lux Rosa herself.

A series of explosions outside followed by the sounding of horns brought her back to reality, informing her that the battle was indeed not yet over. Entering her puddle state once again, she slid off to the party room as quickly as she was able.

Chapter 2

Racing down the citadel corridor, Birdie's senses ran wild as intense magic unlike anything she'd felt before erupted outside. The flavors of magic were all familiar — weak spells that nearly anyone could master, but they were pushed to a level of intensity that would rival even low-tier Radiants.

As she drew near to the banquet hall, she realized that she no longer sensed any of her soldiers within them. Most likely they'd all gone out to combat the assailing force, but that didn't help her now. She strained her senses to detect either Ev or Jax, but there was too much chaos going on outside and too many soldiers casting spells.

Not having any better leads to go on, Birdie set her attention on what she sensed was a mild gathering of soldiers above her with many more on their way. Heading up would help her better assess the situation anyway, so altering her course, Birdie made her way toward a balcony a few floors above the armory.

There, archers and mages fired upon a swarm of pegasus riders while the riders rained brutal spells down on the city below, most of them ignoring the defenders. Jax was nowhere to be seen, but Birdie thankfully spotted Ev behind the archers.

Before she could move to get Ev's attention, one of the riders flew in close and unleashed a spell that caused an eruption of toxic gas to spread over the entire area. The soldiers, including Ev, began choking uncontrollably, many of them falling to the ground.

Unaffected by the toxin, Birdie ran out onto the balcony and grabbed Ev, pulling her back inside away from the poison.

"Wait here," she ordered a disoriented and still choking Ev as she rushed back out onto the balcony. As much as she wanted to make sure Ev was alright, if they couldn't fend off this attack, it was likely none of them would make it out alive.

Back in the toxic cloud, she used her senses to search for a mage that felt strong in wind magic. There were a few to choose from, so she grabbed the woman closest to the doorway and hauled her inside as well.

"You have to blow away that cloud!" she nearly shouted at the woman who was still coughing on the ground.

"Birdie?" Ev choked out from behind her.

Birdie turned to face Ev. Though concerned about her friend, she focused on the task at hand. "Ev, as soon as the cloud is clear, I need you to heal everyone as fast as you've ever healed anyone before."

"I…. What's wrong with your voice?" Ev asked, clearly unnerved at the harsh wheezing sound directed at her.

"I got hit with that spell that defeated Apollyon," Birdie replied, not exactly thrilled at having her condition pointed out.

"Oh, no!" Ev shouted, standing up and immediately casting a healing spell on Birdie through a rod she must have grabbed when the attack started.

"It's not an injury," Birdie told her, though she did feel a great deal of relief as Ev undid the damage that she'd taken in her battle with Lux Rosa, "but thank you. I needed that."

Letting Ev continue her healing, Birdie turned her attention back to the mage. "What are you waiting for? People are dying out there! Help them!"

The mage stood up shakily and prepared a spell. After a second, the mage produced a violent wind that blew away the toxic cloud outside.

"Quickly," Birdie turned to Ev, "get everyone back in fighting condition! Our attackers might have powerful spells, but they're definitely mortal!"

"What about you?" Ev asked. "Can you fight in your condition?"

Birdie didn't answer, instead heading to the edge of the balcony to survey the situation. She might not have been fully healed, but she was leagues better than she had been. From her new vantage point, she could see heated battles taking place in the city streets near the walls, the square, and the base of the citadel. The pegasus riders were mostly concentrating on tearing apart the city, with a few swooping in to take potshots at defending soldiers whenever they were exposed.

After analyzing their strategy, Birdie turned to Ev, who had already started healing the survivors. "I need to take out the pegasus riders. They're spreading panic and scattering our troops. Can you tell me where Jax is?"

Ev shook her head. "He said he was going to rally soldiers on the ground. I don't know where he went after that."

Birdie considered that for a moment. "Alright, I'll worry about him later. For now, I want everyone up here to spread out and concentrate on supporting the soldiers on the ground. Those riders' spells are too dangerous for you to group together. Stay close, but not too close. And you!" she pointed to the woman who'd cast the wind spell. "Stay in the hall and be ready in case those riders are as stupid as I hope they are and cast poison again."

Before anyone had a chance to say anything further, Birdie dropped into a puddle and slid over the side of the balcony. She made her way down the citadel and headed toward the stables. Pegasi might have been the most maneuverable aerial mount around, but there was one that was faster.

Not far from the base of the citadel, Birdie spotted a good portion of the Shadow Guard retreating from a group of twenty or so invaders. Jax wasn't with them, but she recognized Waylen among their number.

Annoyed at their disorganized flight, Birdie sped along through the cracks in the street to intercept Waylen as he darted into an alley with a few others. She popped up in front of him, prompting him to scream and nearly take her head off as he swung his war hammer. Though he missed her, he did knock a door off its hinges.

"Waylen!" she shouted in her wheezy voice, startling him once again but succeeding in calming him a tad.

Still holding his hammer in a defensive position, Waylen cautiously spoke. "Miss Birdie?"

An enemy soldier appeared at the end of the alley.

"Get down!" Birdie yelled, grabbing Waylen and struggling to pull his massive bulk after her through the doorway.

A wall of fire blazed past them as they cleared the entrance. Only one of the other soldiers had managed to make it through before the flames hit, leaving the other two scorched and barely alive. Panting, Waylen stood and stared at the glowing alleyway outside.

"What do you think you're doing?" Birdie demanded. "Why is your entire platoon scattering?"

Waylen's face was pale, but at least his eyes told her he was now confident who she was. "I'm sorry, Miss Birdie, but haven't ya seen what they can do? We can't fight that!"

"Yes, you can!" Birdie returned. "They might have powerful spells, but aside from that they're ordinary nepacs, and you're going to prove it!"

"How — wait, me?" Waylen asked, concerned.

"Grab your hammer and get ready to kill the guy who just did that," she said, pointing at the downed soldiers.

"I, uh…" Waylen hesitated.

"He'll be here in seconds," Birdie said, sensing the enemy rapidly approaching. "I'll distract him, then you jump out and end him! Understood?"

Waylen nervously gripped his hammer and nodded.

"Good," she said. "Then get ready… now!"

Birdie jumped through the hole just as the enemy arrived, startling him.

The invading mage sent another wave of flames down the alley, but she was already on the wall sliding around behind him. She leapt out of her shadow form and took a cheap swipe at the back of the mage's neck, doing minimal damage in her current state but prompting him to spin around and face her.

Before the mage could cast another spell, Waylen burst into the alleyway. He swung his hammer with far more force than necessary, leaving their foe's head significantly less attached to his body and significantly more… well, dead.

"There, you see?" Birdie remarked to a shocked Waylen. "Now get your platoon back under control! These creeps are completely disorganized. The only advantage they have is magic and fear. As long as we steel our courage, we can win this!"

A new look of determination appeared on Waylen's face. Gripping his hammer, he nodded as Birdie melted once more and continued on her way to the stables. As best as she could tell, none of these invaders possessed the spell she'd been hit with. At the very least, she hadn't sensed any of them casting it, nor had she detected any sign of that enchantment that had been on Cray. If that was truly the case, then their enemy were likely without a leader and were only acting on whatever orders they'd been given prior to the assault. That was an analysis she was banking on, because if that was true, then disrupting the assault would be all her Shadow Guard would need to turn the tides back in their favor.

Arriving at the stables, Birdie untied her zodiac and climbed on.

"Alright, Big-Eyes, let's see how well you do in a fight."

Urging the big fish out of its pen and into the air, she made a beeline to the armory. Halfway there, a blinding explosion billowed out from the roof of the citadel, alerting her that the riders had now begun to focus their attacks on the archers and support.

Now rushing even harder, Birdie didn't bother waiting for the zodiac to stop before jumping off and sliding under the armory's door. Inside, she grabbed the nearest bow and arrows she could find. For what she was doing, quality didn't matter. Kicking the door open on the way out, she climbed back onto Big-Eyes and took off into the sky.

"Okay," she told herself, not looking forward to what she was about to do. "This is only temporary. Big-Eyes, I apologize in advance if I do anything that hurts you."

Giving Big-Eyes a reassuring pat, she focused on the task at hand. Once she was sure she had a singular goal in place, she passed that information on to her othermind, relinquishing control of her body in the process.

Immediately, Birdie felt herself push Big-Eyes at top speed down toward the nearest pegasus rider — fortunately one of the ones attacking the balcony. A hundred yards from her target, Birdie's arms readied an arrow in her bow and fired before she even had time to fully process where she was aiming. Augmented with the already blazing speed of her zodiac, the arrow rocketed through the sky and struck the pegasus in the neck, sending it into wild throws that cast its rider careening toward the ground.

Birdie's other-mind redirected Big-Eyes toward another rider. With only slightly more hesitation as she felt it analyze this rider's more erratic movements, another arrow was sent flying.

Her othermind didn't wait to see if the arrow connected as it adjusted Big-Eyes's course to another target. After two more successful snipes, the remaining riders took notice of her assault.

Unease crept into Birdie, but she'd made her decision. Trusting her othermind was her only option now, as risky as that option was.

At her othermind's direction, Big-Eyes sped towards the airspace above the oncoming riders. The invaders cast powerful spells of lightning, fire, and ice, with Big-Eyes' speed the only reason their attacks failed to connect.

Birdie aimed and fired at pegasus after pegasus, only occasionally hesitating should her target change course unexpectedly.

Birdie couldn't keep track of the arrows, but she knew most of them would find their mark. The number of riders around her thinned out rapidly, proving her confidence correct, but her supply of arrows also began to thin.

With one last shot at another of the aerial mages, that supply dwindled to zero. Unfortunately, that still left three more pegasus riders remaining.

Likely predicting that her opponents wouldn't give her the chance to grab more arrows, Birdie's othermind instead directed Big-Eyes straight at one of the surviving pegasi.

The enemy mage countered the charge with a barrage of icy spears. A jerk on the reigns pulled Big-Eyes clear of the worst of the attack, though a stray shard pierced Birdie's torso and sent pain throughout her body.

Her shadow quickly pushed the shard back out.

A second jerk on the reigns, and they were flying directly at the mage. Before her foe could prepare a second spell, Birdie's arm formed a hammer from its shadow and connected hard with the enemy's chest, knocking the woman clear off her pegasus.

As soon as the attack landed, Birdie found herself directing Big-Eyes toward one of the last two riders, this one preparing a fire spell.

Rapidly approaching what could be her and Big-Eyes's doom, Birdie wrested control of her body back from her othermind and pulled the reigns hard, sending Big-Eyes high up into the sky. Her othermind protested, but it had done its job. She wasn't about to let it get them killed just to claim a complete rout.

Flying up above the clouds where she knew pegasi couldn't reach her, Birdie stopped to examine her zodiac's injuries. Several shards of ice — the largest of which were over a foot long — protruded from its face and belly, luminescent goo dripping from the wounds. Big-Eyes didn't seem particularly bothered, but another hit like that would cripple it at best.

After taking a moment to catch her figurative breath, Birdie maneuvered Big-Eyes a few hundred yards south before dropping back below the clouds again.

From her vantage point, it was difficult to tell if the tides had yet turned, but she noticed quickly that the number of pegasus riders had dropped to only one since her retreat, and that rider was currently occupied with a renewed assault on the citadel's balconies.

Such reckless aggression would be that rider's downfall.

Birdie directed Big-Eyes into a downward plunge, aiming to strike from behind, but her maneuver proved unnecessary. Before she even arrived, the balcony defenders managed to down the final rider.

Slowing her descent, Birdie flew in close to the balcony. Circling the citadel once in search of Ev, she halted at the spot where she'd last seen her.

"Where's Eveline?" she demanded.

The soldiers looked around, but none answered.

"Where's Dame Ruthoree?" Birdie reiterated, trying to hide her frustration and concern by the lack of response.

One of the archers answered, shaking his head. "We don't know."

Birdie quickly glanced along the balcony a second time before flying alongside it, straining her senses for Ev's particular flavor of magic. A wave of relief washed over her when at last she detected it. Approaching that spot, she heard Ev call out.

"Birdie!" Ev ran out onto the balcony.

"Ev, thank goodness you're okay," Birdie said, but she quickly covered up her favoritism with a request. "I know right now might not be the best time, but could you please heal Big-Eyes for me?"

Ev rushed forward, pulling out her rod.

"Poor Big-Eyes," she exclaimed as she examined its injuries. "What happened? Are you hurt?"

That last question was directed at Birdie.

Birdie placed her hand on where the ice had struck her. The injury had since equalized throughout her body, but damage was still damage.

Ev recognized Birdie's body language and immediately focused on healing her instead of Big-Eyes. Once she'd tended to Birdie, she then worked on removing the icicles still protruding from the zodiac.

The smaller shards prompted barely a twitch from the big fish as they slid out cleanly, but the larger, more jagged shards caused Big-Eyes to jerk wildly.

"Easy, there," Birdie said as she pat the fish on its side.

Once the ice was removed, Ev made quick work of its injuries.

"That should do it," she said.

"Thanks, Ev," Birdie replied before turning Big-Eyes back to the battlefield.

"Wait! Where are you going now?" Ev asked.

"I need to see what we're up against. My impression is that our attackers are a bunch of power-mad morons, but even if that's the case, they're mad with power because they have it. The only way we'll win this fight is with knowledge, and who's better with knowledge than me?"

Birdie tapped at her temple with that last remark, prompting a frown but also a nod from Ev.

Pushing Big-Eyes into the air once more, Birdie sped over the city buildings in wide circles, taking in the situation below her. The platoon that had made it to the citadel steps had been defeated, so that was good to see. She was also pleased to see that Waylen had managed to rally back his troops and was making short work of several of the smaller groups spread across the city. Best of all, her earlier analysis of the overall situation appeared spot on. While there were two large groups of enemy soldiers that moved as units and appeared well trained, a disproportionate number of the invaders had gone off on their own, wreaking havoc seemingly at random as they generally moved towards the citadel. With aid from her othermind, she counted nearly three hundred enemy forces still alive on the ground. She also noticed something interesting about them.

Many of the ground soldiers bore the red-maned lion of Grandis on their shields. Grandis loyalists had long been the source of a significant share of Birdie's problems. That they would be willing to fight for a new Radiant who had it out for her and Syrus would not be surprising, and it would explain how Lux Rosa might have amassed an army quickly without anyone noticing. The presence of the additional emblem of a white rose — a symbol she'd never before seen a loyalist wear — seemed to confirm that their defection to Lux Rosa was indeed the case.

Her scan of the city complete, Birdie then set out to find Jax and any other officers of her guard. She now knew what she was up against, and while she was sure they could win, she'd likely have to sacrifice a few soldiers to turn the tide.

Her search didn't take long. Birdie spotted Jax fighting alongside a contingent he'd rallied a hundred yards back from the city square, taking cover from one of the larger enemy units as they demolished every obstacle in their way.

Swooping in low from behind, she called to him. "Jax!"

Jax turned around, on guard. "Birdie?"

"Never mind the voice," she said quickly, pointing at her neck. "Bad spell. Not important. Pull your troops back to the citadel. Get them into the citadel itself, not the surrounding buildings. Support from the balcony will provide cover when the enemy follows."

"We can't fall back," Jax protested. "They're destroying everything! We need to stop them here!"

"You don't stand a chance against them here."

"Maybe not, but you do!" Jax shot back.

Birdie narrowed her glowing eyes. "No, I don't. The spell that hit me weakened me to the point where my magic can't even produce a human voice."

Jax stared at Birdie in disbelief.

"I know you hate running," she continued, "but this time you have to. Warn as many as you can to get away, but your priority is leading those loyalists to the citadel steps. Fighting here isn't an option. If you try, you'll die, and if you die, then the city burns anyway."

Jax cursed and slammed his fist against a nearby wall, cracking it. Looking toward his troops, he called out.

"Everyone, fall back to the citadel! Warn as many as you can to follow you! We make our last stand there!" He turned to Birdie. "I sure as hell hope you know what you're doing."

"Of course I do," returned Birdie. "Let's just hope these loyalist scum are too dumb to figure it out."

Kicking off into the air again, Birdie flew back to the citadel to complete her trap.

Upon arrival, it was clear the Shadow Guard at the citadel's base had suffered heavy losses against the invading forces, but there were still at least thirty soldiers on the front steps alone.

Coming in for a landing, Birdie shouted to the lieutenant in charge. "Oswald! Move your troops into the buildings at the entrance to the court and wait! Captain Ruthoree is luring a group of about seventy to the steps. As soon as the balcony starts firing, that's your signal to attack from behind. Don't let a single one escape!"

Oswald seemed surprised by the sudden orders, but his expression quickly turned to one of resolution as he nodded in understanding.

Next, Birdie headed back to where she'd left Ev. Once there, she commanded her soldiers.

"Gather up everyone on the balconies and head to the western side of the citadel. Leave only six soldiers on each of the other sides to make sure we aren't surprised. A hoard of Grandis loyalists is pursuing Captain Ruthoree. They'll be here soon. When he arrives, wait until the enemy is at the steps, then rain hell upon them!"

Ev saluted dramatically. "You can count on us!"

If Birdie'd had lips she would have smiled. As it was, though, she simply nodded, then flew off towards the second large group of invaders on the east of town.

There, she found that Waylen's platoon had formed a blockade, but they were still losing ground. She spotted Waylen himself taking cover behind a destroyed bakery being tended to by a cleric.

"Waylen!" she called before landing beside him.

"Miss Birdie?" he asked weakly. "I'm sorry. We're tryin', but I'm not sure how much longer we can hold 'em off."

Birdie hadn't realized the extent of his injuries from the air. A hole large enough for a cantaloupe to fit in had been burned through his armor on his left side. The cleric worked quickly to mend the damage, but an injury like that was likely going to have lasting complications, healing or no.

"You've done great," Birdie replied to him. "You got your forces back together, and now we're going to use them to put an end to this."

A massive bolt of lightning punched through the building just over Birdie's head, sending bricks raining down upon them. Waylen started to say something, but they didn't have time where they were, so Birdie spoke first.

"Give the order to fall back to the citadel. Lure the enemy to the north side of the court, outside of the buildings. If they won't follow, then wait for them to enter the court on their own and then attack from behind once they've reached the citadel. I'll be watching from above to make sure that either way, they'll have a surprise waiting for them."

Before Waylen could respond, another bolt of lightning arced through the building to their side, collapsing the left half of it. Birdie could sense enemy soldiers approaching rapidly now, and she knew she couldn't stay there, but she also didn't want to abandon Waylen.

She hopped back onto Big-Eyes and directed her zodiac up into the air.

"Alright, Big-Eyes, let's give them something else to shoot at."

Turning sharply back over the building, Birdie unveiled her Radiant wings, the light from their crystalline form standing out like a beacon in the night. If the enemy was comprised mostly of Grandis loyalists, there was no way they'd be able to resist taking a few shots at her.

Sure enough, the enemy forces halted their advance and began firing upon their new target.

"Idiots," she muttered under her breath at the futile attempts to strike her speeding zodiac.

Their spells might have been powerful, but they were useless if they couldn't land a hit.

Birdie made two more passes over the loyalists. By her third flyby, most of them seemed to have caught on to the fact that they had very little chance of striking her, minimizing the effectiveness of her distraction. Unable to do much more good there, Birdie instead returned to the citadel to oversee the efforts against Jax's group of loyalists.

She arrived just as Jax and his soldiers scrambled across the citadel court to the front steps, a number of civilians among them and enemy forces hot in tow. Once they reached the steps, the civilians ran inside as Jax and his soldiers turned to face their pursuers. Knights formed a wall with their shields as spellcasters enchanted them to form a massive barrier at the foot of the stairs.

The loyalists immediately unleashed a barrage of powerful attacks that tore the barrier to shreds but injured surprisingly few. That was actually quite a relief to Birdie. She'd expected at least a quarter of Jax's soldiers to perish in that. If their attackers had better paced their spells, that would certainly have been the outcome.

The Shadow Guard then returned fire with their own spells as the balcony defenders joined in the barrage, raining down explosive arrows and debilitating spells.

Now on the back foot, the loyalists quickly pulled back only to be greeted by Oswald's soldiers as they poured from the buildings behind them and cut off any chance of escape. Jax then led a charge forward as well, and the two groups surrounded the rapidly diminishing loyalist forces.

Birdie swooped in close to see what more she could learn about the loyalists' abilities when they were in direct combat, and to her relief it indeed seemed that the only real advantage they had was their magic. She noticed that enchantments on their weapons and armor seemed more potent than should have been possible, but the Shadow Guard's spellcasters didn't seem to have any more trouble lifting those enchantments than they would have for ordinary enchantments, quickly nullifying that obstacle.

Once the enemy had been routed, Birdie flew down to speak with Jax.

"Nice work, Ruthoree," she remarked. "Ready to do it again?"

"Again? How many more are there?" Jax asked.

"By my estimate, there should be fewer than two hundred left."

"Two hundred!" Jax exclaimed, though after glancing at his soldiers he quickly calmed himself.

"Relax," said Birdie. "There's only one more group that's any sort of organized, and Waylen's leading them to the north of the citadel right now. There's about eighty of them, but if we do what you just did again, that eighty should be zero in the next ten minutes. After that, we'll split the Shadow Guard into groups of eight and clear out the rest of these scum from our city. With me watching their movements from above, we should have the last of them gone within an hour."

Jax clenched his fist as he surveyed the fallen loyalists. "I don't understand. How are Grandis loyalists able to use Radiant class spells?"

"They aren't," Birdie answered. "These spells are definitely low level spells that have been pushed to the extreme. I don't know how she did it, but I'm certain the one responsible is someone named Lux Rosa."

"Lux Rosa?" Jax repeated, frowning.

"I'll explain once this is over. For now, head towards the northeastern wall and wait in the buildings for Waylen to lure the other big group closer. Once they've gone past you, send half your troops to attack from the side and the others from behind. I don't know how long it will be before they arrive, but it should happen soon."

Jax's frown deepened, then he nodded. He turned to the soldiers around him. "Alright, you heard Eclipse! Let's move!"

As Jax led his troops to the far side of the court, Birdie flew up to visit Ev once more.

"That was great!" Ev announced upon Birdie's arrival.

Birdie tilted her head. "Yeah, well, it's still a work in progress, you know."

"Just tell us what to do next," Ev shouted. "We'll make sure no one ever tries to attack Roehelm again!"

Birdie pointed to the buildings surrounding the citadel court. "I want everyone here to spread out across the outer complex. Make sure no more enemy forces make it into the court. Once you're in position, don't leave it unless you absolutely have to, and by 'have to' I mean 'bad guys made it past you and are heading to the citadel.'"

"You got it! We won't let a single one get through."

Satisfied, Birdie directed Big-Eyes out over the city once again for another analysis.

The hundred or so scattered invaders were decimating her city, but until that last big group was taken care of, she couldn't do much about it. Toward the east, Waylen was losing soldiers fast, but he had successfully drawn his pursuers to the north of the citadel. It wasn't nearly as good of a trap as the one she'd set with Jax's group, but with the enemy coming from the east, she couldn't really set up as good of an ambush without making it obvious.

They still weren't quite in position yet, so Birdie took the opportunity to return to the armory and restock on arrows, this time making sure she grabbed the highest quality ones she could find. While she was there, she also swapped out her bow for one that enchanted its arrows with lightning.

Making her way back to the ambush point, Birdie arrived to see that the trap had already been sprung, the loyalists being pressed from three sides. Without support from above, however, the loyalists were mostly holding strong, and were even on the verge of breaking through Waylen's line.

"That's what we got these for, eh Big-Eyes?" Birdie remarked as she flew in from above.

Relinquishing just enough of her self-control to her othermind to allow it to take aim and select targets, she fired three arrows at enemy clerics.

Two of the arrows bullseye'd their targets, striking the clerics' unprotected faces and erupting into streaks of lightning that spread to the surrounding foes. The lightning did little damage to the loyalists' enchanted armor, but enough of it seeped beneath the armor to send them into short spasms, leaving them open. The third arrow bounced off its target but exploded nonetheless, its lightning still doing its job.

Birdie turned Big-Eyes around and let loose another volley, this time focusing on mages.

Some of the loyalists now turned their attention to her, but Birdie was out of range by the time they attacked.

Knowing they'd be ready for her on her next strafe, she pushed Big-Eyes to its top speed. This only gave her time to fire one arrow per pass, but that was enough.

With each subsequent flyby, Birdie could see the loyalists' numbers dropping more and more. She must have actually killed some of the invaders with her attacks, as towards the end of the battle she felt a small bit of her old strength return to her. Her othermind informed her that she'd now be able to mimic human speech once again, which was certainly a welcome development.

Eventually, the last of the enemy platoon fell, and Birdie set down once more to speak with Jax and Waylen.

"Finally," she said in her preferred voice. "Good work, guys. That should be the worst of it."

"How can you say that?" Jax asked. "From what you told me, there's still a hundred of these guys left, and we're down to what? Fifty?"

"We have well more than fifty. Don't forget about the Shadow Guard you'd sent to the balconies."

"That may be, but that—"

"As I told you," Birdie spoke over him, "the rest of Lux Rosa's forces are scattered and disorganized. With me as your eyes, we won't have any problem hunting them down. If any enemies start grouping together, I'll make sure we take care of that before it becomes a problem. Besides, you have clerics. They'll tend to the wounded and get our numbers back up while the loyalists' will only fall."

Jax sighed. "Alright, then. We'll follow your lead. Just tell us where to go, and we'll do the hard part."

Birdie narrowed her eyes at that remark but ignored it. Climbing onto Big-Eyes one more time, she directed the Shadow Guard to ambush every one of Lux Rosa's minions out in the city while Ev and the other balcony defenders dealt with any who felt so emboldened as to attempt to capture the citadel on their own. A handful of the invaders possessed enough intelligence to recognize the change in the battle's tide and fled before the Shadow Guard could reach them, but most were too caught up in their rampage to notice until it was too late. By the time the last of the enemy forces were snuffed out, the city had practically been reduced to ruins. Most of the citizenry had survived, but over half of the Shadow Guard had fallen.

Back at the citadel and after the fires had mostly been put out, Birdie met with Jax, Ev, the surviving Shadow Guard officers, and several members of the city council.

"Alright," said Jax, "you said this attack came from some guy called Lux Rosa, right?"

"Lux Rosa isn't 'some guy,'" responded Birdie, staring Jax in the eye. "She's a Radiant, and I have a bad feeling that what happened here tonight is just a taste of what's to come."

Chapter 3

The sensation of actual clothing wrapped around her body was not a comfortable one for Birdie, but at the moment it was necessary. Whatever that curse that had hit were was, its effects seemed to be permanent. Even after recovering from the battle, she still couldn't maintain a human guise, and while speaking with a human voice was now possible it wasn't yet easy.

Wrapped from head to foot in a tunic, boots, gloves, and a cloak tightly around her, she was mostly safe from the sun, which for the first time in ages overpowered her natural darkness to the point of causing pain. She also didn't want the townsfolk to see her stuck in her shadowy state as she made her way to the stables with Jax and Ev. At her hip was a small bag with a very important letter Syrus had given her long ago. It's contents she'd been told never to reveal to anyone, and after Lux Rosa's repeated demand for Syrus's true name, she could see he had every reason to warn her. How a name could be dangerous not even her othermind knew, but Lux Rosa wanted it for a reason, and it couldn't be good.

Jax opened the gate for Birdie, speaking quietly as she walked past. "Are you sure you can fly all the way to Ars Summis in your condition?"

Birdie turned to look at Jax. "When I first awoke in Nox Lumos six years ago I was in this exact same state. I know how to survive like this. Besides, it's a short trip. Big-Eyes can travel to Ars Summis and back in less than a week."

Inside the stables, a group of stablehands and a mage stood around Big-Eyes' stable speaking frantically to one another. When they noticed Jax and Ev approaching with Birdie, they grew nervous, which in turn put Birdie on edge. Growing closer, Birdie stopped as she caught sight of her zodiac collapsed on the ground in its pen.

"What happened?" she demanded.

The stablehands must have recognized her voice. "W-we don't know, Your Ladyship. It— your zodiac just fell to the ground half an hour ago. We swear it seemed fine just a moment before! We asked Miss Sonya to try sharing her magic with it, but nothing is working."

Birdie, with one hand holding the cusp of her cloak to keep it drawn tight, approached her fallen mount. The stablehands quickly backed out of her way as she moved. The glowing fish looked up mournfully at her as it gave a feeble flop on the ground.

What she sensed couldn't be right. Zodiacs, even dead ones, always overflowed with air-based magic, yet there was not a trace of it in Big-Eyes. Her abilities had dulled, but surely she could still sense every type of magic, right? Yes, of course she could. She'd sensed air magic last night! Something else had to be going on.

She turned to Sonya. "Do you know wind spells?"

Sonya stammered. "I… a few, yes."

"Cast one," Birdie ordered, pointing to the center of the stables. "Right there."

Sonya obediently raised her hand and… nothing. Shock on her face, she tried again, this time thrusting her hand forward. Still nothing.

"I-I don't…" she glanced nervously at Birdie and tried again, visibly straining this time.

"Stop," Birdie said, her voice unintentionally shaking.

Sonya fearfully turned to Birdie. "I swear I can do this! I just— something's wrong."

Trying her best to hide her own concerns, Birdie responded to Sonya. "I know. I believe you."

Relief appeared on Sonya's face as Jax and Ev approached Birdie. "What the heck is going on?" Jax asked. "Do you think Lux Rosa sent someone to do this?"

Birdie held her cloak tightly to her, not answering. She was too busy trying to think of any possible explanation. Her othermind was screaming "Suppression spell! Magic drain!" but she was pretty sure Sonya would have noticed someone hitting her with a spell. There was one way to find out.

"Cast a different type of spell," Birdie ordered. "Nothing air-based. Now."

Sonya hesitated, then lifted her hand again. After thinking for a moment, she channeled magic through her arm and through the air, forming a medium-sized sheet of ice on the ground.

Birdie's othermind was at a loss, and so was she. A suppression spell would have prevented Sonya from casting any type of magic, and Sonya giving magic to Big-Eyes would have undone any magic drain the poor zodiac might have been hit by. Whatever this was, it was something new.

She turned to Jax. "Check on every mage you can find. See if any of them can cast air-based magic. You," she turned to one of the stablehands. "Get me the fastest horse you have available."

"Hold on," said Ev. "You'd better not be thinking about going alone on the ground."

"Agreed," said Jax, "Ev and I will gather up our best soldiers and go with you."

"Absolutely not," returned Birdie. "You are the Captain of the Shadow Guard. I need you to stay here and protect Roehelm. If Syrus returns and Roehelm's been conquered, then he'll only return to be surrounded by Lux Rosa's forces."

Ev stood defiantly before Birdie. "Maybe so, but if you die before you send him a message, how long do you think it will be before he comes back on his own?"

Birdie squeezed her cloak tightly and thought for a moment before turning back to Jax. "Check on the mages, then find me two volunteers I can trust, preferably a spellcaster who can lift enchantments and a knight. I'd prefer for at least one of them to know ice or water magic, but I can make do without it. Make sure they're comfortable fighting without fancy armor. They can only have chain mail. No helmets, no gloves, no boots. Make sure they put ordinary clothes over the armor. They can only bring weapons they can conceal plus hunting bows. We'll need to look like ordinary travelers. I don't want us to risk attracting unwanted attention."

Jax nodded, then turned and hurried on his way.

Birdie followed, stepping around Ev and heading back to the citadel when Ev grabbed her cloak.

"I'm going, too," Ev demanded.

"No, you're not," Birdie returned. "We are short on healers as it is, and you're one of the best we've got."

"Exactly," replied Ev. "I'm also the only one who knows how to heal you if you get hurt. You're the one who decided you didn't need your clerics to learn how to heal shades, remember?"

"And you're the only one who didn't listen to that," Birdie added, making the sound of sighing purely out of habit.

She supposed Ev had a point. Her experience last night had been the closest she'd ever come to death, at least since her former incarnation had fallen. The thought of repeating that experience without Ev around frightened her, but if Lux Rosa had somehow made air magic disappear, there was no telling what other actions she'd take to prevent Birdie from reaching Ars Summis.

"Talk to your brother," Birdie said at last. "If he doesn't object, then you can come."

"And since when do I let him tell me what to do?"

"Ev."

"Fine, I'll talk to him," Ev conceded, "but for the record, I'm coming no matter what he says."

Birdie was tempted to assert her authority. Ev's stubbornness was frustrating, but it was admittedly one of her traits that Birdie was most fond of. That, and it was nice to know there was someone who had her back no matter what.

Turning back to the stablehands one last time, Birdie amended her order. "I've changed my mind. Prepare four of the strongest horses for travel. I'll be back in two hours."

Birdie left a smiling Ev, made her way back to the citadel, and headed towards her room. Along the way she ordered an attendant to gather five hundred gold and forty platinum from the treasury and to have ample food and water prepared and sent to the stables.

Up in her room, Birdie grabbed her old hunting bow from off the wall. She then went to her closet and pulled out a large backpack in addition to the small bag at her side. Next, she went to her desk and pulled out the flask of necromantic magic she'd been gifted the night before. She'd intended for it to be a decadent treat, but now it might mean the difference between life and death. Concentrated necromantic magic would significantly enhance her strength temporarily if the need happened to arise. Wrapping the flask in cloth, she headed down to the Shadow Guard's supply room.

After a brief exchange with the guard, she was allowed inside. There, she grabbed a canteen, uncorked the necromantic flask, and poured its contents into the metal container. There was no point in risking the loss of all that magic by keeping it in a fragile container, after all. Birdie then wrapped the canteen up in the cloth and packed it into her bag. She next grabbed a few restoration elixirs on top of that. She'd probably glean enough magic from her companions and any monsters they came across, but it wouldn't hurt to have a backup source of sustenance, even if it wasn't quite the same quality as natural stuff.

Supplies ready, Birdie headed to the armory to search for a suitable weapon.

Before she'd been weakened, her shadow weapons were absolutely top tier.

Now, however, she would have to rely on her old bow and the equipment of the Shadow Guard, as unfortunately none of the equipment they'd scavenged from the invading forces would be much use to her. All of the loyalists' armor had been plate, which would stand out, and surprisingly, none of their weapons had been enchanted with anything spectacularly special — mostly just physical strength enhancers, which wasn't exactly in line with her preferred combat style. All that wasn't to say the Shadow Guard's equipment was subpar, of course, but having equipment with enchantments of the same level as those spells last night would have been helpful.

Inside the armory, the first thing Birdie grabbed was a suit of chain mail that looked like it would fit. It did, but it was an uncomfortable sensation — even worse than the other clothes had been. It was tempting to simply forgo armor, seeing as it wouldn't do much good if she needed to enter puddle form, but she could always abandon it later if she needed to.

After struggling but ultimately succeeding in getting her other clothes to cover the armor, Birdie grabbed a beautiful dagger enchanted with high level durability and an enchantment breaker property. If she ran into any more of Lux Rosa's puppets, hopefully a strike from the dagger would break her control over them. Depending on how they'd received their enhanced magic, it might also prove useful in removing that threat.

A second dagger also caught her eye, this one with a magic drain enchantment. She next found a belt designed to hold two daggers, put it on, and placed the daggers into the belt. Lastly, she grabbed the most worn-down quiver she could find and stuffed it full of normal-looking arrows augmented with permanent piercing enchantments. She placed the quiver on her free hip and headed out the door.

Before returning to the stables, Birdie made a quick detour to pass instructions on to her staff about what to do in case of another attack. Once that was done, she was finally ready to go.

Back at the stables, Ev and Jax had already returned, along with Waylen and that Tallis kid. All of them, save for Jax, were packed and ready to go. Birdie's attendant was there waiting for her as well with the supplies Birdie had requested.

Upon seeing Birdie, Jax approached, a dire expression on his face. "Birdie, I had the other mages try casting air spells. None of them could do it. How the hell is that possible?"

Birdie had been thinking about that as well. "I've seen two spells that shouldn't exist, about ten pushed far beyond their known limits, and now air magic has disappeared. The only explanation I can think of is that Lux Rosa has somehow managed to gain some of the power of the Masters."

Jax's eyes widened. "That can't be possible. Syrus has been trying for years to do that."

"And apparently this Lux Rosa's beat him to it," Birdie stated. "If that's really what happened, then we have to get Syrus back now. He has to figure out what she did so he can do it, too. Otherwise we won't stand a chance against her."

Jax swallowed, and Birdie looked over once again at the soldiers he'd brought her.

"Are you sure you'll be able to manage without Waylen?" she asked. "We lost several officers last night."

"I know," said Jax, "but you wanted a knight, and he's one of the best. I've already sent messengers to bring more forces here. Once they arrive, we should be fine."

"Speaking of forces," Birdie said, "do we have any across the sea? I'd like to send a message to Dezeroth once we've crossed."

Jax shook his head. "We've stayed out of Atsia since he started his stupid war. You wanted us to remain neutral."

Birdie nodded subtly. "I was afraid of that. I'll have to make contact with his army at some point, then." She then looked at Tallis. "What about him? Was that kid really the best you could find?"

Jax followed her gaze. "Tallis wasn't exactly my first pick, but he was very insistent. Waylen also vouched for him, and I know the two of them work well together, so I agreed. Besides, he knows ice magic, and none of his spells rely on the air. He also knows earth magic and has studied a bit as a spellcaster. He's not so good at breaking enchantments, but he's got a few of his own he can cast. I thought they might prove useful to you, especially his shrinking spell. He's already helped Waylen pack his favorite war hammer into a satchel."

Birdie cocked her head as she looked back at Jax. That wasn't exactly what she'd asked for, but she supposed it was good enough. "And Ev? What did you decide about her?"

Jax glanced away for a second before returning his attention to Birdie. "As much as I hate it, I think she should go. If you get in any battles, you're going to need a healer."

Birdie let out the sound of a sigh. "Fine, but you'd better tell your Gram that this wasn't my decision."

"I'll tell her we both tried to stop her. I'm not taking the blame for this either."

Birdie let out a very small chuckle, then made her way over to Ev and the others. "So," she called out, "the three of you have volunteered to go with me to Ars Summis."

"Yes, ma'am!" Tallis blurted out. "It would be our honor and our privilege to escort you to the City of the Divine."

Annoyed at the outburst but choosing to ignore it, Birdie continued. "Before we go, I want everyone to be aware of what it exactly is that we're doing. We must head south and cross the Sea of Rezin to the nation of Atsia. From there, the fastest route will be through the Crystal Desert, and even after that we'll have a long road ahead of us. Lux Rosa likely expects that we're heading to Ars Summis, which means she'll try to stop us. She's already shown us that she can do things only the Masters have ever done before, so let me ask you: knowing what we are up against, are you sure you want to come with me?"

Ev answered before Birdie even finished. "Absolutely!"

"With certainty!" said Tallis.

Waylen stepped forward, all two hundred and fifty pounds of him. "You gave me a second chance after I betrayed Lord Syrus because of Grandis."

Waylen's beard shook as he pounded his chest. "I took an oath to serve you, and serve you I'm gonna do."

Birdie looked from Ev to Tallis to Waylen in turn. At last she nodded, then tilted her head. "Alright, then. Let's make sure we have enough supplies for all of you. I've been told you have a shrinking spell," she said to Tallis. "We might as well make use of it and pack as much as we can. Let's try and make it quick, though. It's a long ride to the Sea of Rezin."

✳ ✳ ✳ ✳

Twenty miles out from Roehelm, Birdie, hunched over, pulled her cloak tightly around her head. The noonday sun beat down upon them with such intensity that she could feel it burning through the hood of her cloak. All the while the light reflecting off the road scorched her face any time she tried to look up.

The pain gave way to relief as Birdie felt Ev's healing magic surround her. "Maybe we should travel under the trees for a while," Ev said from beside her.

36

"The trees would be slower," Birdie replied. "Even with luck it will take us twelve days to reach Ars Summis. We don't need to make it twenty."

"Maybe not," replied Ev, "but we won't exactly be making good time if we have to stop because you've passed out, either."

Birdie hesitated before answering. "It's just a little pain. I'll be fine."

Waylen spoke up now. "Ya know, we have been pushin' the horses for a long time now. We really ought to give 'em a break."

"Fine," Birdie agreed. "Next stream we come across—"

"How about that one?" Ev interrupted.

Birdie glanced over to see Ev pointing through the trees to their right. Sure enough, there was a tiny stream not too far in.

Reluctantly, Birdie directed her horse over to the woods. The relief of the shade was immediate. Letting go of her cloak, she dismounted and led her steed to the stream. Ev and the others followed closely behind.

As soon as the horses saw the water, they started moving on their own. Each of them drank for nearly a minute, and Birdie realized she might have been pushing them too hard.

Waylen noticed as well. "These horses are pretty tired, Miss Birdie. I know you want to hurry, but I reckon we should give 'em a half hour."

Birdie nodded, then took a seat at the base of a particularly shady tree as her human companions took the opportunity to refill what they'd drunk from the canteens they had with them. She'd often wondered what it must be like to have to consume material substances for sustenance, but she assumed it wasn't all that different from what she did. It seemed more annoying, seeing as physical beings had to consume multiple types of material to stay healthy. It also was likely less pleasant having to deal with odd textures. Other than that, though, she guessed the only difference was that they received the benefits of consumption from the inside out rather than the outside in.

Once Ev was done with the stream, she joined Birdie by the tree.

"So, tell me," she began quietly. "How are you really doing? What exactly did that spell do to you?"

Birdie hesitated before answering. She didn't like admitting weakness, but she also knew Ev would see through any bluff. "Honestly," she said, glancing over at the others to make sure they couldn't hear, "I feel like I'd never left Nox Lumos. It's like every ounce of strength and skill I've ever gained is gone. The only abilities I have left are the ones that are natural to a shade, and even those I can't do very well."

Arms over her knees, she looked over at Ev. "I'd say that spell reset me to my weakest state, but it also worked on Apollyon. Because of that, my guess is that what it really does is zero out every way that the Masters' systems augment living things."

Ev looked confused. "Wait, are you talking about magic or proficiency?"

Birdie shook her head. "Those, too, but the Masters did more than just give the world magic and rules for gaining new skills. I'm talking about the way nepacs and Divine grow stronger from fighting and overcoming trials."

Ev looked a mixture of surprised and concerned. Birdie guessed she must not have realized those routes of gaining strength were unnatural. That wasn't surprising. It was such an intrinsic part of life few would likely question how it worked.

"Well," said Ev, now looking down in thought, "if you got… 'zeroed out,' do you think maybe you could get your strength back again by hunting some monsters?"

Birdie glanced sideways at Ev. "I think so. Why?"

"Because if we can get you stronger, why are we sitting around here when there are monsters to hunt? Come on!"

Ev grabbed Birdie's arm and attempted to pull her to her feet.

Birdie looked up tiredly at Ev. "You know we need to get moving again soon. We'll have time to get my strength back after we contact Syrus."

"Waylen said the horses need to rest half an hour. That's thirty minutes. Come on. Do you really want the sun to keep hurting you the whole trip? What about when we get into town? You can't even disguise yourself right now."

Birdie glanced deeper into the woods. She supposed it was worth a shot. There was no way any of the local monsters would give her enough strength to maintain a human appearance before they reached the port, but it might help her fight off the sun by then.

"Alright, you win," she said with a sigh before standing up. She turned to Waylen and Tallis. "You two stay here and watch the horses. Ev and I will be back before it's time to go."

Tallis jumped up at this. "W-wait, where are you going?"

"I'm just going get some exercise," Birdie answered.

Waylen walked up behind Tallis and placed a big hand on his shoulder. "No worries, Miss Birdie. We'll be waitin' for when ya get back."

Birdie could see that Tallis wanted to say more, but he refrained. Not wanting to give him the chance to change his mind, Birdie crossed over the stream and headed deeper into the woods with Ev following. The monsters around here didn't possess strong magic. That, coupled with her now weakened perception skills, meant that she didn't have any good way to detect potential prey.

"Let's go this way," Ev suggested, pointing off to their left.

Birdie didn't object. At this point, Ev was the one in better shape for tracking down monsters. She'd been hunting beasts in the area for the last five years as part of her crusade against monsters, so Birdie trusted her abilities.

After following Ev's lead for a good five minutes, Birdie finally began to sense new magic nearby.

"Wait," she said, grabbing Ev by the arm. "There are volecans nearby."

"I know," replied Ev, smiling. "I could smell the smoke two minutes ago."

Birdie released Ev's arm. Of course. Smell was a sense she often wished she had.

"I'm not sure I can fight volecans," Birdie said, the various possible scenarios entering her mind.

"Maybe not on your own, but that's why I'm here," Ev said as she pulled out her bow and an arrow. "Come on. Where's the confident Birdie who made slaughtering hordes of bublobs look easy?"

"I'm only confident when I know I can win," replied Birdie, annoyed.

Pretty much every scenario in her head ended with her fleeing or relying on Ev to survive. As much as she liked Ev, she didn't like putting her life in anyone else's hands.

"Look, I know how to fight these things," Ev said, seeing Birdie's reluctance. "We peg 'em with an arrow if they pop up far away and stab them if they try to get close."

"I know how to kill a volecan," Birdie replied. "That's not the problem."

"Come on. Let's at least see how many there are. If you still don't want to do it, we'll back off."

Birdie reluctantly agreed, and the two of them made their way to a scorched clearing in the middle of the woods. Holes and upturned ashen earth sprinkled the area. At its center were three child-sized, narrow-headed rodents with fire dribbling from their mouths and nostrils sniffing around their little hill. Birdie knew there had to be at least one more hiding underground. Volecans always had a leader that was larger than the others, and none of those three fit the cut.

Straining her senses, she picked up on the magic of two more volecans underground. She didn't think she sensed more, but it was difficult to tell if there was anything past the visible trio.

"I think there are only five," she told Ev quietly, not wanting to alert the monsters.

"So, what do you say?" Ev asked, her bow still ready. "Shall we give it a shot?"

Her othermind informed her that the odds of her under-detecting the volecans by more than one was next to zero. She would still need to rely on Ev, but she felt their prospects looked fairly good.

"You know what?" she answered, pulling out her own bow and nocking an arrow. "I think we shall. Middle one first?"

"Middle one first," Ev confirmed, and the two of them took aim and let their arrows fly.

The two arrows struck side by side in the center volecan's chest, with Birdie's flying clean through thanks to the penetration enchantment on the arrows she'd packed. Their target thrashed about as the other two beasts let out high-pitched shrieks to alert the ones underground that there was danger.

Ev and Birdie let loose another pair of arrows, each hitting one of the other two volecans. Ev's reacted by diving into a nearby hole, whereas Birdie's entered a suicide charge. Ev fired another arrow, crippling the giant rodent. Birdie quickly followed up with yet another to finish it off. The two of them then backed up to put some distance between themselves and the nearby holes.

Birdie sensed one of the creatures rapidly approaching the closest of the holes and ran to position herself behind it, drawing both of her daggers in anticipation.

Sure enough, just as Ev unleashed another arrow, a huge volecan the size of a bear burst from the ground.

Birdie was ready for it. She jumped on the monster's back and dug her blades deep into its sides. It spun around quickly, throwing her off as it spewed fire from its mouth in a wide circle. Birdie scrambled out of the way of the flames, then held her daggers out defensively as she stared down the great beast.

She was not in a good position. To her left she could sense the other two volecans approaching rapidly underground, and she couldn't defend against all three at once. Still, she was here to fight, so that's what she'd do, even if it meant leaving herself open.

The big one charged. Its attack was interrupted as an arrow struck its neck, drawing its attention away from Birdie. It focused on Ev instead just as the other two emerged from the tunnels. The injured one went straight for Birdie's hip.

Birdie slashed at it with her right-hand dagger, landing a glancing blow against its eye and chasing it away. The other one managed to sink its red-hot teeth deep into her shin even as she struck it, sending pain shooting up her leg. Birdie reacted by slamming both her blades into the rodent's neck before tearing them upwards, killing the thing.

Birdie felt a small surge of strength as the other small volecan spit flames in her direction. She nimbly leapt out of the way, easily avoiding the attack.

The oversized rodent seemed set on not getting within range of her daggers again, choosing instead to continue spitting fire at her from a distance.

That was fine with Birdie. As she danced out of the way of the next blast, she readied her arrow and shot it straight into the creature's mouth.

The volecan gasped, staggered, and fell over dead.

Birdie then turned her attention back to Ev and the large one, but that battle was already over. Ev stood beside the dead monster, a smug look on her face.

"See?" she called. "I told you we could do it."

"Yeah, yeah," replied Birdie, the pain in her leg now dissipated evenly throughout her body. "Would you mind healing me now? One of them got my leg pretty bad."

Ev hurried over and pulled out a pocket-sized rod that she pointed at Birdie's torso, a dark glow emanating from it.

"Thanks," said Birdie, the relief immediate.

Ev stepped back and looked at Birdie eagerly. "So, feeling any better?"

Birdie paused for a second, realizing that the sun wasn't bothering her quite as much. "Actually, I think I do," she replied, a bit relieved.

Ev gave a little clap. "That's great! Do you think you can disguise yourself as a human again?"

Birdie shook her head. "Maybe in the dark, but not likely. I'm afraid it will take a while before I can maintain that kind of illusion indefinitely."

Ev looked disappointed, but ultimately shrugged. "Oh well. At least we know we can fix this. What do you say about going on a hunt every break from now on?"

Birdie crossed her arms and tilted her head. "I say, 'I knew there was a reason I let you come with me.'"

Ev smiled, and the two of them made their way back to where Tallis and Waylen were waiting by the stream. Apparently the two of them had had a nice time of their own, if the lack of prying by Tallis was anything to go off of.

That was good. Her talk with the kid the previous night had her worried he'd be a nuisance, but perhaps this journey wouldn't be so bad after all.

Chapter 4

Deep in the Hall of Champions, amidst tapestries and statues depicting once renowned Radiants long gone, Lux Rosa sat comfortably on a lavish throne surrounded by shimmering ripples in the air. Her reflection looked back at her from the silver armrest — an indigo-eyed beauty with long blond hair, or at least as much of a beauty as these human bodies could be shaped into.

Her hand deep inside one of the ripples, she felt for the system of air magic she'd discovered. Channeling her will, she reactivated the system. She'd given her troops more than enough time to conquer the city before turning it off and given Eclipse enough time to give up on flying to Ars Summis should they have failed. If Syrus's little pet yet lived, there were now few routes left open to it.

The grinding of stone signaled the arrival of Vellic, the self-proclaimed Grand Curate and leader of the group of Grandis loyalists Lux had taken under her wing. The old man, clad in his gold-trimmed white robes, approached her throne reverentially.

"You summoned me, Lady Rosa?" Vellic asked, bowing.

"I did," replied Lux. "A situation has developed. While I was able to successfully weaken Eclipse, I'm afraid your choice of soldier lacked the strength to split it."

Vellic looked up in shock. "Sir Richman is—"

"Dead, yes," Lux finished. "Now, we must prepare a second assault force against Roehelm."

Vellic opened his mouth in surprise. "A second force, my lady? Surely the rest of our battalion must have been sufficient. Roehelm certainly burns as we speak."

"Is that so?" Lux Rosa smiled sweetly, crossing her fingers in her lap. "Tell me, have you seen its ashes yourself?"

"Well, no—"

"Then send another battalion to make certain of it!"

Vellic bowed low to the ground. "A-as you wish, my lady."

Vellic stood and turned to go, but Lux called after him.

"Now, now, don't be so hasty."

Vellic looked up, shocked. "Lady Rosa?"

"We now have two potential threats that we must deal with. We must take decisive action against Roehelm, yes, but if Eclipse lives, we also must make certain that it does not reach Ars Summis. We would gain nothing from Roehelm's conquest if Syrus is alerted any other way. If he expects an ambush on his return then he simply won't return."

"Forgive me, my lady, but is that not a desirable outcome?"

"NO!" Lux shouted. She leaned forward, towering over Vellic from her throne. "If we cannot strike him with my inhibitor, we cannot remove his ability to create avatars in Ars Summis. He would become an active and nigh irremovable threat if he knew about us!"

Vellic nearly trembled. "What would you have me do?" he inquired.

Lux leaned back again, then smiled. "First, I require another… volunteer. I'll need someone with a good grasp of fire magic this time."

She waved him away.

"As you wish, Lady Rosa." Vellic made a feeble attempt at hiding his reluctance, but he obeyed, and that was what was important.

Lux shifted her attention back to the swirling shimmers around her as Vellic left the room to fetch her a new host. It would take at minimum eighteen days for her forces to reach Roehelm. The possibility that Syrus would return before then was a very real one, but it cost her nothing to be proactive. Nonetheless, she needed to find ways into more of the so-called Masters' systems as soon as possible, lest he return before she had a chance to stamp out anyone who might inform him of her existence. Of course, Syrus was not *that* great of a threat. If he were, he would have already made at least some of the same progress she had. Still, his creation of Eclipse was proof that he did have the potential to compromise her ambitions, and that was something she would not risk. She'd waited a hundred and fifty years for the opportunity now before her, and she would allow none the chance to take that away.

Some number of minutes later, Vellic returned with a soldier in tow. That meant it was time for the performance to begin.

Lux stood, removing her hand from the nearby shimmer. "Welcome, brave warrior. Pray tell, what is your name?"

The soldier kneeled before the throne. "I am Dame Lotree. I am humbled and honored that you would consider me to serve as your next champion."

Lux raised her arms outward. "Dame Lotree. Grand Curate Vellic has brought you here before me. You have proven yourself to him. Now, it is time to prove yourself to me. I ask you now: will you pledge your life to carrying out my will, that we may purge this land of the evils of Eclipse and its vile creator Syrus?"

The soldier raised its head. "I will serve you with all my might. Whatever power you give me, I will wield with righteousness."

"Then," Lux brought her hands together, "it is time. Close your eyes and allow the Grand Curate to purify your mind in preparation for the power which I will soon bestow upon you."

The soldier obeyed, and Vellic stepped forward to perform his little ritual. He placed his hands on the soldier's head and cast a little spell Lux had created for him, forcibly and permanently suppressing all conscious thought from the soldier.

The ceremony over, Lux stepped down to her new puppet and placed her own hands on its head, casting the only spell that actually mattered in the process. The deed complete, she returned to her throne, sat back down, and closed her eyes. She reopened them to see herself upon her throne in all of her beautiful glory. Her new body then stood as her original opened its eyes once more.

"Now," Lux stated from her body atop the throne, "we have three situations we must address. First, the matter of Roehelm. For that, I want you to gather five hundred soldiers and prepare them to ride. Send thirty pegasus riders with them. When they reach Roehelm, they are to leave no survivors. They are to find Syrus's marker and prepare a trap for his return. Make sure they are aware that if they split him, I will personally erase them from existence. I do not need him resurrecting someplace where we have no presence. Also, bring me a soldier whom I may bless with a special version of my inhibitor spell. It will cripple Syrus, but not to the same extent that my full inhibitor would. Nonetheless, it will remove a portion of his Divine abilities. That should be sufficient for containing him.

"Second is the matter of Eclipse. There are six likely routes that creature might take to reach Ars Summis. Five of them require visiting specific ports; one travels up a river. We must cover all of them. We have sixty-two other pegasi available. I want nine riders sent to each of those ports and to the mouth of the river. Make sure at least one in each group is able to detect different types of magic and have them on alert for illusion spells. They are to remain at their assigned location until they either destroy Eclipse, or I send word otherwise. Once they have been sent out, send one more rider to our camp nearest Ars Summis and have them ready to rally at the city's gates if need be.

"Finally, dealing with those two problems will leave us short on soldiers here. See to it that recruitment and training is accelerated. I don't care how you do it, but do not draw soldiers from our pool of laborers. Am I clear on all of this?"

Vellic bowed his head but glanced at her puppet. "I will do as you command, Lady Rosa, but—"

"Does something concern you, Vellic?"

"Forgive me, but for what purpose did you request a new… champion?"

Lux's puppet smiled and leaned close to Vellic. "Simple. There is one port in particular I find likely Eclipse will visit. That is a town I would like to pay a visit to as well."

Understanding appeared on Vellic's face. He nodded, then escorted her puppet body towards the door.

"And Vellic," Lux called after him from her throne.

Vellic stopped and looked back.

"Do be a dear and have your workers increase their productivity in exacerbating the degradation. The closer this world is to falling apart, the easier time I will have in fixing it."

Vellic bowed and left the room, leaving Lux alone with the shimmering distortions. This degradation was the key to getting around every safeguard the Masters had ever created to prevent other Divine from seizing control of their world.

Lux placed her hand back into the waving light. Whether Roehelm had fallen or not, she knew Eclipse would have escaped. She'd made the mistake of underestimating the artificial intelligence Syrus had placed in Eclipse, and now she had to deal with the consequences. She would not succumb to such overconfidence again.

Chapter 5

Ev's idea of hunting monsters every rest stop had proved a fruitful one, allowing Birdie the opportunity to regain some of her other skills that she had lost. After two days, she could manage minor illusions such as conjuring darkness and light. After four days, Birdie had managed to recover enough of her strength to keep a human guise up indefinitely — when light levels were low, at least. It was a marked improvement, and it was proving invaluable now that they'd entered into the harbor town of Roeport late in the evening. She'd put on a short-haired brunette look this time, as that was a disguise she was sure no one would recognize.

Arms crossed, Birdie addressed Waylen. "Maybe we should ask someone if he's even in town? We'll need to find a room for the night if we have to wait much longer."

"I reckon we'll need a room anyhow," responded Waylen, peering once again through the clouded windows of his captain friend's home. "It'll take time for 'em to get a ship ready, ya know."

"I'm going to look for Ev and Tallis then. There's no point in buying supplies now if we're just going to have to store them all night anyway."

"Jus' give him a few more minutes, Miss Birdie. Captain Dragmun's no drinker. Reacts poorly to the stuff, if I remember. Whatever he's doin' I'm sure he'll be back shortly. The boys at the harbor said he's home, after all."

"That doesn't change the fact that we'll be stuck hauling around a week's worth of feed until morning."

"I'm sure he'll hold onto it for us if we ask nicely," Waylen said, waving his hand dismissively. "Besides, I'd bet when he hears Lady Eclipse wants his service, he'll be rather wantin' to meet ya for himself."

Birdie sighed, then leaned back against the side of the building. They'd already been waiting thirty minutes. Though, now that she thought about it, that meant that Ev and Tallis had likely already bought everything. In that case, she supposed she didn't have anything better to do. She'd rather they ask around a bit more instead of wait, but she could last until the others returned before doing that.

Three minutes later, Waylen piped up.

"Ah! There he is!" he shouted as he stepped into the street.

Birdie looked in the direction Waylen was headed and spotted a large, gray-bearded man carrying a large sack over his shoulder. His left eye was missing, replaced with a cloth wrapped around a piece of clay with an eye painted on.

"Dragmun, ya old codger!" continued Waylen. "Where've ya been? We've been waitin' all day for ya!"

Dragmun stopped as a flash of recognition filled his eye. "Waylen?"

A large grin spread across his face as he set his sack on the ground.

"Waylen!" he shouted again as he stepped forward and the two large men embraced, giving Birdie the impression of two bears wrestling.

Dragmun took a step back. "Lords, man, how long has it been? Why didn't you send word you were coming? I would've gotten' the place ready for ya!"

Solemnity appeared on Waylen's face. "I'm afraid this visit ain't a fishin' one. Somethin' real bad's goin' on, and we need to hitch a ride across the sea soon as possible." Waylen motioned towards Birdie.

Dragmun followed Waylen's gesture, his eye landing on Birdie. "And who might this be?"

"That's—" Waylen began, but Birdie cut him off.

"Let's talk about that once we're inside."

Waylen stopped, then nodded.

"She's right," he said quietly. "If the wrong people found out she was here, there could be trouble."

Dragmun looked between Birdie and Waylen before sighing and picking up his sack again.

"Lords, Waylen, what have ya gotten yourself into this time?" he muttered as he headed to his door and unlocked it.

Pushing it open, he motioned for Birdie and Waylen to step inside. He set his sack down on a table in the center of what looked like a kitchen, then lit a pair of lamps on opposite sides of a room further back. He beckoned for his guests to follow. They did so, taking seats in a room filled with ship parts and large fish heads lining the walls.

"Alright," said the still standing Dragmun, arms folded, "so who is this woman that's causin' you so much trouble?"

Waylen glanced nervously at Birdie. "Dragmun, this is Lady Eclipse."

Dragmun raised an eyebrow, then burst out laughing. Waylen looked apologetically at Birdie, who rolled her eyes before standing up.

"Let's just get this out of the way, shall we?" she said, displaying her Radiant wings to Dragmun.

Dragmun's mirth ended the moment he noticed her wings. He dropped down to the floor and stammered, "I-I... Your Ladyship, forgive me. I thought —"

"It's fine," Birdie said, putting her wings away and sitting back down. "If I wanted people to know who I am, I wouldn't look like this right now."

Dragmun was clearly confused. "Your Ladyship?"

"Would you please get off the floor? And please don't call me that. Right now, it's just 'Birdie.'"

Dragmun took a moment to process that before rapidly rising to his full height again, confusion still on his face as his eyes darted to Waylen.

Waylen gestured to a third chair in the room. "Please sit down, my friend. Like I said, there's some bad tides afoot, and we could use your help."

Dragmun looked once again between Birdie and Waylen, though he was beginning to calm down. "I don't understand. How can an old sailor like me help...?" He trailed off while staring at Birdie.

Waylen explained to Dragmun what had happened to Birdie and how air magic had disappeared.

"That's incredible," Dragmun said after Waylen had finished.

"And it's why we need your help," Birdie stated.

Dragmun placed his hand on his beard as he looked down in thought. "You said this Radiant's name is Lux Rosa?"

Waylen nodded, then leaned forward. "That's right. You haven't heard of her, have you?"

The prospect had Birdie's attention as well.

Dragmun stroked his beard. "Heard of her, yes. Can't say I know much, though. Can't even remember the last time I heard the name. Probably back before the whole brouhaha with Syrus turnin' on the other Radiants."

"What do you know about her?" Birdie pressed. No one back at the citadel had been able to tell her much. Whoever this Lux Rosa was she couldn't have had much of a presence in the region, not even in the old days.

Dragmun shook his head. "I'm sorry. It's been years since anyone's... wait a minute." He looked up. "I remember where I heard that name. Old Patches used to sail to her citadel. It was down in the Southern Isles."

Well, that partially explained why no one in Roehelm had heard of her. The Southern Isles were about as far away as possible, and Radiants who lived there rarely gathered much of a following. Still, if Lux Rosa had indeed worked with Syrus at some point, she should have been known to at least a few people.

Birdie pressed further. "Do you know what her relationship is with Lord Syrus?"

"Sorry, Lady Eclipse—"

"Birdie," she interrupted.

Dragmun blinked.

Waylen spoke up. "Er, we don't know if there are servants of Lux Rosa about. We think it's best if everyone just calls Lady Eclipse 'Birdie,' just in case."

Dragmun seemed to accept this. "Yes, well, as I was sayin', Miss Birdie, I don't recall Old Patches ever sayin' much about it."

"Where can we find this 'Old Patches'?" Birdie asked, leaning back in her seat.

"I'm afraid Old Patches passed away three years ago," Dragmun answered. "If ya want I should, I can ask his old shipmates if they know anything."

"Yes, please," replied Birdie, "but only if it won't take much time. Right now we need a ship to take us to Noontide Bay, and the sooner we leave the better."

Waylen spoke up again. "Whaddaya say, Dragmun? Do ya think you can help us out here?"

Dragmun shifted in his seat. "Aye, well, I can take ya, I suppose, but it's gonna be a long journey. It's too risky to sail straight across the sea these days, and I'm not sure how soon I can put together a crew willin' to go that far."

Birdie leaned forward. "We can't afford any delays. We brought twenty platinum to pay for the voyage. That's nine hundred gold for each member of a crew of twenty, plus some extra to cover costs. How quickly will that get your sailors together? "

Dragmun's eye opened wide. "Twenty platinum? Well, I suppose I shouldn't expect less from a Radiant. I hate takin' your money for somethin' like this, but I'll wager for that amount I could probably convince enough hands by mid-afternoon tomorrow."

Birdie leaned back in her seat again. That was acceptable, but they still couldn't afford to travel all the way around the sea. "Thank you, but if I may ask, what makes crossing the sea so dangerous?"

Dragmun adjusted his fake eye with his hand. "I'd have wagered you of all people would know that, given your reputation. The sea's too full of monsters without any Divine patrollin' it. Folks in this town aren't equipped to fight off the kinds o' demons that rise up from the depths."

Waylen leaned forward and pounded his chest. "A few monsters ain't a problem for us. We've got three of the finest Shadow Guard travelin' with us, yours truly included!"

"Mm," grunted Dragmun, "that may be, but you'll still be havin' a hard time convincin' sailors to travel across deeper waters."

"Even if ya tell 'em we've got the blessing of a Radiant on board?"

"A Radiant who's lost all her power," Dragmun frowned before looking quickly over at Birdie. "Erm, no disrespect, your ladyship."

Birdie cocked her head and smirked. "I might not be at my best, but like you said, I know more about monsters than anyone, and I know there's only a handful of things in that sea we aren't prepared to deal with."

"Is that a fact?" Dragmun asked, unconvinced.

Birdie's othermind went through the list of creatures too dangerous for them and where they were located. "I admit things might get rough, but the only monsters out there we'd likely lose to are storm titans, lurkers, and Scylla. If you let me navigate, I can make sure we stay clear of those regions."

Dragmun frowned. "With all respect, I'm aware of where those monsters live. The problem is everythin' else. Are you sayin' your three soldiers can fight off ghost ships and hordes of man o' wars?"

Birdie smiled as she shifted into a more comfortable position. "We have a cleric who can handle ghost ships, and I can deal with man o' wars."

"You?" Dragmun blurted, and even Waylen seemed surprised.

"Man o' wars live in colonies with a collective intelligence. Kill the leader, and they all die. I know how to spot said leader, and I'm more than capable of killing it. Besides, I said I can navigate to avoid monsters. That means all of them."

Dragmun seemed unsure, which Waylen noticed.

"There, ya see?" he offered, motioning to Birdie. "With us on board, you ain't got nothin' to worry about."

Dragmun stroked his beard once more. "I dunno. This Lux Rosa sounds like she might be trouble, but it won't help anyone if we all end up chum for the fishes."

"Oh, come on, now, Dragmun," Waylen said, standing up and pulling out a tiny war hammer he kept in his satchel before holding it out in front of him.

"Look, we've got the finest weapons in Doxla."

Dragmun was unimpressed. "That? Ya couldn't even hammer a nail with that thing."

"Oh, not now," responded Waylen, palming the hammer. "A pal of mine put a spell on it to keep it shrunk down, but when this little beauty's big it can shatter dragon bones."

Dragmun sighed and stood up. "Look, I can't make any promises, but I'll try and see if I can round up a crew willin' to sail over deep sea."

Birdie stood as well. "Thank you. That's all we're asking for," she said, cocking her head. "Besides, I'm sure lots of sailors would love the chance to see me in action."

Birdie and Waylen shook Dragmun's hand, and he escorted them to his front door. Before leaving, Birdie handed over a small bag of twenty platinum coins.

Dragmun opened the bag to inspect the coins. Satisfied and seemingly impressed, he tucked the bag into his pocket.

"Meet me at the docks at noon tomorrow. Straight across or through the shallows, I'll have Your Ladyship a crew."

"Thanks, Dragmun," replied Waylen. "When we get back from Ars Summis, I'll treat ya somethin' special for this. Before we go, though, mind if we store our supplies at the shipyard?"

"Really? Ya couldn't have asked me sooner?"

Waylen shrugged.

"Fine. Bring your stuff to my ship in an hour and I'll help ya load up. Anything else?"

Birdie did have one thing. "Maybe try a little harder to not refer to me as 'Your Ladyship'?"

Dragmun blushed. "I'll do my best."

"Alright then, we'll see ya tomorrow, Captain!" Waylen slapped Dragmun on his shoulder before he and Birdie took their leave.

Outside, Ev and Tallis had returned, the horses loaded up with supplies for the journey.

"So, how'd it go?" asked Ev.

Birdie smiled faintly. "Well, we have a ship. That much is certain."

Tallis raised a fist excitedly. "Excellent! Ars Summis, here we come!"

The outburst took Birdie aback. "Maybe don't announce that to the whole world," she scolded.

Tallis looked back at her sheepishly.

Birdie sighed. "Well, for now let's find a place to stay for the night. Even if we travel straight across the sea, it's going to be a while before we sleep on a bed again."

* * * *

The next day, the group gathered at the docks near Dragmun's ship — a three-masted vessel about twenty-five yards in length and eight yards wide. The letters *WINDFALL* had been burned into the port side. Dragmun stood on the dock supervising a group of sailors as they loaded supplies.

"It's about time," Dragmun crowed as the group approached him. "I thought ya were in a hurry to set sail."

Birdie stepped forward with her hand on her hip, though she kept her hood on tight in the noonday sun. "We're in a hurry to get to Ars Summis. Is this a crew that can help us do that?"

"Aye. I found enough souls who were willing to cross over deeper waters, but not by much. We've only got a crew of seventeen, and a few of 'em only 'cause they're green and don't yet know what's out there waitin' for 'em."

"As long as they can sail the ship, that's good enough for me."

"They don't know who ya are, mind ya." Dragmun looked over his shoulder, then back to Birdie. "I jus' told 'em you're ex-soldiers. Some folks blame ya for the famine goin' on, ya know."

Birdie tsked. "Good for them. If that's easier than accepting that the world is simply dying, then they can keep clinging to their delusions. I'd rather not reveal myself, anyway."

Dragmun shifted uncomfortably at that and cleared his throat. "Yes, well, I also asked Old Patches's old shipmates about that Lux Rosa woman. I'm afraid they didn't know much. Only one of 'em ever even laid eyes on her — said she was a real beauty."

"How good to know," Birdie quipped.

Dragmun frowned. "The only thing they had to say that might be interestin' is that she abandoned her citadel not long after Syrus started his war. No clue as to why. She just up and disappeared."

Birdie sighed. "I see. Well, you're right that it doesn't tell us much, but I appreciate you asking about it. It's certainly more than we knew about her before today."

An hour later, they, their horses, and all of their supplies were safely on board the *Windfall*. Dragmun barked a series of orders, and the deckhands scurried about getting the ship underway.

Tallis was practically giddy. "I can't believe I'm finally going to see Ars Summis!" he shouted from the bow of the vessel.

"This isn't a field trip," said Birdie as she joined him up front. "You can't even enter the city."

"Maybe not," replied Tallis, turning to Birdie, "but I can get right up close to it! How many nepacs can say they've even laid eyes on the City of the Divine, let alone gotten close enough to see the guardian?"

Birdie looked the young man in the eye. "Tallis, please tell me you didn't volunteer just so you could take a trip to Ars Summis."

Tallis's smile disappeared as he stammered. "What? N-no, of course not! I mean, it's a perk, but of course I didn't volunteer just for that. I mean, this is important that you send a message to Syrus, right?"

Birdie stared at Tallis for second — an act that clearly made him uncomfortable — before sighing and turning to face the other way.

"Just promise me you won't do anything stupid like upset the guardian when we get there," she said as she leaned onto the railing, only half looking at him.

"Oh, uh, right, of course not. I mean, of course I wouldn't do that," Tallis replied before settling into awkward silence.

That suited Birdie just fine. That gave her more time for her own thoughts and to enjoy the view of the sea as the *Windfall* pulled away from the docks. The endless expanse of waves gave way to the realization that this was the first time she'd ever been on a ship, at least since her reincarnation. Actually, she wasn't sure that her former self had ever ridden on a ship, either. Now that she thought about it, she hardly knew anything about what her past self had done. Syrus had never told her more than she'd asked, and she hadn't exactly asked much. It hadn't ever seemed important, and she supposed it still wasn't. She did wish she had her old memories from time to time, but her last incarnation had been split — the closest a Divine could come to death. As a false Divine, apparently only part of her mind persisted through that, unlike the entirety of a true Divine's mind. Regardless, the breeze on the sea and the sound of the waves was a pleasant experience, and that was a memory she intended to keep for as long as she was able.

"So," prompted Tallis after a few minutes of peace, "I've always wondered about something."

"If it's about the Divine or Ars Summis, I can't help you," Birdie responded, not in the mood for a chat.

"Oh, no, it's nothing like that," Tallis spat out quickly. "It's about you, actually."

Birdie glanced in his direction and raised her presently nonexistent eyebrow.

"It's just… you're a shade, right?"

"Oh, you noticed that, did you?"

Tallis blushed. "Yeah, I mean, I knew that already. I was just wondering, why do you always take on the appearance of a woman?"

Birdie stood up straighter and turned to face Tallis but kept one arm on the railing. "First of all, I don't. Second of all, I don't see why that's your business."

Tallis blushed harder, but seemed intent on pursuing the question. "I'm sorry. I only wondered because stories say you used to always take on a man's appearance."

Birdie turned back to the sea again, this time her arms crossed over the railing. "Yeah, well, that's reason enough, wouldn't you think? I wasn't always a Radiant, you know. I used to be just as vulnerable as I am now, and people wanted to kill me. It's a lot easier to hide when you don't look like what others expect you to."

Tallis blinked. "That makes sense." He paused before turning to ask another question, but Birdie cut him off.

"I think that's enough questions for now."

She barely looked over at him, hoping he'd take the hint.

Fortunately, he did. After a moment's hesitation he turned his attention back to the sea, not saying another word.

A short time later, once the ship was well out to sea, Dragmun approached her. "Alright, Miss, you said ya knew a path across the sea safe from monsters. Seein' as we're underway, now might be a good time to chart it out."

Birdie followed Dragmun back to the cabin, passing by Ev on the way. Apparently she wasn't taking too well to the sea, as she was presently occupied with leaning over the railing and reducing the weight on board. Birdie stopped long enough to give Ev a small pat on the back before continuing on.

Inside his cabin, Dragmun directed Birdie to one of his maps. Stepping over to it, she drew a wobbly line from Roeport to Noontide Bay, then marked where each of the different types of threats were located.

"That's an awfully precise course there," Dragmun commented when she was done.

"I know," replied Birdie, "but if the weather stays good it's possible. Even if we do hit a storm, the only place we'd be in trouble is down here." She pointed to a spot about a hundred miles from Noontide.

"Mm," grunted Dragmun. "Lurkers on the left and a storm titan on the right. I don't like it. A fight with either would destroy this ship."

"It's the most direct route we can take while avoiding everything," Birdie stated. "The regions east and west of them are swarming with man o' wars, knife fish, and other lesser monsters."

"Well, I'm sorry, Miss, but if a storm titan's livin' there, then there's a good chance there will be a storm, too, and I'm not risking my ship and crew just to save a few hours."

Birdie wanted to argue, but she also wasn't completely confident in their odds with the route she'd proposed. That, and she did need Dragmun to manage the ship. After a few moments of letting her othermind do its thing, she scribbled a new path across the map and updated the threats they'd pass either near or through. It wasn't quite as quick of a route, but it would have to do.

"There," she said. "This route goes nowhere near any storm titans. There's a narrow region where we'll have to pass through some knife fish territory here, but that's the only place where we'd have to deal with any monsters."

Dragmun studied the new route before looking back at Birdie. "What makes you so sure you're right about where all these sea devils are, anyway?"

Birdie shrugged. "You'd have to ask Lord Syrus that one. Somehow he gifted me knowledge of every monster in existence, including the territories they patrol. For as long as I can remember, I've yet to be wrong about them."

"Is that so?" Dragmun looked skeptical but didn't voice it, instead turning his attention back to the map. "Well, you do have a reputation for dealin' with monsters. In all my years I can't recall another Radiant doin' as much to keep their numbers down as you have."

"You ought to thank my friend Ev for that," Birdie said. "I can't stand the damage they do to the land, but she's the one who's taken charge of organizing the hunts. Whenever she's not helping Syrus, she's figuring out better ways to deal with them."

"Well, it's a shame your friend hasn't done much about the monsters on the sea, but I know it's not easy to convince common folk to risk their lives for that sort of thing, let alone doin' so out on the water." Dragmun gave the map one more look over. "Alright then. The men-at-arms I hired ought to be tough enough to manage a few knife fish. We'll follow your path, but you'd better be right about these monsters. I'm puttin' a lot of faith in ya here."

"And I appreciate it," returned Birdie with a smile. "Don't worry. I told you I'll get your ship safely to Noontide, and that's what I'm going to do."

* * * *

The next four days were smooth sailing across the sea. One night the Windfall did drift a bit too far east, attracting the attention of a group of starcrabs, but it was hardly an issue. Between Birdie's group and Dragmun's two men-at-arms, the spindly legged beasts were dealt with as quickly as they climbed aboard the ship. The distraction also seemed to have temporarily helped Ev with her seasickness, though the cure lasted only as long as the starcrabs.

The morn of the fifth day opened with a worrying sight, however. In a span of just three hours, dark clouds had arisen seemingly out of nowhere and blotted out the sky.

Dragmun growled. "I thought you said there weren't any storm titans along this path."

"There aren't," Birdie replied.

"Well we sure have a storm brewin', don't we?"

That was inarguable. Before long, the winds had picked up to the point where they had to retract the sails, putting them at the mercy of the sea — not that they could navigate without seeing the sky, anyway. Birdie wasn't entirely sure where they were at this point, but she knew they were close to the region of knife fish they had to cross. If they were lucky, they'd continue straight along their course. If not, they could end up with quite a fight on their hands.

Rain ripped across the bow as waves tossed the ship to and fro. With the rain came the knife fish, and Dragmun ordered most of his crew below deck as the wolf-sized monsters began launching themselves at the ship. The ones that landed on the deck used their fins as makeshift legs and charged with their razored heads at anyone that remained up top.

Despite the thrashing boat, the knife fish weren't particularly difficult to deal with, especially with Tallis's ice magic. The rain made it easy to freeze the already vulnerable fish solid, allowing Waylen to easily smash them with his now enlarged hammer any time he was able to get his footing. Birdie and Dragmun's men-at-arms easily managed the rest — the fish's mindless tactics making them easy foes to best. This left Ev mostly waiting by the wayside as her magic was only useful for healing injuries and combating ghostly creatures. An unstable ship deck also wasn't exactly the best place to use her bow, meaning the only weapon she had available was a dagger. She took up a position near Dragmun at the helm to protect him in case any fish landed nearby. Holding to the railing, Ev didn't look well, but Birdie was confident Ev would be able to hold her own against simple foes such as these.

Chunks of ice and fish guts sprayed Birdie from the side as Waylen swung a particularly enthusiastic blow at one of the unwelcome guests.

"Watch it!" she shouted.

"Sorry, Miss Birdie!" returned Waylen. "I'm tryin' to break 'em up good so they'll wash back over the side!"

"That's very thoughtful of you," she called back as she dodged a bladed charge, countering with a slice deep into the side of her attacker. "Maybe try and aim *not* at the other people on board?"

Waylen pounded a single fist against his chest, presumably in acknowledgment of Birdie's request, then turned to deal with another fish freshly frozen behind him. It was good to see him still able to fight well after his injury back at Roehelm. Birdie had been sure it was something he'd never fully recover from, but he seemed to be doing just fine right now.

After about fifteen minutes of a steady stream of fish, both the onslaught and the storm finally began to subside, though it was still far from over.

Taking advantage of the lull, Birdie rushed up to the the helm to speak with Dragmun.

"How far off course do you think we've gone?" she asked him, eyeing his compass.

"How the blasted devil should I know?" was his response as he struggled with the wheel.

"Well, which way do you think we're going?" she pressed.

"Madam, I'm a sailor, not a fortune teller! All I know is the wind's blowin' westward, so we're bound to be driftin' that ways somewhat."

Birdie didn't need to consult her othermind to know what that meant. "We need to take advantage of the calm to get the sails up. We have to go southeast!"

"It's too dangerous for the crew to manage the sails in these conditions. Once these fish stop comin' aboard, then we'll hoist the sails."

"If we keep going west, we're going to end up in man o' war territory!"

"I thought you said ya could handle man o' wars!" Dragmun shot back.

"I can," returned Birdie, "but I can't promise they won't do much damage before I stop them!"

Dragmun cursed and spit, then ordered one of the men-at-arms to fetch the rest of the crew from below deck. As soon as they returned, Dragmun began barking out orders. At first they hesitated, but the moment he mentioned man o' wars, the sailors jumped onto their tasks.

Dragmun turned to Birdie. "They won't be able to fight and manage the ship at the same time."

"You leave that to us," Birdie replied before turning to Ev. "Keep watching the captain's back, but be ready in case we need you to heal someone."

Ev nodded, holding fast to the railing near Dragmun.

Birdie darted back down to where Tallis and Waylen were busy splattering more knife fish. On her way, she spotted the unsettling sight of large blobs floating in the waves off to her right.

"Tallis, Waylen," she began when she reached them, "I need you to spread out and cover as much of the ship as you can. We need to protect the sailors."

"Leave it to us!" shouted Waylen, who immediately charged off towards the bow.

"Where do you want me to go?" asked Tallis.

Birdie glanced around at the situation. Dragmun's men-at-arms were both midship, and Waylen was at the front. That left just Ev guarding the aft.

"Get back up by Ev. Watch for anything coming aboard the back and use your magic to assist anyone having trouble midship."

Tallis obeyed, and Birdie took up position on the starboard side where she'd be able to monitor their distance to the man o' wars.

The arrangement worked beautifully. Tallis and Waylen were more than capable of fending off any knife fish on their thirds of the boat, while the two men-at-arms protected the middle with Birdie occasionally assisting by casting darkness over the eyes of the fish monsters and stabbing any that came too near to her.

The sailors worked quickly, drawing the sails up in a matter of minutes, but it was clear that the man o' wars had already noticed the ship. The gelatinous blobs rapidly approached through the waves, and before the *Windfall* was able to pull away, a number of them had latched onto the sides.

The first of the monsters heaved itself up on board near Birdie — a six-foot tall man-shaped monstrosity with an enormously bulbous head of jelly and whip-like tentacles for arms.

Birdie readied her blades, but before she could strike, the beast's head crystallized in a thick layer of frost.

From the corner of her eye she caught Tallis smirking, clearly thinking he'd helped, but by freezing its head solid he'd essentially given it a helmet against her daggers.

No matter. Birdie ducked as the creature shot one of its tentacles in her direction and sliced a dagger overhead, severing its tentacle.

The monster repeated its attack with its other tentacle to the same result, leaving it wide open as Birdie charged it before it could cast any spells. With a quick thrust of both of her blades to its abdomen, Birdie tore upwards, spilling slime across the deck and killing the monster.

In the time it took her to slay the man o' war, three others had already climbed on board. A loud clink rang out as one of the men-at-arms' swords bounced off another frozen head.

Birdie turned to Tallis. "Stop freezing their heads!" She yelled up at him.

Tallis looked shocked at the reprimand.

"Aim for their arms and legs! Stop them from attacking and moving and focus on the ones still climbing on board!"

Tallis hesitated, then nodded in understanding as he turned towards another man o' war climbing aboard near the back.

Birdie turned back to the battle at hand. Several sailors had retreated from their stations. A shock wave from one of the monsters blasted one of the men-at-arms to the far end of the deck, sending his sword flying. All the while, more creatures climbed onto the ship from all sides.

This situation wasn't sustainable. Birdie needed to find the leader of the man o' wars.

Turning her attention to the sea, Birdie strained her senses for any sign of what she was looking for.

There, about a hundred yards away, was a blob that looked like it had a different tint than the others. From this distance it was hard to discern, but she was sure she could sense a slightly different flavor of magic from that direction as well.

Stripping out of her clothes and wrapping her daggers in them before tossing them down into the hold, she turned back to Dragmun.

"Don't you *dare* leave me!" she shouted at the confused captain.

"Wha—?" she heard him begin, but she was already underwater.

Dropping her human guise, Birdie shaped her form as best as she could into something fish-like to move quickly through the water. She kept well below the surface to stay out of reach of the other man o' wars as she homed in on her target. As she grew closer, her senses confirmed that she was indeed approaching the leader. Once she was directly under it, she took on a humanoid form once again and formed a large, hooked spear from the shadow of her arm. With a savage thrust upwards, she impaled and hooked the creature.

The lead man o' war thrashed about, having been caught completely off guard. Her shadow weapons weren't as potent as her daggers, but they were sufficient for this.

Holding tight to the shaft of her spear, she formed another non-hooked spear and thrust repeatedly up into the body of the man o' war.

By now the others would have been alerted to the attack and would come stop her, but it was too late. With her seventh strike, the lead man o' war ceased flailing, lying limp and leaking ooze out into the sea. Almost immediately, Birdie sensed the life of all of the surrounding creatures fade away, and an immense surge of strength filled her body.

Reabsorbing her weapons back into herself, Birdie floated up to the surface and restored her human appearance.

All around her the man o' wars floated dead. Off in the distance, the *Windfall* was still sailing away. If Dragmun abandoned her here, she would be royally pissed.

Hoping that they would have noticed the man o' wars dying and that Dragmun would have the sense to realize they weren't a threat anymore, she raised an arm and emitted a bright light from it.

A wave of relief washed over her as the ship turned around. She could have made the journey to shore on her own, but she would have hated every grueling minute of it.

At last, the *Windfall* pulled up alongside her. A rope was tossed down to her, which she promptly grabbed before being pulled back up.

"Are you crazy!" Ev shouted as soon as she was on board again.

"That was amazing!" Tallis chimed in.

Birdie ignored both of them. Wearing only illusionary undergarments, she could feel the eyes of everyone aboard staring at her. Without a word, she made her way back to where she'd left her physical clothes, taking stock of the situation along the way. It appeared that everyone had made it out of the attack relatively unscathed.

Good. She'd told Dragmun they'd make it to Noontide Bay safely, and at this point she'd effectively kept her word. As long as the storm didn't pick back up, they were in the clear.

Down in the hold, she dressed herself before returning once again to the deck.

Ev was waiting for her, arm outstretched against the bulwark to keep steady in the still violent waves.

"Really?" Ev asked.

Birdie shrugged. "It was either that or fight them one by one for an hour."

Ev shook her head, clearly not feeling well enough to engage in further conversation.

Out on the deck, the sailors were back to managing the sails now that they were no longer under threat from any monsters. Soon they'd be arriving at Noontide Bay, and hopefully the rest of the journey would be a smooth one.

Chapter 6

By late afternoon of the fifth day aboard the *Windfall*, the group finally spotted Noontide Bay. The skies and sea had cleared up considerably, though the sun was presently well behind a large cloud. A nice breeze similar to the one Birdie had felt when leaving Roeport welcomed her back to the shore. In the distance, another large ship approached the port from the west.

Ev and Tallis joined Birdie up at the bow. Waylen stayed towards the back, chatting with Dragmun.

"Finally," remarked Ev, "I can't wait to be on dry land again."

"I'll bet," remarked Birdie. "You seem to be doing better, though. I think another day out here, and you'd get used to it."

"It's not the being sick part. It's *boring* out here," Ev responded as she leaned over the railing. "There's nothing to see, just sea."

Birdie smirked as Tallis chimed in. "Ha! I get it! Sea as in water, right?"

"Yes, Tallis, that is the joke," remarked Ev, rolling her eyes.

The sound of now-familiar footsteps signaled Dragmun and Waylen's approach. Birdie turned to greet them.

"Ya know," Dragmun began, "I have to admit, I had my doubts about followin' your course, but here we are, safe and sound. I guess there's more to bein' a Radiant than just raw power."

Birdie smiled and cocked her head. "I don't know. I get the impression that a lot of the old Radiants didn't feel that way."

"Aye, it's true. Back in the old days, most Radiants were content to sit about in their citadels, putting nepacs in charge of everythin' important while they either feasted or went off to that Colosseum of theirs. I swear it's as if it was all a big game to them. I don't know what makes you different, but it's nice to finally see a Radiant who's willin' to risk her own life for someone else. Not that I suppose ya can actually die, can ya?"

Birdie shrugged. "I just did what needed to be done. I told you I'd see you safely across the sea, and I did."

"Mm," Dragmun grunted. "Well, regardless, ya have my respect, and not the kind a man has to give to a Divine. I mean real respect. If ya ever need a ship again, I'll be happy to oblige."

Head cocked again, Birdie crossed her arms and smiled. "So that respect you showed me back in Roeport wasn't real respect, then?"

Dragmun just smirked and grunted, then turned away and headed back to the helm. Waylen opted to stay up front, leaning back against the railing.

"Ya know, I have to thank ya, Miss Birdie. It's been ages since Dragmun and I have sailed together. I really appreciate ya lettin' me come along."

Birdie shrugged. "What can I say? You are my favorite knight, after all."

Waylen blushed a tad. "Hah! Well, even if you're jus' sayin' it, I appreciate that, too."

A short time later, the *Windfall* dropped anchor about a hundred yards off the port. There, Dragmun ordered his crew to row some lines out to the dock so they could pull in the ship. While the crew worked, Birdie and her companions went below deck to get their horses ready to be pulled up. When they returned up top, however, Birdie sensed something amiss. The ship she'd spotted earlier had anchored a short time prior near the next pier over, and something unusual was definitely happening over there. The distance made it hard to sense exactly what, but she was sure she sensed the presence of shades and other immortal creatures on board. That in itself was unusual, but there was other powerful magic over there as well. Despite the occasional spike, both flavors were fading away — the immortals' unquestionably disappearing faster. Birdie wasn't sure what to make of it, but she was sure it wasn't good.

Whatever was going on, Birdie didn't want to get involved. She turned to Ev, Tallis, and Waylen.

"Something's not right. We need to leave town as soon as we reach land."

"What? Why?" Tallis asked

Ev's face echoed Tallis's words, but Waylen appeared serious.

"Should we get our weapons ready?"

"I don't know," Birdie answered.

She turned her attention back to the ship and focused. It was hard to tell from this distance, but were those…?

Her heart sank. A number of pegasi were on board the other ship.

"Captain, get us out of here, now!" Birdie shouted at Dragmun.

Once they were clear, they could sail to a shallow location away from town and disembark there.

Dragmun looked surprised and started to question her order when an explosion rang out from the other ship. Spinning towards the sound, Birdie caught sight of smoking shrapnel flying out from the side of the ship as electric arcs sparked across the surface of the sea.

Dragmun didn't need any more convincing. He immediately started barking out orders. "Pete, Jonesy, tie those dinghies back up. Bart, raise the anchor!"

The sailors obeyed, and as they went about their duties Birdie turned her attention back to the other ship. The pegasi had taken off from the wrecked ship and were now flying towards them. The only explanation for how they could fly was that Lux Rosa had restored air magic for them, which meant either they had special treatment, or Lux had tricked them into giving up on flying so that they'd fall right into her hands.

"Ev, Waylen, grab your bows!" Birdie shouted as she dashed to the hold to grab her own.

Waylen and Ev followed right behind her, and the three of them returned to the deck in half a minute. While they did that, Tallis unshrunk Waylen's hammer for them, just in case they needed to fight up close. During that time the pegasi had already closed nearly half the distance to the ship. Birdie counted seven in total.

She addressed Tallis. "Tell me you have a spell that can knock things out of the air."

Tallis glanced between the pegasi and Birdie. "Well, I have an earth magnet spell, but there's no way I can cast it from this distance."

"Can you place the spell in an enchantment vector?" she pressed.

Tallis blinked, then nodded confidently as he realized what she was asking.

Birdie thrust a handful of arrows toward him. "Do it. Try not to remove the piercing enchantment on them."

Sweating, Tallis took the arrows and began enchanting the first one. The moment he was done Birdie snatched it away and took aim.

"Don't wait for Tallis to finish! Keep them away from the ship and watch out for any spells they cast!"

The riders were now only two hundred yards out, and Birdie did not want to see what they could do. Birdie loosed her arrow at the one she'd kept an eye on. Fortunately, the arrow's augmented piercing was sufficient to break through her target's leather armor. The man was immediately yanked from his pegasus, sending him screaming into the water below where he disappeared, leaving the pegasus to fly off into the distance.

Ev and Waylen fired upon the attackers as well but without any enchantment on their arrows. Both of them struck pegasi, but only Waylen's struck with enough force to bring another rider down.

A mage at the front raised his hand to cast a spell.

"Watch out!" Birdie cried.

A massive arc of lightning ripped across the helm, shattering the rear mast and sending splinters flying everywhere.

"Dragmun!" Waylen shouted in horror as the captain's scorched body landed with a thud on the deck.

Enraged, Waylen grabbed an arrow from Tallis just as the enchantment was complete and fired it at the man responsible.

He missed.

With a mighty roar, Waylen fired again, again missing.

The pegasi had now surrounded the ship. Another blast of lightning tore across its front, downing another mast and injuring several sailors.

Birdie took aim at the first of the lightning mages, sending his pegasus into the sea.

A fiery explosion from the center mast threw Birdie to the deck and rained flaming debris around them. Waylen grabbed Ev and pulled her out of the way of a falling beam.

"Tallis, are they close enough for you now?" Birdie shouted as she took aim at the second lightning mage from the deck.

A piercing beam of heat shot through Birdie's wrist, causing her shot to go wild.

Tallis fortunately picked up the slack. Though sweating profusely, he raised his hand and unleashed his earth magnet spell at the lightning mage as she prepared another attack.

Tallis's spell only glancingly hit the rear of the pegasus, but it was more than sufficient. The steed was pulled into the deep as the rider let loose another bolt of lightning, scorching the side of the ship on the way down and ending abruptly with a sickening sizzle as its caster hit the water not far from where the other lightning mage had fallen.

That left only three. Birdie turned her attention to the source of whoever had struck her and froze

At the front of the ship, a woman with a sadistic grin and solid plate armor had landed and was now approaching, her arm outstretched and ready to cast again. Birdie had no doubt about what she sensed from the woman. The same enchantment that had been on that Cray fellow was here as well, which meant this was Lux Rosa's new puppet.

One of the men-at-arms charged the woman.

She pointed her other hand at the warrior, and before he even made it three steps, a wave of fire reduced him to ash. Despite the ferocity of the attack, Birdie couldn't help but notice that Lux's puppet didn't actually possess that much magic. Now that she thought about it, most of the loyalists back at Roehelm had only been low-to-mid level in their abilities. Somehow Lux Rosa was manipulating the magic system to enhance her soldiers' abilities without actually instilling them with magic of their own.

Every other sailor nearby scrambled away from the woman as she stepped around the burning debris in her path. Not for a moment did she take her eyes off of Birdie, nor did she lose her sickening smile.

Two small explosions rocked the ship as the other two pegasus riders landed attacks near Ev, Tallis, and Waylen. The three were sent flying towards the center of the ship near Birdie, and the two riders landed on each side of them, ignoring the sailors and surrounding the group.

"Well, well, well, well, well," Lux Rosa mused, her arm still pointed at Birdie. "What fine happenstance for us to meet here this day. Wouldn't you say so, Eclipse?"

If Birdie had the ability to spit, she would have. "What loyal followers you have. Are they aware that you use them as puppets?"

"Such negative phrasing. I gift my most loyal followers with my intimate presence and power. It is truly an honor, and frankly I'm impressed you noticed. Indeed, even the mere toys that the Masters discarded were impressive. Aren't you?"

Lux's comment struck something deep inside of Birdie. She knew she shouldn't let it bother her, but it did. "What the hell are you talking about?"

Lux tilted her head. "Oh? Didn't Syrus tell you what you really are? You're a tool. An artificial intelligence the Masters discarded long ago, made for no other purpose than to concoct challenges for the Divine. Syrus found you and with a bit of help was able to attach you to the body of an automaton that's just as soulless as you are. Surely you must have wondered where all the knowledge you possess actually comes from."

No. No, that couldn't be right. Syrus had created her the same way the Masters had created other nepacs, hadn't he? She'd always assumed so, but Syrus had never actually divulged to Birdie how he'd done it.

"I know what you are," Lux narrowed her eyes, "and deep down so do you. Why don't you tell everyone? Tell them about how when you fight you give yourself over to a heartless killing machine — your true nature and what you will slowly become the more you embrace it."

Birdie's couldn't help but lose herself in Lux Rosa's words. The description of her othermind was accurate, but she wasn't slowly becoming it, was she? The only people other than her who knew of her othermind were the Divine who'd aided Syrus; he himself had said so. If that was true, then Lux's claim of being one of her creators must also be true, which meant Lux would know if her othermind was corrupting her....

"You lie!" Ev shouted, rising to her feet and snapping Birdie out of her thoughts. "Birdie isn't some mindless tool! She cares more about our world than any other Radiant, especially something horrible like you!"

Feigned hurt appeared on Lux's face. "Oh, sweetie, how cutting! But if your 'Birdie' really does care, then why hasn't she told me Syrus's name yet?"

Lux raised her hand above her, forming a small fireball with a frightening amount of energy above it.

Forcing her concerns aside, Birdie took a step closer to Lux, one hand resting on the hilt of her magic-draining dagger. "You still haven't told me why you want his name. What does that even matter?"

"For you?" Lux smiled sweetly. "It means your little friends here get to live. They seem to believe they mean something to you. I'm sure you'd hate to disappoint them." Her face suddenly twisted with rage. "So tell me his true name, or I will blow away this entire—"

As quick as lightning, Birdie flung her dagger at Lux. The dagger wedged itself between Lux's helmet and cheekbone, slicing into her flesh, and the ball of fire immediately disappeared.

With no reason to pretend not to be what she was anymore, Birdie brandished her enchantment-breaking dagger with a tendril of shadow and charged as Lux pulled the first dagger out.

She could sense the other riders preparing their own spells and her comrades engaging them, but whatever happened behind her was not her concern now. Defeating the monster in front of her was all that mattered.

Lux backed away and raised her hand to blast Birdie, but the distance between them had been closed.

Ignoring the loud blasts behind her, Birdie crashed into Lux and slipped more shadowy tendrils between the plates of her armor, removing the straps holding it together. With her other tendril, she slammed the enchantment breaker into the puppet's hip the moment the gap was opened wide enough.

The woman's eyes opened wide in shock and confusion as Birdie felt Lux's possession vanish.

Birdie allowed the former puppet to stumble backwards, not sure what to do with her. Lux had said her followers viewed possession as an honor, but that didn't mean it was true.

True or not, Birdie didn't get the chance to find out. The surviving man-at-arms jumped up behind the woman and ripped off her helmet to deliver a fatal blow. That was probably for the best. Right now, the loyalists behind Birdie were her priority, and she didn't need to risk that one still wanting to aid them.

Turning back to help her friends, the scene before her appeared dire. One of the pegasi had been frozen to the deck and the other killed by a blow from Waylen's hammer, but both soldiers were very much alive. Ev had been tossed down a hole in the deck, Tallis had suffered severe burns, and Waylen had collapsed to his knees, his left arm completely seared off.

The mage atop the frozen pegasi raised a fiery hand toward Tallis.

In a single motion, Birdie picked up her magic-draining dagger and lobbed it at the mage.

The mage ducked aside, and Birdie followed up with her other dagger. The blade cut his face, but failed to stop him. The intensity of his magic held strong, meaning that whatever Lux had done to make them so powerful was *not* a normal enchantment.

The mage grimaced and pointed his hand at Birdie in retaliation.

Birdie tensed, but the attack never came. The rider had been distracted long enough; an icy spear from Tallis and an arrow from a hole in the deck simultaneously connected with the mage's sternum and neck, respectively.

Birdie metaphorically breathed a sigh of relief. The fire in the rider's hand fizzled in and out as he wobbled sluggishly before toppling to the deck, leaving only one enemy remaining.

The surviving enemy, meanwhile, had her sights set on Birdie. The woman's face twisted in fury as her palm opened above her, revealing the same fireball Lux's puppet had conjured earlier.

No time to counterattack, Birdie dove in desperation to the side as the woman lobbed the fireball.

The maneuver proved pointless. The world slowed as the fireball hurtled through the air. The energy in that spell was such that Birdie had no chance of surviving.

Then, movement.

Just below the fireball, Waylen rose upward, his war hammer in hand. With a wide swing, he struck the fireball mid-flight, setting off an explosion that engulfed half the ship.

Even from halfway across the deck, the heat was scorching. When the smoke cleared, a quarter of the center deck was erased and half of it was on fire. Everyone near the blast had been blown away, and those that had been nearest its center — Waylen, and that cursed loyalist — were gone.

Slowly, Birdie pushed herself back to her feet, staring at the gaping hole in the deck. She didn't have time to mourn, however, before another explosion rocked the ship. Running to the side, she spotted one of the other riders still alive in the water near the front of the ship. And down there, floating about midship, were the smoldering remains of the woman who'd cast the fireball.

Barely even thinking, Birdie raised her bow once again, gripping it so tightly she wouldn't have been surprised if it cracked. Not caring whether Lux had told the truth or not, she let her othermind take over completely and landed an arrow directly between the survivor's eyes.

Her othermind was satisfied, but she wasn't. She turned her attention to the fireball woman. Knowing full well she'd be wasting arrows, she shot at the still figure in the water, this time without the aid of her othermind.

She missed.

She fired again.

Again a miss.

Birdie froze. Did she really depend on her othermind that much? Time seemed to stand still as Lux's words came back to her. Was that why she so often viewed her soldiers as tools rather than people? Because she constantly relied on her othermind? Was that why she was upset about Waylen's death — just because he was valuable to her?

No, she knew she had been fond of the old man. But would she have cared more if she didn't have her othermind?

A voice calling out behind her pulled her back to the situation at hand. It was Tallis, heavily injured and stumbling across the deck.

"Waylen, what happened to Waylen?" he asked shakily.

Birdie opened her mouth but didn't answer. Instead, she just closed her mouth back and looked somberly at the flaming hole in the ship.

Tallis shook his head. "No. No, it can't be…" he muttered.

Tallis used his ice magic to put out the flames between him and the hole.

Dropping down near its edge, he yelled weakly into the hold below.

"Waylen!"

Birdie walked up behind him and put her hand on his shoulder.

Tears ran down his cheeks.

Comfort wasn't exactly something she was good at, but Birdie did share in his sorrow, regardless of what that sorrow stemmed from.

"Birdie! Tallis!"

The two of them nearly jumped at Ev's voice.

Birdie repositioned herself to peer down into the hold. There, she spotted Ev, already recovered and in the process of healing one of the now injured horses.

As soon as Ev saw Birdie, she stopped what she was doing and pointed her rod deeper into the hold at the front of the ship.

"We're sinking!"

Birdie shoved her head into the hold and followed Ev's finger. She cursed.

Water sloshed in through a hole where that last rider had struck the ship. Thankfully the hole was small, but that was still another problem to deal with.

Birdie pulled herself back up and surveyed the situation. Most of the crew had been injured or killed, and fires still crackled across much of the ship. The dock was only a hundred yards away, though. Getting to shore would be easy. Getting the horses to shore, on the other hand....

She put her hand on Tallis again. "Tallis, I'm sorry, but this isn't over yet. We need to put out these fires before they bring down the last mast. Do you think you can do that?"

Tallis clenched his fists and wiped away his tears before slowly pushing himself up. Without a word, he turned toward the crackling sails and went to work.

Birdie felt bad for him, but she couldn't dwell on that. She called back down to Ev.

"There are a lot of hurt people up here. Don't worry about the water. We need to save as many as we can. Maybe they can still pull us to shore before we sink."

Ev nodded and hurried back up, darting from sailor to sailor and helping who she could along the way.

While Ev and Tallis worked, Birdie dropped down into the hold and searched for a spare sail. She first found spare boards and nails, but that was more effort than she felt necessary at the moment. She was many things, but a carpenter was not one of them. Besides, she only needed to slow the water, not stop it. The sailors could work on salvaging the ship later if they deemed it worthwhile.

Eventually she found what she was looking for, and after dragging the heavy thing from one side of the hold to the other, she forced the spare sail into the big hole. Satisfied that would easily buy them enough time to reach the dock, she made her way back topside.

Up on deck, Tallis had made good progress dousing the fires. Many of the sailors had joined him in his endeavor, though many still appeared in pretty bad shape.

Birdie looked for Ev and spotted her near the back of the ship surrounded by several other survivors. One of the sailors shifted slightly, letting her see whom Ev was working on. To her surprise, it was Dragmun, who'd somehow survived the blast to the helm.

Jumping over one of the holes in the deck, Birdie ran up to Dragmun and filled him in on what had happened. Upon hearing of Waylen's passing, the old man closed his eye. By the time Birdie finished, so had Ev, who'd gone off to help other survivors.

"We need to pull the ship to shore before it sinks," Birdie told him. "That little plug I made won't keep the water out forever."

Dragmun stood up but said nothing, instead surveying the damage somberly. Seven of the crew had perished in the attack — most of them noncombatants, and the rest were understandably distraught. After a moment, Dragmun opened his mouth again, his eye still fixated on the scene before him.

"That kind of magic — were those Radiants?"

Birdie was surprised by the pragmatism of his question and a tad annoyed that he seemed to ignore her comment.

"No," she answered, "they were nepacs. Lux Rosa's found some way to magnify their abilities."

Dragmun nodded almost imperceptibly, his gaze shifting towards one of the fallen riders. "I see now why you and Waylen made such a fuss about takin' action against her. This kinda thing ain't natural, and this brutality... they were attackin' every ship that came to port."

"Captain," Birdie pressed.

Dragmun's eye swept across the ship and stopped at one of the dingies on the side. "It looks like at least one of the dingies still floats. I'll have a crew draw up a line to the dock. No point in us stayin' out here any longer."

Birdie nodded solemnly and stepped back. She was more than ready to let someone else take over.

* * * *

Once the ship had docked and all of the supplies and horses had been unloaded, Birdie stood before Dragmun. Against her better judgment, she handed over an extra five platinum to the captain.

"What's this for?" Dragmun asked.

"It's my fault you're stranded here. If I'd just been smart and asked you to take us to a nearby beach, your ship wouldn't be dead in the water now, and neither would Waylen."

"Horse rubbish!" Dragmun returned, surprising her. "Waylen didn't sacrifice himself just for you to start second guessin' yourself! Of course it seems obvious in hindsight, but if we all knew the future I'd still have this eye here."

Dragmun pointed up at his not-at-all convincing fake eye, then handed the money back to Birdie.

"The money ya gave us at the start o' the journey will be more than enough to get me and my crew back to Roeport. I've seen what you're up against, and if you keepin' that money means you've got a better chance, then you'd better keep it."

Birdie looked down at the platinum and pocketed it once more. "Thank you. When this is over, I'll make certain I find some way to repay you."

"If you get rid of that monster, Lux Rosa, and make her pay for the lives of Waylen and my crew, that will be all the repayment I need."

Birdie nodded solemnly, then shook hands with Dragmun as they parted ways. Once they were away from the docks, she led Ev and Tallis to the western edge of the city.

"Where are we going?" asked Tallis somberly as they crossed the city border. "Shouldn't we be heading south?"

"We weren't the only ones attacked by Lux Rosa's forces," Birdie replied stoically.

"What does that have to do with anything?"

Ev spoke for Birdie. "Tallis, if Birdie wants to help people, we help people," Ev answered.

"I don't want to help them," Birdie stated. "I want them to help us."

"Wait, what?" Ev and Tallis asked almost in unison.

Their surprise was almost enough to prompt Birdie to smile. "You'll see. Wait here with the horses. I'll signal you if I need you."

Ev didn't seem to like that. "Are you sure?"

"Positive," said Birdie, giving a small smile to reassure her.

No one protested further as Birdie climbed over the rocks separating her from the source of the magic she'd been keeping track of since she first noticed it on the other ship.

On the other side, three faces looked up at her. She'd have been more surprised if she'd caught them off guard, what with one of them being a fellow shade. The other two were a revenant with gray hair, emaciated flesh, and her right eye glazed over; and a horned, red-eyed, gray-skinned demon whose pointed tail twitched restlessly. Both of them appeared half drowned and heavily injured. The trio stood on guard, with the revenant holding a spear and the demon a short sword, but Birdie wasn't concerned.

Dropping her human appearance, she hopped down from the rocks to speak to them on even ground. Even if she was still covered in human clothes they could clearly see what she was.

"Aren't you a motley crew?" she remarked. "Soldiers of Dezeroth, I presume?"

"Who do you be!" the skinny demon demanded, dark flames rising off of him.

Birdie cocked her shadowy head, bringing out her normal persona. She needed these people's help, and the great Radiant Eclipse wasn't supposed to show weakness.

"Me? My name is Birdie, but most people seem to know me as Eclipse."

"Eclipse?" The revenant spat on the ground. "You expect us to believe a lie such as that? Prove it."

Spreading her arms dramatically, Birdie unveiled her Radiant wings.

"Bah! So what?" the demon shouted. "Any shade can do that. Show us real proof, or a liar you be!"

The shade of the group walked towards Birdie, prompting odd looks from its fellows. When it reached her, it raised its hand and touched her wings. Birdie stayed silent as it did so, waiting for it to speak.

The shade turned back to the other immortals and spoke in a male voice. "These wings belong to a Radiant."

The revenant was clearly taken aback by the statement. The demon was somewhat less convinced.

Still, it was good enough for Birdie. She put away her wings and brought back her favorite black-haired human guise. She'd finally regained the strength to maintain the illusion in the sun and had every intention of doing so. Upon her transformation, the shade took a step back from Birdie, apparently taking in her human appearance.

"So," Birdie began, placing a hand on her hip, "now that it's been decided who I am, who are all of you?"

The group hesitated a moment before the shade decided to answer.

"We are sailors," he stated matter-of-factly.

Birdie merely tilted her head, waiting for more.

A moment and some nervous glances later, the revenant stepped forward. "My name is Nephira," she stated before motioning to the demon and shade in turn, "and these two are Helcant the Infernal and Umber Blight."

"There, now was that so hard?" asked Birdie, smiling and crossing her arms. Her smile quickly disappeared as she continued, however. "I saw that you were also attacked by Lux Rosa's forces. I don't sense anyone else nearby. Are you the only ones who survived?"

Nephira narrowed her eyes. "We might be. Who is Lux Rosa?"

Birdie frowned. "She's a Radiant who's somehow acquired some of the powers of the Masters. She's been using them to create new spells and take control of certain kinds of magic."

"A Radiant?" repeated Helcant, a suspicious tone in his voice. "Eclipse is the slayer of Divine! All Radiants are supposed to have been purged from Doxla!"

"You know I'm right here, right?" Birdie countered what she took to be an odd attempt at an accusation. "And all Radiants? Haven't you heard of Syrus? Have you ever seen a map of how big Doxla is? I'm one person. I can't police an entire world on my own."

Nephira spat again. "So what is this Radiant's intent? Is it another Grandis?"

Birdie shook her head. "I don't think so. Grandis wanted to end the world. Lux Rosa wants to control it; that much I'm sure of. She also said she wants to rid the world of immortals."

That announcement shook the trio in front of her, though they tried to hide it.

"Ha... haha... mayhap this Radiant will try," Helcant laughed nervously, "but we return always."

Birdie gave Helcant a glare that wiped his feeble smile away. "Lux Rosa disabled air magic across my entire city if not the whole world, all to force me to travel by ship. She clearly hasn't gained all the power of the Masters yet, but how long do you think it will take before she learns to put an end to your cycle of resurrection?"

Nephira narrowed her eyes. "You believe she can do this?"

Birdie turned again to Umber. "I know you sensed the magic her soldiers wielded. Have you ever felt anything like that in the four centuries since you were created?"

"No," Umber stated.

"There you go," Birdie said to the clearly unnerved immortals before her. "This Radiant who's been in hiding for years is reshaping the world around us as we speak. If we don't act now, we could lose everything."

Birdie could practically see the thoughts racing through Nephira's head.

"You do not need to fight them," Birdie reassured her. "I only need you to send word to Dezeroth that I need his aid."

Nephira looked up. "That's it?"

Birdie nodded.

"We can't do that!" Helcant shouted. "Have you no knowing of the war going on?"

"I'm aware that Dezeroth has been expanding his kingdom, yes."

"Helcant's right," Nephira stated. "We'd have to pass by armies of humans to reach him."

Birdie tilted her head. "And yet you sailed a ship to a port town of humans?"

"That's why we kept brigands and shades in our crew," Nephira returned angrily. "They do the trading, we do the sailing."

Birdie couldn't help but smile slightly. "That's both clever and ambitious of you. Clearly you have a passion for what you do."

"What bearing does that have on anything?" Nephira demanded.

"Not much, I suppose," Birdie answered. "I just think it's nice to see people who've lived for centuries as the 'villains' finally coming out to live ordinary lives. It's a shame it won't last long if Lux Rosa has her way."

Nephira and Helcant exchanged looks with one another, but neither spoke.

"I will deliver your message," Umber offered. "I can travel quickly at night."

Nephira jerked her head around. "Umber, no, you don't have to do that."

"I believe I do," Umber replied. "I have been without purpose since the battle against Grandis. I sought one sailing with you, and now I have found one."

Umber turned to Birdie and repeated himself, more resolutely this time. "I will deliver your message. Tell me what I must say."

Birdie allowed a brief smile to come and go before she spoke again. "I need you to inform Dezeroth about Lux Rosa. Tell him everything I've told you, and tell him that I need him to send as many of his forces as he can muster to the northern border of Ars Summis. Tell him I will arrive at Bailey Town within ten days from now, and I expect him to be there when I do."

"I will do as you say," stated Umber, unmoving aside from the wisping of his shadow.

His stare hinted that he had more to say, however, and after a moment he voiced it. "I would like to ask you something."

"And what's that?" asked Birdie.

"Why do you take on this human appearance?"

Birdie tilted her head, then shrugged. "It helps with body language, humans seem to prefer it when I do, and honestly, I just like the way it looks."

"Interesting. You cannot see it, yet you prefer this appearance regardless?"

"I don't have to see it to know what I look like, and yes, I do."

Umber stood silent for a moment before repeating, "Interesting," but then said nothing more.

Birdie smiled at Umber.

"Well, I want you to know that delivering that message will help me tremendously. Thank you. I'm glad to see someone has the courage to do what's necessary," she remarked, though she avoided looking in the direction of Nephira and Helcant.

She didn't have to.

"Do you call us cowards?" Helcant demanded, flames erupting down his back.

"I don't believe I did, no," said Birdie, turning away from them, though she looked back again at Umber one last time. "Please be safe. I'd rather my message arrive late than not at all."

"I will arrive safely and as quickly as possible."

Birdie nodded, then started back up over the hill.

"Wait!" shouted Nephira, prompting Birdie to look back over her shoulder.

"Where are you going?"

"I already told you," replied Birdie, "I'm heading to Ars Summis. Now if you'll excuse me, every minute that passes is another Lux Rosa comes closer to the power of the Masters."

With that, Birdie made her way back to Ev and the others. She knew she couldn't rely on Dezeroth, but if he did come to her aid it would make her journey much easier. Lux Rosa undoubtedly had even more forces waiting at their destination.

When she rejoined her companions, Tallis was the first to speak up. "What happened? Who were you talking to?"

"Survivors of the other ship and citizens of Dezeroth's empire."

Tallis blinked and opened his mouth to speak, but he had trouble finding any words.

Ev scowled at the mention of Dezeroth's name, but quickly hid her displeasure.

"Will they help us?" she asked, having already put two and two together.

"One of them will," answered Birdie.

"No!" Nephira's voice called from behind. "All of us will."

Tallis nearly stumbled backwards as Birdie turned to see Nephira and Helcant atop the wall of rocks.

"Is that so?" asked Birdie. "So you're going with Umber after all?"

Nephira hopped down from the rocks, Helcant following close behind her. "There's no point in us going with him. We'd never keep up. You, however, already have companions that will slow you down."

"W-we don't slow Miss Birdie down, revenant!" Tallis stammered, holding his hand out in preparation to cast a spell.

Ev pushed his hand back down before he could do anything stupid.

Ignoring Tallis's drama, Birdie continued her conversation with Nephira. "Are you saying you want to travel with me?"

Nephira approached Birdie, Helcant still on her heels and eyeing Tallis warily.

"It's as you said. We've spent centuries being monsters for Divine to fight against. We've finally been given the chance to try and live a different life, and you're telling us a new Divine has appeared and wants to take it away from us."

Nephira spat on the ground again. "We will do whatever it takes to help you split this Radiant and slaughter every one of her followers. This would be the will of King Dezeroth."

Tallis had apparently worked up the courage to step closer to the two visitors. "Yeah, well, you can't. We don't have enough horses."

"Good point, Tallis," Birdie said, turning back to him. "We can try to find one in town before we set out. If we can't, I can ride with Ev. Neither of us weigh that much."

"Wait, what? That's—" Tallis began before Ev nudged him to be quiet.

Helcant seemed equally incredulous. "Truly? You would procure a steed on our behalf?"

Birdie forced a smile back at him. "I'd like to keep our group small, but just two more travelers shouldn't draw too much attention. Besides, once we're done here we'll be mostly steering clear of human towns. I'm not taking any more chances than necessary after the attack that just happened. So sure. We'll have to restock on food and water before we go through the desert, but Tallis is really good at packing thanks to his shrinking spell."

"The desert?" Nephira repeated. "You're traveling through the Crystal Desert?"

Birdie placed a hand on her hip. "It's faster than going around it, we'll be able to spot enemies coming from miles around, and there are caves we can seek shelter in everywhere. Do you have a better suggestion?"

Nephira didn't.

"Alright then, it's settled. We'll grab some more supplies, see if we can get another horse, and we'll be on our way. Also, Ev's a pretty good healer, and the two of you look like you could use some of that. Ev?"

Ev whipped out her rod at the prompt. "If they're helping us, I'll help them."

"Thanks, Ev," Birdie stated. "I'll leave you with our new allies, then. Tallis and I have some shopping to do."

Chapter 7

The great stone door at the entrance of the Hall of Champions slid open, briefly drawing Lux Rosa's attention. She lost interest immediately, however, as the interruption was merely one of Vellic's servants delivering a new sample of degradation to her collection. The servant moved quickly as it used a spell she'd developed for all of her laborers to push the shimmering ripple up near her throne, and was welcomely gone as soon as its job was done.

With Vellic still taking his sweet time arriving, Lux turned her attention back to the degradation beside her — her hand deep within as she sifted through the Masters' systems in search of more signs of their database of registered Divine. If they'd been even half competent at organizing their systems, then all of the Divine would have been listed in one place, which would have allowed Lux to simply purge the world of all of them at once, removing the threat of Syrus and leaving her as the sole inheritor of Doxla.

But no, of course they hadn't. Lux supposed she shouldn't have been surprised, considering where the Masters had constructed this ramshackle world and how poorly it was all held together. Now she was stuck sifting through their systems line by line looking for anything that might be a seitti name, then making certain it truly was another entry in the Divine registry before purging the entry permanently.

Well, she supposed she should take a break from the tedium long enough to at least take a look at the new piece of degradation that had been brought to her.

Moving her hand into the new ripple, Lux was disappointed but not surprised to find nothing new within it. Perhaps it was time to move her efforts to a new location. Unfortunately, relocation would take weeks, and she could not simply abandon her existing collection of degradation to go off on her own.

No matter. Once this Syrus problem was dealt with, she would have all the time in the world to find what she was looking for.

The stone door slid open again, and at last Vellic made his appearance.

"You summoned me, Lady Rosa?" Vellic bowed.

"I did," replied Lux, growing weary of this same exchange every time she called for him. "I need you to prepare all but two of the remaining pegasus riders and send them to Ars Summis, then bring me someone well-versed in light magic. I require a new vessel."

Vellic's expression told her he was unprepared for those instructions. "What? But what happened to Dame Lotree? What about Eclipse? Surely you must have felled the fiend this time. You said it was weakened from our last attack!"

Lux rested her weight on her left arm as she deigned to look down at the man who seemed to be growing too comfortable in her presence. Unfortunately, he was useful, so for now she would cater to his concerns.

"I felt it worthwhile to attempt reason one last time before bringing down my unbridled wrath upon Eclipse. That attempt failed. Now, I will correct that mistake. I will gather up the riders we sent to the other ports and strike without mercy and without hesitation. Eclipse will be split at the gates of Ars Summis. But Vellic?" Lux eyed the nepac sweetly.

"Yes, Lady Rosa?"

Lux was pleased to see a hint of nervousness in her servant.

"Eclipse was accompanied by a mage who knew spells no hired hand should have known. Do you know what that means?"

Vellic shook his head. "No, my lady."

"It means the Shadow Guard was not eliminated. Either our assault failed, or some escaped, in which case reinforcements will arrive soon to retake the city."

"I have already sent a battalion of five hundred to Roehelm, as per your orders."

"And how many more do we have to defend the Hall of Champions?"

Vellic hesitated. "Lady Rosa, I do not believe—"

"I did not ask you what you believe, Vellic, I asked you how many soldiers remain."

Vellic stood up tall, a vain attempt at appearing confident. "We have three hundred stationed here who are trained to fight, but we are doing our best to gather more. We haven't had time to—"

Lux held up her hand to silence him. "In that case, I've changed my mind. I still desire a vessel proficient in light magic, but illusion is the priority. Bring me someone who has at the minimum the ability to disguise their appearance. If they possess the magic of a paladin as well, all the better. You can do that for me, can't you, Grand Curate?"

Vellic tried to hide a frown. "May I ask what you need with such a vessel?"

Lux held her hand to her chest in mock hurt. "Oh, dear. Vellic, do you doubt my intentions? Surely you don't think I would allow another champion to lose their life in my service. I do hope you don't have such little faith in me."

Vellic squirmed. "Not at all, Lady Rosa. I merely—"

"Good." Lux leaned back against her throne. "In that case, do be a dear and fetch me what I asked for."

Vellic frowned once again, but ultimately bowed and obeyed. A short while later, he returned with an older soldier whom he introduced as Sir Grunsworth.

Lux put on her usual show of praising her new vessel before allowing Vellic to apply his little consciousness suppression spell — just to keep her pet complacent with the whole proceedings. Once she had completed the possession of her new puppet, she sent Vellic on his way to prepare the other riders to fly to Ars Summis. In the meantime, Lux made her own way to the pegasi stables using her puppet's body. Once there, she ordered the stable hand to give her the fastest steed available.

"Under whose authority?" the stable hand had the gall to ask.

Lux smirked, then with a raise of her puppet's hand she triggered a small earthquake using her actual body and the distortions around her throne.

"Under no one's authority," Lux's puppet stated. "I am the supreme authority."

Trembling, the stable hand bowed low to the ground. "F-forgive me! I didn't realize—"

"Yes, yes, yes," Lux waved her hand dismissively. "Just get on with it. I am in a teensy bit of a hurry."

The stable hand obediently ran off to one of the farther pens and retrieved one of the pegasi. After placing a saddle and bridle on the beast, it backed away to give Lux the space she deserved.

"This is the fastest of these animals?" she asked the nepac.

The stable hand bowed low once again. "It is the fastest, Your Great Ladyship."

Lux smiled. "Great Ladyship" was a new title for one of these creatures to call her, and one she could get used to. Perhaps she would make such reverence a decree after her victory over Syrus. It would certainly make the remaining time she was forced to spend in the presence of these finite beings more enjoyable.

"Good," was all she said in return before climbing aboard.

With a strong kick of her puppet's heels, she set off into the sky and pointed her steed in the direction of Grandis's old citadel. There was one stop she had to make before gathering her forces to deal with Eclipse once and for all.

Chapter 8

The day after leaving Noontide Bay, Birdie and her companions arrived at the edge of the Crystal Desert. Before them lay a seemingly endless sheet of solid glass rolling as if the gentle waves of some ancient ocean had frozen in time. The passage of time had not been kind to the land. Seventeen years without the Masters using their abilities to repair damage had left much of the surface scratched, chipped, and covered in broken shards of what must have once been a beautiful sight. The desert looked as torn apart as Birdie felt. As sad as she was about Waylen, her thoughts were on Lux Rosa's words and her own discovery about her limitations.

Without her othermind, she was helpless. If she continued to embrace her othermind, on the other hand, she might become the very thing she wanted to keep out of Doxla. Though likely not an immediate concern, how far off was it? If only she'd bothered to train herself to fight without her othermind, the solution would be simple. Now, however, she'd have no choice but to rely on it for the foreseeable future.

Further into the desert, bits of life began to appear. Sprinkled across the mostly green and orange glass were clusters of crystalline tubes jutting high into the air with feathery plant life protruding from each tip, though most of the tubes were damaged or destroyed. Tiny holes pockmarked even the healthy tubes and surrounding glass near the tubes' bases, with larger craters scattered about that led deep beneath the desert. What few areas remained where the surface stayed yet pristine allowed distorted glimpses into the labyrinth of tunnels below.

"Okay," chimed Birdie in an attempt at sounding cheery, "who's ready for three days of warmth and sunshine?"

Helcant grumbled something under his breath in response, which Tallis quickly seized on.

"What's the matter, demon? Is the sun too much for you?"

"Not so much as the heat will be for you, human!" Helcant shot back.

"Guess again, fiend. My magic can freeze the air in seconds!"

"Fiend? I was corrupted, not created, you newborn cur!"

"Will you two shut up!" Birdie interjected, sick of having to listen to this nonsense all day.

She understood that both of them were upset after the attack at the bay, but so was she, and their taking things out on each other didn't help.

"You know what? New rule. The next time either of you opens his mouth you're *walking* this desert."

"You can't be serious," blurted Tallis.

"He was the inciter!" proclaimed Helcant.

Birdie pointed two fingers with her right hand at the two of them and then pointed downward. "Now. One hour."

Both of them protested.

"Do you want to make it two hours?" Birdie asked, glaring.

"You can't force me!" spat Helcant.

Nephira stepped in. "Helcant, get down."

"Do you jest at me? I—"

"I've had to listen to you two bickering since we left the port. If you're going to act like a child, maybe Birdie's right to treat you like one."

The look of utter brokenness that appeared on Helcant's face almost made Birdie feel bad for the little demon. Without another word, he slipped from his horse to the ground, the tiny glass shards crunching beneath his boots as he did so.

Tallis glanced between Birdie and Ev, both of them giving him stern expressions. Growling under his breath, he too dismounted from his horse.

The group continued in relative silence for a while, the only real sound being that of the crunching glass beneath hooves and boots. After a few hours, it became clear that the horses were approaching their limit.

Birdie couldn't blame them. The desert was absolutely sweltering. The tunnels below acted as an oven as sunlight passed into them from above, warming the chambers that had few routes from which heat could escape. As the day went on, that heat made its way back to the surface, making the ground hot enough to cook on. The only things adapted to live on the surface were those tube plants and a handful of reptile and insect species that lived in and around the holes near said plants.

"It really is fascinating," Birdie mused to Ev as she motioned for everyone to stop. "The desert itself is crumbling without the Masters, yet the life within it persists."

Ev looked to the batch of tube plants Birdie was eyeing. "Yeah. The

Masters may have been awful, but at least they left us with a world still filled with beauty."

She turned back to Birdie. "Why are we stopping? To look at the lizards?" she smiled playfully.

Birdie returned the smile, though lacking Ev's sincerity. "We need to rest the horses. They can't continue on like this. Tallis," she called.

Tallis, still stinging from the earlier reprimand, didn't answer, but his eyes told Birdie she had his attention.

"Could you work on cooling off the area for a bit? If you run out of magic, I've packed some restoration elixirs that should help. Please use them sparingly; I don't have many. Ev, could you empty out all the canteens except for mine into that dip over there so the horses can drink? When you finish, bring the canteens and meet me at that hole over there, please."

She pointed to a large opening in the ground.

Ev nodded. "Sure thing. Is there more water down there?"

Birdie nodded back. "There should be. If I'm wrong, we're only half a day into the desert. We still have time to go back if we need to."

Ev set to work, as did Tallis. After a few of his spells, the only things colder than the glass they stood on were the looks he kept shooting at Helcant and Nephira.

Birdie ignored that and grabbed one of the elixirs for herself as she made her way to the hole in the ground. The drop into the tunnel below wasn't far, but the heat she sensed coming from it was immense, as was the humidity. She wasn't sure she wanted her human companions accompanying her for risk of passing out. They'd probably be fine if they took breaks between trips, but why risk it when she didn't have to?

"Helcant, Nephira, would you mind helping me bring water up?"

Helcant waited until Nephira started over before sending a sideways glare to Tallis and slinking along himself. Ev followed shortly after, carrying an armful of empty canteens with her.

"Thank you," Birdie told her. "Just leave those here and wait for us to come back. If the horses need more water, empty them as needed and we'll keep refilling them."

Helcant scowled as Ev put the canisters near the edge of the pit. "Is this what the great Eclipse takes us for? To fetch water for horses and humans?"

Birdie returned the scowl. "As I recall, it was only yesterday that *you* asked to come. If you don't want to contribute, you don't have to be here."

"Ignore him," Nephira interjected. "It has not been easy to let go of the past, especially when most of the world refuses to try."

Birdie sighed. "Believe me, I'm well aware. There's been more attempts on my life than I can count since I defeated Grandis. I don't know how long it will take for people to get over it. Maybe they never will, but…" she looked to Ev, "I know there are at least some people who don't care about those things. That's enough for now. Once this Lux Rosa catastrophe is over and Syrus finishes his research, then we'll worry about fixing the rest of this world."

"Research?" Nephira repeated, incredulous. "What research is more important than ending centuries of injustice and persecution against immortals."

Birdie tilted her head and narrowed her eyes. "Oh, I don't know. Maybe figuring out how to take over the systems created by the Masters? You know, so we can stop the world from literally falling apart and keep its creators from taking back control in case they ever return?"

Nephira stared at Birdie, looking as if she couldn't decide if Birdie was serious or not. Helcant held a similar expression, though tinged with interest.

"Come on," said Birdie, grabbing her weapons and a pair of canteens under her arm. "The path to the water is straightforward from here. Bring your weapons and be careful not to slip down there; it's going to be a bit wet."

Helcant and Nephira exchanged glances before also grabbing their weapons and some canteens. They followed Birdie down into the tunnel — a narrow passage only about five feet in diameter.

Despite being underground, the tunnel was well lit. A surprising amount of sunlight penetrated into the crystalline underground of the desert despite the layer of powder and glass shards covering most of the surface. A decent bit of additional light was provided from the opening of the tunnel as it reflected deeper along the walls of the passage. Every foot further they stepped, the path grew more coated with condensation from the water below. About twenty feet down, the light became noticeably dimmer, and the path became slick from condensation. Another ten feet below that, the light somewhat returned as they entered the lowest level of the labyrinth. Here, thousands of tiny holes dotted the ceiling; a small portion of them letting in pinpricks of light as they stretched to the desert surface. Roots spread out over every inch of the ground. Most belonged to thick ferns adorning the sides of deep channels, while the larger roots attached to the tube plants up top. The bottoms of said channels held small streams of water that seeped in from the Waterfelled River.

Scurrying amongst the plant life were a number of tiny newts, frogs, slugs, and other tiny creatures that thrived in the sweltering humidity.

"Alright, let's fill these up fast," Birdie instructed. "We don't want to be down here for longer than we need to be."

"Bah," replied Helcant. "Yet have I to see a creature in this desert that threatens me."

"Well, if you want to see one, start making a lot of noise and wait. In the meantime, I'll be back on the surface out of the way."

Helcant clamped his mouth shut, and the three of them filled their canteens and returned to the surface. Ev proceeded to empty them out once again for the horses, and the trio made a second trip. Then, a third. Then a fourth. By the time they'd gone down for their seventh load, Birdie was kicking herself for not thinking to bring buckets with them.

Eventually the horses managed to get their fill, and soon afterward so had everyone else. After a few more minutes of rest up in Tallis's bubble of cool, Birdie had the group pack up and continue on their way. Four hours later, they needed to stop and water the horses once again.

"You surely jest at me," growled Helcant after Birdie called him over to another hole she'd found. "A waste of my time is what you ask, dipping in and out of these pits, and nasty at the bottom! Those plants possess a stink!"

"And tell me," replied Birdie, growing agitated with the demon, "just what else were you planning on doing with your precious time."

Helcant growled as small flames began to crackle on his back, but Ev stepped in before he could say more.

"Did you say there are plants down there?"

Helcant spun around toward Ev. "'Tis a jungle! Smelly roots and leaves and slimy things everywhere!"

"Really?" replied Ev excitedly before turning to Birdie. "Can I go, then?"

Birdie sighed. "I'm sorry, Ev, but it's too hot for you down there."

"Oh, balderdash," returned Ev. "How long does a single trip take? Five minutes? I'm pretty sure I'll survive, and Tallis can cool me off when I get back."

"Aha! See?" exclaimed Helcant as he pointed at Birdie. "She makes us fetch water when the humans can do it themselves! I refuse another trip!"

Birdie threw her hands up in the air. "You know what? I don't care! You want to go? Fine. You don't? Whatever! Stay here and complain about how it's so unfair that you aren't bothered by the heat and other people are. You must have made a great sailor if people expecting you to do things is such a bother to you. So, anyone who wants to help, come on in, because I'm not wasting any more effort talking about this."

Birdie snatched up a pair of canteens and dropped into the pit without waiting for anyone to say anything further. This hole had multiple branching paths down to the bottom, so she took the one that had the gentlest slope. A few seconds later, she heard two others jump in after her. She didn't bother turning around. She could sense well enough it was Ev and Nephira who'd followed her.

When Birdie entered into the root level of the labyrinth this time, she found herself in a sprawling cavern. On the one hand, this meant it more likely that monsters would be nearby. On the other, it meant she'd be able to see them coming with ample warning. In fact, she could see several giant flowers scattered about the cavern, but they were all far enough away to not pose a threat.

"Wow," she heard Ev whisper from behind. "This is incredible. It's like a giant, natural greenhouse."

"It's also incredibly dangerous," warned Birdie, pointing at the flowers. "See those plants over there? They're blooming dagger lilies. They'll attack anything that gets within twenty feet of them, and they're deadly."

Nephira joined Ev and Birdie in observing the lilies. "They don't look much different from normal dagger lilies. What makes these so dangerous?"

Birdie sighed and prepared to allow her othermind to explain the lilies' capabilities, but she stopped herself. Nephira's question might have been genuine, but Birdie was tired of having to argue and explain herself. That, and the thought of giving her othermind control again unnerved her, even for something as small as this. What Lux Rosa had said about her othermind taking over her personality… it was probably a lie, but what if it wasn't?

"Just stay away from them," Birdie stated without looking at either Ev or Nephira.

She took her canteens and filled them in the stream below, the whole time feeling Ev's eyes watching her.

"I'm fine, Ev," Birdie said without looking up.

"Are you sure?" asked Ev as she and Nephira climbed down into the stream as well. "You haven't been yourself since, well, you know."

Birdie stayed silent.

"I'm sad about Waylen, too, but you can't blame yourself for what happened."

Birdie scowled. "First of all, I can, and second... never mind. I just need some time to think."

Ev paused for a second before an unwelcome look of realization appeared on her face. "Wait, this isn't about what that woman said on the boat, is it? Come on, since when do you let what some random person says bother you?"

"That wasn't...!" Birdie spun towards Ev. "That was Lux Rosa!"

Ev looked taken aback, but quickly recovered. "So what? She was obviously just trying to get under your skin."

"Hold on," Nephira stepped in, "did you just say you spoke to Lux Rosa on your ship?"

"What? No, she wasn't actually there."

Nephira looked confused.

Ev continued. "What do you care what she thinks, anyway? She doesn't know anything about you!"

"She knows everything about me!" Birdie yelled back, surprising both herself and Ev.

The two of them stared in silence for a moment before Birdie held her arm across her waist.

"Ev, there are things you don't know about me — things no one should know, but she does."

"What are you talking about?" Ev asked, growing defensive. "I've known you for five years. What could you possibly keep secret from me that's such a big deal?"

"It's not that important," Birdie answered, looking away.

"Oh, really, because it sounds—"

"We really should get moving. It's too hot for you down here. You're sweating as much as you're collecting in the canteens."

Ev glared at Birdie, then plunged her canteens into the stream before climbing back up into the glass tunnel they'd come from. Nephira dipped her canteens into the water as well, gave Birdie a backwards glance, then followed Ev.

Birdie sighed again before also making the climb back up.

At the top, Ev climbed all the way out of the tunnel.

"Here," she stated as she thrust the canteens into a surprised Tallis's hands before marching off toward a cluster of tube plants a short distance away.

That was fine with Birdie; she didn't want Ev down in those tunnels anyway.

Seeing as Tallis had apparently taken on watering duty, Birdie handed her canteens to him as well. She started back down the tunnel again when she realized Nephira was still following her.

Neither of them said anything to one another as they repeated the trip several times over. On the eighth trip, however, Nephira finally broke the silence.

"I don't understand. Why are you concerned about that human's feelings toward you?"

"That 'human' is the closest friend I've ever had," Birdie retorted. "I trust her more than anyone."

"If you trust her so much, then why are you keeping secrets from her?"

"It's complicated," answered Birdie, "and frankly it's none of your business."

"Maybe not," replied Nephira, "but let me guess. You're afraid that she'd be afraid of whatever it is you're hiding. It's a story many corrupted have shared. We go to extreme lengths to reclaim our humanity — makeup, disguises, illusions — and we find a group of mortals we try to befriend, knowing full well that if they ever learned what we really were, we'd be their enemy. Inevitably, that fear is always eventually realized. It is why King Dezeroth's conquest is our only path to salvation. When the land is controlled by immortals, humans will no longer be able to deny us the lives we deserve."

Birdie frowned at Nephira. "That's not what this is. Ev knows what I am. At least…"

Nephira waited for Birdie to finish.

"…at least she knows as much as I do."

"You don't know what you are," Nephira stated, skeptical.

"Do you?" Birdie replied. "I'm a nepac and a Divine at the same time. I'm a shade, but I'm nothing like any other shade I've ever met. And on top of it all, there's—"

"You're secret," Nephira finished for her.

Birdie nodded. "Ev knows a little about it, but I've never told her the whole story."

Birdie crossed her arms and sat down, looking up at the points of light in the cavern ceiling. "I suppose it's like you said. I'm afraid to tell her, but not because I think she'll be afraid. I'm afraid because I think she won't be."

"Should she be?" Nephira inquired, still standing.

Birdie shook her head. "I don't know."

The two waited in silence for a while, listening to the sound of the stream burbling by.

"Well," Nephira said at last, looking away, "I can't say what you should do one way or another. The only thing I can say is what not to do, and that's let some vile Radiant control what you think. Whatever you were told on the ship, true or not, you shouldn't let it affect you. If you do, you are playing into that Radiant's hands."

Nephira filled up her canteens and started back up the tunnel. Birdie simply watched her go as she contemplated Nephira's words. After about thirty seconds, she stood up as well, recognizing that her new revenant friend was right.

Filling up her canteens, Birdie climbed up the roots toward the exit when she froze. An irregular clicking sound echoed down the tunnel. Her senses confirming what was coming, Birdie raced forward in an attempt to escape before the creature cut her off.

Just before she passed the branch in the tunnel, an enormous glassworm thrust its ugly head in front of her. The beast blocked the tunnel entirely. It's transparent flesh allowed Birdie to see clearly into its insides where backwards pointing teeth lined its throat all the way down.

The glassworm opened its maw and lunged at Birdie, its thousands of needly legs clicking madly against the glass.

Birdie retreated as quickly as she could back into the cavern, fortunately outpacing it. Once clear of the tunnel, she pulled out her bottle of elixir and threw herself down into the stream, frightening an army of frogs away in the process.

Birdie had only one idea for how to defeat this thing. She wouldn't be able to maintain the illusion for long, but if the glassworm's bloodlust was strong enough, perhaps it would fall for it.

Dropping her human guise, Birdie held out one hand and focused her magic to conjure an image of herself up on the raised area of the cavern near one of the dagger lilies. She could feel her magic supply dropping rapidly, so she dabbed a bit of the elixir on her head, which she quickly absorbed, refueling her.

The worm burst out of the glass tunnel and charged at the illusion. Birdie splashed on the last of the elixir as she directed her false self to run past the dagger lily.

The worm followed, and as soon as it was in range the dagger lily attempted to ensnare the worm with its roots as it launched an endless supply of razor sharp stamens into the worm's hide.

That was all that Birdie needed to escape, but she felt her othermind directing her to finish the job. The glassworm was more than a match for the lily, but it was also wide open. If she did manage to kill such a powerful creature, it would go a long way to bringing her strength back.

Against her better judgment, Birdie pulled out her bow and took aim at the creature while it was distracted with tearing apart the lily. Focusing on one of the worm's five "hearts," she let one of her arrows fly.

She'd made the right choice bringing enchanted arrows; the penetration enhancement helped it pass clean through the beast's gelatinous flesh, bursting the first of its hearts.

The worm thrashed about and spun around to attack Birdie. She used the last of her spare magic to create another doppelganger, but to her horror, the worm ignored it and charged straight for her.

She dashed to the side, and the monstrous worm slammed its head into the side of the channel near her.

Spinning around, she fired another arrow and struck a second heart. The worm flailed again but didn't slow its attack, changing its course before Birdie could ready a third arrow.

Scrambling out of the channel, Birdie made a dash toward another lily when the glassworm whipped its tail around and slammed her to the ground. She cried out in pain as the giant monster dug its needly legs deep into her own.

Before she had time to slip into puddle form, dread overtook her as the worm lifted her into the air and swung her toward its mouth.

Suddenly the monster released its grip, and Birdie fell to the ground with a thud. She looked up with relief to see Nephira atop the worm's back, her spear dug deep into its crystal clear hide.

The worm rolled over violently, sending Nephira to the ground.

They were now committed to this fight. Birdie took the opportunity to send another arrow through another of the worm's hearts.

Nephira jumped back to her feet and roared as she skewered the worm once more.

As wounded as the creature now was, its rage propelled it to keep fighting. Sweeping its front across the ground, it knocked Nephira to the floor and promptly slammed its bulk down upon her. Nephira cried out in pain as the worm's legs gripped her tightly and bashed her to the ground repeatedly.

Realizing she had to act immediately, Birdie rushed to a better position to take aim at another one of the monster's hearts.

The fourth heart ruptured, and the great beast released Nephira from its grasp as it turned its attention to Birdie once more.

Its movements now significantly slowed, Birdie had more than enough time to dodge its next swipe and fire one last arrow through the creature.

The worm spasmed on the cavern floor before finally falling still. Soon after, Birdie felt another influx of strength, though that did nothing for her exhaustion or injuries.

Turning her attention to Nephira, Birdie immediately regretted her decision to fight the worm. Not only was Nephira not moving, but the necromantic energy that sustained her had vanished from her body.

Hurrying over, Birdie was horrified to find Nephira had been impaled many times over by the glassworm's dagger-like legs.

Glancing around for she knew not what, Birdie's thoughts raced as to how to fix this situation. Revenants required both necromantic energy and a relatively intact body to live. Nephira's body was heavily damaged, but was it too far gone? Maybe if she received more necromantic energy she could be revived now, or could they only resurrect on the Night of Darkness? Birdie's othermind informed her that the former was the case, which meant she could still salvage this.

Picking Nephira up over her shoulder, Birdie carried her back to the surface. Almost immediately after she set Nephira down, Helcant ran over screaming.

"What have you done!"

Birdie ignored him and looked for Ev, whom she spotted feeding insects to one of the local lizards.

"Ev," she shouted, "we need healing, now!"

Ignoring Helcant had been a mistake, as to her shock, the scrawny demon grabbed her by the neck and lifted her into the air, flames erupting from his arms and back.

"What have you done!" he repeated.

"Let go of me!" Birdie yelled back.

Helcant involuntarily obliged when a blast of ice slammed into him from behind. The demon spun around and faced off against Tallis.

This was not what Birdie needed right now.

Helcant roared. "You will regret that, hum—!"

Birdie struck Helcant with a shadowy maul before the situation could escalate any further. As the demon fell limp, she worried that perhaps she'd underestimated how much strength she'd regained and put too much force into the attack. She still sensed life within him, however, so whatever damage was done, Ev could heal later if needed.

Tallis ran over and prepared another spell. "I knew we shouldn't have trusted them. Monsters, every one of them!"

"Excuse me," hissed Birdie, grabbing Tallis's arm, "but the only reason I'm alive right now is because of her!"

She pointed at Nephira.

Tallis was at a loss for words. "W-what? But—"

Birdie let go of Tallis and turned back to Ev. "Ev, please tell me you can heal her," she almost begged.

Ev had already made it over. Birdie couldn't tell if Ev was still angry from before, but that wasn't really her concern at the moment. She knew Ev wouldn't let tensions between them get in the way of what mattered.

Ev leaned over Nephira and examined her before shaking her head and looking back at Birdie. "There's nothing I can do. She's already gone."

"What if she's not?" Birdie asked.

Ev frowned. "She is, though. I just told you that."

Birdie sighed in exasperation and hurried to her horse where she pulled out her personal canteen. Returning to Ev, she held it out.

"Necromantic magic. If I use it to revive her, can you heal her?"

Ev blinked. "Where—?"

"A gift from Zun-Roven. I thought it would come in handy, but not like this."

Ev paused, then nodded. "As long as she's animate, I can heal her."

"Good," said Birdie, and she popped open the canteen and poured it over Nephira.

The glowing dark liquid seeped into the revenant's flesh and soaked her clothing. Shortly after, Nephira began to stir.

"We'll have to work fast. Hold her still," Ev commanded, and Birdie did so.

Ev pulled out her rod and pointed it at the holes in Nephira's chest, a black and white aura emanating from her arms down to the tip of the rod. The holes began to close up, and Nephira awoke. She immediately tried to sit up, but Birdie held her down.

"Don't move; you're hurt," Ev stated.

Nephira pushed herself up regardless, proving stronger than Birdie could hold, but she stopped when she saw the holes in the rest of her torso.

"I told you to hold her still," Ev growled.

"I tried," returned Birdie. Now wasn't the time for Ev's sass.

Ev sighed exasperatedly and continued working. A minute later, she sat back.

"There. That's as much as I can do."

Nephira pushed herself to her feet and felt herself over, seemingly deep in thought. Whether she was aware or not that she'd perished, Birdie didn't know, but she didn't see any point in bringing it up. After a moment, Nephira looked up as if she'd suddenly thought of something. Looking around, she stopped when she spotted Helcant on the ground. Ev had apparently thought he was in good enough condition to let be and went back off to her tube plants instead.

"What happened?" Nephira demanded.

"He attacked me when he saw you hurt," answered Birdie. "He's just knocked out. He'll be fine."

"Typical," Birdie heard Nephira mutter under her breath. "I suppose I'll wait with him until he awakens," she said a bit louder.

"Hey," Birdie said to Nephira, and she waited until Nephira looked at her. "Thanks for the help down there."

Nephira just turned away again and sat next to Helcant.

Birdie then turned her attention to Ev, who was once again feeding the lizards.

Birdie headed over and asked, "Mind if I sit?"

Ev scooted over, spooking the lizard and causing it to hide behind the plant.

Birdie sat down and sighed. "Ev, do you remember how I once told you Syrus gifted me with knowledge of just about everything in the world?"

Ev raised an eyebrow.

"That wasn't the whole story. I don't know what it is, but there's something else inside of me. Something just like what Lux Rosa described. That's where my knowledge comes from."

"What are you talking about? How can you not know what it is? Couldn't Syrus tell you?"

Ev was definitely still upset, but at least she was talking.

Birdie shook her head. "He did, a little. I should have asked more, but I'm not sure I want to know what it is. I call it my "othermind," because it's like there's another mind in my head that's not me. It tells me things; it helps me plan and fight; it even takes control of my body if I let it."

Birdie looked Ev in the eyes. "And it doesn't care about anyone. Not you, not Syrus, not even me. It only cares about achieving victory. The closest it comes to caring about people is seeing them as tools to be used and exploited, and again, that even includes me, the very being it's inside of."

Ev looked skeptically at Birdie. "But you're the one in control, right? Not this 'othermind.'"

Birdie blinked, then sighed. This was exactly how she was afraid Ev would react.

"I'd like to think I am, but who knows what kind of effect it might be having on me over time? You heard what Lux Rosa said. The more I use it, the more I'll become it."

Ev rolled her eyes. "Bah, so what? Why should you believe anything she says?"

Birdie paused. "Ev, I think there's a chance Lux Rosa might have helped Syrus create me."

Ev opened her mouth and closed it again, temporarily at a loss for words. She closed her eyes and waved her hands in front of her.

"Whoa-whoa-whoa, WHAT? How? Why?"

"When we first met, she claimed as much. Then on the boat, she proved she knew about my othermind. No one should know about that other than me and those who played a role in creating me."

Ev swiped her hand in front of her again. "No! Just no! You can't believe what someone like that says! Maybe she found out a different way."

"Ev—"

"And who cares, anyway? Even if she did help make you, that doesn't mean she's telling the truth about your othermind! She's scared of you! Wouldn't it make sense that she'd tell you that kind of thing to mess with your head? Have *you* noticed it changing you, because I sure haven't."

Birdie blinked. "You haven't?"

"The only big change I've seen in you is how stressed out you've been since the attack on Roehelm, which I thought was because, you know, there's a Radiant trying to decide the fate of our world again? But now I see it's because your letting this wannabe Master get inside your head."

"But what if she's right?" protested Birdie.

"What if she is?" returned Ev, lifting her hand dismissively. "Once we've kicked her out of Doxla, Syrus will have the whole place to himself. I don't think you realize just how close he is to taking control of the Masters' systems, and he was able to create you without *any* of the power of the Masters. Don't you think that if this othermind really is a problem, he'll be able to fix it?"

Birdie supposed that was a good point.

"Besides, if you're really worried, why don't you just ask him about it once we get you to Ars Summis?"

Birdie nodded. "Yeah, I think I should. No matter what the answer is, I'm not sure I can stand not knowing anymore."

"Good," said Ev, plopping her hand on Birdie's shoulder. "Now, isn't it much better when you aren't keeping your existential worries all bottled up?"

Birdie picked up Ev's hand and gave it back to her. "Yeah, yeah, don't milk it. Come on. Let's get back to the others before Helcant wakes up and tries to kill someone again."

Chapter 9

The rest of the journey through the desert went far better than that first day, at least for the most part. At some point Nephira must have had a little chat with Helcant, because he didn't voice any more protests about being asked to help with water retrieval. Helcant also kept a healthy distance from the rest of the group, so that made travel far less of a headache. A random pack of monsters would occasionally show up, but aside from diamond dogs, none were remotely a problem. The diamond dogs weren't much of an issue, either, to be honest. The problem was that they attacked at night and went straight for the horse carrying their rations. Thankfully, the horse was able to survive with the help of Ev's healing, but their food stock had been ruined.

The third day in the desert also had one dangerous moment when the wind picked up and kicked off a glass storm. Without much warning of the deadly weather, the group was left scrambling to get to a hole large enough for the horses to fit in to take shelter. Once inside, the glass storm was remarkably beautiful as bits of twinkling colored glass flew by overhead, but it was nonetheless an issue Birdie would have rather avoided.

Once the desert was behind them, the only major hurdle that remained between them and Ars Summis would be the distance. Before that, however, they would need to stop somewhere to restock on supplies.

Breaking in a forest whose trees had all died long ago, Birdie directed everyone to empty the satchels of three of the horses. Once that was done, she stood in front of the others with both hands on her hips.

"Here's the plan," she announced. "Ev, Tallis, and I are going to head into town to buy supplies while Helcant and Nephira stay here with the stuff we already have. Any questions?"

"I have one," said Nephira. "Why are you even going there? Didn't you say we would stay away from human towns?"

"I said we'd *mostly* be staying away," Birdie corrected. "Besides, we need food. Don't worry. This town isn't on the most direct route to Ars Summis. Lux Rosa obviously knows our destination, but the fact we weren't attacked in the desert tells me she either wasn't prepared for a defeat at the port, or she lacks the resources to cover every possible path we might take. I suspect both of those are the case, so I doubt it's likely she has soldiers waiting for us here."

Ev spoke up when Birdie had finished. "Maybe not, but maybe you should stay here, too, just in case? You're the only one who can enter Ars Summis. What if there *are* soldiers here?"

"Then we'll be careful not to arouse suspicion."

Ev frowned.

Nephira spoke again. "And how long are we supposed to wait here for you?" she asked.

"Until either we return, or I send a signal that we need help," Birdie replied, then smiled. "If you hear a bunch of big loud kabooms, that means we're in trouble."

"I see," said Nephira, not at all amused.

"Alright, let's go," Birdie said to Tallis and Ev before climbing back on her horse. "Also, for the record, I'll be going by the name 'Dusty' while we're there. Ev and Tallis, if anyone asks, you're my kids."

"Wait, what?" Tallis asked, visibly confused.

"Well, of course," responded Birdie before shifting her appearance and voice to that of an older man's. "Everyone knows Eclipse always takes on the form of a woman, so what better disguise is there than this?"

The shocked expression on Tallis's face prompted a chuckle from Birdie.

"What? I told you I don't always take on the appearance of a woman, remember?"

"I mean, I—" began Tallis before clearing his throat. "Of course you don't. Who doesn't know that?"

Birdie grinned.

"Yeah, yeah. You can make a good disguise," added Ev. "I still don't think it's a good idea for you to go."

"I knew you wouldn't, but maybe I can do something to help you feel better about it," piped Birdie, prompting Ev to raise an eyebrow.

On the way out of the forest, Birdie took a moment to kill a small bird she spotted, which she then tucked into her sleeve.

"Uh, whyyy?" asked Tallis.

"Because last I checked Dezeroth's forces were getting close to the Crystal Desert. There's a good chance they'll have guards checking for shades, loyalists or no."

"And a bird helps how?"

Birdie smiled, then retracted her hand back into her sleeve and popped it out again. Her hand then turned into the dead bird, which she waved around in front of her.

"See? Bird hand! Now, if they check to see if I bleed red, I will."

"Huh," remarked Tallis, "that's very clever, actually."

"Of course it is," replied Birdie before turning to Ev. "Feel a little better about me going now?"

Ev shook her head. "Let's just get this over with."

Birdie's smile faded, but she really wasn't surprised. Ev's concerns were valid, but she very much doubted they'd have trouble. Well, she supposed they'd find out soon enough.

$$* * * *$$

Considering how close it was to the borders of Dezeroth's still expanding kingdom, the town of Wayworth appeared remarkably at ease. The guards at the town gates barely even gave Birdie, Tallis, and Ev a once over before letting them through, making the dead bird pointless. Within the town itself, families and businessfolk went about their routines without so much as a glance at the newcomers.

"Alright," remarked Birdie in her new voice. "Looks like this is going to be even easier than I'd hoped it would."

Ev said nothing.

Birdie stopped and looked at her friend. "What's wrong? You don't think so?"

Ev shook her head. "I don't know. I just don't like it."

Tallis spoke up. "What are you talking about? Everything looks fine."

"I already said why I don't like it. Can we please just do this already?"

"I'm all for that," Birdie stated. "No need to leave our new friends waiting."

Tallis frowned at that remark but said nothing. The trio then headed further into town in search of food, which actually proved more difficult than Birdie had expected. The marketplace had scarce offerings, likely due to the ongoing famine, but Birdie hadn't realized it had gotten this bad yet. Still, after a little less than an hour, they'd bought and loaded their supplies onto their horses and were ready to head back out of town when Birdie sensed a frighteningly familiar magic building up.

Tallis noticed Birdie jerk her head.

"What—" he began, but an enormous arc of lightning cut him off as it stretched into the sky from behind some nearby buildings.

The townsfolk around the group all gazed up at the sky, some with surprise but most in awe — a few even cheering.

Birdie, Ev, and Tallis all glanced around as they took in the odd reaction. A sinking feeling made its way into Birdie's chest.

Ev stared at Birdie with a mixture of anger and fear. "What did you say about coming here?" she whispered.

"I think we should get out of here," Tallis muttered.

Birdie nodded in agreement, but couldn't help but look back at where the lightning had come from. After taking a few steps, her curiosity got the better of her.

"Wait with the horses," she ordered.

"What are you doing?" hissed Ev.

"Don't worry," answered Birdie, "I'll be fine."

Birdie didn't even take two steps before her ears picked up on a male voice shouting from a couple of streets over. At first it was hard to make out what was said, but as she drew nearer the words became clear.

"…rid the world of the likes of Dezeroth and all immortals forever! Pledge yourselves to the last true Radiant and you will also be blessed with the power of the Divine!"

Birdie rounded the corner and spotted a pair of soldiers with red-maned lions and white roses emblazoned on their armor, as if the magic they wielded hadn't already been enough to inform Birdie of who they were. They stood atop a hay cart — one a mage and one a knight — shouting to a packed street of onlookers.

"The vile treachery of Syrus and Eclipse still festers in Doxla," the knight continued. "Too many have sold their humanity and sided with their wickedness, all for empty promises of safety and power! But you have seen firsthand their true colors. They lie in bed with the Undead King himself! They have sold your lands to literal demons, let your crops and forests die! 'All in the name of peace,' they say, but have any of you known peace since the Dark Radiant murdered your protector and savior, Supreme Lord Grandis?"

The crowd erupted into angry shouts and jeers, causing Birdie to involuntarily duck down as if someone might recognize her through her disguise. Discomfort quickly made way for intrigue, however, as she noticed a third loyalist cast the oddest flavor of spell she'd ever sensed before pushing a strange shimmering ripple up towards the other two.

The knight raised his fist into the air. "Yes, all of you know the true color of the traitor Syrus and fiend Eclipse! Their hearts are blacker than the darkest night, and that darkness can only be fought with the light of a true Radiant — the light that Exalted Lady Lux Rosa has, in her endless cunning, wisdom, and benevolence, found a way to share with all who would stand against such villainy.

"Behold!" the knight shouted as the third loyalist raised her shimmer level with the knight's shoulder. "This tiny light contains the blessing of the Masters themselves! Lady Rosa has shared this blessing with all who will serve her in the battle against evil. With but a small ritual, any pure-hearted nepac can wield the power of a Radiant."

"*That's* how they get their magic?" Ev's voice nearly made Birdie jump.

Birdie spun around to see both Ev and Tallis standing behind her.

"What are you doing here?" she hissed. "I told you to wait with the horses."

"We've got the horses," Ev patted one of their steeds, grinning defiantly. "Did you honestly think I'd let you go off on your own?"

Birdie shook her head slightly before turning back to the spectacle before her. The information on display could well prove to be invaluable.

The knight went on with his speech. "You all know why we are here. Too few have heeded the calling of Lady Rosa, and now Dezeroth's hoards claw at your very doorstep! So I ask you again, who will put down their plows and take up a sword?"

The crowd roared enthusiastically — their reaction very much unnerving. Birdie had known she wasn't exactly popular in most circles, but to see a whole town cheering for her death — she almost wanted to turn and slink away. Yet, she knew she couldn't miss this. These loyalists threatened everyone and everything she cared about, and this might be her only opportunity to learn about them.

"Blind sheep," Tallis muttered behind her.

Birdie turned to silence Tallis before he got them caught, but she was happy to see Ev already signaling to him to shut it.

"Such willingness to stand up to injustice!" the knight shouted, raising both hands out to the crowd. "But I must ask you again. Who here is willing to leave their homes to learn the ways of the Guardians of Light? We will grant this power to a few brave defenders of your town, yes, but only if enough others are willing to dedicate their lives to the service of Lady Rosa and the obliteration of the vile Syrus and Eclipse. If you are willing to travel to the Hall of Champions and march against the Shadow Guard, then declare it so and step forward!"

"I am!" shouted a young man at the front of the crowd.

"And me!" shouted another.

One by one about fifteen villagers — ranging from teenagers to one man at least in his forties — pushed their way to where the loyalist knight smiled down triumphantly.

"The bravery shown by these men and women is admirable!" declared the knight. "But are there truly no others in a town of this size willing to fight for this world's future?"

The crowd exchanged looks with one another. After a moment, three more stepped forward.

"Very good," stated the knight. "It is a pity no more are willing to join, but I know that not everyone in this town has come to hear my words. We shall remain until the morning comes, lest any others summon the courage to fight for justice. At that time, we will depart with all who take an oath to serve Lady Rosa. Spread the word throughout your town, and let it be known that for every ten who march with us, we will grant the power of the Radiants to one defender of this town, up to at most five. I am truly sorry that we can offer no more, but the blessings of the Masters are limited, and there are many towns yet who still have no defense against Dezeroth's twisted hoards.

"To those of you who have stepped forward, go and bid your farewells to your families. Let them know that you go on to serve the highest of causes. Come to the eastern gate of town at morning tomorrow, and bring your champions who will defend your town at that time as well. Be warned, however, that only those who already possess some skill with magic can use our blessing. To the brave warriors who travel with us, this will not matter, as they will all be granted this power when we arrive at the Hall of Champions!"

The knight and his fellow loyalists departed, and the crowd dispersed. Birdie watched as the three soldiers walked alongside an older woman — possibly the town elder — to what appeared to be an inn. The spellcaster kept careful control of the shimmer before her, walking between the other two as she kept both arms around but a decent distance from whatever that thing actually was.

Ev leaned close and whispered, "There, they're done. Are you ready now?"

Birdie nodded an affirmative, frowning. She led the way back out of town, dropping the dead bird into a small bush once they were clear. She could always get another if needed.

She glanced back at the town as they entered into the forest. Birdie wasn't close to done with this group of loyalists yet. What they'd learned just now could prove vital. The loyalists apparently had some connection to the Hall of Champions, and their power came from some strange shimmering thing. They would apparently be using that shimmer in the morning, and Birdie was going to be there when they did.

* * * *

"Are you sure this is a good idea?" Ev asked again the following morning.

"Yes," hissed Helcant, "our impression was that much haste was needed, yet you delay us half a day."

"And my impression was that we already talked about this yesterday," countered Birdie, arms crossed. "We have an opportunity to learn firsthand just how the hell Lux Rosa is giving common nepacs magic on par with Radiants. If we can figure out how she's doing it, then maybe we can do it, too."

Tallis spoke up. "Those bastards killed Waylen. I say it's time we turned the tables on them."

"Exactly," said Birdie.

"I get that," protested Ev, "but maybe you should take me instead? I'm smaller than Tallis."

"Not by enough to make a difference," replied Birdie, slipping a pair of elixirs under her shirt, just in case.

"But—"

"Ev, I said 'no.' Please wait here with Nephira and Helcant until we get back."

Ev pouted but held her peace.

Birdie turned to Tallis as she shifted her appearance to that of a young redheaded man. "Remember, you'll need to stay close to me. Are you ready?"

"Absolutely," Tallis answered.

"Then let's go," Birdie replied. "We don't want to risk missing the show."

Birdie and Tallis made their way through the forest to a point east of the town before exiting and heading south to the road. Once there, they turned back west to arrive at the eastern gate. As they drew near, Birdie began casting a small illusion on Tallis to change his eyes and hair to blue and blond. The effort was relatively minor. The only problem was the fact that a small bit of dark magic wisped steadily from her left hand, but she kept that hidden by keeping the arm flat against her beneath her shirt. She then forced a small nub out from her shoulder to give the appearance of an amputated arm under her sleeve.

At the town, they seemed to have arrived early, so they headed in and made a show of shopping around until Birdie noticed a number of townsfolk heading to the gate.

"Looks like it's time," Birdie murmured to Tallis before addressing an old street vendor. "Excuse me, ma'am, but is something happening here? I keep seeing people walking that way."

The vendor almost chuckled. "Oh, you're in for a treat, deary. The Guardians of Light have visited our town and are soon to bestow the blessings of the Masters upon us. I'd be going myself if these old legs could still carry me."

"Interesting," Birdie mused. "I'd say that sounds like something worth seeing, wouldn't you agree, cousin?"

"Why, yes, I think I'd love to see it," Tallis said with just a bit of a tone Birdie'd have preferred he'd left out. "Thank you so much for telling us."

The vendor nodded. "I'll be waiting here. Do come back and tell me all the details."

"Oh, we sure will," Birdie said with a smile and a wave goodbye, and she and Tallis were off to the gate once more.

Outside the town, a crowd much larger than the one yesterday had gathered. Birdie and Tallis slid around the side of the crowd to get a clearer look at just how this "blessing" thing was done.

At the front of the crowd was the village elder flanked by twenty-something villagers, some of whom Birdie recognized as having volunteered yesterday. The loyalist knight stood before them. His mage and spellcaster companions stayed several feet back — the strange shimmer still floating between the spellcaster's hands.

For a time, the loyalists, elder, and volunteers all stood silent. The only words spoken were murmurs and whispers by the rest of the crowd, which continued to grow as the morning dragged on. Eventually, another handful of volunteers pushed their way up to the front to join the elder, who gave them a glare and said something to them Birdie couldn't hear. A brief conversation then took place between the knight and the elder, and once it was done, the knight raised his hands high.

"Such a courageous gathering of noble folk whose hearts are those of warriors! Before me today are thirty-one brave souls come to take an oath to serve the last true Radiant and purge the world of all evil! I ask of these heroes now, which of you will be the first to take said oath?"

The young man who had been first to speak up the day before once again stepped forward and shouted, "I will!"

The knight smiled. "In that case, stand before me and declare your name!"

The man approached the knight. "My name is Thomas Faux!"

The knight drew his sword and held it pointing upward in front of him. "And, Thomas Faux, do you swear fealty to Exalted Lady Lux Rosa, to obey her commands, and to dedicate your life to ridding this world of the villainy of Syrus, Eclipse, Dezeroth, and all immortals?"

"I swear it," declared Thomas.

"Then kneel," ordered the knight.

Thomas obeyed.

The knight placed his sword on each of Thomas's shoulders. "From this day forward, you will no longer be known as Thomas Faux of Wayworth, but as Sir Thomas Faux of the Guardians of Light! Stand, Sir Faux, and take your place with your fellow warriors behind me."

Birdie noticed Tallis was practically quivering, his fists clenched tightly. Birdie gave him a nudge and very subtly shook her head, her eyes warning not to do anything that would draw attention to them. She wasn't exactly thrilled with the clear manipulation of these villagers either, but she also wasn't surprised it was effective. Syrus had long ago made a deal with Dezeroth to allow him to expand his empire in exchange for assistance in defeating Grandis, and both Syrus and Birdie had upheld that deal. They'd tried their best to make the expansion peaceful, but longstanding loyalties, fears, and animosities had doomed such efforts before they even began. These people would likely sell their souls if it meant destroying the bogeymen that threatened the way of life that they knew and held to so desperately.

The villager named Thomas had now taken up position near the other loyalists, and the knight repeated his little ceremony with the next volunteer. Then the next. Then, the next. Once all thirty-one volunteers had been "knighted," the knight put away his sword and the spellcaster walked forward. The frustration Birdie had felt with the whole proceedings thus far finally gave way to anticipation. This looked to be exactly what they'd come for.

The knight addressed the elder. "Your village has proved themselves loyal to the cause of Lady Rosa. For this, you have earned the blessings of the Masters. You have given us thirty brave soldiers, so we will grant three champions the power to defend your town from Dezeroth's hoards. Let them step forward now."

The elder and two others — a middle-aged man and a young woman — approached the knight.

"Very good," said the knight. "Please, before we grant you the power of the Radiants, demonstrate for your fellows your most powerful spells."

The elder raised her hand and cast a small fireball about thirty feet away that exploded into a small bonfire when it hit the ground. The man did the same with a ray of light that left a decent scorch mark on the ground; the young woman cast a weak lightning bolt that arced about twenty feet before popping a small hole in the grass about a foot across.

The knight raised a hand towards the three "champions." "Behold, the extent of your champions' powers without the gifts of Lady Rosa. I ask them now to touch the light of the Masters and let it flow through them. Absorb its power, then cast your spells once more."

The elder moved first. She approached the spellcaster and reached out her hand to the floating shimmer. Even from this distance, Birdie could see the elder hesitate, but ultimately she steeled herself and touched the center of the odd light. The moment her finger contacted it, a thin, iridescent ripple shot out and enveloped the elder, distorting the air around her in a quick flash before vanishing as rapidly as it had appeared. Birdie could sense that there was a subtle change in the magic inside of the old woman. She hadn't noticed it before in the other soldiers she'd fought, but having witnessed the transformation directly, it was now clear that those who possessed such power did have a clear signal of its presence. The elder jerked back and looked at her hand as she opened and closed it a few times.

"Now," said the knight, "cast your spell again so that the power of Lady Rosa shall be known!"

The elder stepped away from the others and raised her hand to the field once more. A fireball many times larger than her first erupted from her hand and streaked into the distance, erupting into an explosion large enough to demolish a house when it finally landed.

"Impossible," Tallis couldn't help but mutter.

Birdie frowned, but caught herself. The rest of the crowd had erupted into cheers, so she made an attempt to do the same, smiling and raising her "good" arm as she gave Tallis another nudge and look to join in.

The elder stood stunned, staring at her hand and the fire burning in the field. Her attention was brought back to the knight as he made another announcement.

"Very good! Now, let the other two champions receive Lady Rosa's blessing so that they may also wield the power of righteousness!"

The other champions touched the ripple as well. Just as with the elder, each of them briefly flashed with an iridescent distortion. Just as with the elder, each of them cast another spell. Just as with the elder, the second cast was magnitudes more powerful than what they had done before.

The display of power here sent Birdie thinking back to the battle at Roehelm. Were those soldiers they'd fought against then just like these here — random people given extraordinary magical abilities? It made sense, now that she thought about it. Some of the enemy soldiers had seemed disciplined, but most of them had been disorganized, as if they'd had very little training. If Birdie was right, Lux Rosa must have begun putting her army together very recently, or at least wasn't bothering to train them properly before sending them off to battle.

The knight had started off on another speech, but Birdie wasn't listening. It was all more propaganda, and she'd seen what they'd come here to see. Whatever that ripple the spellcaster possessed was, it held the power to enhance the spells of anyone who touched it.

The moment the loyalists prepared to leave, the crowd began to disperse. Birdie tapped Tallis and motioned that they should be on their way as well. Taking their horses back through the town, they followed the road west a short distance. Once they were well clear, Birdie changed back to her preferred appearance before heading back north to the forest where the others were waiting.

Ev was the first to speak upon their return. "Finally! When we heard those explosions, we were worried something had happened."

Helcant chimed in before Birdie had a chance to respond. "Well? What knowledge did you acquire?"

Birdie frowned, but her frown quickly turned to a smile as she cocked her head. "Oh, we learned a lot."

The group waited eagerly for Birdie to continue, who delayed saying more to enjoy how rapt their attention was.

Helcant broke the silence, scowling about being made to wait. "Well? What do you now know?"

Birdie tilted her head the other way, still smiling. "We learned how Lux Rosa is giving her soldiers that crazy magic, and better, we learned that we're going to be taking a detour to Ars Summis."

"A detour?" Nephira seemed skeptical. "What manner of detour?"

Birdie grinned slyly. "The kind of detour that will take away Lux Rosa's advantage. She's sending soldiers out to share the gift of enhanced magic, and I think it would be very rude of us if we didn't accept it."

Chapter 10

Through the dead forest, Birdie led the way as they stalked the loyalist party. She knew attacking them would be dangerous, but none of the villagers that had volunteered to join Lux Rosa had touched the shimmer, at least not at that little ceremony. So long as that hadn't changed, they had a decent shot, but they would need to make their move soon. Birdie doubted the loyalists had come all this way out here on their own. Most likely, they had a camp near one of the crossroads between towns, and if they got back there then the chance for stealing that shimmer would vanish.

Fortunately, the loyalists made slow progress with the villagers all walking on foot. Thanks to the forest's barrenness, Birdie and her group were able to move ahead of them in pretty good time. As far as she could tell, their targets had yet to spot them through the trees.

Once Birdie was confident they were far enough ahead, she dismounted from her horse, removed her physical clothing and equipment, and put it all up for her horse to carry.

"Just keep going at the current pace," she said. "I'll catch up easily."

Ev shifted on her horse. "I'm not sure I like this plan."

"Relax, Ev," Birdie returned. "If they could sense my magic, they would have done so back at Wayworth. I won't be in the slightest danger of getting hurt."

"*This* isn't the part I'm worried about," Ev muttered.

Birdie placed her hand on her hip. "Ev, we'll be fine. If I sense they've been using that shimmer, I'll call the whole thing off. Okay?"

Ev growled slightly, but held her peace otherwise.

"I'm going now," said Birdie. "I'll see you all again up ahead."

Birdie melted down into a puddle and slid out of the forest through the grass. Maintaining that form in the sun took all of her effort, but the grass was tall enough to keep most of it off of her, allowing her to reach a small boulder beside the road. There, the rock shaded her well enough to let her stay hidden while she waited for the loyalist band to arrive.

About fifteen minutes later, they did, and they walked right past her, oblivious to her presence. Birdie's suspicion proved accurate, as best as she could tell. While it was beyond her ability to sense all of the village recruits while they were bunched up like that, none of the ones close to her possessed that subtle yet distinct flavor of magic marking the use of the shimmer.

Once they had continued on for another five minutes, Birdie felt comfortable enough to venture back to the trees once again. The sun was up higher now, and its increased pressure forced her out of her puddle form before she could reach the trees, but none of Lux Rosa's band spotted her as she scurried the rest of the way to cover.

Her mission accomplished, she ran as fast as she could to meet up with the others. When she finally arrived, she gave them the news.

"It's just the three of them," she said. "If we play this right, we shouldn't have any problem."

Ev frowned. "Am I really the only one who thinks this is a bad idea? If you get split, we lose everything."

"As long as everyone follows the plan, we won't have any trouble," Birdie repeated. "Lux Rosa *will* be waiting for us at Ars Summis. There's always a chance Dezeroth either won't get or won't heed our message. If that happens, this power might be our only chance at getting past her."

Ev swung her arm wide. "Then let us get it! You wait here and we'll take Helcant with us."

"And then what?" countered Birdie. "You'll never get to the carrier before she starts using that shimmer on their volunteers. I have to go."

Nephira directed her horse alongside Ev's. "As much as I agree that this attempt is borderline foolish in its recklessness, I unfortunately must also concur with Birdie that her role is essential to success, as is Helcant's."

The expression she directed at Birdie was clearly one of disapproval, but that mattered not. Birdie had already made up her mind.

"Ev, I appreciate your concern, but I'm not budging on this." She looked from Ev to Tallis to Nephira. "Now, are the three of you ready?"

Ev pushed herself off her horse, defeated. "I guess I have to be."

"Absolutely," answered Tallis, a determination Birdie hadn't seen before now in his eyes.

Nephira dropped down from her mount but said nothing.

"Good," said Birdie before turning to Helcant. "Remember. Wait until at least two of the armored loyalists are in swinging distance of the rest of us. When they are, watch out for their spells. I know they have a lightning one.

There's no telling what else they can do."

"I know my role," shot back Helcant. "My fire shall outshine the sun!"

Birdie nodded and slipped back into her armor and clothing. She and Ev left their bows and arrows with the horses. She then led Ev, Tallis, and Nephira to the side of the road, making certain to keep an eye in the loyalists' direction as they went.

So far, the loyalists were still out of sight, and if her estimates on their speed were right, then they still had roughly fifteen minutes to get everything prepared.

"Alright, ready?" Birdie asked the others as she held out her enchantment breaker to Tallis.

Tallis took the dagger and stared at it with determination. Ev held out her own dagger, eyeing Birdie unhappily but clearly ready.

"I'm sorry for asking you to do this," Birdie told them, "but it has to be convincing."

"I'll do whatever it takes," Tallis muttered, "though I don't see why we couldn't have used the horses."

Ev spun on him. "We are *not* hurting a horse!"

Tallis ignored her. Gripping the dagger tightly, he ran it clean through his left hand, surprising Birdie with his utter lack of hesitation. Tallis struggled to hold back a cry through his clenched teeth as he removed the blade once again, holding his hand to his chest and spilling blood all over it.

Ev recoiled slightly at Tallis's fervor, but not to be outdone quickly followed suit, letting out a suppressed gasp as the blade sliced through.

Once the two of them were coated quite thoroughly in blood, and several splatters stained the ground, Ev went to work at healing the wounds.

"You two look horrible," Birdie said. "Now we just need to put on the finishing touches and we'll take up our positions. Mind if I have my dagger back?"

Birdie held out her hand, into which Tallis placed the borrowed blade. Birdie then flipped her enchantment breaker in the air as she grinned.

"Right then. Don't move," she commanded.

With a few quick slashes she tore a set of holes in Tallis and Ev's clothing at the locations they'd spilled most of their blood. Once done, she addressed Tallis.

"Okay, time to make a hole." She turned to Nephira. "You ready?"

"Why are you wasting time with conversation?" Nephira asked.

"I'll take that as a yes," responded Birdie, nodding to Tallis.

Tallis turned a steely gaze to the ground nearby, and with a flick of his glowing arm pushed the grass and soil aside to form a shallow grave. Wordlessly, Nephira took her spear and lay flat in the hole before Tallis buried her again, careful not to leave a mound that might have signaled the earth had been disturbed.

Checking over her shoulder to make sure their quarry had yet to crest the hill, Birdie then ordered Ev and Tallis to take up their positions.

"Alright. Tallis? You go over there," she pointed about ten yards farther down the road. "Ev? Lay down right near Nephira."

Tallis obeyed immediately, laying flat on his back halfway into the grass on the side of the road furthest from the forest.

Ev hesitated. "You know, we don't have to do this."

Birdie crossed her arms. "This might be the only chance at this we'll get for a long time, if ever. We kind of do."

"That's not what I mean. What about all those villagers? They don't even know what's going on. Are we just going to kill them?"

Birdie frowned. "They took part in this the moment they swore an oath to Lux Rosa. If we let them go, we'd just have to fight them later after they've been given obscene powers."

"So, that's it then? Just because they're making a mistake now, you aren't going to give them a chance to realize it and do better?"

"Ev—"

"What about Waylen? He used to serve Grandis before you took over, and so did Tallis!"

Tallis called out at that. "And we realized our mistake as soon as Grandis's treachery was made known! What he tried to do is no secret to anyone, but those villagers would rather cling to their false hero than accept the truth."

Birdie sighed. She didn't have time to discuss this further.

"Look, I'm not going to simply kill them all. I never said I was going to. We kill who we have to, Ev. That's how we've always done it, and you know that. Now please, lie down," she ordered.

Ev lowered her eyes, but obeyed.

Birdie then hurried to take up her own position in the grass about twenty yards closer to the approaching loyalists where she dropped into the grass, staying on the same side as Tallis. Concentrating, she projected an illusion of blood soaking her clothing, making sure her appearance was that of an older woman whose throat had been slit. Producing convincing blood on the ground was still beyond her ability, but she could approximate it by spreading her shadow out a bit and tinting it red. The fact that she didn't breath or have a pulse would also certainly help with the illusion, though hopefully she wouldn't have to keep it up for long.

Less than a minute later, Birdie spotted their targets cresting the hill. The only real hitch in the plan was the possibility that only one of the loyalists would investigate the horror scene that had been laid out for them. If that happened, they might have to resort to using the villagers as cover, but her othermind assured her they could win this.

As the enemy group approached, that possibility seemed more and more remote. Though their steps grew cautious shortly after coming into view, the entirety of their band stayed together as they drew well within firing distance of Tallis's spells. It wasn't until they'd come within ten feet of Birdie that the lead knight held up his hand and directed his mage to investigate the scene.

Birdie watched every moment, making certain to keep her illusion steady, including the appearance of dead eyes staring blankly into the sky.

The mage first approached her, staring at the apparent gash in her throat and tapping her lightly with his boot.

"She's dead," reported the mage, his forensics skills truly admirable.

"I can see that," returned the knight, eyeing the nearby forest suspiciously. "What about the others?"

The mage turned his attention to Ev, who was the next closest to him. As he walked, the rest of the loyalists edged forward as well, the recruits from the village all glancing around nervously as their shadows fell over Birdie's body.

"Bandits," she heard one of them say.

"Dezeroth scum," another spit.

In a sense, they were both right, Birdie mused, but they wouldn't find that out until it was too late.

"This one's still alive," the mage called to the knight.

The knight's attention snapped back to the mage as the latter kneeled down to investigate more closely, risking the ruse being blown early.

Tallis must have noticed this, as he started moaning. The mage stepped away from Ev almost immediately and hurried over to Tallis.

"This one's alive, too!"

The knight's curiosity now piqued, he approached Ev and Tallis. Birdie almost let a grin slip onto her face by sheer habit. The spellcaster guarding the shimmer still kept her distance, but otherwise the plan was unfolding almost perfectly. All they needed now was for Helcant to make his move.

Right on cue, one of the village recruits let out a shout. "Demons!"

The knight and mage both spun towards the shouting recruit and just as quickly followed said recruit's finger towards the woods. There, Helcant charged toward the group on horseback, sword raised high into the air and a trail of fire blazing behind him.

The mage jumped forward to cast what Birdie sensed would be a lightning spell, but he soon found himself on the ground as Ev kicked hard at the back of his knee.

The knight saw this and drew his blade.

"It's a trap!" he yelled as he moved to impale a still prone Ev.

His attack was halted by a blinding sheet of ice wrapping around his face.

At the same moment, Nephira burst from the ground and plunged her spear into the toppled mage's exposed neck.

Some of the braver recruits rushed in to help, but Ev leapt into their path and brandished her knife, leaving Nephira and Tallis to deal with the knight. The "heroes" paused momentarily before the first of them made the mistake of pressing further. Ev might have been a cleric-turned-scholar, but she was still a soldier with several years' experience under her belt.

Her assailants never stood a chance.

Most eyes now off of her, Birdie made her move. Using her othermind to control the force and trajectory of her throws, she lobbed both of her daggers high into the air in the direction of the shimmer's guardian.

This immediately resulted in the nearby recruits retreating from her, but packed together as they were, they couldn't go far.

Birdie melted out of her armor and slipped into the recruits' shadows, prompting shouts of surprise and terror from them as she zipped along toward her target. She materialized behind the spellcaster in her shade form, caught the knives, and plunged the magic drainer into the loyalist's neck. A few recruits tried to jump her as she did so, but Birdie tripped them all up as she swept her shadow along the ground around her and her target.

After a few seconds of struggle, the spellcaster's movements ceased, and Birdie let her drop to the ground. The recruits around her all backed away, terrified of the shade that had erupted in the middle of them.

As Nephira and Tallis worked in tandem to finish off the lead knight, Helcant arrived and charged the horses through the cluster of recruits to where Birdie waited with their newly claimed shimmer.

One of the recruits made a dive for the shimmer, but Birdie shot a shadowy spear from her arm and impaled the attacker's shoulder, stopping her in her tracks. Birdie then threw the recruit to the ground and retracted the spear.

Now alongside Birdie, Helcant raised a fiery hand in preparation for a scorching attack on the survivors.

"That's enough, Helcant," ordered Birdie in as deep and intimidating of a voice as she could muster. "We've secured what we're after. I don't think any of these humans are foolish enough to throw their lives away in a fight they know they can't win."

Helcant sneered down at the trembling village recruits around him and seemed ready to relent, but just as it looked like Helcant would cooperate, he instead swiped a wave of flames along the ground, scorching the legs of several villagers.

The attack sent nearly half of the villagers running, with a few dropping to the ground as they struggled to douse their flaming pants and shoes before ultimately fleeing as well. After the attack, only fourteen of the villagers still stood before a now furious Birdie.

Frankly, Birdie didn't know what she'd expected from him. She'd deal with Helcant later, however, as right now she needed to continue her performance.

She pointed her dagger at the young man directly in front of her, whom she recognized from the village as that Thomas fellow, and made sure she spoke loud enough for everyone to hear.

"Begone from here. Our quarrel is with Lux Rosa, not with you. Unless you serve her, you are free to go."

None of the villagers moved.

"Now!" Birdie shouted, jerking toward Thomas.

Thomas fell backwards, and several of the remaining villagers fled. As they fled, so did others, until only the woman Birdie had skewered and a few of the ones Ev had defeated remained.

"And what are you waiting for?" Birdie asked the woman. "Go home."

The woman glared at Birdie, holding her bleeding shoulder. "I will not."

Birdie cocked her head and narrowed her eyes.

"Is that so? Tell me, then, what good do you think it does anyone for you to throw your life away?"

"I will not run from a monster!" the woman yelled before lunging for the shimmer a second time.

She fell dead before she reached it, Nephira's spear buried deep in her back. Birdie spun her head toward Nephira.

"That wasn't necessary," she growled.

Nephira returned stoically, "She had her chance to flee. She refused it."

Birdie left her eyes on Nephira for a second before turning to the others. "Ev, are those villagers dead?"

Ev looked down at the three bodies before her. "Not yet. What do you want me to do with them?"

Birdie glanced briefly at Tallis. "Heal them. Send them home. They aren't a threat to us."

Ev nodded and obliged, pulling out her healing rod and pointing it at the wounded. The three villagers arose to find themselves surrounded by five figures — any one of whom could have ended them on the spot. Their earlier bravado utterly quashed and replaced only with fear and confusion, Birdie directed their attention to the woman Nephira had killed.

"Your friend died because she tried to touch this shimmer after I gave her a chance to return home. You are free to take her body back to town, but if any of you try to make the same mistake she did, you *will* meet the same fate."

The three kids stared back at the shade speaking to them, clearly distrustful of what she said.

Tallis opened his mouth to speak, but Birdie raised her hand to cut him off before tilting her head.

"Let me put it to you a different way. Do you honestly think we would have healed you if we wanted to kill you? You clearly don't know much about shades if you think we play games like that. We don't. We also don't like wasting time, so I suggest you go now before we decide it's not worth waiting for you to make up your minds."

Birdie stepped a bit to the side and gestured once more to the fallen woman.

The villagers still looked skeptical, but they at last decided that sticking around maybe wasn't the best decision. Once they'd taken their first few steps past Birdie, two of them broke into a sprint and fled down the road at full speed. The third tried to stop and grab the woman, but when he noticed the others were leaving him behind, he took one look back at Birdie before dropping the girl and running off as well.

"Cowards," Tallis said quietly, disgust dripping from his voice.

"Whatever," Birdie shrugged, returning to her favored guise. "Let's clear away the bodies and see what we can do with this thing."

The group quickly pulled the fallen into the grass where Tallis used his earth magic to bury them.

The thought of repurposing their foes' armor was now a tempting one, seeing as they'd be staying well away from human settlements for the remainder of their journey, but they'd also be heading into Dezeroth's territory soon. Wearing anything with Grandis's emblem would not be a wise decision, so as nice as the enchantments may have been, she decided it best to pass on that for now.

Once the bodies were dealt with, the group gathered around the floating shimmer, with Birdie, Tallis, and even Ev putting their faces right up near it.

"What do you think it is?" Ev asked.

"It can't be what they said it was," Tallis answered, likely referring to the statement that it was a blessing from the Masters.

Birdie remained silent. This glowing ripple was an enigma to her. It clearly held some powerful connection with magic, but even inches away from it she could sense absolutely nothing, or at least not anything that touched her usual senses. Something felt very wrong about it, but perhaps it was simply her imagination.

"We don't know that for sure," Ev commented. "It's possible the Masters left something behind. Maybe."

"I don't think that's what this is," Birdie remarked stoically.

Tallis seemed validated by her agreement.

"Well, what else could it be?" Ev asked.

"I don't know," Birdie admitted, "but the knight said its power is limited. It sounded like only a few people can use it before it stops working."

Tallis straightened slightly at this. "So who did you have in mind for using it?"

"Duh," Ev answered for her, "Birdie, obviously! Maybe this thing can give her back her full power!"

Birdie frowned, not wanting to appear uncomfortable at the prospect of touching the thing.

"I don't think it will do that either. From what I've seen, it only magnifies the power of spells someone can already cast; it doesn't actually increase their magical abilities, let alone any other skills or strength."

"Well, it can't hurt to try," Ev insisted. "Besides, even if that is all it does, think how powerful you'd be once you do get your strength back!"

"I don't know," Birdie muttered.

Many of her abilities were tied to being a shade, not to learned magic. She wasn't sure if the shimmer would even affect those skills.

Nephira added her thoughts. "Your friend speaks well. A Radiant with the power of the Masters can only be fought by another of the same."

Birdie stared at the shimmer for a moment before shifting her gaze to Tallis. She could see in his eyes that he wanted to try it himself, but he nodded in agreement at what Ev and Nephira had said.

Birdie sighed. "Alright, but after me, it's Tallis. If the shimmer still works after that, then Ev, then Helcant, then Nephira. Understood?"

Everyone save for Helcant and Nephira nodded in agreement, and no one disagreed.

Not seeing any point in delaying any further, Birdie slowly reached forward.

Her fingers passed the threshold of the swirling ripple, greeted by a cold sensation that seemed to pull her fingers in all directions at once.

Pressing deeper, she touched the center of the pale, rainbow light. Birdie barely had time to register the conflicting sensations of a solid barrier tugging her finger into an empty void before an iridescent sheen raced out and along her body, covering her completely.

The world flashed white as for one terrifying moment she felt her othermind vanish from within her before reappearing just as quickly.

Birdie jerked back from shock, wide-eyed and trembling.

"Birdie?" Ev asked, taking a step forward. "Are you okay?"

"Did it work?" Tallis prodded, but Birdie answered neither, instead staring at the palm of her hand, still shaking.

Ev took another tentative step forward. "What happened? Are you hurt?"

Birdie blinked, slowly coming back to the moment. Turning her head toward Ev, she shook it in the negative.

"I-I'm fine, I think," she answered.

"Are you sure?" Ev pressed.

Helcant butted in. "Enough talk. Show us this power!"

Her anger at Helcant resurfacing enough to partially push her concerns from her mind, Birdie frowned harshly at the demon. Birdie very much wanted to rip into Helcant for his blatant disregard for her orders earlier, but she knew now wasn't the time for that. She also wanted to see what this shimmer power could do, and she didn't like the idea of standing out in the open for long.

Putting off her reprimand for the next time Helcant inevitably refused to cooperate, Birdie put on a show of her usual bravado. Wiping a hair from in front of her eyes and turning away from the others, she raised her hand, wisps of dark magic swirling around it.

None of the spells she currently possessed would benefit much from the shimmer, but she knew one way to test its effectiveness — her remote illusions would normally be highly transparent out in the sun.

Conjuring an image of herself a few feet away, she felt far more magic than she actually used surge out from her hand to form a fully opaque other Birdie. The burst of magic came from seemingly nowhere, its energy so immense that Birdie could feel herself actually feeding from the very spell she was casting.

She ceased her casting and stared at her hand once again, this time in amazement.

Tallis wasn't impressed. "Wait, that was it? You'd think you'd be able to conjure a whole army after what those loyalists could do."

Birdie stared daggers at Tallis. "You have no idea how much power was in that spell," she said before turning her attention back to her hand.

Tallis recoiled at her tone. After a moment, Birdie turned back to him once again.

"Your turn. Just make sure you cast far away from any of us."

"Wait, really?" Tallis asked.

"That was the plan, wasn't it?" Birdie returned before turning her attention back to herself.

She could sense the effect of the shimmer within her. Consulting with her othermind, her conclusion was that it didn't actually affect her or her spells directly — the conclusion being that it must be some sort of permanent boon that magnified the amount of magic put into any spells cast without actually taking extra magic from the caster. That would make it similar to how Radiance was a permanent boon given to the Divine who attained it.

While Tallis absorbed the shimmer's light behind her, she tried conjuring another illusion. Her false self flashed in and out of existence as she practiced management of the flow of energy pouring from her, but with assistance from her othermind it turned out not to be too difficult. It did worry her about how well Tallis would be able to manage in the heat of battle, but as long as he was aware of what kind of power he was presently taking onto himself, she did have confidence he would learn to use it responsibly, or at least she hoped he would.

A spike in magic and a blast of frigid air informed her he'd just tried one of his ice spells. Birdie glanced over to see him staring at his hand with as much amazement as she had, prompting a small smile that left as quickly as it came.

While Tallis played with his magic, she still had one more thing to test. Imagining a foe in front of her, she tried extending her shadow outward to engulf them. The effect was far from impressive. As she'd suspected, her natural shade abilities were no stronger than they had been. It seemed that the shimmer indeed only affected learned spells.

Satisfied, she turned to Ev. "Alright."

Ev had already stepped forward to touch the light. Helcant had also dismounted from his horse, eager to take his turn right after. Ev placed her hand into the shimmer and… nothing.

Ev blinked, then tried again, going so far as to try to grasp the central light.

"It's not working," she stated, withdrawing her hand from the light.

Helcant panicked. "What do you mean, 'not working'? It must work!"

He rushed forward, grabbing at the shimmer with both hands. Failing repeatedly, he spun towards Birdie.

"Why does it not make rainbows anymore? He broke it!" Helcant spat, thrusting a finger at Tallis.

Ev came to Tallis's defense. "Don't be ridiculous. We knew it had limited uses."

Birdie added to that. "The knight said they could only use it on five people. It looks like he told the truth."

"Foolishness!" exclaimed Helcant. "Only two have touched it."

Birdie crossed her arms. "And three of the villagers got it back in town. That's five."

Helcant growled, but relented.

Ev, on the other hand, confronted Birdie once again, sidling up close to her.

"Really, though," she said quietly, "are you okay? That look you had…"

"I'm fine, really," Birdie returned.

Ev frowned. "I thought we agreed no more secrets."

Birdie sighed and looked around at the others, making sure to project the illusion that she was only looking at Ev. "I don't remember agreeing to that, but I'll tell you. Just not here. Wait until dark. I promise it's nothing that can't wait."

Ev seemed satisfied with that, so Birdie rounded up the others.

"Nice work, everyone. Mission successful. Now, let's get out of here before anyone else comes by." She cocked her head and grinned. "Our next stop is the Waterfelled River. I hear the swarms of dead souls look lovely this time of year. I'll bet they'll look even better from deep inside their eternal blanket of mist, which makes viewing rather difficult from the sky. I, for one, am looking forward to paying it a visit."

Chapter 11

"Here we are," announced Birdie as they reached the lip of a great canyon. "The Waterfelled River. As I'm sure you've all heard the fanciful stories, I'll spare you any dramatic speeches about it ferrying the souls of the drowned to the afterlife."

Below them, the canyon was flooded with thick enchanted mist, completely obscuring the bottom. The morning sun still low, they could see the occasional light bobbing to and fro beneath the mist's surface — part of the aesthetics each of the five Rivers of the Dead possessed to give the appearance of souls floating through it. A short ways to the south was located one of the very few ways down.

This place was not to be traversed lightly — successfully traveling it from end to end was part of the post-lord trials that fledgling Radiants had to conquer to further themselves in the Radiant hierarchy. Only eight paths in or out of the canyon existed — two on each side in four locations — escapes for those who lacked the capacity to survive the full ordeal.

"Once we reach the bottom, we'll need to be extremely cautious," warned Birdie, looking at Tallis. "Nepacs were never meant to pass through this place. The Rivers of the Dead are swarming with monsters, some of which are among the strongest found in the surface world. The worst of them will try to pull you into the river. If they succeed, you will be taken to the depths of the Netherworld."

"Relax," Tallis said. "There's nothing down there that's a match for my new magic."

Birdie narrowed her eyes. "Don't let power get to your head. This is *not* going to be an easy journey. Reckless casting of earth spells might bring the canyon down on us, and a number of monsters here are highly resistant to ice magic. Wet wights can pass through ice like water, and hell ferries' fire protects them from ice and lets them feed from fire spells. We will need to be on constant guard. That mist suppresses perception and magic sensing abilities, including my own."

Nephira moved her horse closer to Birdie. "I have concerns regarding this plan. The likelihood of encountering enemy forces in the fields is slim. Is it really worth the risk just to travel out of sight?"

Birdie turned to Nephira and tilted her head ever so slightly. "It's not about the cover. Weird shimmer powers excluded, I still haven't even gotten back the strength I had prior to my ascent to Radiance. I know Lux Rosa will be waiting for us at Ars Summis, and I want to be as prepared for that confrontation as possible."

Birdie heard Ev attempt to suppress a growl and turned to see a scowl on her face. Birdie wasn't surprised. Presumably, the only reason Ev didn't protest further was because it was Ev's idea for Birdie to fight monsters to regain her strength in the first place.

Tallis spoke up again. "You don't really think she'd try fighting at Ars Summis, do you? She'd risk pissing off the guardian."

"And?" asked Birdie. "For her, that could be beneficial. I sincerely doubt she's above sacrificing her puppets if it means wiping us all out."

"Bah!" spat Helcant. "Cursed snake! Long ago the city would have been ours were it not for its presence."

"Hardly," chided Ev, albeit quietly. "The guardian is just to scare people. Nepacs wouldn't able to pass through the barrier anyway."

"Let's try to focus," interrupted Birdie. "The message I sent to Dezeroth was to have forces ready at Bailey Town within four days from now. Assuming he receives it and listens, that gives us only three days we can spend on the river. We won't have any time to delay. Come on."

As they made their way down, the visibility approached near zero. The mist wasn't so bad on its own, but at this early hour, so little light pierced through from above that it seemed like night. The darkness was welcome for her, but it would be an impediment to her comrades. Fortunately, Birdie's new boon allowed her to produce so much light it was nearly painful. Ev could also channel healing magic into her rod to serve as a makeshift torch, and Helcant's flames would also work in a pinch.

The group soon reached the end of the long, winding trail to the bottom of the glowing river's canyon. No sooner did the first horse set hoof on the muddy ground than a horde of ghostly corpses burst forth all around them. In the haze, it was difficult even for Birdie to see how many had risen, but she spotted at least twenty.

"Here we go!" shouted Birdie, her othermind excited, though she was admittedly nervous.

She hopped down from her horse and brandished her daggers. "Watch out for their ice breath, and you should be fine. Wet wights might be hard to bring down, but they're predictable and stupid! Tallis, see if you can funnel them to us, so we can take them one at a time! Helcant, guard the rear!"

Tallis glanced nervously at the barely visible canyon wall but obliged, casting a pair of earth rift spells that created two jagged columns of muddy stone through the middle of the wet wights. The walls separated about ten of them from the rest of the group, and Birdie ran to meet them.

Nephira joined Birdie on the ground, spear at the ready as she took up position on Birdie's left. Tallis raised another rift a bit too close nearby that caused Nephira to stumble, but it served its purpose of dividing the wights even further. Once finished, he joined Helcant in protecting their rear, with Ev being relegated to creating light for the others to see.

The vile corpses shambled ever closer, and Birdie rushed forward to engage. Dodging every swipe, lunge, and icy spray, she countered with blow after blow, spinning like a whirlwind. Exploiting the broken powers of the shimmer, she cast pointless illusions for the sole purpose of feeding on them, supplying her with effectively infinite stamina as she whittled down wight after wight.

Her rampage only faltered when she sensed Tallis unleash a massive earth attack. With a deafening rumble, the ground around her shook as she dealt with one final foe before turning back to see what had happened.

Behind her, the land had been split in twain — the river pouring in as spooked horses bolted away. Ev and Tallis held fast to their steeds and managed to stop them before they ran too far, but Helcant had been tossed to the ground. A number of the shambling corpses that had appeared from behind stepped mindlessly into the chasm, but as undeniably effective as the attack was, it was also intolerably reckless.

More wights still approached from the front, however, so Birdie couldn't deal with Tallis at the moment. She'd have to leave him to Ev to make sure he didn't do something like that again.

Once the monsters had been dealt with, Birdie climbed atop one of the rifts Tallis had created. She scanned the area for the horses, but in the thick fog could only spot three of them. Since their mounts lacked magic, she couldn't sense the missing one, though in the enchanted fog she likely wouldn't have been able to regardless. That meant they'd have to go looking for the stupid thing.

And speaking of stupid, "Tallis!" Birdie shouted. "I told you to be careful with your magic. Now we're missing a horse, and you could have gotten us all killed!"

Helcant pounced on Tallis as well. "Yes, fool! Your dirt casting sent me to the floor!"

Tallis huffed atop his mount. "I wouldn't have *had* to cast that spell if *you'd* bothered to help me, you twitchy hell spawn!"

"Ho-ho, the mortal needs my help now, does he?"

"Enough!" erupted Birdie, placing a hand to her forehead. "We are trying to save the whole damn world, and you two can't even try to get along in the middle of a fight!"

"Me? I tried—"

"What insults—"

"Shut up!" Birdie cut off the both of them, then pointed to Tallis and Helcant in turn. "*You* should know better, and *you* are pushing my patience to its limit! If you ignore my orders or do anything that threatens us again, you are done traveling with us!"

Flames erupted down Helcant's back. "Of course Eclipse disfavors me. She always sides with her precious mortals!"

"What did you say to me?" Birdie hopped to the ground and started towards Helcant.

The demon stood his ground as Birdie walked up to him and pointed a finger at his face. "Let's make one thing absolutely clear. The only sides right now are those who are for Lux Rosa and those who are against her. If you have a problem with mortals being on our side, then I have bad news for you. Mortals are the only reason I ever beat Grandis in the first place, and that girl right there is one of the ones who made it possible," she yelled, pointing a finger at Ev.

"Do you know what that means?" she continued at a glaring Helcant. "It means none of us would even be here right now if it wasn't for them, not even you. So if you can't get over whatever little hangups you have about mortals or my care for them, then you're no different than all the humans who refuse to believe that people like you are the reason they didn't all die five years ago when Grandis tried to betray them to Apollyon. Are we clear?"

The air around Helcant practically sizzled. The tiny demon clenched his fists, his mind clearly racing for something to retort with. Birdie didn't give him the chance, though. She still had more to say, but not to him.

Spinning back to Tallis, she continued her verbal assault. "The same goes for you. Helcant and Nephira are our allies, and if you continue to keep using terms like "hell spawn," then I will have a serious talk with Jax when we get back regarding your continued service in the Shadow Guard."

The smug look that had appeared on Tallis's face while she'd yelled at Helcant vanished to one of shock, hurt, and anger. Tallis opened and closed is mouth, stammering for words.

Helcant started to growl, and Birdie turned a steely gaze back at him.

"You... you—!"

"Helcant, be silent!" Nephira hissed through clenched teeth. "Remember what we are doing this for. Nothing. Else. Matters."

Helcant growled and stared daggers at Birdie, but ultimately doused his flames and stepped back, saying nothing further.

Birdie tried to get a read on Nephira's attitude on all of this, but aside from reigning in Helcant, Nephira remained stoic.

Birdie couldn't tell if that was a good thing or a bad thing, but thus far Nephira had been a stabilizing force for Helcant, so that was good enough for her.

For the rest of the day, both Helcant and Tallis kept almost completely silent, the tension between them and Birdie as thick as the fog all around. To their credit, neither of them acted up or disobeyed her orders after her reprimand. Most subsequent battles were more difficult than what the wights had presented, but Ev swooped in with her healing the moment any of them were injured, though Birdie couldn't help but notice a growing irritation in her friend with each injury, especially after one particularly successful ambush had nearly resulted in Tallis's death. While Birdie could understand Ev having apprehension about this place, she was starting to get annoyed by Ev's lack of faith in Birdie's ability to get them through the area.

As the group grew used to the local monsters, the only creatures that managed to pose a consistent threat were the winged, flaming skeletons that were the hell ferries. Immune to fire and ice and safe from most earth spells, that left traditional weapons as the only means of reliably harming them. Fortunately, they only encountered two pairs of such foes, and never on one of the small bridges they occasionally had to cross. That gave them plenty of room to maneuver and avoid being caught and dragged into the river.

Eventually night fell, and the darkness of the canyon grew ever towards absolute. The group began searching for a place to set up camp for the night. What they found was a cozy little alcove in the canyon wall amidst some long dead trees that had fallen from above, giving them a nice, safe buffer from the river. The rotten wood made for poor fuel for a fire, but with a bit of work from Helcant, they were able to dry it out and set up a steady smolder. Soon after, night took over, which left the weak flames and eerie river lights as the only illumination around.

Ev, Tallis, and Helcant all pulled out some bread and fruit to munch on before Tallis and Helcant went to separate sides of the camp and sat silently, both of them well away from Birdie. Ev took up a spot near Birdie, while Nephira sat in the middle, sipping on some water — essentially the only sustenance she needed to keep her undead body "healthy."

"So," Ev said after several minutes of awkward silence, "seeing as how we're nearly at Ars Summis, what do you think it's like?"

Birdie shrugged, not in the mood for conversation after all the attitude she'd dealt with today.

"Well?" Ev pressed. "Surely Syrus must have told you something about it."

Birdie noticed Tallis perk up at that. "Not really. You know we don't talk much. You'd know more about it than me."

Ev sighed. "Look, I don't know what happened between you two, but he's doing the best he can. If he succeeds in his work, you don't have to keep being Doxla's protector anymore."

Now Birdie sighed. "It's more to it than that, Ev, and I don't want to talk about it."

Ev crossed her arms. "Okay then, how about I tell you what *I* think Ars Summis is like?"

Birdie looked up at that, admittedly curious.

"Like you said, I've been helping Syrus a lot, and he's told me a lot about where he comes from. I'll bet Ars Summis is pretty similar to that."

Now Ev had caught even Helcant and Nephira's attention.

"He said his world is called Veravis, and there are machines there that can do anything, like send you halfway across the world in an instant, or show you visions of history from long ago, or keep track of an entire world's population. It sounds like there are even machines that can pass as people. What do you think? Think there might be machines like that at Ars Summis?"

"You mean machines like me?" replied Birdie dryly.

Ev stammered. "W-what? N-no, Birdie, you're *not* a machine."

Birdie chuckled. "And what if I am? Would it really make a difference to you?"

"No! Of course it wouldn't!"

"Then what does matter?" Birdie stared at the fire.

Out of the corner of her eye, Birdie could see that Ev was searching for something to say, but words escaped her. Tallis, on the other hand...

"H-hey," he said, approaching Ev. "You said Syrus told you about the world of the Divine? What else did he say?"

Ev scowled. "Tallis, now isn't the time. It's not a big deal."

"Yes, it is!" Helcant shouted from across the camp, surprising everyone but Nephira. "Speech of other worlds was the greatest taboo of the Masters! Divine who spoke it were banished. Nepacs who learned were erased!"

Helcant bounded across the camp to Tallis's side. "The Masters are gone. Their secrets you must share!"

A dumbfounded Tallis quickly joined his unexpected ally. "Exactly! If the Masters didn't want people to know this stuff, then it's probably something we should know, right?"

Ev scoffed. "Excuse me, but I'm trying to talk to Birdie right now."

"Ev," Birdie pressed, not about to let this one thing those two were getting along about slip by, "there's no harm in sharing. I'm fine, really."

Ev looked at Birdie to check her expression, but she already knew Birdie's expression only revealed what Birdie wanted it to.

Sighing, she gave in to Tallis and Helcant's demand. "Alright, fine, but don't expect too much. The only reason the Masters didn't want people knowing about other worlds is because they didn't want people finding out that they aren't special."

"Not special?" repeated Tallis. "They're the Masters! They're the most powerful beings in existence!"

Ev almost laughed. "Uh, no, that belief is exactly what I'm talking about. The Masters are no different than any other Divine. They only have power over this world because they created it. Every other Divine has the same abilities as the Masters, and many have even greater. Even more, the Divine only have their abilities because they are granted them by a higher power, but Syrus wouldn't tell me much about that. All he said is that he's sure if the things the Masters did to our world were ever discovered by that higher power, they'd be stripped of their abilities and banished to another realm."

"What you say is blasphemy," said Helcant, grinning maniacally. "Beautiful! I knew the Masters were but charlatans. Their great deception showed us all their true colors."

Tallis seemed at a loss for words. "Are you seriously implying that our world was created by rogue Divine? I mean, I know they endangered and abandoned us, but—"

"But nothing, human! It is as we have long said. When the Masters came to us, they promised power and immortality, then they turned us into *this* instead!"

Helcant spread his arms, letting a flash of flame ignite around him.

"They created monsters! They created Apollyon! They made us into what we are and spread lies to make us villains. Mortals believed them and drove us from our lands with the help of the Divine, worshiping the very beings who enslaved them!"

Tallis shook his head. "I just don't understand."

"What's not to understand human?" Helcant mocked. "Does it hurt to know you were wrong?"

"No!" shouted Tallis. "I don't understand why they would do this. If what they did was forbidden to them, why do it? What could beings like that even have to gain?"

Helcant's grin faded. He had no answer.

"Well?" Tallis pressed Ev, his arms open.

Ev shook her head sadly. "I only know what Syrus suspects, but it would only make you angry."

"I'm already angry!" Tallis shouted. "Every time I find out something new about the Masters, it's always something worse."

Ev's sadness gave way to a frown. "Do you really want to know?"

"I asked, didn't I?"

"Fine then. The reason was money, or at least the Divine equivalent to it."

"M-money?" Tallis could barely spit out. "H-how, wh-"

"Not money like you and I know. Syrus just used money as a comparison to explain it to me. I'm still not sure I understand either, but Divine have somehow turned the idea of prestige into a sort of currency. The more they have, the more they're allowed to do."

"Well, if they're rogues, why didn't Syrus just turn them in?" Tallis erupted. "He could sure as heck have saved us a lot of trouble."

Ev shook her head. "He can't. The Masters hid their true identities."

Birdie jerked her head up, suddenly fully attentive. Lux Rosa had asked for Syrus's true name. Could this have anything to do with her reasons?

"So that's it, then?" asked Tallis. "The Masters made our world into a game for Divine, profit from it, and get away with everything?"

Ev crossed her arms. "If Syrus can take control of the world, he thinks he can find out who they really are. Until then, yes. There's nothing he or anyone else can do."

Tallis let his arms drop. He appeared frustrated but accepting of the situation. With a minor sigh, he turned and went back to where he'd been sitting, clearly turning over what he'd just heard in his head. Helcant watched him curiously for a moment before casting a final glance back at Ev, smirking, and doing the same.

After a few minutes of silence, Birdie whispered to Ev. "Is all of that true?"

"Of course it is," Ev answered huffily. "You'd know that if you'd ever ask him about it."

Birdie took a second to reply. "I wasn't supposed to ever need to know it."

Ev sighed, then shrugged. "Well, it's not like it really makes any difference, I guess. The Masters are gone. It's Lux Rosa we need to worry about."

"Yeah," replied Birdie, still pondering the reason Lux Rosa wanted Syrus's name.

If a Divine's true name was required to report them to some higher power, could it be possible that Syrus was also a rogue? He did dare to dabble in things no other Divine had attempted to, at least until Lux Rosa. That likely wasn't the reason, seeing as how Lux was doing the same thing, but it was a possibility.

Still, she supposed that was a question for another time. Right now, she was ready for sleep.

* * * *

The next morning, Birdie awoke in darkness. Their fire had not lasted long, and the mists of the Waterfelled River permitted not the morning sun to shine through.

As comfortable as it was, these were not ideal conditions for her companions to travel in. Nonetheless, they were still two days out from their exit and needed to get an early start to compensate for the inevitable battles ahead.

Shaking Ev awake, her favorite human immediately broke the darkness by concentrating healing magic into her hand, emitting a soft, ghostly glow.

"Birdie? What happened?" Ev asked softly, concern rising rapidly.

"Nothing," Birdie replied gently. "It's morning, is all."

Ev looked around at the wall of black surrounding them. "Are you sure about that?"

"Positive," answered Birdie before moving on to the others.

As expected, the only one to put up a fuss was Helcant.

"What, what, what? Why do you wake us in darkness?"

"Because it's going to stay dark until nearly noon," Birdie returned, answer ready. "Remember yesterday?"

Helcant grumbled, but didn't argue.

In a matter of minutes, they were on their way again, this time with Ev providing light through her rod while Birdie rode alongside her in case of an attack. After half an hour, Birdie decided to test the water of that pot she'd stirred yesterday.

"Helcant, you take the lead. Ev's running low on magic." She wasn't lying.

"I'm fine," called Ev loudly before Helcant could react.

"No, you're not," Birdie replied. "You're almost out."

"I know how to gauge my own magic," Ev shot back. "I can easily go another ten minutes."

"And what happens if we get attacked again toward the end of that? We need your magic for healing."

Why Ev had suddenly become so argumentative, Birdie didn't know, but this was neither the time nor the place for it. Thankfully, that seemed to be the end of it for now, as Ev stopped her horse, though the look she gave Birdie showed she wasn't happy about it.

"Alright, Helcant," Birdie tried again, "You're up."

Helcant obliged with a suspiciously cheerful tune. "Happily so, but if Miss Ev wishes to stay forward, I would welcome her company."

"I think I do wish that," Ev remarked without a beat, casting a defiant look back at Birdie.

Birdie frowned but allowed it. Arguing over something like this wasn't worth it, especially this early in the morning.

"Can I come up, too?" Tallis piped up from behind.

"No more than two horses side-by-side," Birdie answered as she pulled her own mount back to follow immediately behind Ev.

Helcant grinned back at Tallis but mercifully kept his mouth shut, instead doing his job of lighting up the path with a fireball he conjured in his hand. A few seconds later, Helcant looked over at Ev.

"Tell me, hu— Miss Ev, what other secrets of the Masters do you know?"

Ev frowned, it now clear why Helcant had wanted her to stay. "I told you everything I know about the Masters last night."

"Then speak of the Divine! Your Syrus must surely have spoken more of them and their treachery!"

Birdie could see that Ev was uncomfortable with this line of questioning. "I hope asking questions about the Divine isn't the only reason you wanted Ev to stay at the front."

Helcant turned a glare back at Birdie, almost like a child who was both shocked and angry he'd been caught doing something he shouldn't have.

Ev spoke before Helcant could respond. "Oh, I don't mind. I do know a little more about the Divine, actually."

Tallis immediately pushed his horse forward to ride beside Birdie, but she paid him no mind. Ev's attitude was unacceptable. Friend or no, this was something she'd have to put an end to immediately.

Then again, it was giving Helcant and Tallis a common thread over which they might finally put aside their differences, at least to a degree. She'd allow them to have their little conversation, but as soon as it was over, she was going to have a serious conversation of her own with Ev.

Figuring she might as well give them some space until then, Birdie pulled her own horse back to ride alongside Nephira. Tallis and Helcant together could provide more than enough cover for Ev to retreat if there was another attack.

Not particularly keen on hearing more about the Divine, Birdie asked Nephira about something that had been bothering her.

"Yesterday you told Helcant to remember what you're doing this for. What were you referring to?"

"I told you when we joined you," replied Nephira. "We want to live the lives we had before the Masters took them from us. It is why we fought against Lord Grandis. Not to save ourselves from a permanent death, but for the promise that King Dezeroth would be allowed to reign in fertile lands once again. If Syrus had not already betrayed the other Divine, we would not have believed his promise, nor would we have helped overthrow Grandis."

"Are you serious? But if Grandis hadn't been stopped, Apollyon would have killed you permanently."

Nephira paused. "I don't expect you to understand. You never lived life as a human. You don't know what it's like to have your world taken away from you, then dangled before your eyes for centuries while your former countrymen turn their backs on you and call you 'monster.'"

Birdie looked down. She could hear Ev saying something about "countless worlds" and "anther," whatever that was, but it was essentially noise.

"You're right," she replied. "What I am is all I've ever been, and I haven't exactly been it for very long. I can't say I see the appeal of being human. It seems to me like too much maintenance, but you're wrong about one thing." Birdie locked eyes with Nephira. "I do know what it's like to be betrayed. After my reincarnation, Grandis sought me out, and to save themselves, my fellow shades tried to hand me over to him."

"So, you know the fury. You know the pain."

"I know the confusion and hurt," Birdie corrected. "I can't say I've been angry about it for a long time."

"Of course you haven't," spat Nephira. "You have everything anyone could ask for. You have power, money, followers. You aren't stuck looking like a corpse for all of eternity."

"I-" Birdie stopped, having noticed their horses had just stepped onto a narrow bridge.

"Ev, wait!" she shouted. "Tallis, Helcant!"

The trio in front stopped and looked back.

Birdie cursed at herself for not paying more attention, hopped off of her horse, and walked to the front.

"We've been over this," she said. "Any bridges we come across, I go first. Wait at the bank until I check for hell ferries."

She waited for the others to make it all the way back off the bridge before proceeding herself.

The old brick bridge stretched diagonally across the river, running over a hundred feet in length. The water of the Waterfelled sped by just inches below, splashing regularly up onto it and feeding the thick layer of moss that had made the bridge its home. The eerie lights of the river passed by underneath, traveling steadily upwards against the current.

About halfway across, several orange glows appeared beneath the waves, and Birdie's fear became realized as not one, not two, but *five* flaming skeletons burst from the water.

"Hell ferries!" she shouted to the others as she broke into a sprint back to shore.

The first of the ferries was on her in seconds, wrapping its grisly fingers around her head, hoping to drag her down into the depths.

Birdie partially melted back into shadow and slipped from the creature's grasp. Spinning around, she sliced at the ferry's exposed vertebrae.

The spine cracked but held together. The other four ferries sped past to the shore while the first flew upwards before lunging back down.

Birdie sidestepped and slashed upward. Another hit. Another dodge and swipe, and at last the skeleton's lower half fell to the ground. Its torso still kept up the assault, but the fire burning in its chest and skull faded to half its former size.

Just then, Birdie sensed Tallis casting a powerful earth magnet before hearing a scream.

Ev!

Unable to help herself, Birdie spun back toward the shore just in time to see Ev being carried through the air by one of the other ferries.

Dropping her dagger, she reached for her bow when the ferry she'd been fighting grabbed her arm and yanked her toward the edge of the bridge.

"Let go of me!" she roared before plunging her arm deep into the skeleton's fiery chest.

She wrapped her shadows around its ribs, ignoring the searing pain of the fire as she squeezed with all her might. The ribs cracked, then caved, and the flame of the hell ferry faded from existence.

Immediately afterward, Birdie aimed and fired her bow at the hell ferry carrying Ev, but it was too late. The arrow struck, but it wasn't enough to kill the skeleton. Before she had the chance to fire again, it had dived down into the river, silencing Ev's pleas for help as it pulled her deep beneath the waves.

"No!" shouted Birdie as she ran toward where Ev had disappeared and dropped to her knees.

Cursing loudly, she slammed her fist against the bridge before another cry pulled her back to the situation at hand.

On the shore, Birdie spotted one ferry dead, one struggling to lift a prone Tallis from the ground, and a third carrying away Nephira. Helcant roared as he leapt onto the back of the one holding Nephira and started hacking at it with his sword. The skeleton dropped Nephira as it struggled to throw off Helcant, eventually succeeding in tossing him into the river. The creature then sped toward the demon, but a single arrow from Birdie was enough to shatter the already injured skeleton.

Helcant sputtered as the river swept him downstream. Nephira raced after him and stretched out her spear. The demon grabbed hold, but as Nephira pulled him toward the shore, an orange glow appeared beneath him before he too disappeared into the river.

"Helcant!" Nephira shouted, though she dared not get any closer to the water.

Birdie stood frozen, staring at where Helcant had vanished. In an instant, everything was falling apart. She never should have risked coming here.

She shook herself out of it. The battle was still ongoing.

She grabbed her dropped dagger and darted over to Tallis, where she jumped up onto the hell ferry that was still trying to lift him. With four quick swipes, she'd hacked through its wings. The skeleton fell to the ground where Birdie made quick work of it. She then stabbed Tallis in the arm with her enchantment breaker, freeing him from the overpowered earth magnet he'd cast on himself. She could only imagine he'd tried to ground himself but failed to realize just how strong his boosted enchantment would become.

Tallis jerked up, gasping for breath. "Thanks," he got out weakly.

"Stay here," Birdie ordered.

"What?" he asked.

"I said stay here!" she shouted. She removed the bag at her hip containing Syrus's letter and tossed it to Nephira. "Do not follow me, do not leave, and *do not* lose that bag!"

Nephira stood shocked at the command, but before she could say anything Birdie was already running to where an orange glow grew beneath the river. Diving in, Birdie latched onto the hell ferry that had taken Ev and Helcant. The burning skeleton grabbed her in turn, and she found herself speeding ever deeper into the river depths.

Soon, darkness thicker than even she could see through swallowed her whole. The water vanished shortly after, replaced by cold emptiness.

The hell ferry had taken Ev to the Netherworld.

Birdie was going to get her back.

Chapter 12

The darkness broke around Birdie, revealing an endless cavern in all directions. The cavern had no visible ceiling — only a dark cloud punctuated with shimmering green ripples. A handful of massive stone towers stretched up into the dark cloud — narrow paths wrapping around them and weaving in and out of the pillars themselves — providing the only routes out of this dreadful place save for passing through the fiery Underworld. Sprinkled across the landscape were countless specks of blue and green light. Some indicated the presence of truly terrifying foes, others merely luminous stones, though the stones had clearly dimmed in the years since the Masters had abandoned the world.

The hell ferry flew with insane speed down along one of the towers as it headed to the deepest depths of the Netherworld. Breaking away from the tower, it aimed toward a barren shore on the edge of a goopy black sea. In seconds, it traveled more than a mile over the jagged landscape. As it slowed to a stop on the beach, Birdie spotted both Ev and Helcant standing beneath a stone outcrop. A few feet above the ground, the skeleton released Birdie from its grip, but she wasn't ready to release it from hers. This thing had forced her to come to this awful place, and it was going to pay.

Latching onto it with her shadow, she slashed again and again at its neck until at last its head departed its body. She and the pile of bones fell to the ground, its flame extinguished. Picking herself up, Birdie hurried over to Ev and a clearly panicking Helcant.

"Birdie?" exclaimed Ev.

"Hey, Ev," Birdie cocked her head, trying to act cool in the situation. "You ready to get out of here?"

Ev's face went from surprise to relief, then unexpectedly to anger.

"Wait, did you come down here just to save me?"

Birdie frowned and crossed her arms. "Well, if you don't want me to, I can always head back with just Helcant."

Ev grabbed at her hair in frustration. "Why? *Why?* Why do you keep doing this? First it was the ambush, then the river, now the Netherworld itself! What happened to being cautious? Have you even *thought* about what will happen if you get split before you reach Ars Summis?"

"Excuse me," countered Birdie, "but you were the one who told me to take risks to get stronger."

"I told you to hunt monsters. I never said to take us into places only Radiants are supposed to go!"

Birdie uncrossed her arms. "We've done very well against the river monsters. This is just… a little hiccup."

"A *hiccup?* You call half of us getting dragged into the Netherworld a *hiccup?*"

"I admit I may have miscalculated the danger a bit, but we can still get out of this. If we just climb to the top of one of those towers, we can get back near where we were dragged into the river."

"And then what? Get pulled back in again? Get killed?" Ev stretched an arm up toward the mountainous tower, her face pained. "We can't keep going this way. I don't know if you've noticed, but we've barely made any progress since entering that valley. Do you really think we'll reach Ars Summis in three days at our current pace?"

Birdie paused. It was true they were going more slowly than she'd hoped, but they could still make it in time. That assumed they traveled at night and avoided any more trips to the Netherworld, of course, but on the other hand, they were already a full day into the valley, so turning around would also put them behind.

Helcant interrupted her thoughts. "Can we discuss later?" He looked around nervously. "We must not stay here. The Netherworld is unsafe. We must flee to the Underworld. Yes, we must go now!"

"We can't travel to the Underworld," Birdie scoffed. "It would take weeks to get back to the surface, let alone Ars Summis!"

"Fool! Only death lies in this place. The darkness is home to the Spawn of Apollyon! The Underworld is our only escape!"

Birdie crossed her arms again. "Okay, then. Let's go. Just remind me. Where exactly is the Underworld from here?"

Helcant glanced down the beach into the distance, then the other way, then turned around and looked up at the mountain behind him. It was clear he had no idea where they were.

"That's what I thought. Considering where we fell in, I'd say we're at least a day away from any of the Underworld portals. So, we can either spend the next two hours climbing up that tower, or we can spend the next two days going your way. What's it going to be?"

Helcant spun back at Birdie and pointed at her. "We cannot go up the tower! Great shadow beasts lurk in the rocks. The sand has only tentacles. We follow the water, we stay safe. The Underworld will show eventually."

"Yes, it will," replied Birdie, "but if we stick to the beach it won't be two days to the Underworld, it will be a week! Neither you nor Ev can go that long without water."

"Bah! I fear not death. I will return, but you will not! I know Eclipse's secret. Your memories are lost on death. If you are split, all is lost!"

"He's right," said Ev softly. "Even if you get to Ars Summis late, at least you'll get there."

Birdie and Helcant both froze, staring at Ev.

"Ev, I am not letting you die here."

"And what happens if Lux Rosa wins?" Ev countered. "Have you thought about how many people will die then?"

Birdie shook her head. "Do you even hear yourself? You're asking me to take a three week detour to get to Ars Summis. That isn't late, that's *too* late! If Syrus isn't back on his own by then, then Lux Rosa will certainly have already taken Roehelm. It would be pointless!"

"No more pointless than if you die," returned Ev. "At least if you live, you can get your strength back. You can still fight her."

Birdie sighed. "I think you know just as well as I do that's not true."

Ev's eyes softened ever so slightly.

Birdie continued. "Look, you're right. It was stupid to try to go through the Waterfelled. If we make it back, we'll turn around and take a safer route. No more risks."

She looked up at the tower and narrowed her eyes. "But we have to take this one. For all we know, Lux Rosa is only a few days away from unlocking the full power of the Masters. We can't afford to let her have three more weeks to do it. Besides," she turned back to Ev, "even if I do make it to Ars Summis, I can't contact Syrus without something I left up with Tallis and Nephira. We don't have a choice."

That announcement clearly surprised Ev, but she didn't look happy about it.

Birdie shifted her gaze to Helcant. "We're climbing that tower. If you don't like it, you can travel to the Underworld on your own, but I'd prefer if you came with us."

A small bit of flame spread down Helcant's arms. "You insult me greatly.

Already have I stated I fear not death. If Eclipse insists on entering peril, my sword will follow."

A small smile graced Birdie's lips. "Well, I'm glad to hear it. Ev?"

Ev nodded, her expression unhappy yet understanding.

"Okay, then. We'll need to be extra careful to avoid encountering any monsters down here. I doubt we'd stand much chance against even a single one of them. As long as we're quick and smart about it, though, we should make it through without attracting unwanted attention."

Birdie led the way from the ebon beach into the craggy landscape beyond. Crumbling ridges of obsidian formed archways and tunnels over the branching, weaving path toward the great tower before them. Pockmarked along the corridors were numerous glowing rocks — some glowing bright green, most much fainter, and some almost completely extinguished.

Rounding a corner, Birdie stopped and held up her hand.

"What is it?" Ev whispered, edging up to get a look herself.

"We need-" Birdie cut herself off as she saw Ev brush up against one of the faint glowrocks.

A brilliant and painful light bathed the area, forcing Birdie out of her human guise as she instinctively retreated away from it. Pushing through the pain, she ran back to grab Ev and pull her back down the path.

"What did you do?" Helcant yelled, following quickly behind.

"Quiet!" Birdie hissed, pulling them into a small alcove near the ground where they'd hopefully be out of sight. Her whole body ached now that the damage had equalized throughout her.

Seconds later, a trio of front-half emaciated, back-half skeletal horses rode past, each carrying a hulking cloaked figure wielding a butcher's knife so large that it dragged along the ground. The figures stopped just a few yards past the group's alcove, fiery eyes searching for whatever had caused the disturbance. After a few seconds, the night butchers turned back, moving far more slowly.

Birdie could feel Ev's heart beating against her arm as the undead horses walked past them. The sound of metal scraping on stone reached their ears; the green glow from the skeletal halves of the nightmare steeds lit up the their faces. The butchers stopped again, then again turned around and passed back the other way.

"Why aren't they going back?" Ev whispered, her breathing tense. "Can they sense us?"

"No," answered Birdie, but she had to admit even she was on edge.

The nightmarish hooves stomped by once more, then again, then again, the creatures seemingly having decided that this was their new patrol area.

"What should we do?" Ev asked, her heart still pounding but her breathing slower, though Helcant's breathing was only picking up.

Birdie waited for the butchers to pass by once more before answering. "Get ready to run."

Birdie stretched out her hand and focused. Traveling through the Waterfelled may have been a bad idea, but she had succeeded in gaining back a significant degree of strength from the experience. She was at last as powerful as she'd been just prior to obtaining Radiance, which meant she did have one trick that could get them out of this.

Right behind the butchers, Birdie conjured a doppelganger of herself and swung at the rear rider with her knife. The blade dug deep into the rider's side, and though the damage it caused was only illusory, the pain was real enough.

The butcher immediately swung its large knife up and around, which Birdie's lookalike nimbly avoided before running back down the path toward the beach. The riders gave chase but could not catch the speedy illusion.

"Run! Now!" Birdie hissed as she clambered out of the alcove, her smoking hand still outstretched toward her illusory self.

Birdie let Ev and Helcant run on ahead, not wanting to get out of casting range until she was sure they'd be able to make it to safety. She sent her doppelganger down a side path to make sure she'd at least have a few moments before the riders returned. Night butchers might not have been the most intelligent of enemies, but they were smart enough to recognize an illusion if they could catch it.

Once she'd pushed her spell as far from her as she was able, she dropped her hand and ran. The light from the stone had faded, so there was no danger there, and she soon caught up to a waiting Ev. Helcant had stopped to wait for her not much further down.

Rounding the corner, Birdie made a beeline across an open area and through a nearby archway. "This way!"

Ev and Helcant followed, and the three of them took shelter on the other side of the stone while Birdie waited to sense if the butchers had followed.

Sure enough, their stalkers reentered the open area, still atop their nightmares, but that was as far as they went.

After a minute of waiting, Birdie was comfortable that they'd given up the chase and motioned for the others to follow her.

Once they were safely away, Helcant hissed at Ev.

"Stupid, that was! Careless touching of glowrocks attracts death!"

"How was I supposed to know that thing would light up like that?" Ev countered.

Birdie stepped in before the fight could escalate further. "It's alright, Ev. It's my fault for not telling you about them. Those rocks are useful for fighting shadow beasts, but they attract pretty much everything else around here."

Helcant fumed. "We are lucky no Spawn of Apollyon was around. Our journey would have concluded in death!"

"But it didn't," Birdie said. "The incident's behind us. Let's focus on what's ahead. We've still got a long way to go."

* * * *

Two hours and several close encounters later, the group arrived at the base of the tower. Over that time, the all-encompassing darkness proved more than sufficient for Birdie to recover naturally from the damage the glowrock had caused her. She supposed she could have asked Ev to take care of it, but as it was hardly necessary, she opted not to.

"We'll need to be extra careful here," Birdie stated, one hand against the opening of a cave leading into the tower. "There won't be much room to move around once we get near the top."

Helcant groaned, but otherwise stayed silent. His tail seemed extra twitchy as he gazed up at the great tower.

"Just stay calm, and we can do this," Birdie told him. "The only thing that can get in our way now is a shadow beast, but as long as we stay sharp, we can use the glowrocks to outrun them. Just stay alert and don't panic, no matter what happens."

She decided it best to leave out the fact that they would indeed likely run into one near the top.

The trio made their way into the colossal structure. The inside was only slightly darker than the outside, with glowrocks scattered about the cave providing just enough light for a human to see by. The group followed the path up and eventually out the other side, where they looped a quarter of the way around the exterior before entering once again about thirty feet higher up. A pair of night butchers patrolled the second level, but a quick illusion from Birdie drew them out of sight beyond a wall of ebon stalagmites, letting the group pass by undetected.

The next several chambers went similarly — an illusion here, a side path there, the odd hole in the ceiling they could climb up to avoid a room altogether — all went well as the three weaved in and out of the chambers of the tower. As Birdie led the way up an interior slope, that all changed with the sensation of a shadow beast up above them.

Birdie immediately reversed direction and practically tackled Ev and Helcant down to the bottom of the slope.

"Wha-?" Helcant cried before Birdie placed her hands over both his and Ev's mouths.

They might have been well out of the shadow beast's earshot, but the basilisk they'd just snuck by was yet another creature they didn't want an encounter with.

Birdie held still as she looked back over her shoulder. The shadow beast would have felt her presence as much as she had sensed it. After a moment of nothing, Birdie felt comfortable that she'd reacted quickly enough to avoid notice and removed her hands from her friends, though she also felt stupid for not moving more cautiously to begin with.

"What is it?" Ev whispered as Helcant rubbed his mouth.

"There's a shadow beast about a hundred yards above us," she answered.

Helcant's eyes opened wide, then he threw up his hands as he exclaimed quietly, "Wonderful! We climbed the pillar of horrors for nothing."

"We climbed this 'pillar of horrors' to escape," replied Birdie.

"We cannot sneak past a shadow beast," Helcant returned. "It will smell our magic. Your illusions will do nothing!"

"If we reach the top, it can't follow us. That's only thirty yards past the shadow beast." Birdie pointed to a nearby glowrock. "We can use those to slow it down. It will probably come down the side of the tower once it senses us. If we can get outside before then, their light might make it fall. That will give us the time we need to make it up."

"And what if it doesn't fall?" Helcant demanded. "We-"

"Then you would have both died anyway," Birdie answered coldly.

Helcant blinked. "Wh-what?"

"You've both made it very clear your only concern is my getting back to the surface. I'd prefer to do that with my equipment and even more so with you, but if we can't avoid an encounter with that thing, I can still get away in my shadow form."

Helcant was speechless. Ev eyed Birdie with a mixture of shock, suspicion, and just a touch of hurt.

"Would you really run, or are you just saying that?" Ev asked.

Birdie avoided looking at Ev, choosing instead to gaze at the nearby glowrock. "I can't fight that thing any more than you can. If it's a choice between none of us and just me, there's really only one option, isn't there?"

Birdie looked back at Ev. She could see Ev was sad, but her eyes were determined. "You'd better not be just saying that."

Birdie turned back toward the slope. "I'll run on ahead. Use Helcant's sword to break off a piece of glowrock once I'm out of sight and follow quickly. Try to keep the light covered until the shadow beast gets close. If it's close enough, it will fall. If we're lucky, it will fall all the way to the bottom. If we're not, we'll need to give it a push as soon as it hits the path. If it gets a chance to recover…" she gave one more look back at Ev as she trailed off.

Birdie half-expected Ev to frown, but instead, Ev just nodded, her expression unchanged from its deterministic melancholy.

Helcant looked back and forth between the two of them. "Er… wait, let us not be filled with haste. There are other towers, yes? Mayhap a better route waits for us elsewhere. A route that does not involve shadow beasts who desire to tear apart our limbs."

Birdie answered Helcant. "We were lucky not to run into any of those creatures in the valleys. Towers without shadow beasts are rare, and we would be tempting fate tremendously to reach one. That's not even counting the fact that this is the tower we were brought down from. If we travel up another, we would not reappear back on the surface world where the others are."

Helcant clenched his fists and closed his eyes, cursing repeatedly. When he was done, he looked to have made peace with the situation.

"Alright then," Birdie said. "Grab that stone the moment I'm out of sight and follow as quickly as you can. I'll be waiting for you at the next exit."

With that, Birdie ran into the chamber above her. As she hopped over a low natural wall, a brilliant light lit up the room from behind her. The light soon faded, and Birdie kept running, casting an illusion along the way to distract the creatures in the chamber.

Outside, she could already sense the shadow beast speeding toward her. She may have also been made of shadow, but many of the illusions she cast were not natural to a shade and merely possessing those spells would attract the beast. Ev and Helcant soon joined her, the glowrock gleaming brightly even beneath Ev's mail and tunic.

"Wait for it," Birdie said, hand out and neck craned upwards.

A large blotch of smoking darkness raced down the side of the tower, fifty yards out, then forty, then thirty. Ev likely couldn't see it, but Birdie could.

Only twenty yards out, Birdie shouted "Now!" and covered her face as the blinding light of the glowrock bathed the area and burned her exposed hands and head.

Birdie felt the ground shake as the great beast crashed down beside her, having been forced from its puddle form by the light.

"Push it off!" she shouted, and she ran half-blinded toward the beast, ignoring the pain of the light as she slammed into the still stunned creature.

Ev and Helcant crashed into the beast as well, and with a great shove they were able to slide the monster partway over the edge.

The shadow beast was having none of it, however, and quickly retaliated, slashing clean through Birdie's armor with its claws and throwing her back. The pain was no worse than that caused by the light, but she knew she wouldn't survive a second blow like that.

"Birdie!" she heard Ev shout, and soon both the light and the shadow beast had gone, toppled over the edge.

Ev ran up to her, touching her rod to Birdie's chest to heal her.

"Are you okay?"

Birdie stood back up. "What happened? How'd you knock it off?"

"I fed it the rock," replied Ev matter-of-factly as she kept healing. "It didn't like that."

"And I stabbed its foot!" Helcant roared triumphantly.

"You—" Birdie cut herself off with a quick laugh, but she soon grew serious again. The shadow beast's energy had taken a grave hit, but it was still alive and far too strong to face head on.

"We have to keep moving. That will slow it down, but it won't take long to catch up."

"Impossible!" cried a no longer jovial Helcant. "Nothing could survive such a fall."

"It didn't fall all the way. I feel it only thirty yards down. It will soon be coming back. Now move!"

Ev and Helcant didn't need to be told twice. The three of them charged up the path and into the next chamber where a pair of basilisks slept on either side of the room. The group sped through without conflict, though by the time they reached the far side, Birdie could already sense the shadow beast having entered behind them. It had clearly managed to rid itself of the glowrock Ev had given it, so Birdie figured it could use another one.

Before emerging onto the path outside, she kicked a glowrock on the edge of the exit. If it was going to follow them, it wasn't going to do it in its speedy puddle form.

At the top of the path waited the entrance to yet another room. Before them this time stood a lone night butcher in the center. Behind, however, the shadow beast was nearly upon them, even with the light having slowed it down.

"Ev, hit another rock!" Birdie shouted.

Ev adjusted her course toward a series of columns on the right and brushed one of the glowrocks to set it off. With no cover from the light, the pain was immediate, but Birdie had no choice but to endure it.

Spinning around, Birdie pulled out her bow but couldn't bring herself to turn her face toward the light. She shifted control to her othermind. It cared not for the damage the light caused her, and for the first time Birdie gazed directly upon the the massive creature. Standing just over her height, the shadow beast's shape resembled that of a tiger crossed with a salamander.

Birdie fired a single arrow at the creature. It would do little to stop it, but it would draw its attention toward her. Taking back control of her body, Birdie turned her attention to the now enraged night butcher. She casted an illusion of herself directly in front of the butcher, grateful that the shimmer's power allowed her to do so even in this light.

The butcher began attacking the illusion, and as Birdie ran past it she lured it into the path of the shadow beast.

The beast bulldozed right over the butcher, but it stumbled mightily as Birdie sensed its energy drop even further, the night butcher's massive blade proving to perhaps not be the wisest thing to charge blindly into.

Ahead of her at the chamber's exit, Helcant cracked off another piece of glowrock, setting off another blinding light.

Birdie recoiled, but managed to push past it while Helcant shoved the chunk under his cloak. It was a good idea on his part, but she wasn't sure how much more of that light she could take. Already she could feel her body beginning to break apart. Despite Ev's healing, that swipe she'd taken earlier did nothing to help in that matter.

Ev must have noticed Birdie's condition, because the next thing she knew,

Ev was running right alongside her, rod pointed at her side.

"Thanks," Birdie grunted.

"You can't keep this up," Ev returned out of breath. "You have to make it to the surface. We'll hold it off."

"No," Birdie shot back, but hesitated as she spotted the shadow beast burst back out onto the path. "It's hurt. If it takes much more damage, it will start running from the light. Even it's smart enough not to kill itself chasing us."

"Then let us give it more damage!" yelled Helcant beside her.

He spun around and lobbed a volley of fireballs down at the creature. Each ball exploded in flame, but the attacks only enraged the monster further.

"Run!" Birdie shouted as the beast charged up the path.

She grabbed Ev by the arm and headed into one final chamber.

Helcant followed quickly behind, but not before tossing his chunk of glowrock at the beast. The light caused Birdie to flinch, but she didn't stay to see what effect it had on the monster.

The inside of this chamber proved more of a labyrinth than most, but her othermind was quick to pick out a path through the stone formations. Fortunately, the chamber was the lair that the shadow beast had first come from and was completely devoid of foes.

"This way!" Birdie pulled Ev past a row of low-hanging stalactites to the right of the entrance.

Helcant followed close behind, and after more time than Birdie would have expected the shadow beast roared into the chamber.

"Ha!" shouted Helcant, panting. "I damaged it! It fears the light!"

Birdie felt a touch of relief at that. The madman had actually pushed the monster over the edge. Still, they were a good thirty yards from the top of the tower — far from safety yet.

The shadow beast ran straight toward the group, not even bothering to turn into a puddle. It crashed hard into a row of pillars separating it from its prey, toppling them as it swiped at Helcant.

Helcant retaliated with a blast of fire to the beasts giant maw and dodged aside as it pushed through the rubble and slammed its head into the wall.

Ev reacted quickly, running to the nearest glowrock and striking it.

The beast roared and stumbled briefly before darting back behind the natural columns once more. The pursuit had taken its toll on the creature to the point that Birdie's othermind began flirting with possible ways to kill it.

Birdie herself, on the other hand, knew she was in no condition to attempt such a thing. She cried out as the light blasted her yet again, pressing herself against the wall to try and minimize her exposure to it.

Ev took quick notice of this and stepped between her and the glowrock, giving Birdie the chance to run to cover.

Outside the exit of the final chamber, Birdie waited long enough for Ev to trigger one final rock just inside before leading the way up the path to the freedom.

Near its top, the tower rapidly grew narrower — one side far more so than the other — giving the top a lopsided appearance. The path turned inward to run along that top to the far side, where at last the glowing portal to the surface world waited.

The trio sprinted toward the light until Ev stumbled and fell. She was panting profusely, her human body nearing its limits of endurance.

Birdie turned back to help when she spotted the smoking puddle of the shadow beast spill up and over the edge. There were no glowrocks up here to hold it at bay, and it would be on them in seconds.

"What are you doing?" panted Ev as Birdie lifted her up.

"Fool!" cried Helcant. "The beast is upon us!"

"I'm not leaving Ev!" Birdie returned. "Not when we're this close!"

She barely made it ten steps, however, before she felt the shadow beast rise up behind her. She spun back in time to see it leap toward her, claws outstretched.

An explosion of flame interrupted its attack, and Helcant leapt between Birdie and the monster, sword drawn.

"Flee!" he shouted. "Flee with your precious human!"

He slashed at the great beast, but with a quick swipe of its claws he was thrown to the ground several yards away. The monster turned its attention back to Birdie and Ev, crouching in preparation for another attack.

Birdie drew her daggers, ready to fight despite Ev's pleas to escape.

A second fiery blast struck the creature. Off to the side, a bloodied Helcant pushed himself to his feet.

"Do you insist on failing the world?" he cried. "I said flee!"

He threw another fireball at the shadow beast, now capturing its full attention.

Birdie stood in shock before Ev yanked at her arm.

"Come on!" she shouted, and the two of them ran toward the portal.

Just before passing through, Birdie looked back to see a battered Helcant get tossed toward the edge of the tower, the shadow beast moving in for the kill.

She stopped and drew her bow. She doubted there was anything she could do, but she wasn't going to leave without trying.

"What are you doing?" demanded Ev, pulling on her.

Birdie didn't answer and didn't budge. She released her arrow, but it was too late.

The beast had already lunged. Helcant tried to dodge the attack, but though he avoided the jaws of the creature, he could not escape entirely. The monster bashed him with a swipe of its head, sending him over the side.

The arrow pierced the beast's flank, prompting it to roar and turn its attention back to Birdie.

She didn't care. She was only two feet from the portal. It could come for her if it wanted, but it would never catch her. All it would obtain would be the sting of her arrows.

She fired again, struck again, and the beast dropped into a puddle and sped towards her.

Ev pulled harder against Birdie, but she still refused to move, drawing her bow for another attack.

The shadow beast erupted into physical form mere feet in front of her.

Birdie struck it point blank, and before it could attack in turn, she jumped with Ev into the portal.

The two of them floated through cold, dark nothingness for several seconds. Then, water.

The portal launched Ev and Birdie with tremendous speed up into the Waterfelled River, shooting through then out of the water and onto the shore. The two of them landed hard, with Ev coughing up water she'd swallowed from the rapid ejection.

"Miss Birdie? Ev!" Tallis shouted in surprise before running over and looking around. "What happened? Where's Helcant?"

Birdie pushed her aching body to its feet before offering Ev her hand.

Ev accepted it, but as soon as she was standing she pushed Birdie away.

"What were you thinking! After everything that happened, you just stood there at the exit? Helcant sacrificed himself so you could escape, and you nearly wasted that chance!"

"I was *trying* to give him a chance, too," Birdie replied, turning toward the water.

"What chance? He was already gone!"

"No," she answered. "He wasn't."

Ev clenched her fists, tears nearly welling up in her eyes before she turned away in a huff.

Nephira quickly stepped forward. "What is she talking about? What happened to Helcant?"

Birdie didn't answer, her eyes on the water, hoping her demon ally would soon emerge.

"I demand to know what transpired below." Nephira was now only inches behind Birdie.

Birdie still didn't answer, but Ev did. "Helcant— we were being chased. Helcant distracted the monster so we could get away, but then…"

The water erupted as Helcant burst from the surface onto the shore. Blood poured from his wounds as he sputtered weakly. All but Birdie stared in shock at his arrival, with Birdie sighing in relief before turning a stern look at Ev. She could see Ev noticed the look, but rather than respond, Ev rushed over to help Helcant up and tend to his wounds. Nephira was right behind her.

"How did you escape?" Ev asked Helcant as she worked on him.

"Ha… ha," Helcant laughed weakly. "Of course I survived. That beast was no match for such as I."

Birdie raised an eyebrow. "Wait, you didn't actually kill it, did you?"

"Ha! No!" Helcant replied, wincing at his own exclamation. "But I am clever. I won the battle of wits!"

He proudly dropped a chunk of exhausted glowrock onto the ground.

Birdie smiled. "I'm glad to see you made it. Ev and I owe you our lives."

"No," Ev interjected, turning on Birdie. "The only life he should have saved was mine! You… you…!" Ev sighed and looked defeated. "Thank you for coming for us."

Birdie nodded. She appreciated Ev's gratitude. Of course, Birdie knew that Ev was right to be angry with her, but that didn't make that anger any less frustrating. She also knew she'd need to do better at putting her mission first.

"You're welcome, and I promise: no more big risks. We'll go back the way we came and travel to Ars Summis on a much safer route. We might get there a day later than intended, but that's my fault. Some of you expressed concern about going this way, and I should have listened."

She glanced at both Ev and Nephira, neither of whom were smiling.

"From now on, getting a message to Ars Summis is our only goal. Striking at the loyalists, getting my strength back — that can all be done after contacting Syrus. If you will continue to help me do that, I promise you I will not let you down."

"Well of course we're going to help you!" exclaimed Tallis. "Why wouldn't we?"

"I did not climb to the top of the Netherworld for you to leave now," added Helcant.

As confusing as his wording was, Birdie knew what he meant.

Ev didn't answer, but she did switch to healing Birdie now that she was done with Helcant.

Nephira was the last to speak. "We already said we will travel with you. Let us be done with this drivel and continue our journey."

Having already cleared the path of dangers, the trip back to where they'd entered the Waterfelled was an uneventful one. With any luck, so would be the rest of their journey, at least until they reached Ars Summis.

Chapter 13

The next three days were free from excitement. Though they had abandoned the route along the Waterfelled River, they stayed close to its canyon's edge to avoid other towns and travelers. The off-road travel was slow, but with far weaker monsters than down in the mists, their pace was still better than it had been below, nearly making up for the day they'd lost from backtracking.

At the morn of the fourth day, the party broke away from the river and headed to Bailey Town — the closest settlement to the northern border of Ars Summis. They were well within Dezeroth's territory now, so Birdie had no fear of Lux Rosa's forces lurking about. By noon, they'd arrived at their destination.

"Stay close," Birdie told Ev and Tallis. "We're just going to see if Dezeroth got our message, then we're leaving."

Ev grumbled at that. "As if he'd listen if he did."

None of the others seemed to hear her, so Birdie let that slide.

"Um, maybe we should wait out here," Tallis suggested, eyeing a gaggle of gargoyles staring at him from just within the town walls.

"Oh, grow up," Ev chastised, her expression sour.

Helcant cackled at that.

"We'll be fine," stated Birdie. "No one's going to…" she trailed off as she sensed a familiar magic rushing toward them.

Tallis looked at her nervously as he waited for her to finish, but she never did. Instead, she dismounted her horse to meet a puddle of shadow sliding from the town. The puddle stopped and took on the shape of tall, muscular revenant, though one who's body appeared completely healthy, albeit colored gray.

Birdie smiled. "Well, well. I see you're trying out other appearances. How do you like it?"

"It is odd," replied Umber, "but I believe you may have been mistaken regarding the benefits. I have found minimal improvement in the quality of conversations since beginning this practice."

"That so?" Birdie tilted her head. "Have you been using facial expressions when you talk? It takes practice, but that makes a big difference. Also, make sure you don't change appearance in front of people. In my experience most folks aren't a fan of that."

"Interesting. I will attempt to incorporate that advice." Umber looked over to Helcant and Nephira with a very awkward, toothy smile. "Greetings, Helcant, Nephira. It is good to see you have traveled safely."

Helcant laughed. "What is that? A smile?" he quipped before continuing his laughter.

"Ignore him. You'll get used to it," Birdie told Umber. "I found it helped me to keep a small mirror on hand to practice with."

"Never mind that," interrupted Nephira. "What word have you from King Dezeroth?"

Umber went back to a blank expression, though he kept his revenant guise. "Dezeroth will not send assistance."

"What?" Birdie, Tallis, and Helcant shouted in unison.

"Why the hell not?" pressed Birdie. "You told him what Lux Rosa is trying to do, didn't you?"

"I did," replied Umber. "He agreed to send a small contingent upon receipt of my message."

"But you said—" Tallis started, but Birdie put up her hand to stop him.

"What happened?" she asked.

"I am unsure," Umber answered. "The morning after receiving my message, King Dezeroth had changed his mind. He claimed he wanted more evidence before moving his forces away from his war effort."

"That stupid…" Birdie clenched her fists and trailed off. She'd known from the beginning she couldn't rely on him, but his help was something she desperately could have used.

Nephira frowned at Birdie. "I am certain King Dezeroth has a good reason for his hesitancy."

Birdie sighed and relaxed her hands. "It doesn't matter. If he wants evidence, we'll give him evidence. We're only a few hours from the mountains surrounding Ars Summis. I know Lux Rosa will be waiting for us, but I doubt even she has the forces to guard the entire border of the city."

"But what if she does?" asked Tallis. "How would we get past them without Dezeroth's help?"

"We don't have a choice," Birdie glared at Tallis. "We're a full three days away from his citadel. Assuming we could even convince him to help us — a big assumption, mind you — that would be at least another week before we could get inside."

Tallis cursed. "This is what we get for relying on that decrepit old tyrant."

Nephira turned on Tallis. "I would watch your tongue, if I were you, mortal," she hissed.

"I don't know," Ev said, "that seems about right to me."

She received a death stare from Nephira in response.

"That's enough," Birdie said. "There was always a possibility Dezeroth never would have even received our message. We would have had no choice but to sneak into Ars Summis in that scenario as well. With any luck the five of us will be able to do it on our own."

She turned to Umber. "Unless you'd care to make it six?"

Umber directed his eyes to Birdie. "I delivered your message as you requested. I am now in need of a new purpose. I believe further aiding you would be a worthy one."

"Thank you. We'll see about getting you a horse while we're here." Birdie glanced at the others as she changed into a revenant version of her favorite appearance. "Let's get some fresh water and a bite to eat while we're here."

Tallis spoke up. "Actually, I think I'm good. We should probably hurry to Ars Summis, anyway."

Birdie smiled at Tallis. "Going slow, it will only take eight hours to get from here to the gates of Ars Summis. Our best chance of getting in will be at night, so there's no reason to hurry."

"Oh. What a relief," Tallis muttered.

Ev spoke up, ignoring him. "Well, if we've got time, maybe we could try to recruit some of the townsfolk to help us. I'm sure a lot of them would do it."

"That's…" Birdie started. It wasn't a bad idea.

"What purpose would that serve?" interjected Nephira. "If our plan is to use stealth at night, greater numbers would do nothing for us."

"It also wouldn't hurt us," Ev shot back.

"We would travel more slowly and be more easily seen. That hurts us," Nephira returned.

Birdie sighed. "It does." She looked over at Ev. "Sorry, Ev. It's a good idea, but Nephira brings up good points."

Ev huffed and shrugged. "Whatever."

Birdie led the group into town past the gathering of gargoyles still eyeing Tallis. No one stopped them, but they did get a number of stares from the locals.

It had been a while since Birdie had visited a town under Dezeroth's control. The diversity of its inhabitants was just as impressive as she'd remembered, ranging from corrupted beings such as revenants, brigands, and gremlins, to artificial fiends such as gargoyles and, well, her and Umber. A few humans yet lingered about from before Dezeroth's takeover, though they appeared miserable and kept to themselves. At the center of town was the marketplace — large for a town this size, but considering the range of needs of its varied populace, that seemed fitting.

Birdie handed out a good chunk of gold to each of the others.

"If anyone sees something they want, feel free to get it. Just don't wander out of sight," she warned Ev and Tallis. "When evening comes around, we'll head out. Consider this a little break."

"Oh, how nice," said a very uncomfortable Tallis as he looked around the area, clearly unsure about getting anything at all.

Ev rolled her eyes before beginning her own perusal of the market. She stopped at a stall operated by a pair of gremlins. Slabs of meat hung from hooks above the stall, mushrooms lined the table, and a fire crackled behind it all. A number of sharp sticks had been set against the wall behind the fire.

"Kabobs, I assume?" Ev asked.

The gremlins eyed her suspiciously.

"You are not brigand," the larger one remarked. "Why is mortal human buying from us?"

"She smells like brigand," the other gremlin croaked, and both of them burst out laughing.

Ev took their remarks in stride. "Oh, please. Considering how long it's been since I've had a bath, I'm sure I smell worse than any brigand you've ever met."

The larger gremlin ceased her laughter and scowled, though the other's laughter renewed.

"And what business does mortal have in our town?" pried the larger gremlin.

"Well, right now I'd like to buy some food. Roasted meat and mushrooms sounds pretty nice."

"We will not sell-"

"Five gold!" the smaller gremlin squealed.

"No!" the larger shouted at him, but then she saw Ev pulling out a handful of gold coins and growled. "Ten gold."

Ev flashed a frown, but quickly hid it and handed over twenty. "In that case, I'll take two, please."

The larger gremlin grabbed the gold and counted it as the smaller one eagerly looked on. Satisfied, she tossed the gold under her stall and grabbed a small slab of meat and equally small mushroom to roast. The other goblin grabbed another chunk of meat and mushroom — each substantially larger than what his counterpart had taken — and went to work cooking a second kabob.

Birdie frowned as she watched but opted not to get involved. Though neither had said anything since the Netherworld incident, Birdie sensed a bit of tension yet remained between Ev and her. As such, she figured it might be best to give Ev some space for now.

Instead, Birdie made her way over to a small building from which she felt a great deal of magic emanating. With her new ability to generate unlimited magic, she had no need for extra rations, but that didn't mean she couldn't enjoy a nice treat. Pushing the door open, Birdie stepped into the potion shop.

The shop's owner seemed to be in the back at the moment. It was just as well, she supposed. Nothing particularly stood out to her, at least not until she spotted one of the ingredients behind the counter. Crystal roses — she hadn't expected to see something so exotic in a small-town shop. That got her curious as to what else might be in stock.

"Hello," she called out. "Paying customer, here."

To Birdie's surprise, a bored-looking half-snake man slowly slithered out from the back room and leaned onto the counter.

"What does this one seek?" the shopkeep asked.

Well, this at least explained the crystal roses, though what a naga was doing this far north was beyond her. She could only imagine it was somehow related to Dezeroth's campaign of expansion, not that it mattered. What did matter was this presented her with an opportunity she couldn't ignore.

Placing her hand on her hip, Birdie addressed the naga. "I couldn't help but notice the crystal roses on display, and I wondered if you might happen to also have junghoul blood and dream frog tears."

A bit of life sparked in the shopkeep's eyes as he straightened his posture. He grinned.

"We see this one is knowledgeable of the alchemical arts. Unusual for a revenant. For what purpose do you seek such a brew, may we ask? Surely you know its effects would be ill-served in a body of dust."

"It would be even less suited for a body of shadow," Birdie replied, flashing her shade appearance briefly. "Then again, it's not for me."

The naga seemed unfazed by her revelation. "Even more unusual. The treasures you seek are not found here. My stock is all of such in Atsia. For one potion of invisibility, you must part with two thousand gold."

"Money isn't an issue," Birdie replied, pulling out eight platinum and placing it on the counter. "I'll take four."

The shopkeep gave an odd expression that was somewhere short of surprise and halfway to amusement. He took the platinum then headed to the back, grabbing four roses and jars of black and clear liquids on the way.

Five minutes later, he returned and placed four crystal vials on the counter, which Birdie snatched up.

"Does this one seek further services?" the shopkeep asked. "Perhaps a wardrobe's accompaniment? For you, the price is equal in measure."

"That would be ideal, yes, and appreciated," replied Birdie, handing over another eight platinum.

The naga took the money and once again headed to the back. This time he took with him a jar of creep vine seeds in addition to the same ingredients as before. Another five minutes passed, and he brought back four glass, star-shaped containers, each fastened to a string like a pendant.

"We trust this one is knowledgeable of this potion's method of application."

"Indeed I am," replied Birdie.

"Is that all this one desires today?"

"It is all that I require," Birdie answered, "but it has been a long time since I have enjoyed the delicacies of Seboul. Might you also have star dew and kirin scales? I do not see them on display."

The naga grinned as he reached under the counter and pulled out a container of gelatinous cyan ooze and a bowl of glistening silver scales.

"The price of astral ether is three hundred gold."

Birdie pulled out the last platinum coin she possessed and handed it to the shopkeep, receiving seven hundred gold back. They didn't have enough to afford a ship back across the Sea of Rezin as it was, so she didn't have any reason to hold onto it. They were very nearly at their destination, and they would still have more than enough to buy a horse for Umber.

Upon handing over the ether, the naga bowed to signal the end of their business.

Birdie returned the bow, then exited the shop to look for the others and get Umber his horse..

* * * *

Six hours after departing Bailey Town, the group stopped at a small pool halfway up the mountains surrounding Ars Summis. A steady stream flowed into and out of the pool as it made its way down the mountain, providing a relaxing ambiance in the midst of the pine forest as they settled in for very late dinner. The forest itself was a neon paradise. The needles of the lumine pines glowed bright blue — the sap leaking from their bark a brilliant orange. Beneath the glowing canopy, Ev, Tallis, and Helcant all pulled out various vittles they'd procured from the market. They found a nice, large rock to sit on — one clean of the sticky sap constantly dripping from the trees.

Birdie was surprised to see Helcant sitting with Ev and Tallis rather than Nephira, who'd wandered off with Umber to a particularly large tree a short distance away. Birdie wasn't about to complain. She did want to speak with Umber, however.

Making her way over to her fellow shade, she leaned against a large boulder that had somehow also avoided being coated with sap and crossed her arms. "Nice place, wouldn't you say?"

Umber looked over at Birdie. "It is interesting. I am surprised by the amount of magic held within these trees. I would not agree that the magic is pleasant."

He brushed his hand against the bark of the tree and rubbed a bit of sap between his fingers, absorbing the magic from within it.

Birdie cocked her head. "Lumine pines are filled with light magic. It's an acquired taste, to be sure."

Umber's face remained expressionless as he continued to examine the tree.

"Here," she offered her astral ether to him. "If you don't like the trees, you can have some of this. It's a potion common to the region of Seboul. It does have some light magic in it, but it's far more pleasant than the pure stuff. I figured we should enjoy ourselves on what might be our last night together."

Umber examined the flask of sparkling, sky-blue liquid, then poured about half of it onto himself before returning the rest to Birdie.

"Interesting," he stated. "The sensation is pleasing." After a moment's thought, he gave a decent attempt at a smile.

"There are a lot of nice things in the world if you know where to find them," said Birdie. "Once this is all over, you should try and experience them. I'd be more than happy to give some suggestions."

"Yes," said Umber, "I discovered in my time as a sailor that my existence prior failed to provide me with adequate knowledge of life beyond the catacombs. I would like to correct that failure."

Nephira cleared her throat, interrupting their conversation. "Now that we are here, what's our plan? How do you intend to enter Ars Summis?"

Birdie looked at Nephira and shrugged. "I'll have to see what we're up against before I can answer that, but ideally I'll leave most of my gear with you guys and climb over the wall in my shadow form."

Umber stared blankly. "How would that be possible? My understanding is there is a ravine surrounding the city."

"There is," Birdie replied, "but if I can climb up, I can climb down. My concern is that there will be patrols circling the city. If that's the case, I'll likely need some help distracting them while I make my way up."

"So we're to be bait," Nephira stated.

"You're a diversion," Birdie corrected. "Don't worry. I picked up something that might be helpful in that regard."

"And what would that be?"

"I'll tell you once we get to the top of the mountain and see what Lux Rosa has waiting for us," Birdie answered. "Just know that I've got you covered."

Nephira grunted but didn't press any further.

The break over, the group decided to leave their horses by the pool, tying them to nearby trees. The rest of the climb would be steeper, and horses would only slow them down. They could carry all of the supplies they might need the rest of the way.

An hour later, the party reached the summit. Below them, the massive city stretched out well over fifty miles, glistening in the light of the evening sun. Huge buildings of gold, silver, white stone, and glass reached nearly as high as the mountains surrounding them. Most buildings stood as great cylinders topped with domes, spires, and gardens. Enclosed pathways raised high in the air connected the taller buildings, and at the center of it all an enormous, curved tower stood above all the rest, growing narrower as it reached the top. At its peak, the building bubbled out into a ring surrounding a central lobe. Encompassing the city was a great white wall and nearly invisible dome. Circling that was a ravine and the guardian of Ars Summis — a great serpent that stretched around the entire structure, ready to destroy any who would dare assault the city.

Birdie stepped out onto an overhang to gaze down at her destination and spotted numerous pegasus riders patrolling the city borders. The rest of her group soon joined her.

"Incredible," murmured Tallis.

Ev agreed, "It's absolutely massive."

"It was designed to house a hundred thousand Divine," Birdie stated. "It was the hub of their activities and connects to important locations around all of Doxla. It's the only place where they can instantly send messages to one another even beyond our world."

Tallis jumped in excitement. "I can't believe we're actually here! Can you believe the size of the guardian? I mean, I'd heard stories, but—"

"Tallis, please, let's try to focus," Birdie interrupted.

Tallis calmed down, but Birdie could tell he was having trouble doing so.

"What are those?" Helcant asked, pointing to numerous bright lights floating above the ground near the city.

Birdie frowned. She'd never seen them before, but she had a feeling what they were for.

"A complication," she answered. "Looks like we won't have the cover of darkness to help us. I also won't be able to slide up the wall with those lights there."

"What should we do, then?" asked Nephira. "We cannot enter through the main gates. Even from here I see their forces waiting."

Birdie could see them, too. A good thirty soldiers stood before the northern gate. Presumably the other gates held similar guards. There was no way they'd be able to break through that. Their only real options were to either head back and build an army, or somehow build a bridge.

Birdie turned to Tallis. "That ravine around the city— do you think you can make a bridge across it?"

"What? M-me?" Tallis stammered. Then he thought for a moment. "Possibly? How far do you think it is?"

"On average, fifty feet," Birdie answered. "The wall is half that height."

Tallis looked at his hand in thought before answering. "I should be able to do that, but even with my new magic, it might take a minute."

"A minute might be all we have," Birdie stated dryly before stepping a few feet away and turning back to the others.

She placed her hands on her hips and tried but failed to speak in a chipper voice. "Alright then. As much as I really, really don't like it, I think I have a plan."

Chapter 14

Working their way closer to Ars Summis, Birdie's little band made sure to stick to denser woods to avoid being spotted by the sentries circling above. Birdie and Umber stayed vigilant — quick to absorb the magic of any sap that dripped on their companions. The last thing they needed was to be covered in bright dots as they slunk through the darker undergrowth.

Two-thirds of the way down, they stopped, and Birdie handed Ev and Helcant each two vials of the invisibility potion and two of the star-shaped potion-pendants that would give the same effect to their clothing and equipment.

"Remember," Birdie cautioned, "they'll only last ninety seconds each. Once you've triggered the alarm, use them to escape and find a safe place to hide, and be careful not to break both pendants at the same time. The durations won't stack."

The two took the potions. Ev smiled up meekly at Birdie.

"Don't worry about us," she said. "You go contact Syrus, and give him a kick from me for being gone so long."

"Oh, I will," Birdie smiled back, hugging Ev. She then turned to Umber. "Are you sure you're okay with this?"

Umber quickly shifted his appearance to match Birdie's before cocking his head and speaking in her voice. "I will aid you in protecting this world. A task of such importance is worth a year's wait for revival."

Birdie nodded, then looked to Ev, Tallis, Umber, Nephira, and Helcant in turn. "I don't normally say things like this, but just in case things don't turn out well, I want you all to know how much I appreciate each of you coming on this journey with me. I hate to admit it, but I never would have made it this far on my own. So, thank you."

"Absolutely!" Tallis chirped. "It's been nothing but an honor!"

Helcant grinned. "Whatever it takes to punish the worshipers of the Masters!"

Nephira said nothing, but kept her eyes on Birdie.

Birdie noticed, and figured now was as good a time as any to offer her bow and arrows to Nephira. "Would you like this now or when we get closer?"

"It makes no difference," Nephira answered, taking them. "Are you now ready?"

Birdie nodded, then looked again to Ev, Umber, and Helcant. "Good luck."

"Same," replied Ev, and the three of them started off down the mountain eastward, heading to a location about a thousand yards from the northern gate.

Birdie then led Tallis and Nephira down the mountain in the opposite direction, heading west, about a third of the way between the northern and western gates of the city. They moved quickly so as to get in position before Umber reached his destination.

As they drew near their target, Birdie peered up from beneath the trees at the pegasus riders zipping by overhead.

Tallis looked up with her. "Wish we had some of those potions to use right about now."

Nephira spit. "Stop sniveling. It is unbecoming."

"I'm not sniveling," Tallis retorted. "If you want to talk about unbecoming, let's talk about you spitting all the time."

Nephira simply spit again.

"Knock it off," Birdie said sternly, then dug into her bag and pulled out the last of the restoration elixirs and handed them to Tallis. "Here, just in case."

Tallis pocketed them. "Oh, uh, thanks."

The trio continued onward to the edge of the forest, stopping just short of the hundred yards of flat, barren land between them and the ravine circling the city. Two of the the lights Lux Rosa had set up floated ten feet above the ground to her left and right, exactly halfway between the forest's edge and the wall and separated from one another by about a hundred yards. Even from here, the stupid things were painful — almost as bad as those glowrocks had been.

"I can't believe we're so close…" Tallis started, but after a look from Birdie he cleared his throat and redirected his attention to the lights, shielding his eyes. "So, uh, do you think we can break them?"

"Maybe," Birdie answered, but she doubted it.

She sensed immense magic energy from those lights and suspected they were the result of a spell. The only way to destroy them would be to absorb their magic. She certainly couldn't stand to be in contact with that light long enough to do it, though her little dagger could potentially do the job.

"Should we try?" Tallis asked.

"No," Birdie answered. "If a light goes out, they'll know we're here for sure."

Tallis glanced up at the sky, then the wall, then back at the sky again, a combination of excited and nervous. Nephira kept her gaze steady, Birdie's bow already in her hands.

A few minutes later, a bright red flare lit up the sky to the east. Immediately, all the riders in the area sped towards the flare. Tallis started out from the woods, but Birdie placed her arm in front of him. A moment later another few riders flew by. Tallis looked anxiously at Birdie, waiting for her permission.

She winced as she heard a series of explosions in the distance. It had been stupid of her to send Ev as a decoy. Sure, Lux Rosa knew Birdie'd had two companions, but Umber on his own would still have been enough to sound the alarm.

"You should move," Nephira said from behind.

Birdie snapped out of it and nodded, and she and Tallis sprinted across the rocky terrain while Nephira readied her bow from the woods.

As soon as they drew near the ravine, Tallis halted, staring nervously at the guardian serpent down below.

"Come on!" Birdie shouted. "We have to hurry!"

Tallis swallowed, then cast a spell that forced a large, jagged chunk of stone out over the ravine. The stone only stretched about thirty feet.

"Is that as far as you can go?" Birdie asked him.

"I don't want it to collapse," Tallis answered defensively. "That stone has to come from somewhere."

He then cast again — another spell, another piece of bridge pressed up tightly against the first. This time Birdie felt the ground beneath her sink downward, and she understood what Tallis meant. Caution was definitely wise, then. They did *not* want to annoy the guardian by dropping a boulder on it.

Birdie looked around while Tallis worked, making sure no other riders were coming. It was hard to tell in the darkness above, but her othermind assured her it also detected no movement. That was a relief, but time was still of the essence. The sounds of devastating spells in the distance continued, telling her Lux's forces were still occupied, but that was of little comfort.

"Can you go any faster?" Birdie pressed.

"Do you want this to break?" Tallis shot back, surprising Birdie, and from the look on his face surprising himself as well.

"Sorry," he said, pushing out another large block of land over the ravine before casting something directly underneath.

Birdie couldn't see what the effect was, but she definitely heard and felt the ground moving. She could only assume he was moving more earth around underground to push it nearer to the ravine's edge. Hopefully he'd soon work on making the bridge longer, because as of now it still only stretched thirty feet — only half the distance to the top of the wall.

Once Tallis finished shifting stuff around underground, he cast a series of spells that thickened the bridge from below. He then took a swig of one of the elixirs before finally sending out another jut from the bridge, this one extending nearly within six feet of the wall.

"That's good!" Birdie shouted, and she bolted past Tallis onto the bridge.

"Get to safety!" she called back to him, but before she could take another step she felt a powerful spell incoming and quickly reversed direction, her path disintegrating in a flash of light and dust.

The ground was bathed in red as another flare burst overhead. Birdie looked up to spot three pegasus riders descending slowly from above, led by an older man grinning wickedly. A chill coursed through her body as she sensed the telltale magic of Lux's possession enchantment.

Lux's puppet spoke condescendingly. "Now, now, Eclipse, didn't anyone ever tell you that stealing is wrong? I do believe that's my power you're using."

In a flash, Tallis launched his earth magnet spell at Lux. Lux sneered and swung an enchanted blade at the spell, sending it flying back at Tallis, who jumped out of the way with only inches to spare.

"Did you honestly think I wouldn't come prepared for that this time?" Lux called out in mock disappointment. "Really. And here I'd thought you thinking I'd fall for that pathetic excuse of a diversion was insulting. Your doppelganger and pals barely even put up a fight, much less made any attempt to get into the city."

Birdie clenched her fists. "What did you do to Ev!" she roared.

Lux's puppet tilted his head, feigned confusion on his face. "I have no idea who that is, but don't worry."

The puppet pointed a glowing palm at Birdie, grinning wildly. "When you reincarnate, neither will you."

Birdie's eyes opened wide as a huge burst of light rocketed toward her, too large and fast to avoid. She held out her arms, knowing full well it would do nothing to save her, when the light briefly darkened before exploding in a storm of rock and dust that nearly knocked her clear off the bridge.

Birdie held tight to the stone, dangling over the ravine and unsure as to what had happened, but a quick glance around answered that. A massive wall of rock had appeared between her and Lux, though that massive wall now had a gaping hole in the center of it as the whole thing toppled into the ravine below, striking the guardian and causing it to stir. To her left, Tallis stood tall with his arm outstretched, panting.

"Kill him!" Lux Rosa ordered.

The two riders flanking Lux turned their attention to Tallis, but their attention was quickly redirected as an arrow shot clean through the side of one of their pegasus's chests.

Birdie spotted Nephira from the corner of her eye, having run out to help. They were running out of time, however, as the guardian had now awoken *and* a swarm of riders sped towards them.

Birdie turned her focus to Lux's puppet, raising a glowing arm. The possibility that Lux's possession would override Birdie's illusions was very real, so she picked the next best target. Her othermind informed her that pegasi had organs in their flank and in their ears that regulated their balance, so that's where she struck.

As Birdie cast a spell of illusory pain, Lux's pegasus immediately began thrashing about, quickly losing altitude. Lux struggled to maintain control but only succeeded in crashing into the ravine wall. Unfortunately, her puppet was able to grab the ledge and pull himself up.

Birdie took advantage of the time to climb back up as well, but she wasn't sure what her next step would be.

The bridge was broken, more riders had arrived, and the guardian's enormous head had swung around to examine who had been responsible for striking it. Her only hope was for Tallis to try and extend the bridge again before it was too late.

"Tallis, the bridge!" she called, but he was busy defending against attacks from the new riders, raising great earthen barriers around himself and Nephira.

Lux wiped her puppet's bloodied chin and grinned. "What bridge? Do you mean *this* one?"

Lux's puppet swung his blade, slicing clean through the stone outcrop with a wave of light.

Birdie darted toward solid ground, her othermind the only reason she reacted quickly enough to move before her footing fell out from under her. With a final push, she leapt toward the edge of the ravine.

Lux moved just as quickly, swinging a second arc of light at Birdie. Her othermind saw the movement and twisted her body, but it was impossible to avoid the attack entirely.

Birdie cried out in pain as she landed hard onto the ground, her legs severed and lost to the pit below.

Lux pointed her puppet's sword at Birdie's face and practically sang.

"Bye-bye, 'Birdie.'"

A loud crash. Sudden pain. A dizzying jolt. The next thing Birdie knew, she was flying through the air, having been launched by the earth with enough force to crack her armor. She slammed hard into the top of the wall of Ars Summis. Herself dazed, her othermind took control and grabbed the ledge, not wanting to give up the fight.

On the edge of the ravine, Lux Rosa screamed and fired another great ball of light.

Birdie quickly pulled herself up, passing through the city's barrier. The world flashing white as her othermind temporarily vanished before she flopped onto the top of the wall less than a second before the blast hit.

The light exploded against the barrier. Immediately, the guardian erupted with a terrifying roar, it's body now glowing and crackling with electricity. It dove toward Lux's puppet, mouth wide open. The last Birdie saw of the puppet was his face twisted in rage as the guardian's breath disintegrated him in a wave of prismatic energy.

The other pegasus riders turned and fled, but it was too late for them. The guardian was enraged, and not one of them escaped as the great serpent chased after them and blasted each and every one of them from the sky, devastating the mountainside in the progress. It continued its rampage out of sight, presumably having spotted more targets for its wrath, before ultimately returning back to where Lux had struck the barrier. As the dust settled, the guardian swiveled its head around the area, searching for any further sign of intruders. Seeing none, its glow faded as it retreated back to its resting position.

The carnage over, Birdie pushed herself up and concentrated on reforming new legs. Her body screamed in pain, the loss of so much of her shadow nearly ending her. Fully reformed but barely holding together, she shakily stood up, staring out at the destruction and clouds of dust now obscuring the brilliant lights.

She'd made it. Despite everything, she'd made it to Ars Summis. She'd accomplished her mission. Though, at what cost, it was still too soon to be sure.

Feeling her bag with Syrus's letter to make sure it was still intact, she gave one last look out to see if somehow Tallis or Nephira had survived. Without them, she certainly wouldn't have.

A bit of movement in the rubble caught Birdie's eye. She smiled as Tallis and Nephira stumbled out from behind a crumbling wall of earth Tallis had erected in the battle. Whether the guardian had simply not seen them or had recognized that they weren't with the ones who'd attacked the city, Birdie couldn't be sure. Either way, she was glad to see they'd made it as well.

Birdie raised her hand to signal to them.

Tallis saw her and raised his hand in turn, shouting triumphantly. Nephira quickly covered his mouth, saying something to him Birdie couldn't make out. Nephira then pointed emphatically at at the city, and even from here Birdie could make out the word "Go" on her lips.

Birdie smiled again and nodded. She was worried about Ev, but a part of her dared to hope that between the potions, Umber's aid, and the guardian's rampage, she and Helcant would have managed to survive as well.

With as much confidence as Birdie could muster, she turned to face the city before her. Taking one step toward the glistening buildings, she let the otherworldly magic of the place flow into her.

The only thing that remained was finding that communication thing Syrus had told her about. That should be easy enough. All she had to do was let her othermind—

Birdie blinked. Her othermind was turning up blank. For whatever reason, it didn't have any information on the interior of Ars Summis!

"Really?" Birdie groaned. Maybe she should have taken Syrus up on his offer the last time he'd invited her here.

Whatever. She'd find his little communication device one way or another, and when she did, she'd also ask him why he left that important bit out of her othermind.

Oh, yes, and she'd give him that kick Ev had asked her to. Right about now, Birdie definitely agreed he deserved it.

Chapter 15

Birdie's footsteps echoed in the silent streets of Ars Summis. White stone buildings decorated with silver, gold, and precious stones rose up into the sky around her. Strange symbols adorned their exteriors. Light from unseen sources illuminated their empty interiors, revealing marble floors, exquisite furniture, and lush gardens that had somehow neither died nor wilted from the years of neglect. Lampposts lined the white-bricked road, lit not with flame but with the same magical lights erected around the city by Lux Rosa. These, fortunately, possessed far weaker intensity. Despite her weakened state, her magic had not lost its potency, shielding her from the light and allowing her natural healing to run its slow but steady course.

Birdie had absolutely no idea where she needed to go, so she pulled out Syrus's letter to see if maybe it would offer her some clue.

The only thing that stood out as potentially useful was the line "Find a terminal in one of the communication hubs. Ask the guide to help you. Most buildings have help desks where you can contact it."

Birdie took another look at the buildings around her. She had no idea what a "help desk" or "terminal" was, and she certainly saw no one else around, let alone a guide.

Well, whatever. She shoved the letter back into her bag and picked a building to explore. Maybe she'd find this guide, maybe she'd find this "terminal." Either way, it beat standing around like an idiot. As she approached her building of choice — the largest one on the street — she noticed it didn't seem to have a door, only windows.

"Good enough," she muttered, pulling out a dagger.

She struck the window as hard as she could but couldn't even nick it. Stepping back, she then formed a mace from her shadow and hit the window with that.

Birdie winced in pain, but succeeded in making a small crack in the window. Unfortunately, said window repaired itself almost instantly.

"What the…?" Birdie placed her hand up against the window.

She didn't *sense* any enchantments on it, nor any magic whatsoever.

Something else was going on here.

Not wanting to bet her health outlasting the wonder window, Birdie chose instead to see if there was some other way in. She walked along the edge of the building, searching for any indication of a possible entrance. Noticing that two of the windows seemed slightly more indented than the others, Birdie approached the building once more.

Without warning, the two windows slid apart at her approach. Birdie paused, then stepped cautiously inside, watching the moving windows as they closed again behind her.

"Huh." That turned out to be easier than she'd made it out to be.

Inside was a cavernous room — the temperature unusually cool. All around her were chairs and tables spread evenly about on the ground floor with potted plants lining the sides. Halfway across the room was a wall and a set of stairs leading up to a second floor — still part of the same room and serving as a sort of balcony. More chairs and tables were on the second floor, but so were a number of what appeared to be stalls of some sort set into the upper floor's wall. A hallway on the second floor went further back into the building.

Not seeing anything interesting on the bottom floor, Birdie made her way to the second and checked out the stalls.

Pictures of food — some she recognized and some she didn't — were plastered on white boards at the back of the stalls, along with more of those unrecognizable symbols Birdie assumed must be the language of the Divine.

None of that was of any use to her, however, so she headed back to the hallway and made her way deeper into the building.

The hallway opened up into another large room, this time circular. Though it was nowhere near as wide as the outer room with the tables, this one stretched up many stories high — nearly as tall as her citadel — with balconies circling the room every floor up. At the center of the room was a circular stand, and in rings around the stand were a number of very plush couches facing inward and outward in pairs and accented with ornamental plants at the end of each couch. The stand at the center only had a few unknown symbols plastered on a sign above it with no accompanying image. While it almost appeared to be some sort of stage with the seating arrangement, Birdie somehow doubted that's what it was. It was clearly important, however, so she figured it wouldn't hurt to give it a closer look.

She barely made it five steps, however, when she nearly shouted at the sight of a person laying hidden on one of the inward-facing couches and staring right at her.

Birdie instinctively reached for her dagger but quickly caught herself. Even she knew that combat in Ars Summis was impossible. How? She had no idea, but Syrus had distinctly told her it was impossible for Divine to harm one another within the city's walls. Honestly, it was fortunate, given the circumstances. Her injuries right now meant a confrontation with even a non-Radiant Divine would be risky.

Trying her best to play it cool at the sight of a Divine actually being here, Birdie brushed back her hair and gave an awkward chuckle.

"Hi, there. You startled me. I didn't know anyone else was here."

The reclining Divine said nothing.

Birdie cleared her throat. "Um, anyway, I was just looking for the help desk. Do you know where that is?"

The Divine still said nothing. It was at this point Birdie noticed he wasn't really looking at her, either.

She turned around to see what he was staring at but saw nothing. She turned back to him.

"Hello?" she waved her hand.

Still no response.

Birdie then approached the Divine and waved her hand right in front of his face. When that did nothing, she gave the cushion he was laying on a little push with her foot.

Odd. He certainly wasn't dead, but it was like he wasn't here either. Birdie was sure that when Divine temporarily withdrew from their worldly vessels they only left behind a crystal marker to return to, but perhaps things worked differently here in Ars Summis?

She shrugged. Whatever the case, she clearly wasn't getting any help from him. She turned her attention back to the stall.

No sooner did she place a hand on the counter than a ghostly figure emerged up from the ground, startling her nearly as much as the Divine had. The glowing blue woman then proceeded to speak to Birdie in a language she didn't understand.

Birdie froze, not sure how to respond.

After a moment, the woman spoke to Birdie again, still in that same language.

Birdie shook her head. "I'm sorry. I don't know what you're saying."

"Acknowledged," the woman replied. "We will correct our records regarding your language of preference. May I ask for your correct language of preference?"

"Um, Doxlan," Birdie replied, eyeing the woman suspiciously. "Are you a water elemental?"

The woman smiled. "Thank you. From now on all compatible services will be presented in Doxlan for your convenience. To answer your question, yes, I am indeed a water elemental."

Birdie was confused, but intrigued. "How is that possible? I thought only Divine could enter Ars Summis."

"Nepacs are generally forbidden from Ars Summis. However, some, like me, have been appointed to special positions to aid in the city's upkeep." The elemental smiled sweetly. "But don't worry. All of us are very friendly and are happy to be working here."

Something about this woman unnerved Birdie. She'd never once heard anything about nepacs working in Ars Summis, and the way this one spoke to her was just… off. Elementals were just another flavor of shade, and every one she'd ever met before had a personality similar to Umber's. Yet, this one was disconcertingly cheery. That, and the fact that the woman didn't seem at all interested in Birdie's presence despite the fact that the only other Divine she'd seen since arriving was in a catatonic state, screamed to her that something was deeply wrong.

Birdie glanced around the room quickly, a part of her having to make sure this wasn't some sort of trap. As she shifted her eyes up toward the balcony, she had to do a double-take at the sign on the stall, now completely legible.

It read "Help Desk." She didn't know how the words got changed, but presumed it had something to do with saying she spoke Doxlan. Either way, it wasn't something to dwell on now.

"This is—" Birdie began, but she realized pointing out she was at the help desk was a dumb statement. "Are you the guide?"

"I am Rime Thawfate," the elemental replied. "I am one of several guides located around Doxla, and I am an expert on all subjects that might be useful to Divine. Even more experienced Divine may be able to learn a thing or two from me."

Rime smiled that same sickeningly sweet smile. "Is there something in particular I may help you with?"

Birdie decided she may as well just go with it. "I'm looking for a communication terminal. Can you tell me where one is?"

"Absolutely," Rime answered, and gestured to her left. "Communication terminals can be found in all community buildings except for those designated 'local only.' However, it is advised that communication terminals only be used to contact friends who are currently out-world, as amulets of instant transmission are a much more convenient option for in-world communication. Amulets of instant transmission can be purchased for the price of one thousand platinum in in-world currency or for the much better deal of any out-world payments equivalent to ten prestige vouchers."

"I think the terminals are good enough for me," Birdie replied, not sure what the heck this woman was talking about. "Where can I find one of these 'community buildings'?"

"You are currently in the largest community building in the Water Sign sector."

Birdie raised an eyebrow. "Okay, so where can I find a communication terminal, then?"

Rime gestured to her left.

"Communication terminals can be found in all community buildings except for those designated 'local only.' However, it is advised—"

"No," Birdie cut her off, frowning. "I mean, where can I find one of them here, in this building?"

Rime placed both her hands across her waist, smiled, then gestured once more to her left. "Communication terminals can be found on the twentieth floor. It is advised that you use the teleporters down the hall for more convenient travel. The cost is five gold per trip, or you can purchase unlimited teleporter usage for out-world payments—"

"I'm good," Birdie interrupted, now understanding just what this thing in front of her really was. Ev had been right on the money, literally, about her ideas of machines here passing as people.

Frankly, it was disgusting. Birdie had known for years that the Masters had created their world just to entertain Divine, but she never would have guessed how blatantly unabashed they'd been about the whole thing when out of view of nepacs. Seeing it for herself, she completely understood Ev and Helcant's disdain for the Masters. Syrus had likely shared all of this with Ev during their lessons together, and Helcant would have been unfortunate enough to experience it for himself. Well, Birdie wasn't going to give the Masters a single coin. She'd traveled hundreds of miles to get here; she could afford to climb a few stairs, her injuries be damned.

Birdie looked around, then begrudgingly addressed Rime one more time. "Okay, last question. Where are the stairs?"

*** * * ***

Upstairs, it didn't take long for Birdie to find what she was looking for. The entire floor was essentially a series of crisscrossing hallways lined with nearly empty rooms, all of them seemingly identical and labeled "Com Room" with various numbers.

After checking a few and seeing that they all looked the same — a dark room with an odd glowing machine in front of a glass-covered wall — Birdie entered one and pulled out Syrus's letter to see what she was supposed to do next.

"Touch the 'out-world' button on the display."

Birdie wasn't sure what that meant, but the only thing in here was that machine in the middle of the room, so she assumed that was the "display."

Sure enough, the words "out-world" were written on the glowing part of the device, along with "in-world" and "shop," all of which sat above what appeared to be a map of Doxla.

Not seeing anything else she could do, Birdie tried pushing on the glass above "out-world." She retracted her hand as the display changed in an instant.

The words and map disappeared, replaced with numerous lines of strange symbols in gray boxes with a glowing, spinning structure behind them. At the top of the list of gray boxes was the only line she could read, simply saying "voice." She didn't know why the stupid thing wasn't translating everything for her anymore, but whatever. She was sure Syrus would have accounted for that.

Birdie checked the note again. It now told her to press a specific group of symbols. After some examination she was able to find a matching set on the display.

With another touch, the display changed again, this time showing a screen of almost nothing but foreign symbols, most of which were in individual boxes. The only image here was a tiny globe on the bottom right, and above the symbol grid was a single white rectangle.

Birdie had now reached the final instruction on Syrus's note: "Now, you need to write my name. Once you've pushed the following keys, touch the globe symbol, and the terminal will contact me. It might take a while for me to answer, so please be patient."

Right below that were more symbols, so Birdie pressed them all one at a time, making sure not to mix any of them up. As she pressed them, they appeared in the white rectangular box.

Once she'd put them all in, she pressed the image of Doxla's globe, and the glass-covered wall in front of her lit up. It displayed only "Calling…" followed by the symbols she'd entered — Syrus's true name — the thing Lux Rosa had sent entire armies to obtain.

The window also started making an annoying series of beeps which it kept repeating every few seconds. Birdie didn't know if this was what the world Syrus came from was like, but if it was, she couldn't say she was particularly fond of it.

After enduring the relentless beeping for over ten minutes, Birdie started to fear that maybe she'd done something wrong, but just as she began looking for a way to stop the machine and try again, the wall changed it's display, revealing a dimly lit yet brightly colored room and the top half of a loosely dressed being not even her othermind could identify — a being she could only assume was…

"Syrus?" Birdie asked, nearly dumbstruck.

Syrus raised one of four arms in a wave, smiling with a surprisingly feminine, blue-tinted face before swiping back long locks of green hair on both sides, placing them behind what looked like two pairs of pointed ears.

"Hello, Birdie," Syrus responded in a voice Birdie couldn't place as either male or female. "My apologies if I took long to answer. I'm afraid you caught me sleeping. That's also why I might look a bit of a mess."

Birdie didn't know how to respond. She wanted to be angry, but at the same time she was so caught off guard that the strangeness of everything she'd experienced since entering Ars Summis was now catching up to her.

Syrus chuckled. "What's the matter? You didn't expect I'd look like my avatar, did you? Where's the fun in that? As a prifae, I'd be remiss not to take advantage of the opportunity to try out a new look."

"A prifae?" Birdie repeated, words beginning to return to her. "Is that what Divine call themselves outside of Doxla?"

"My dear, I'm afraid it's not that simple." Syrus leaned forward and placed a chin on his top two hands. "As I'm sure Ev has told you, it's rather taboo for me to speak of what lies beyond your world, but suffice it to say that there are essentially two types of what your world knows as Divine. There are seitti, and there are various races elevated by seitti. I belong to one of the latter."

"Elevated?" Birdie frowned. "What do you mean, 'elevated'?"

"I mean we have been granted some degree of access to the technology and abilities of seitti, typically on the condition of assisting them in their work. I'm afraid that's all I can tell you about that. Once I finish my efforts at liberating your world, perhaps then I will be able to tell you more." Syrus tilted his head in sort of shrug. "Bureaucracy and all that, but I'm sure you didn't call me just to chat about Divine. Did Ev's experiments yield any results?"

"What? No!" Birdie almost yelled. "We've been attacked! Another Radiant showed up and is using the power of the Masters! What the hell have you been doing? You've been gone for over a month!"

Syrus looked both shocked and hurt, lowering one of his chin-supporting hands. "That shouldn't be possible. It wasn't until just prior to my departure that the modal schisms began leaking any substantial degree of degradation. No one should have been able to claim the Masters' abilities in that time."

"Well, she did! Maybe not all of them, but she's created new spells and enchantments, she can possess other people, she can turn air magic on and off, and she has these lights that grant magic on par with Radiants to anyone who touches them."

Syrus tapped a finger on his chin, frowning. "I see. You say she turned off air magic. How long ago did this happen?"

"It was over two weeks ago now. You'd know this if you ever came back!"

Syrus sat back up. "My apologies for my absence, but as I recall, you were the one who told me you needed some space after our last conversation."

"Oh, no," Birdie countered. "Don't you blame this on me. You're the one who keeps putting more and more responsibilities on me. You're a Radiant, too. It shouldn't be my job to take care of Doxla by myself!"

"Of course it shouldn't. That's why I helped you get a system set up. You have the Shadow Guard, a loyal staff, diplomatic connections—"

"That's still me in charge of everything! How about you pull *your* weight for a change?"

Syrus sighed. "Birdie, I never wanted any of this either. Doxla isn't my world. I have a life that I abandon every time I take on the persona of Syrus. It has cost me tremendously in more ways than one to aid Doxla as much as I have, and I can't keep doing this forever. Prifae are mortal. That is why I and others created you, so that even after we are gone, there will always be a Radiant watching over your world. I only hope that before then we are able to transfer the Masters' control of the world to you or to other Doxlan natives."

Birdie looked down for a moment and clenched her fists before returning her gaze to Syrus. "Is that so? Well, apparently not everyone who created me wants that."

Syrus raised an eyebrow. "What do you mean?"

"The Radiant that attacked us. She's one of the ones who created me. She said her name is Lux Rosa."

Syrus frowned. "I see. Give me a moment, please. I need to check on something."

Birdie, surprised, watched as Syrus stood up and walked out of view, her eyes moving to what looked like four tentacles protruding from a fleshy skirt hanging down from his waist. She could hear him talking to someone else in a language she couldn't understand. After about five minutes, Syrus returned and sat back down, holding some sort of device.

"Thank you for waiting. It has been over ten years since I last spoke to most of my co-conspirators, and there were many who played only a tangential role in our attempt to put you in charge of Doxla."

"What does that—?"

"The name Lux Rosa is unfamiliar to me. Fortunately, those of us most involved made certain to catalog everyone who assisted us in any way." Syrus looked at his device as if he was reading from it. "The Radiant you named was not involved in your creation. She joined up with us briefly in our initial purge of the other Divine after your creation, but disappeared after your former incarnation was defeated."

"But she knew about my othermind!" Birdie insisted, leaning over the machine between her and Syrus. "Those weird little light thingies almost made my othermind disappear when I touched them!"

Syrus put down his device and leaned forward, once again placing his chin on the backs of his upper pair of hands. "It wasn't exactly a secret as to the general concept of how you came to be. It was only the details that a select few of us were privy to. As for these 'light thingies,' the only thing I can think of that would do that is cosmic degradation. Although, I'm honestly surprised just touching it would have that effect. You should only lose connection to your othermind if the entirety of your physical being were to be immersed in degradation. Perhaps because you are a shade, with your mind not localized to any one part of your body, any contact results in instability in your connection and desynchronization between your conscious thoughts and othermind."

"What the hell does any of that mean?" Birdie asked, swinging her arm in frustration.

She then remembered her conversation with Ev. She took a deep breath and grabbed the top of the device in front of her, closing her eyes for a second before opening them again.

"Just tell me one thing. My othermind — is it dangerous?"

Syrus tilted his head. "How do you mean?"

"I mean," Birdie realized she was raising her voice and stopped herself, "will it take over me? Lux Rosa said the more I use it, the more I'll become it."

Syrus let out a small chuckle, then a larger one. "Oh, did she now?"

Birdie blinked, not expecting that reaction.

Syrus shook his head. "I'm afraid it's already too late for that. The 'you' that you are, that only came to be because of the effects of your othermind. Your original personality was the same as every other shade. What I find interesting, though, is how different your current personality is from that of your first incarnation. That tells me that your othermind was merely a catalyst for your development, and that you became 'you' from your own experiences with the world."

Birdie blinked, but found she couldn't help but look away from Syrus. This was the first time she'd ever really discussed her creation. It was awkward, to say the least. Still, after everything that had happened, she felt like she needed to know more.

"So, if I keep using it, it won't take over me?"

"Of course not," Syrus answered. "Your othermind is a separate entity with which you can share thoughts. It will only ever 'take over' you if you permit it, and even then only for as long as you permit it."

Birdie took another deep breath, then looked back at Syrus. "So what is my othermind, anyway?"

Syrus picked his head up, his smile giving way to sympathy. "This Lux Rosa has really affected you, hasn't she?"

"A lot has happened," Birdie responded, thinking back to her recent recklessness, her reliance on her othermind's knowledge, her inability to even aim a bow without its help.

"I see," said Syrus. "In that case, how about we continue this conversation in person?"

"I'd prefer for us to talk about it now," Birdie replied, irritated. This was *her* existential crisis, after all.

"I promise I won't be long," Syrus replied. "You're in room 7-C of the Water Sign Central Community Building, correct?"

Birdie blinked. She wasn't sure, but that sounded about right. "How—?"

"All out-world communications tell the out-world speaker where the in-world speaker is located to make it easier to meet in Ars Summis. The Masters wanted people to spend as much time in Ars Summis as possible."

"Of course they did," Birdie tilted her head, unamused. "To buy more of their 'conveniences,' right?"

Syrus chuckled at that. "Oh, so you noticed that, did you?"

"It was hard not to," Birdie answered, "but how does knowing where I am help you? Your marker is still all the way back in Roehelm."

"I told you," Syrus answered with a wry smile, "the Masters wanted Divine to spend as much time in Ars Summis as possible. Once a Divine completes their first pilgrimage to the Golden City, they are able to create avatars local to the city at any point afterward. Such avatars can't leave the city, but that shouldn't matter for the business we must conduct. Give me about thirty minutes, and I'll meet you down by the help desk. If Lux Rosa has already made as much progress as you claim, then there is much we need to do."

Chapter 16

Lux Rosa sat steaming atop her throne in the Hall of Champions. Not once, not twice, but thrice had that cursed construct escaped from her grasp. Now, it was only a matter of time before that fool Syrus began taking steps to counter her progress. To be sure, at this point he had little hope of stopping her, but another seitti competing for the world was an irritation she could do without.

No matter, she assured herself. Though Ars Summis had been a loss, her work at Grandis's old citadel had been most fruitful indeed. There were now but a few matters left to attend to in preparation for Syrus's inevitable assault — matters that she would see done as soon as that damn Vellic finally showed his face.

Eventually, the stone doors slid open, signaling the arrival of her pet.

"Ah, my dear Vellic," Lux cooed before he could give his usual greeting. "Thank you for coming on such short notice. I'm afraid we have much work to do."

Vellic bowed. "How may I be of service."

"A situation has arisen. Syrus will soon prepare an attack against us. We must prepare in kind."

Vellic stood up straight, though his lack of surprise was irksome. "May I ask how you know this?"

Lux struggled to suppress a scowl. "Those accompanying Eclipse possessed the powers I have gifted to our soldiers. They used them to find an unorthodox route into Ars Summis. My question for you," Lux narrowed her eyes, "is how they came to possess such a gift."

Vellic frowned. "My lady, I have no idea how that happened. I have received no word of incidents from any of our camps."

"Of course you haven't," Lux chided. "Eclipse is five days away even by pegasus. I want to know what measures were in place to protect such resources from falling into evil hands."

Vellic grew defensive. "Lady Rosa, I assure you that all camps were given your exact orders on how to handle your blessings."

"Oh, my dear Vellic, do tell me that you aren't suggesting this is my fault."

"N-no, of course not," Vellic stammered. "I am merely stating that all camps were told the proper procedures to follow. Perhaps one of them did not follow your directions."

Lux let just the slightest smile slip before hiding it. Seeing Vellic squirm under her authority was one thing she would miss.

"Perhaps," Lux leaned back in her throne, "but I suppose ultimately it is of no matter. We have much we must do to prepare. There is no point in dwelling on the past."

Vellic bowed slightly. "My lady, before we continue further, may I ask what happened to the soldiers sent to Ars Summis?"

"I don't know," Lux responded dismissively. "My champion was surprised and slain before I could see the end of the battle. I assume they are still there."

Vellic clenched his jaw in a poor attempt to hide his displeasure with that news.

"I assume you desire a new champion," he almost growled.

"No," Lux answered, pleased to see the surprise on his face. "What I desire is a volunteer."

"A volunteer? For what?" he asked warily.

"How large is our army?" Lux asked him.

"We still have only three hundred—"

"I mean in total, Vellic. How many soldiers do we have across Doxla?"

Vellic frowned. "After our defeat at Roehelm, we have nearly twenty-five hundred remaining, but we are well into the process of recruiting more as we speak."

"And how many do Syrus and Eclipse have at their disposal?"

"I... across all of Doxla, we estimate at most two thousand."

"Humans," Lux stated.

"Excuse me?"

"Two thousand humans," Lux repeated, placing her weight on her left arm. "That says nothing of the countless immortals who have pledged loyalty to them. I have already taken steps to mitigate the immortal threat, but even with my efforts we must be prepared for numbers far greater than ours. They already know of our enhanced magic. That is why we must prepare something they will not expect. That is why I need a volunteer."

Vellic looked up defiantly. "With all respect, Lady Rosa, you have not answered my question."

Lux placed her hand over her chest. "Oh, my dear Vellic, such little faith in me. You need not fear for their safety. I merely need someone to help me complete a new blessing I have been working on. It will not only increase the recipient's magical abilities, but their strength as well."

"I do not understand. How can a nepac help you complete a blessing?"

"You do not need to understand," Lux answered impatiently. "I have assured you of their safety. Is that not enough for you? Find me someone weak and sickly so that we may best demonstrate the fruits of my labor."

Vellic stared at Lux for several seconds before yielding.

"Very well," he bowed, "I will return shortly."

Lux watched as Vellic trudged out of the chamber. Once he was out of sight, she reached into the degradation surrounding her throne and touched the spot where she'd implemented her new "blessing." She made a copy of her creation and pulled out a small shimmer. With any luck, it would work without requiring much tuning. If it ended up harming the test subject, well, Vellic had been useful, but he was far from a necessary tool.

After some number of minutes had passed, Vellic returned with a scrawny soldier.

"This is Sir Petwick," he said. "He has volunteered to help you test your new blessing."

Lux Rosa waited for the stone door to close once more before she stood and brought her glowing orb down to her test subject.

"Sir Petwick, I am pleased to see such willingness to serve. As a reward, I will make you the first nepac to possess not only the magic of a Radiant, but the strength of one, as well."

Her subject bowed. "It is an honor and a privilege, Your Ladyship."

Lux smiled. "Reach forward and touch the light. Let its power flow through you."

The soldier obeyed.

Vellic stepped back as the soldier's entire body began to glow, concern clearly on his face.

The test subject's muscles expanded, its skin tightened. It stared at its hands in awe of its newfound strength, when suddenly it winced, then began crying out in pain. The soldier buckled over, collapsing to the ground.

Vellic stepped forward. "No! Stop it!"

Lux smirked, then stretched out her hand to her subject. Touching it, she felt what effects her tool had enacted within its body. Though it was unfortunate that this trial was a failure, the information she would glean from it would pave the way to a successful enhancement technique.

At last the glow died down, leaving the soldier gasping and whimpering on the floor before ultimately falling silent.

"You gave your word it would be safe!" Vellic shouted, standing defiantly before Lux.

Lux stood back up and graced Vellic with a sideways glance. "Oh, Grand Curate. You must know that there can be no progress without sacrifice."

"No! No more! My people are not tools to be exploited!"

"Do you want to rid this world of Eclipse or do you not?" Lux responded coolly.

The old man growled. "I want order restored. Lord Grandis kept order. He protected us! You promised us you would bring back that order, but you have done nothing of the sort! You have only obsessed over Syrus and Eclipse and that cursed degradation. You have used us to further your ends, but I will no longer stay quiet as you throw away the lives of my people!"

Lux suppressed a yawn as she turned to face Vellic. "You say I have done nothing to help you. What changes can we make that would remedy this?"

Vellic scowled. "I am taking back control of the Guardians of Light. If you wish to aid us, we will support your 'degradation' machinations, but from now on, I decide the path we take."

"I suppose that's fair," Lux replied absently, flicking off a piece of dirt she'd picked up from touching the fallen soldier. "You rallied the Light Guard after Grandis's defeat and established the Guardians of Light; it's only sensible that your people's orders should come directly from your mouth."

She looked up at Vellic, a feeble old man still standing his ground. She could tell from his expression that he didn't trust her words.

"They are my people," he stated. "You would do well to remember that. You may be a Radiant, but our loyalty is to Lord Grandis. If you will not stand for what he stood for, then they will choose to follow me, not you."

"Of course I don't stand for what he stood for," Lux responded, growing tired of this conversation.

"Then our partnership is—"

Lux leapt forward, squeezing Vellic's head in her hands as she lifted him into the air before draining him of his magic and slamming him to the ground. She stepped on his throat to stop him from calling out — not that it mattered. Her chamber guards knew well not to defy her.

Vellic clawed pathetically at her legs, but she merely pressed down tighter.

As pointless as it may have been, the action was cathartic.

"What you sycophants don't understand is that Syrus's claims were true. Grandis did want to destroy your world. He was a fool who failed to recognize a golden opportunity when it presented itself. He saw a dying world and feared what the Masters intended it for. Whether through incompetence, sloth, or stupidity, he could not fathom taking control of it for himself. That is the truth of your 'hero.' That is the truth of your precious 'Lord Grandis.'"

She removed her foot, giving Vellic the opportunity to breath again.

"You… you lie…" he choked, rolling onto his side.

Lux grabbed his head again and pressed it against the floor, leaning her head close to his as she spoke directly into his ear. "You say you are not my tools, but that is all you have ever been. The Masters created you to be toys. Grandis used you as weapons. I will use you to liberate this world and achieve greatness. You should be honored. Though your existences are ephemeral, at the end of your lives you can die knowing you contributed to something beautiful and eternal. Me."

Lux channeled her possession spell into Vellic. As inconvenient as losing her willing mouthpiece may have been, an unwilling one would suffice for the time being.

Lux stood up in Vellic's body and tested out his voice, talking to him.

"Don't try to fight it. Even with your consciousness still active, my spell's control over your body is absolute. Enjoy the ride. We have so much work to do."

* * * *

Using Vellic as her puppet, Lux Rosa ordered a pair of guards to clean up the mess of her failed experiment. The excuse that he had been in too poor of shape to survive the enhancement placated her workers for now.

Once that was taken care of, Lux summoned the top officers of her army to Vellic's quarters to inform them of her plans.

"We have been instructed to recall all available soldiers to defend the Hall of Champions," she said in Vellic's voice. "Send messengers to the army en route to Roehelm and have them return immediately. Recall them from Ars Summis, our outposts, and our recruitment camps as well."

"That would remove our presence from vital regions," one of the commanders protested. "The immortals will take control of too much land!"

"Immortals will soon no longer be a problem," Lux assured her commander. "Lady Rosa is developing a weapon that will erase countless of them forever."

The commanders looked at one another at that statement. One of them breathed a huge sigh. "It's about time."

"Indeed it is," Lux responded, "but the weapon will not stop the Shadow Guard that will soon be marching against us. We must be prepared. Therefore, it is critical that messengers be sent out immediately."

The commanders all nodded in agreement. "We will see that it is done."

"Very good. That leaves one more matter," Lux told them. "We must find equipment for our laborers to take up arms on the day of battle. Should any of those traitors breach our walls, I don't want our people to be left defenseless."

"That won't be a problem," the nearest commander replied. "We have a surplus of weapons available. Maybe not enough for everyone, but it won't be hard to forge a few more."

"Good. I will leave you to it," Lux stated before leaving. "My apologies for gathering you all for such a short meeting, but we must begin preparations immediately. I myself have a special task that I must begin work on."

"We understand," the nearby commander replied. "We will see to it that Lady Rosa's will is done."

Lux smiled, bowed slightly, then departed. She did not want her new puppet to spend more time around those who knew him than was necessary. While she was familiar with Vellic's mannerisms and with her higher-profile servants, she did not know what relationships Vellic had with them. Improvisation would only get her so far. For now, it was best to minimize the risk of any unfavorable incidents. She could rid herself of the issue after the battle was over.

Lux took Vellic's body back to a position overseeing the Colosseum adjoining the Hall of Champions where she looked down on the soldiers training below. Once she adjusted the mechanisms of her physical enhancer, she would need a new volunteer.

After picking out a few promising-looking candidates, she turned her attention to beyond the outer wall where her laborers worked on procuring more degradation. Most of the new samples had provided very little in terms of new entry points into the Masters' systems. Perhaps it was time to reallocate her workers to more productive efforts. After all, she'd already found the key to her coming victory.

Back in her throne room, Lux's actual body caressed the iridescent shimmers around her. Absolute control over all magic in Doxla was now nearly at her fingertips. Though she had yet to find a way around the Masters' safety measures protecting said magic, it was only a matter of time before that final obstacle was breached.

Chapter 17

Back at the help desk, Birdie was unnerved to see that the Divine she'd spotted earlier no longer rested on the nearby couch. She looked around but saw no sign of him anywhere.

Great. One more thing to worry about. At least that guide didn't bother her so long as Birdie kept her distance from the desk.

After about half an hour, Birdie heard footsteps coming down the hallway with the teleporters. Turning to see who approached, she at last saw Syrus in the form she was familiar with — a bespectacled, dark haired man in a black cloak with a jeweled rod he used as a cane.

"Greetings once again," he said as he drew nearer, now with a decidedly male voice.

"Ev said I should kick you for being gone so long," she responded.

Syrus stopped, hands placed on his rod. He smirked as the two of them stared at one another for a moment before he broke the silence.

"Well, if you must, I won't stop you, but it might be more productive if we start walking. Even with a teleporter, we're going to have a bit of a trek ahead of us."

"And where exactly are we headed? This place is almost deserted."

"A testament to the efforts we've made against other Divine and to the failures of the Masters," Syrus stated. "We are going somewhere we can speak in private. As interested as I am in meeting this Lux Rosa, I believe it would not be in our interest for her to overhear our conversation."

"What? You think she can listen in on us?"

"Of course she can. All she would need do is create a local avatar and eavesdrop. Though I think it unlikely she would herself actually find us, we cannot rule out the possibility that she has enlisted the aid of other Divine who yet linger here. Come."

Syrus motioned for Birdie to follow him, then led her to the teleporter room.

"Do we have to use these?" she asked, eyeing the circular platform with suspicion.

"I assure you they are perfectly safe," Syrus stated, pulling out ten gold.

"That's not the problem," Birdie said, though admittedly it was *a* problem. "Why should we give the Masters any more money after what they've done to us?"

Syrus chuckled. "Don't worry. In-world currency has no value to them. If they so chose, they could produce infinite amounts of it in an instant. Seitti society revolves around a concept best described as prestige and prestige vouchers, which is essentially staking one's reputation to vouch for another's. There are, of course, more traditional currencies in exchange as well, though they are merely complementary to the prestige system. A seitti's reputation is of utmost importance to them, as that is what determines the extent of their permitted activities."

"Permitted? So there really are beings higher than seitti?" Birdie asked, recalling what Ev had said earlier.

Syrus placed the coins into a slot and pressed a few buttons as he answered her. "I am aware of a hierarchy amongst the seitti and have reason to believe that there are indeed higher powers, but I am not privy to details of such information. Apparently whoever is above believes it to be very important that those created by seitti have a degree of mystery in their lives. The one who created and elevated my race told us as much, saying that it leads to more diverse cultures and philosophies."

Birdie instinctively covered her eyes as the teleporter flashed. An instant later, the two of them reappeared in a shiny silver and blue hallway.

Syrus continued speaking, now looking at Birdie. "My ultimate goal is to unmask the true identity of the Masters and expose their crimes. I do not know if this is something I can even do, but if it is possible to gain true control over this world, it should be possible to discover their identities. I have very good reason to believe they are in blatant violation of seitti law — not just in how they've abused your world, but also in where and how they created it."

Birdie shook her head. This was a lot to take in. As curious as she was about what Syrus meant, however, it sounded like an issue that was not of immediate concern.

"About my othermind," she prodded. "You said you would tell me what it is."

Syrus nodded. "I will. It is honestly not that complicated. Come, let us walk as we talk."

He led her out into what appeared to be a vast open-air garden with paths of white stone and structures of silver and blue. Gorgeous fountains lined long streams cutting across the landscape, but what caught Birdie's attention the most was that the sky was now bright as day.

Syrus must have noticed her expression. "These are the Radiant Gardens; only Divine who've reached Radiance are permitted here. Day and night are but illusions in this garden. What is shown to us depends on what those of the Supreme rank decide. Are you happy with day?"

Birdie looked around the garden in amazement. It was the first place since entering the city where she'd seen more than just plant life. A kaleidoscope of butterflies flitted about amongst the flowers; large and small multi-colored fish swam about in the streams and ponds they passed by. Dragonflies flew above the waters, and frogs and turtles basked on the banks or on rocks. Birdie hated to admit it, but this was a place she could enjoy spending time in. It was tempting to just stop and let her aching body rest beneath one of the trees against the nearest stream.

"I'll take that as a yes," Syrus said. "Very well. Let me know if you change your mind."

Birdie looked at him sideways. "I thought you said only Supreme Radiants could alter the sky."

Syrus smiled wryly. "Well, I hope you don't think I've been doing nothing in my absence. I've made regular visits to this place, and I may have given myself a promotion as a reward."

Birdie stared at Syrus. She had to admit, she hadn't expected he'd accomplished much of anything. Perhaps they would have more of an advantage over Lux Rosa than she'd thought.

Syrus led the way across an ornate bridge, heading towards what Birdie recognized as the central tower of the city.

"There had always been a small faction of Divine interested in finding ways to exploit the systems the Masters built into your world," he stated, "though we did not all share the same goals. For my part, something about the world and the way the Masters managed it always seemed unusual, but such things can't be proven without peaking behind the curtains.

"Before the Masters abandoned Doxla, they made certain to double the protections of their systems so that the lingering Divine could not access them. I believe they even scrambled the components of their systems to this end, making the entire thing a convoluted mess. With your world where and what it is, however, it was only a matter of time before even those protections broke down. Once inside, any sufficiently dedicated Divine would be able to piece everything back together. I believe it was purely a matter of overconfidence that the Masters did not simply destroy your world outright when they were done with it."

"Wha—" Birdie stopped herself. This wasn't what she wanted to discuss, and not just because of the sheer unpleasantness of the topic. "What does this have to do with my othermind?"

Syrus gave her a look that told her he was getting to it, but he paused long enough to open a small gate in their way, motioning Birdie through. Once on the other side, he continued.

"One thing they did little to protect were unused assets. Things they created but never used. Your othermind is the result of combining two such creations. The first of these was an intelligence. I can only guess as to its intended purpose, but I suspect it was meant to be an intelligence belonging to the world itself."

Birdie stared at Syrus. That was insane. "What the hell does that mean? How can they give a world intelligence?"

Syrus smiled. "I do not mean the literal ground that you walk upon or the sky above you. I mean the fabric of your reality would have had an intelligence embedded within it."

Birdie stopped. "That makes even less sense!"

Syrus stopped as well and looked at Birdie, both hands on his rod. "It may seem outlandish, but as one who has worked with the tools used to create such things, I assure you it is more than possible — in some circles even common."

Birdie said nothing. She had no reason not to believe him, no matter how strange it sounded.

Syrus began walking again. Birdie followed.

"Also in the repository of unused assets," he continued, "was information regarding every aspect of your world, or at the very least every aspect of your world as of eighteen years ago, excluding information about Ars Summis. I believe that omission had to do with the fact that the intelligence's influence was supposed to remain outside of this city, though again, that is only speculation. Regardless, the Masters had already done part of the work of connecting the intelligence to said knowledge. With assistance from a few others, I was able to complete the connection, and what you know as your othermind was born."

"And then you connected it to me," Birdie stated, looking straight ahead.

"Yes. Eventually," Syrus answered. He paused before adding. "I do not believe the intelligence was ever truly completed. We tested it before searching for a suitable host to see what it was. From those tests we hypothesized that its primary purpose was to provide a challenge for the most experienced Divine. We thought it perfect for augmenting a protector capable of defeating the Radiants who ruled Doxla at the time."

Birdie stopped again. This conversation had suddenly gotten very uncomfortable.

"Is that why I'm a Divine?" she asked after a moment. "Because of my othermind?"

Syrus hesitated. "No," was all he said.

"Then what makes me a Divine? Why aren't other shades Divine?"

Syrus looked at her with concern. "Are you sure you want the answer to that? You've avoided this conversation for years. I fear you may not like what you hear."

"I have a right to know what I am," Birdie responded, staring him in the eyes. "It was my choice to hide from it in the past; it's my choice to face it now."

"Very well." Syrus took a breath and resumed his walk, Birdie following. "When new Divine first arrive in this world, they are placed in the body of a special variety of shade. These shades are classified as Divine and even have a Divine's Heart. This is what makes a Divine actually a 'Divine,' at least according to the systems of the world. The new Divine use their shade bodies to decide an appearance for themselves, and the bodies are then converted into human ones. The bodies are completely normally completely mindless — meant to be piloted by an outside intelligence — but they always revive immediately after death."

Birdie kept her eyes on Syrus. She had an idea where this was going, but wasn't sure how she felt about it.

"All of those shades were copied from a single entity," Syrus continued, now locking his eyes with Birdie. "That entity is your body. We found a way to disconnect it from the system that allows new Divine in, awoke its suppressed intelligence, and connected it to your othermind. I would say the result is you, but as I've said before, the 'you' that you are now is not the same as your original incarnation."

Birdie stayed silent for a while as she processed everything. Not much of it was new from what Lux Rosa had told her, but hearing it from Syrus —

hearing the actual details — was different. Both her othermind and body were tools created by the Masters — soulless automata, just as Lux had stated. Furthermore, from the sound of it, even what she was now was just a collection of tools put together by Syrus.

Syrus looked at Birdie with concern, but continued walking. "Is that knowledge something you would have preferred not to have?" he eventually asked.

"No," Birdie answered. At the very least, she no longer had to wonder.

A few minutes later, the two of them arrived at a shimmering gate set into a low wall. Syrus set his rod against the wall before placing a hand on an oddly hazy piece of the gate. He paused there for a second, staring at nothing, then reached back to Birdie with his other hand, an equal shimmering haziness now covering it.

"We're almost there. If degradation does upset your othermind's connection, this may be unpleasant for you, but I believe it will prove invaluable for us to continue further. Please take my hand for a moment."

Birdie looked from his hand to the gate and back again before reluctantly obliging. Almost as soon as she came into contact with him, she felt... something. The world did briefly flash white, but it was far from the reaction she'd had to the magic-boosting shimmer.

"There," Syrus said with a smile, "congratulations on your new title, Supreme Lady Eclipse."

Birdie took her hand away and looked at it before looking back at Syrus. "What are you talking about? What did you do?"

"This gate separates the part of the garden that Esteemed Radiants may enter from the part that Exalted Radiants may enter. There will be another gate that only Supreme Radiants may pass through, so I went ahead and just gave you that designation to save ourselves some trouble later."

Birdie flexed her hand a little, surprised that Syrus was able to do such a thing. She then looked him in the eye. Her existential crisis could wait. "Do you think you can give me back my Radiant abilities, too?"

Syrus looked confused. "I beg your pardon?"

Right, she hadn't ever told him about that. Birdie explained Lux's ability to reset her foes' strength to zero, as well as how she'd regained some through touching the shimmer.

"I see," he stated, appearing deep in thought. "She really has been busy."

"Can you fix it?" Birdie asked.

Syrus shook his head sadly. "Unfortunately, I know nothing about that. There are likely several ways to do what she did, and each would require its own remedy. Even if I knew how she did it, it would take time to figure out a safe way to reverse it. That said, I may have an alternative to restoration for you."

Birdie raised her eyebrow. "Is it a way to depower Lux Rosa?"

Syrus shook his head as he led the way through the gate. "Not exactly. She has used the tools of the Masters against you. I think it only fitting that you reciprocate in kind."

Syrus now had Birdie's curiosity, but after twice avoiding telling her directly what he had planned, she knew he had no intention of spoiling whatever surprise he had waiting. Instead, she contented herself with taking in the sights and sounds of the Radiant Gardens. If there was any good place to learn that she was essentially an amalgamation of toys created by the beings she despised the most, a garden attesting to the capacity of the Masters to produce beautiful things as well was likely it. The area beyond the gate was even more extravagant than that which came before. As impressive as the sculptures and fountains may have been, though, Birdie found herself preferring the more natural look of the former area. Nonetheless, the trickling water and tweeting birds helped to calm her mind.

As they approached the base of the central tower, Birdie felt the need to ask about one final matter.

"There's one more thing that's bothering me," she stated, figuring she may as well get it over with. "Lux Rosa told me that I'm essentially an automaton. From what you told me, it sounds like that's true."

"Can you think for yourself?" Syrus asked flatly.

Birdie blinked. "Of course I can, but—"

"But nothing," Syrus interrupted, frowning at her for the first time since arriving. "If you can think for yourself, you are not an automaton. You made the decision to help me defeat Grandis. You made the decision to protect this world."

"But you *made* me to do that," Birdie argued. "How can I know I actually made those choices?"

"Five years ago, when I found you traveling with Jax, Ev, and that Gare fellow, what were you planning on doing with your Heart?" Syrus asked.

"I... I hadn't decided yet," Birdie answered honestly after taking a second to remember.

"So, would you say there was a real possibility that you would have handed it over to Grandis had I not accosted you?"

Birdie bristled at the suggestion, but she could see what Syrus was leading her towards.

"Fine, so maybe I have a degree of autonomy, but how do I know my actions aren't influenced by something you did to me?"

"I do not have the power to force mindsets into individuals through any means other than actions and words. The fact that you so oppose the responsibilities I have placed upon you should attest to that. Even if I did have such power, ask yourself: are you happy with the choices you have made in your life?"

Birdie paused. She supposed she was, more or less. Sure, she'd made mistakes she wasn't proud of, but those were poor choices she hoped not to repeat.

She sighed. "Let's just get this over with," but glancing sideways she added quietly, "thanks."

Syrus nodded, then led the way to a pair of large, stained glass doors at the base of the tower.

"Beyond these doors is the Supremacy Plaza. Only Supreme Radiants may pass through them. I warn you now: What you will see on the other side is nothing like anything you will find anywhere else in Doxla."

"I could say the same about the rest of this city," Birdie said as she looked back over her shoulder the way they'd come.

Syrus smirked, then stepped forward, prompting the doors to slide open. "Then let us proceed. We are very near our destination."

* * * *

Inside the enormous circular room, Birdie couldn't see anything that stood out to her as stranger than what she'd already seen. Though the decorations were fancy — glass tables, exquisite seating ranging from leather to fur to metal, great chandeliers — it all seemed like the logical next step up from the outer buildings.

"Here it is," Syrus said, waving his hand over the scene before them, "hypocrisy at its finest, or perhaps stupidity would be a more accurate term."

Birdie simply raised an eyebrow at him.

Syrus strolled over to one of the tables. "Look at this," he said in disgust.

Birdie walked over to see a number of shapes and words appear in the glass of the tabletop. Syrus tapped a few of them and a drink materialized atop the table.

"What the—? How did you do that?" Birdie asked.

Syrus took the drink and threw it to the floor, shattering the glass holding it. A fire elemental appeared immediately from the floor and cleaned the mess with its flames before disappearing just as quickly.

"Do you know why the Divine stopped coming to your world?" Syrus asked.

He tapped on the table further, and a ghostly miniature version of Roehelm's citadel formed above its surface.

"Because of this," Syrus answered himself. "Because of this and because people started to catch on to what the Masters had actually done with this place."

He turned to Birdie, who was surprised to realize she was intrigued. "The appeal of your world was that it was an escape from the technological utopia most of us live in. It was filled with its own variety of magic, danger, excitement, beautiful and exotic landscapes. It was a simpler world with simpler problems. It gave us a chance to actually live out the role of hero; it let us live lives most of would never be able to in our own worlds.

"Yes, we had... other options, but your world is one of the few with actual inhabitants that we could engage with. We thought it a brilliantly crafted system — something truly special."

Syrus slammed his fist onto the table, cracking it briefly before the cracks repaired themselves.

"I'm ashamed to say how long it took me to suspect the degree to which your world had been abused. Even though such thoughts had long been whispered before I ever came here, I was like so many before me, refusing to believe that seitti would mutate the very people they were responsible for, all for the sake of stirring a centuries-long conflict to keep other Divine engaged.

"When Divine began leaving in protest, the Masters' response was to make things more 'convenient.' The teleporters you saw, the automated doors, all of *this*," Syrus waved to the room again, "they thought that bringing in tidbits of the technology we sought escape from would entice us to stay. If anything, it drove us away faster. Only the most conceited individuals approved — those who thrived on praise from their status as a Divine and cared little about actually helping. For them, these conveniences were an improvement. Soon, only those selfish Divine remained. They, and the stubborn few of us who thought we could actually make a difference for the people trapped in this now obviously dying world."

Birdie crossed her arms, a scowl on her face as she cocked a sideways glance at Syrus. "I guess they weren't all that stubborn, then, seeing as how you're the only one left."

Syrus shook his head. "We concluded Doxla had and still has little chance of survival. We believe it was created in a place where sapient life isn't meant to be housed. Worlds there are temporary by nature. We thought that maybe if we could drive the other Divine from your world, a few of us could stay behind and take away the Masters' control, giving it to a suitable inhabitant to wield. It would have given you a chance, however small, but when Grandis defeated your previous incarnation, you weren't the only one to fall.

"Grandis and his allies defeated all of my brothers and sisters-in-arms and guarded our Hearts so we couldn't reclaim our power. At that point we knew that our only chance was if he let his guard down, so we agreed that all but one of us would abandon the world in the hopes that his allies would do the same. His goal was only to hasten Doxla's demise, after all, and I still believe many of those with him only saw our war as a challenge to overcome and cared not for the fate of the world. We took that away from them. Whether the result of our ploy or not, in the end Lady Escalor was the only one who stayed by Grandis's side. I believe you are familiar with how that concluded."

Birdie stopped to process all that. Though it wasn't her concern, she supposed it was interesting how their current situation came to be. That didn't answer one thing that did bother her, however.

"Where does Lux Rosa fit into all of this?" she asked.

Syrus shook his head, clearly bothered. "All I know is what I already told you. She joined us briefly in our initial purge of the other Divine, then disappeared. Whether she had always intended to seek the Masters' power for herself or not, I can only assume that she lingered to witness the outcome of my conflict with Grandis, and that when you and I emerged victorious, she saw the resulting power vacuum as an opportunity to achieve her goals."

"Which are?" Birdie asked. "If Doxla is just a toy to Divine, what would she want with control over it?"

"She likely seeks to take credit for saving it from destruction and exposing the Masters. A seitti could benefit tremendously from such a deed, regardless of their methods of achieving it."

"Is that why you're helping us?" Birdie asked.

Syrus smirked. "As I'm not a seitti, the only benefits I would receive are a pat on the back and possibly material compensation for the effort I've expended. If I had worked on my own, I may have been eligible to be transformed into a seitti myself, but I have admittedly relied on a great deal of consulting to do as much as I already have."

He shook his head, smiling. "No, I'm afraid my reason is simply that I can't stand to see seitti power abused in this way. That, and perhaps the thought of a prifae bringing justice to crooked seitti is something that tickles my ambitions."

Birdie cocked her head. When she'd arrived at Ars Summis, she still held a grudge against Syrus for how much he'd put on her after she defeated Grandis. Now, she realized perhaps her anger had been misguided.

"Okay," she said, looking around. "So, what are we looking for here that will help us bring our current problem seitti to justice?"

Syrus smiled and pointed with his rod to a very large pillar in the center of the room. "That is called an elevator. At the top are the private chambers of the Masters themselves. I found a way to bypass their protections not even a week ago. There is something there that we will need to combat Lux Rosa. There is also something I found that might compensate for your loss of strength substantially."

Birdie perked up at that. She was more than ready to get back what Lux Rosa had stolen from her. She cocked her head.

"Well, what are we waiting for? Lead the way."

Syrus escorted her to the central pillar and pressed a small square on the wall. The wall immediately opened up, revealing an empty yet well-lit room. Once the two of them had stepped inside, Syrus pressed another square, and the walls closed once again. Birdie steadied herself as she felt the floor suddenly lift upwards. After about thirty seconds, the floor halted, the doors opened, and she and Syrus stepped out into a new area.

This new room was smaller than the one below, but still substantial in size. Like the one on the ground, this one appeared to be meant for congregation. Tables and chairs decorated the floor along with other furnishings all in the same style as where they'd just arrived from. The only thing that stood out about this room was the curved, upward-sloping glass wall surrounding it, which allowed her to see out across the entire city in all directions.

"Is this really the Masters' chamber?" Birdie asked, admittedly expecting something more.

"Not quite," Syrus answered, and Birdie turned to look at him, waiting for an explanation. "I'm afraid I haven't figured out how to get the elevator to take me all the way there, but I have discovered other means of breaching their quarters."

"Is that so?" Birdie asked, crossing her arms again. "What are you going to do? Pick a lock?"

"Something like that," Syrus replied before motioning for her to follow him. "Before that, however, let's take care of your weakness issue."

Intrigued, Birdie followed Syrus to a decorative suit of elaborate pearly armor propped against the wall and holding a glowing sword. She noticed there were other suits of different designs on display as well.

Syrus gestured to the armor. "This is a reproduction of Sylvra's armor. All of these outfits were exclusive to the Masters, as were the accompanying weapons."

Birdie raised an eyebrow. "And? How does this help me?"

Syrus placed his hands on his rod and smiled. "Though these armors may be replicas, they are part of the decorations of the Supremacy Plaza. They have massive durability and magic resistance and instantly repair themselves when damaged."

Birdie took another look at the armor. It was certainly not her style, but it did sound potentially useful.

She gave a quick smirk. "So, you're suggesting we steal this, then."

"That's exactly what I'm suggesting, or rather that you steal whichever suit you think would be most comfortable. They lack traditional enchantments and likely can't be imbued with them, but I believe their existing features would put them a level above even Radiant class armor."

Birdie had to admit she was impressed. That did still leave her with the issue of offense, however.

"What about the weapons?" she asked.

Syrus shook his head. "They are the same as the armor, but in my opinion the inability to enchant them would render them less effective than other options overall."

Birdie considered that for a moment and decided she agreed with Syrus. "Alright, then, which one will you get?"

"Me?" Syrus chuckled. "I will not take any. This avatar cannot leave Ars Summis, as I mentioned. Besides, you have the ability to disguise what you wear. I do not. We would not want Lux Rosa to learn that I have breached the innermost protections of Ars Summis until we actually confront her, lest she attempt to do the same. We still must prepare our forces and take them to her, which could take weeks. It would be more than enough time for her to succeed, and we would risk her gaining even more control than she already has.”

Birdie shrugged, then strolled around the central pillar until she found a suit of armor that she liked.

The one she selected held a bit less flair than the others, with few pointy bits and a much tighter frame, but most importantly it looked a good fit for her preferred figure. The only part that stuck out a bit was the helmet, which was decorated with a sort of crown over the brow. The whole thing shone with a silvery purplish tint, but that would be easy for her to hide.

“This one,” she said, standing before it.

Syrus looked it over. “Amethine’s armor. Good choice.” He then walked away.

“Where are you going?” she asked, but decided it didn’t matter.

She reached for the armor but discovered she literally couldn’t touch it. Some sort of barrier was in the way.

“What is this?”

“Step aside, please,” Syrus stated, having already returned with a swirling shimmer in his hand.

Birdie quickly stepped back, eyeing the shimmer with caution. “Where do you keep getting that?”

“Ars Summis is full of locations where degradation is likely to occur. The edge of the Masters’ chambers is particularly prone to the phenomenon,” he stated, and moved closer to the armor.

Syrus squeezed the shimmer and — Birdie wasn’t sure what he was doing. His eyes practically glazed over as he stared at nothing for a few seconds. After a moment, his eyes regained focus as he lifted his other hand and reached through the invisible barrier. He grabbed the armor and pulled the whole thing down onto the floor with a loud crash.

“There we go. Would you care to try it on? If not, we can pick it up on our way back down.”

“Back down from where?”

Syrus pointed upwards. “From the Masters’ chambers, of course. We still need to find out where Lux Rosa is, and I think I might know how to do that.”

“Actually,” said Birdie, “I think I might already know that.”

"Oh?"

"Her soldiers said new recruits go to the Hall of Champions. I would assume she must be somewhere near there."

"That seems probable," Syrus responded. "Still, it would be good to confirm your suspicion, and there is something we need up there, regardless. Help me move some tables, please."

Grabbing one of the nearby tables, Syrus dragged it over towards the window-wall, still carrying his ball of shimmer.

Birdie didn't question it. She grabbed another table, and together the two of them put together a small pyramid that let Syrus easily reach the ceiling.

Once up there, he squeezed his shimmer and entered that hazy-eyed state before dragging his finger in a wide circle across the ceiling, leaving a brief trail of iridescence behind his touch. The circle complete, Syrus struck the ceiling with his fist, cracking the ceiling where he'd drawn the circle. He pushed the slab he'd knocked loose up and onto the floor above, then climbed up himself, beckoning for Birdie to follow.

The room above looked identical to the one below, save for the decorations. Only a handful of seats and tables were present, with most of the decoration being paintings and sculptures of what, judging by the armor they wore, must have been the Masters. A few strange artifacts were also on display, though Birdie had no idea what they were.

Syrus gave Birdie no time to look around, however, as he had already begun piling up another pyramid of tables, this time close to the elevator.

"Again?" Birdie asked.

"As far as I can tell, these upper rooms are meant for Divine to meet with the Masters, though they may have been a meeting place exclusive to the Masters themselves. What we want is one more floor up. Not even the elevator could take us there."

Once again, Birdie helped Syrus stack his tables. Once finished, Syrus made another circle and punched another hole. The two of them climbed through, and Birdie found herself in a room she truly felt didn't belong in Doxla.

"What is this place?" she asked, almost in disbelief of what her own eyes were showing her.

The room had no visible walls or ceiling, instead showing a vast expanse of glowing orange clouds as far as she could see. Above her was an evening sky, pink on one extreme and dark on the other. In the center of the room hovered a giant rippling ball of degradation — presumably Syrus was responsible for it being there. The floor was constructed of a rough greenish metal that glinted in the light, and all around her were strange, circular desks with rings of glass along their edges. Countless strange symbols shone from within the glass along with a few images, one of which she recognized as a map of Doxla. Syrus walked over to the image of the map and vaulted over the desk, passing right on through the glass as if it wasn't there. He then turned and began pressing symbols on the clearly solid glass, speaking to her as he did so.

"I suppose if there is one benefit to the illicit behavior of the Masters, it is that it forced them to keep their control center within Doxla itself," he said. "If it wasn't for that, we would have had no way to take control, and you would be stuck with all of the problems they left with you forever."

"You know I have no idea what you're talking about, right?" Birdie stated, still in awe but getting frustrated at Syrus's constant references to things outside her knowledge.

Syrus elaborated. "Very few seitti directly wield their true capabilities. Controlling such power with the mind alone is more error prone and dangerous than tying said abilities to machines which must be interacted with physically. The Masters created your world in a place that is against seitti law to produce sapient life, so to hide their activities they put their machines within your world. If they tried using their abilities outside of it, their actions would have been immediately obvious, and they would have been stopped long ago. Ah, there we are."

Syrus smiled and pointed at a section of the map. Birdie walked over to view it from his side and saw that he was pointing at a place far to the east of Ars Summis — the Hall of Champions and Colosseum.

"What's all that around it?" she asked, noticing a number of overlapping symbols on the map.

"I did a search for detected points of degradation. The only way to get into the Masters' systems is either through these machines or by entering in through where the world has started to break down. As you can see, the amount of degradation here is far greater than anywhere else," he frowned. "Too much, actually. I know it's possible to move degradation, but that wouldn't explain this. Lux Rosa must have found some way to exacerbate the world's decay. Regardless, I can guarantee that your hunch was correct and that she is indeed operating from there."

"But you can enter the systems, here, right?" Birdie asked. "You can stop her!"

Syrus sighed and dropped his shoulders, and Birdie's heart sank. "I'm afraid not. Different Masters had different degrees of control over the world. The only thing that all of them were allowed to do is monitor it, meaning that is the only operation these consoles provide freely. I have yet to figure out how to trick their systems into thinking I'm any specific one of them, and until I do, my only means of altering their systems is via degradation."

"Then use it!" Birdie yelled. "We have to stop her now!"

"Degradation only lets you enter specific places of their systems. It's an absolute labyrinth in there, and trying to change something without understanding it could literally destroy all of Doxla."

Birdie clenched her fists as Syrus continued.

"I will do what I can with the degradation, but I do believe our best chance of defeating her is to do just that — in battle. We must split her primary avatar and prevent her from using the degradation she's already amassed. That will slow her down and hopefully buy me enough time to take full control of the world before she does. I would also be able to seize her own collection of degradation to see what she may have found that I haven't. If we are lucky, I can find a way to rid her from the world entirely in the process, but without knowing her true name that will be impossible."

So that was why Lux wanted Syrus's name. Birdie sighed and shifted her eyes away from Syrus. She didn't like it, but she didn't see any other options. She looked back at Syrus.

"I don't suppose you have a plan for how to do that, do you?"

"I'll return to Roehelm and rally the Shadow Guard. You need to convince Dezeroth to lend us his forces. The two of us will then meet up here, by Lake Tardele." Syrus pointed to a location about four days' ride from the Colosseum. "I'll do what I can to try and match the magic enhancements you mentioned, but to do that, you'll need to do something that may be a bit unpleasant."

Birdie braced herself. "And what's that?"

Syrus held out his bit of shimmering degradation to her. "I'm going to need to give you the ability to carry this. I will look through my collection to find a few more good pieces for you to take as well, and if you happen to see any on your way out of Ars Summis, please collect them."

"Oh, no," Birdie replied, holding her hand up. "I'm not touching that thing. I'm not risking losing my othermind, not if I'm going to have to face Lux Rosa."

Syrus shook his head. "The only way to truly disconnect from your othermind would be to immerse yourself fully within it. You could actually store this inside of you, and at worst it might inhibit your ability to communicate with your othermind. I assure you it will not leave you."

"There's no way you're putting that inside of me!" Birdie scowled.

"Then carry it," Syrus stated sharply, "but unless you deliver this to my primary avatar, it will be impossible for me to give our forces any of the kinds of enhancements that Lux Rosa's soldiers will have."

Birdie grimaced. She really, really didn't like the idea, but she knew that Syrus was right.

"Fine," she stated reluctantly, "but if anything happens to my othermind, I'm blaming you."

"Fair enough," Syrus replied.

He climbed back over the desk and reached into his large ball of degradation in the center of the room. After pulling out and combining a few bits of it with the piece already in his hand, he approached Birdie and placed a hand on her shoulder. He squeezed the shimmer, and a few seconds later, Birdie felt the same sensation she'd felt when he'd made her a Supreme Radiant.

"There," he stated. "You can now carry degradation. It's not exactly a spell in the usual sense, but it can be thought of as one. It works the same way as levitation. As long as you help it recognize the spell as such, your othermind should be able to use this ability without difficulty."

Birdie slowly reached out to the swirling shimmer and let the magic of her new spell flow through her. The degradation quickly moved towards her hand, stopping a few inches above her open palm. She sighed in relief when it didn't have any noticeable effect on her or her othermind.

"Right then," Syrus said. "Let's gather up a little bit more degradation and put that armor on you. While we work, I'd like you to tell me a bit more regarding what you know about Lux Rosa's accomplishments. Once we are through, you can be on your way, and I will send word to Roehelm. I will then gather up as much degradation in this city as possible and bring it to these chambers. Hopefully it will be out of reach of Lux Rosa should she come here. We will meet at Lake Tardele in twenty-two days. We will attack five days after that. When you leave from here, be sure not to use any teleporters on your way out. The degradation won't travel with you."

Birdie nodded. As much as she'd hoped Syrus would have been able to do more, she supposed she'd known all along things wouldn't be that easy. At least now they had a plan. Hopefully, a way to even the battlefield, as well.

Chapter 18

Dawn had long since arrived by the time Birdie made her way back to the wall of Ars Summis. The lights Lux had placed had fortunately somewhat dimmed, making it safe for her stand atop the wall, so she took a moment to survey her surroundings. She saw no sign of her companions — only the destroyed landscape from last night's skirmish. Prior to them splitting up, she'd told the others not to wait for her, but that was before the guardian had decimated the loyalist patrols. Seeing no sign of Lux Rosa's forces, she called out to the woods, just in case the others had stayed after all.

Several moments passed in silence. Birdie couldn't say she was surprised, though she was a tad disappointed. She started the long trek across the wall down to the nearest gate. Hopefully none of the loyalists were left, because even with her new armor, she wasn't in much condition to fight them. Her body had healed significantly overnight, but it was still not exactly in top condition. She barely made it thirty feet, however, before relief hit her as she sensed familiar magic.

Birdie quickly turned to look back at the forest and waited as the sensed magic drew nearer. Before long, Ev, Tallis, Helcant and Nephira all stepped out to meet her, and according to her senses even Umber had survived, though he understandably opted to stay in the woods away from the still decently bright lights around the city's perimeter.

Birdie smiled wide as Ev spotted her and gave a wave. Birdie returned the gesture.

Ev and Tallis ran toward the ravine with Helcant close behind and Nephira casually taking up the rear.

"Did you talk to him?" Tallis yelled. "Did we win?"

Tallis's eagerness was a welcome return to normalcy after the uncomfortable experience that was Ars Summis. Birdie subtly shook her head, but kept her smile.

"I'm afraid we still have some work to do," she called back, "but at least now we have a chance."

She held out the piece of degradation for them all to see.

Helcant jumped forward. "Yes! At last, my fire shall humble Radiants!"

"This thing won't do anything yet," Birdie called to him, the disappointment on his face immediate. "We need to take it to Syrus at Lake Tardele. He said he'll use it to help us there."

"Lake Tardele?" Tallis repeated. "Where's that?"

"It is far to the east, near the Divine Colosseum," Birdie answered. "He will meet us there with the Shadow Guard, and we need to convince Dezeroth to send his forces with us."

Ev stepped forward. "Wait, does that mean…?"

Birdie cocked her head and grinned. "We know for sure where Lux Rosa is. I say it's about time we brought this fight to her, wouldn't you agree?"

Ev, Tallis, and Helcant all signaled agreement, a fire rekindled within them. Ev was slightly less enthusiastic than the others, but Birdie assumed that was because they were about to have to deal with Dezeroth in person.

"Good. In that case, Tallis? Would you mind making a bridge for me, please?"

Tallis's eagerness faded as he looked at the ravine then back to Birdie. "Um, are you sure we should risk waking the guardian up again?"

Nephira stepped forward. "The Grandis scum have all died or fled. There is no benefit to crossing here."

Ev pointed far to her left. "We'll meet you at the gate, okay? We can travel faster by road, anyway."

Birdie nodded. If the loyalists really were gone, then the gate was definitely the best way to go.

She started along the wall once more, but stopped as she noticed a faint glimmer disrupting the barrier. On closer inspection, she spotted quite a few of them scattered about, extending as far as she could see. Remembering what Syrus had told her, she went ahead and used her new spell to add the ones within her reach to her ball of degradation. How Syrus would benefit from having more of it, she didn't know, but if he said it would help, then he'd get as much of it as she could gather on her way.

Once Birdie had reached the gate and climbed down, Ev promptly went to work healing her.

"I'm glad to see you're okay," Birdie said. "When I heard them attacking you, I couldn't help but fear the worst."

Ev tried to shrug off the comment. "We had things under control. Umber led them away and hid in a rabbit hole he found."

Birdie could tell Ev wasn't sharing the whole story, but she wasn't going to press it. They were safe, and that was what mattered.

"There you go," Ev said when she was done. "I can't believe you're still hurt after a whole night. Are you sure you're okay?"

This time Birdie shrugged it off. "It wasn't pleasant, but I've had worse. I was a bit too distracted by other things to really notice."

Tallis nearly pounced on her. "You *have* to tell us what you saw in there! What was it like?"

Ev pushed him back a bit. "I think we should hear what happened first." She turned back to Birdie. "Nice armor, by the way."

"Thanks," Birdie smirked. "I stole it from the Masters' chambers."

"What?" most of them shouted in unison. Even Nephira opened her eyes wide in shock.

That was exactly the response Birdie had hoped for. She laughed for the first time in a while. Her fun done, however, she figured it best to disguise her armor as nothing extraordinary and expanded her illusion to encompass it.

"I'll tell you about it on the way," she said. "I think it's about time we paid Dezeroth a little visit."

* * * *

It was several hours past noon by the time the party made it back to where they'd left their horses. Fortunately, all of their mounts were still in one piece, having been left alone by the wildlife.

The group untied their rides and made their way back to Bailey Town to rest the night and restock on supplies. While there, Birdie found a metal pot she could hang by her hip and hide Syrus's degradation within. She still had to use his spell to move it, but her othermind was more than capable of having it follow the pot's movements exactly. After that, it was a three day journey northwest to the city of Greater Ascension, renamed from simply Ascension after its conquest. Greater Ascension was the location of what was formerly the citadel of Grandis himself. The citadel now served as Dezeroth's castle, and the city his proclamation of superiority to the world. Ev grew ever quieter as they drew nearer. Birdie supposed she couldn't blame her. Even if what Dezeroth had done to her father and hometown had been for a righteous cause, the Undead King had never once shown remorse for it, nor had he made any effort to curtail his murderous habits since.

Upon arrival at the city gate, a pair of revenants pointed their spears at the group.

"Halt!" they shouted. "No humans may enter this city."

Birdie directed her horse forward and stood tall upon its stirrups. "My Shadow Guard is allowed entrance to any part of King Dezeroth's domain," she announced, revealing her crystalline Radiant wings. "Step aside."

The two guards glanced nervously at one another, but ultimately retracted their spears and returned to their posts.

Birdie put away her wings and kept her eyes forward as she led the way into the city. The sight of a bunch of humans garnered a number of stares from the locals — a far more motley bunch than even Bailey Town possessed — but none caused any issues.

Birdie couldn't help but notice that Dezeroth had certainly been busy redecorating since her last visit here nearly a year ago. Most of the reconstruction was now complete, with the former statues of Grandis replaced with those of the Undead King, and any other depiction of Divine of any sort replaced with figures from the various immortal races.

"Are you okay, Ev?" Birdie asked quietly as they rode through the city.

"Let's just get this over with," Ev answered. "I'll be okay once we're gone."

Birdie didn't press it further. She knew it wouldn't help.

Eventually, they reached the citadel proper, where they were greeted by Dezeroth's chancellor, Zun-Roven, presumably having already been informed of their arrival by Dezeroth's "secret" enforcers.

"Ah, Lady Birdie, what a pleasant surprise," the plump, bespectacled revenant opened his arms wide in greeting. "I do wish you had sent word of your arrival, however. I'm afraid His Majesty is not accepting visitors at the moment."

Birdie dismounted from her horse and approached Zun-Roven. "Well, I'm sorry to disturb 'His Majesty,' but we're at war with a new Radiant, and thanks to him ignoring the message of my friend here," she gestured to Umber, "we nearly lost that war four days ago."

Zun-Roven appeared bothered by that statement. "I'm sorry we were unable to assist you, but we have our own war to contend with. Our forces are being pressed by human retaliation both to the north and the south. His Majesty deemed it unwise to divert our defenses without proof of the threat your messenger claimed."

Birdie crossed her arms. She liked Zun-Roven, but right now, he was the voice of Dezeroth, and she couldn't help but take out some of her frustration on him.

"You want proof?" she replied. "How's this for proof? Tallis, make a mountain. Right here in the courtyard."

Tallis all too eagerly pointed his palm at the stone tiles to his right. With a burst of magic, a hundred foot spire of earth exploded upwards, startling the horses and leaving Zun-Roven speechless.

Birdie tilted her head. "The Radiant called Lux Rosa has found a way to grant any nepac the magical abilities of a Radiant. What you saw there is the result of us stealing one of her so-called 'blessings' and using it on ourselves. Her entire army wields that kind of power, and we need Dezeroth's support if we are to face it."

Zun-Roven adjusted his glasses. "Yes, I can see how this might be a serious issue. I shall inform His Majesty of your arrival right away."

"Good. Thank you," Birdie replied, arms still crossed.

As Zun-Roven walked away, she sighed. Why couldn't he have stayed in charge? The year following Grandis's defeat had been a pleasant one, with Zun-Roven ruling in Dezeroth's stead while the latter awaited resurrection. The chancellor, though surprisingly fierce when angered, had never once attempted to deceive Birdie or Syrus, nor had he tried to push past the boundaries of the treaties made between them. Dezeroth was a megalomaniacal brute who had done all of those things, and the fact that he was responsible for killing Ev's father, who admittedly had been a soldier of Grandis, did nothing to lessen Birdie's utter disdain for the man.

After a few minutes, Zun-Roven returned. "King Dezeroth has agreed to see you. Allow me to escort you to him."

"Thank you," Birdie replied, walking up to him. She briefly turned back to the others. "You all wait here. I shouldn't be long. Tallis, please put that back where you found it," she said, referring to the makeshift mountain.

As Zun-Roven led her between the great stone columns — their original angelic ornamentation long since replaced with busts of seductive demons — he spoke quietly to Birdie. "I must warn you, His Majesty has been in an odd mood since your messenger's arrival. I would strongly advise you not to provoke him."

"I'll try to keep that in mind. That necromantic magic you sent me proved very useful, by the way."

"I am pleased— I mean, His Majesty will be pleased to hear that his gift aided you."

Birdie suppressed a cynical smirk. They both knew Dezeroth had nothing to do with the gift, nor would he have cared.

A pair of guards opened the heavy gilded doors that led into Dezeroth's throne room. Inside, the dark lord himself sat atop a throne of skulls, itself built upon the melted-down remnants of Grandis's old throne. Dezeroth leered at Birdie as he swirled a goblet of wine, his glowing eyes a brilliant orange against the backdrop of his stone gray face.

Zun-Roven bowed as he entered, then turned to leave just as quickly. The doors shut behind him, leaving Birdie alone with Dezeroth.

"I've been expecting you, Eclipse," Dezeroth's gravelly voice echoed across the chamber.

"Funny. I was expecting you at Ars Summis," Birdie replied, disregarding Zun-Roven's warning.

To her surprise, Dezeroth stood and approached her, leaving his wine on his throne's armrest.

"Let us dispense with meaningless prattle. You claim that a new Radiant has appeared — a Radiant named Lux Rosa, according to your messenger. Tell me, what do you know of her, aside from her proficiency at granting magic?"

"I know that she wants control of the world," Birdie replied, standing tall as Dezeroth drew near. "I know that she seeks the power of the Masters, and I know that she wants to purge immortals from Doxla."

"Do you now?" Dezeroth asked almost mockingly. "Tell me this, then. Aside from your claim about immortals, how is this Radiant any different from Syrus?"

"Didn't you hear me? She wants to erase immortals! That includes you," Birdie pointed straight at his chest.

"Answer my question," Dezeroth growled. "What makes her ambitions any different than Syrus's?"

"Because she's doing it for herself!" Birdie exclaimed. "She doesn't care about the people of this world, she only cares about improving her own status!"

Dezeroth laughed derisively. "What difference does that make? If she saves our world from destruction or if Syrus does, how does that affect any of us? Either way, we survive."

Something about Dezeroth's words cut through Birdie's fury. His nonchalance, his immediate line of questions, his responses — something was very wrong.

Birdie had to resist the urge to take a step back, but she did narrow her eyes. "You sound like you've been thinking a lot about something you didn't believe only a few days ago."

"I must always consider what is best for my kingdom, for the future of my empire," he replied. "You claim that Lux Rosa desires to erase immortals from the world, yet offer no evidence of such a claim. Why should I risk my army in a war between Divine when its outcome has no effect on me?"

"She told me herself she wants to get rid of immortals! What more 'evidence' do you need?"

"Is that really what she said?" Dezeroth asked, taking another step forward. "What were her exact words? Try to remember."

The urge to retreat grew stronger, but Birdie refused to show her discomfort.

"She said," Birdie paused as she recollected what Lux Rosa had said in Cray's body, "she said she would make the problem of immortals disappear."

"How intriguing," mused Dezeroth, stroking the beard on his chin. "That sounds very different from your former claim. I can certainly think of other ways to fix the 'problem of immortals' that don't involve erasing them."

He sneered down at Birdie. "But you are clever aren't you? I'm sure you must have also considered such possibilities. It sounds to me like you simply want to use my soldiers for your war and wish to spin the situation in an attempt to convince me to aid you."

"I don't know what you think you know, but her soldiers are Grandis loyalists. They hate immortals! She's using that hatred to control them, I know it!"

"Exactly," Dezeroth stated. "She is using them. That is all."

If Birdie had been human, her face would have gone white. "What—?"

"What would be more valuable to a Divine trying to claim they saved a world?" Dezeroth asked, turning away from her and raising first his right hand, then his left. "The fifty million who would be left if all that the Grandis loyalists despise were slaughtered, or the hundred million who would remain if the loyalists were discarded once done with them?"

"You— you're working with her," Birdie practically spit, glaring at him.

Dezeroth spun back around. "I have been promised freedom from the Masters' corruption if I but convince you that defying her is folly. Consider for a moment all that you stand to lose, for I assure you, you cannot win."

He took another step forward, and this time Birdie did step back.

Dezeroth extended his hand to her. "Give her Syrus's true name, and all of the bloodshed will cease."

"Never!" Birdie swung her arm defiantly.

Dezeroth lowered his hand. "What folly. You still insist on confronting her. You have no hope of victory."

Birdie stood tall again, knowing full well what would come next. "We will stop her, with or without you."

Dezeroth grunted, then stepped back, placing a hand on the hilt of his blade. "You fool. She has power over the very magic that lets beings such as us live. She can end your life with merely a thought. Permanently."

"That's odd. I still feel pretty alive," Birdie remarked, reaching for her daggers as well. She knew she stood little chance of even escaping Dezeroth with her current strength, but little chance was a far cry from no chance.

Dezeroth drew his twisted black blade, eyes glowing like fire. "I will not allow you to jeopardize my empire for your petty sense of justice."

"If justice is petty, then what word describes betraying the world all for a decent face in the mirror?"

Moving like lighting, Dezeroth lunged forward as he swung his sword in a wide arc Birdie just managed to avoid. Before she could regain her footing, he spun around and connected squarely in her chest, striking with enough force to send her halfway across the room.

Thankfully, Syrus had been right about the armor. It had barely even dented, and she could feel it repairing itself already.

Dezeroth's expression showed he'd clearly not expected her to shrug off such a hit.

Birdie decided to take advantage of the moment. With a wave of her hand, she flooded the entire room with illusory darkness.

The illusion only lasted a few seconds before Dezeroth dispelled it with his own magic, but it was enough time for her to reach the door.

Prying the door open, Birdie slipped halfway through before an overwhelming wave of darkness blasted apart the doors and sent her flying.

Birdie cursed as she hit the ground. She couldn't believe she'd missed the subtle scent of Lux Rosa's blessing underneath Dezeroth's corrupt magic. Pushing herself up, she didn't bother looking back. She sensed him coming for her, so she did the only sensible thing she could do.

She ran.

Approaching the courtyard, Birdie shouted to the others. "Mount your horses! We have to go, now!"

She was frustrated to see them all just stand there in confusion. "Didn't you hear me, we have to—"

Birdie was cut off as another wave of darkness tossed her clear from the building, ripping apart the very ground around her.

"Birdie!" Ev yelled, running forward, but she froze when she saw Dezeroth.

A rage boiled up in Ev that Birdie hadn't seen in all the time she'd known her.

"You! What's wrong with you!" Ev screamed, pointing her rod at Dezeroth.

Birdie jumped back up between Ev and the Undead King. Despite the force of Dezeroth's blows, her armor had done its job.

"Ev, run, I'll handle this buffoon," she ordered.

Tallis jumped forward. "No way! No offense, but you can't take him on your own."

"Enough!" Nephira shouted. "Just what the hell is going on?"

"Dezeroth is working for Lux Rosa!" Birdie accused, drawing her magic drain dagger.

"Are you serious?" Ev's voice nearly cracked. "You treacherous slime! After everything we've done for you!"

Dezeroth swung his sword, sending a wave of dark magic over all of them. "Your quarrel with that Radiant is a threat to our existence. She has control over all magic. If we defy her, she will erase necromantic magic. She will erase elemental magic. All undead and all elementals will perish in an instant. I have allied myself with Lux Rosa in exchange for freedom from the corruption the Masters cursed us with. All corrupted immortals will regain their human form while retaining their immortality. All I need from you is Syrus's name, and all of you may go free. Refuse, and none of you leave here alive."

Dezeroth signaled with his free hand, and two dozen soldiers poured from the shadows, surrounding them.

Birdie clasped her dagger tightly, her othermind racing to think of a way out of this, but not even it could see a path to victory.

"Just tell him the damn name," Nephira shouted from behind.

Birdie spun on her. "I can't! If Lux Rosa knows his name, she'll banish him from Doxla forever!"

Nephira spit, grabbed her spear, and took up a position next to Ev. "I guess

I have no choice, then."

Helcant skittered forward a few steps. "This is—"

He was interrupted as Nephira dropped her spear and latched on to Ev, one arm tight around her neck and the other ready to snap it.

"Have you gone mad?" Helcant shouted.

"Say the name!" Nephira yelled, her grip tightening as Ev struggled. "I know you care about this one. Say it or watch her die!"

Birdie's eyes darted from Ev to Nephira to Dezeroth. She couldn't believe this was happening. She couldn't betray Syrus, but she couldn't let Ev die, either. "Nephira, don't—"

"King Dezeroth has told us we cannot win. I will not die in a hopeless battle, not when the alternative is freedom from this cursed life!"

Ev gasped. "Birdie… don't…"

She was cut off as Nephira squeezed even tighter. "Tell him *now*!"

Birdie jerked forward. "If you—"

Helcant roared, swinging his sword with all his might. In a single blow, he cleaved through Nephira's left arm but injured Ev in the process.

Before the arm even hit the ground, Birdie had lunged, striking Nephira with a hammer of shadow and knocking her to the pavement.

The revenant looked up at Helcant in shock and rage. "Helcant… why—?"

"I have not suffered under Divine rule for centuries only for a new Divine to rule over me!" Fire erupted from every inch of his body. "I shall bow to no Divine, nor any king who serves them! Do not bend to her whims, Nephira!"

"You're a fool," Nephira spit, struggling to her feet.

"Look out!" Birdie shouted, spotting Dezeroth signal to his soldiers from the corner of her eye.

Before the soldiers could move, Birdie sent up an illusory cloud around all of them.

A second later, Dezeroth dispelled the cloud, but Tallis was ready with a spell of his own.

The supercharged earth magnet struck Dezeroth square in the chest, and not even the Undead King could resist its pull. He collapsed to the ground, unable to even lift a hand for spellcasting.

That still left the two dozen soldiers bearing down on them, and worse, about thirty more had arrived after hearing the commotion.

Birdie used her illusions to blind those already near, leaving them open to Helcant's fire and Tallis's earth attacks. To Birdie's relief, Umber also joined in the defense. She hadn't expected him to betray them, but she hadn't expected Nephira to, either. Unfortunately, while they succeeded in driving back the soldiers, their horses panicked in the chaos, bolting from the courtyard.

Birdie cursed again. Horses were their only chance of getting away, and now even more reinforcements had arrived — these with bows.

"Tallis, put a barrier around us!" she ordered.

Spinning in place, Tallis sent up column after column of earth.

Nephira charged over to stop him, but Ev, bleeding heavily from Helcant's sword, tackled her, slamming her against the newly formed wall. Nephira's revenant strength was quick to throw Ev back off of her, but before she could recover further she found herself impaled by her own spear against the rock, giving Tallis the time to successfully complete his barrier.

On the other side of the spear stood Helcant, breathing intensely and holding his sword in his spare hand. "You have lost your senses, Nephira. You would trust promises of she who slayed our brethren?"

Nephira grabbed the spear and pulled herself closer to Helcant. "I trust our king's judgment. We have seen her power. It is no stretch to believe she can control necromancy."

"So what if she does?" Ev joined in. "When we beat her, so will Syrus, he can bring it back!"

"You can't defeat her!" Nephira spat. "You cannot triumph over one who controls all magic! All of you will die! Cooperate with King Dezeroth, and you may yet be spared!"

Helcant growled, closed his eyes, and released the spear.

"What are you doing?" Ev shouted.

Nephira removed her spear from herself and leered at Ev. "He is seeing rea-*gurk*!"

Before she could finish speaking, Helcant thrust his sword into Nephira's windpipe, causing her to drop the spear.

"The freedom of death I welcome before slavery to a Divine," he muttered, barely looking at her as he pushed her back against the stone once more. "I remember once you felt the same, but it appears we now travel different ways. Mayhap we will find the same road again one day."

With a jerk of his arm, Helcant put Nephira to rest, her body falling next to her spear.

Tallis could barely speak. "Helcant, y-you—"

"We can talk about what just happened later," Birdie interrupted. She sensed a very big problem arising. "Tallis, do you think you can make a tunnel to get us to safety?"

"A *tunnel*? I can't make a tunnel! There's no spell for that!"

"You can shift earth around, can't you!"

"That's—"

Too late. The side of the barrier nearest Dezeroth exploded inward. Birdie had to dodge to the side to avoid being crushed by the collapsing earthen tower.

Beyond the resulting dust cloud stood Dezeroth, Tallis's enchantment now removed by one of the sorcerers at his side. Raising his hands, Dezeroth unleashed two blasts of dark magic that obliterated all but the far side of the barrier, leaving the group completely exposed to what was now over a hundred soldiers.

Dezeroth pointed his sword at Birdie. "Kill them!"

The soldiers surrounding them drew back their bows; the sorcerers beside Dezeroth conjured humming purple orbs.

Birdie braced herself for the worst.

The sound of bows twanging and spells flying filled the air, but not one attack landed — at least not on Birdie or any of her companions.

Without warning, the soldiers in the back of the lines opened fire on the ones nearest Birdie, attacking the sorcerers as well.

Dezeroth practically screamed. "What is this treachery!"

Birdie didn't know, but she knew an opportunity when she saw one. "Tallis, earth magnet!"

Tallis didn't need to be told twice. He launched another earth magnet at Dezeroth, pinning the roaring tyrant to the ground a second time.

Birdie then launched herself at the still-standing sorcerers, not about to give them the chance to free him from the spell again. Umber joined her in the charge as she pulled out her magic drainer to sap them of their strength while he focused on bringing them down for good.

Behind her, she sensed Tallis and Helcant raising hell with their fire and magic while Ev cast more healing than Helcant or Tallis should have needed. Knowing her, she'd already discerned friend versus foe, and was offering their unexpected allies support in the battle as well.

The fight did not last long after that. In short order, all who had fought on Dezeroth's behalf lay slain — the majority of the forces having surprisingly aided the group instead. Only Dezeroth remained, shouting curses and struggling helplessly against Tallis's enchantment.

As the strangers drew nearer in the aftermath, Tallis looked ready to continue the fight, but a reassuring hand from Ev calmed him… at least slightly.

Birdie herself wasn't sure what had happened, but looking at the faces approaching, she began to put the pieces together.

"Zun-Roven," she said as the chancellor approached her. "You saved us?"

Zun-Roven adjusted his glasses and smiled a broken grin. "I would say you saved yourselves. Dezeroth may be king in name, but it was Syrus who united the immortal races against Grandis, and it was you with Syrus who ended our oppression under the Divine. Compromising stability in your own region, you honored your pact with us to allow us to reclaim the fertile land so long denied to our kind. When I overheard your conversation and Dezeroth's admission to plotting to return rule to a Radiant, as well as his betrayal of those who have only ever stood by our side, it took no convincing on my part to rally immediate aid."

Dezeroth squirmed on the ground. "You treasonous dog! I am king absolute! My kingdom is loyal to me! You will beg for a true death before this day is over!"

Zun-Roven bent down and pried Dezeroth's blade from his grip. Holding it up in the air, he slid his finger along its edge and stated absently, "No, I don't think I will."

He offered the blade to Birdie. "Let us seal our alliance. You may need to make a yearly visit to maintain order, but if you will help us prevent this betrayer from regaining power, I give my word that you will have our aid against Lux Rosa."

Birdie took the sword, ignoring the bile spewing from Dezeroth's mouth. After examining it herself, she looked back at Zun-Roven, understanding what he was asking her to do. "It's a deal, but I believe there's someone else who deserves the chance to send him to limbo more than me."

Birdie offered the sword to Ev.

Ev reached for the sword but stopped before she touched it. She glanced down at Dezeroth in disgust, then ultimately pushed the sword back to Birdie, shaking her head.

"He isn't worth it," she said. "He never was."

Ev's choice didn't really surprise Birdie, but she wanted it to be her choice.

That left it up to Birdie, then. She grabbed the sword's hilt in both hands and frowned. She'd never carried out an execution before, but given the situation, she also didn't see any alternative. After an embarrassing count of five solid swings, silence filled the courtyard as she finally separated Dezeroth's head from his torso, Birdie actually feeling somewhat guilty about the gruesome deed.

Zun-Roven extended his hand, and Birdie returned the blade to him.

"Aren't you worried about what he said?" Birdie asked. "About Lux Rosa controlling necromantic magic?"

"After four centuries of strife and turmoil, I would welcome a release. Whether that release be from true death or peace, it makes little difference to me. Tell me the time and location of the field of battle, and I will send every unit we can spare."

Birdie nodded and told him about Syrus's rendezvous at Lake Tardele.

Zun-Roven readjusted his glasses. "Eighteen days is not much time to travel such a distance, but I will do what I can."

"That's all I can ask," replied Birdie.

A frown crossed Zun-Roven's face. "I must say, though, I didn't expect you to have such trouble with Dezeroth. It seems to me we have much to discuss, including our plan of action. Give me some time to clean house, and we shall speak later.

"Do make yourselves at home in the meantime. As an apology for what has transpired here today, I will see to it that you all receive the finest meals and quarters while we prepare." Zun-Roven then leaned awkwardly to the side as he peered past Birdie towards the gates. "I will also see that your horses are found and returned to you."

"Thank you," Birdie replied, bowing slightly.

Zun-Roven returned the bow, then headed back to the citadel, signaling to the nearby soldiers to dispose of the fallen.

Tallis was the first to speak after that. "So, now what do we do?"

"I suppose we rest," Birdie answered.

She then turned her attention to Helcant, who was staring at Nephira's spear after one of the soldiers carried her body away. "Are you going to be okay?"

Helcant practically jumped, quickly spinning around. "Of course I am unbothered! I have endured countless battles. What is but one more?"

Birdie could clearly see Helcant was far from alright, but she didn't press it. Umber strolled over to him, however, and after an awkward moment of silence, placed his hand on Helcant's shoulder. Helcant accepted it for a second, but ultimately pulled his shoulder away.

Birdie looked back at Ev and Tallis. "We should go. I don't want to stay out in the open until we're well past what just happened."

Ev and Tallis nodded in agreement, and the lot of them followed Zun-Roven into the citadel.

Chapter 19

A full three days passed before Zun-Roven put together an escort for Birdie and her comrades. Birdie couldn't blame him. Even if it hadn't been planned, he had effectively carried out a coup and needed to secure his rule. Fortunately, his claim that most would be willing to rally behind Birdie proved true, making the transition nearly painless. More fortunately still, Zun-Roven had placed gathering an army at the top of his priorities, sending out messengers to rally forces for the battle the very day he'd seized control.

"Are you ready to go?" Ev asked Birdie on the morn of their departure.

Birdie gazed out the window of her room down to the courtyard, her arm resting on the windowsill. "I suppose so. It's not like we have much choice in the matter, though, do we?"

Ev put a hand on Birdie's shoulder. "Are you still upset about what happened with Nephira?"

Birdie shook her head. "I honestly can't say I blame her. You heard what Dezeroth said."

"Oh, come on, do you really believe that?"

"Yes," Birdie answered, having already given the matter a great deal of thought.

The expression on Ev's face soured. "Really? Then why hasn't she already disabled magic? Just think about it. It doesn't make sense!"

"It does if she wants to keep as many nepacs alive as possible," Birdie frowned, squeezing her fist. "She wants this world in good shape when she 'saves' it."

"So? Immortals revive, right? She could turn off magic, then turn it back on when she's done. They'd come back, and there'd still be a lot of people living. So, again, why hasn't she already done it?"

That was a very good point. She supposed it was possible that the thought had simply never entered Lux Rosa's mind, but Birdie somehow doubted that. Still, the possibility that she did possess such power was a real one, and was definitely something she'd have to tell Syrus about the next time they met.

Ev must have seen in Birdie's expression that she'd eased her concerns to a degree. "See? You can relax. I'm sure Syrus will be able to use that shimmer to make our soldiers just as powerful as Lux Rosa's. With Zun-Roven's help, we'll finally be rid of her for good."

Birdie sighed. "Will we though?" she asked, looking tiredly at Ev. "Even if we do split her, she can still send an avatar to Ars Summis. She can keep doing what she's doing there, and no one will be able to stop her."

"Maybe so, but if she hasn't already done it, doesn't that tell you she prefers working where she is? Even if we can't stop her completely, we'll definitely slow her down."

Birdie looked back out the window. "Maybe. It did sound like it took Syrus a while to figure out how to get into the Masters' chambers."

"And it will take her just as long. Besides, that's not what you need to be worrying about. Let Syrus handle all that 'systems' stuff. We just need to focus on the coming battle."

Birdie nodded and gave a weak smile, if only because there wasn't any point in discussing it further.

Ev gave Birdie's shoulder a swift pat. "Let's get going, then. Everyone else is already downstairs waiting."

* * * *

With an entire company of Zun-Roven's army as her escort, Birdie's journey to Lake Tardele proved extremely uneventful. Though they did pass through territories hostile to immortals, few were foolish enough to try and pick a fight. Those who did rapidly regretted their decision.

During the journey, Helcant remained exceedingly quiet. Birdie wanted to say something, but she had her own worries to deal with. Thankfully, both Umber and, to her utmost surprise, Tallis, offered him quiet support. Neither of them said much to him either, but they respected whatever signals he gave off, which was something Birdie never thought Tallis would do. Ev, of course, was more vocal in her sympathy, but Helcant would merely pretend nothing was wrong anytime she did.

It was a relief when they arrived at the lake, and even more of one when Birdie saw that a contingent of about six hundred Shadow Guard was already waiting for them. Their forces were far smaller than Birdie had hoped, but the march against the Colosseum was still three days out — plenty of time for more to arrive.

"Do you think Jax is here?" Ev asked Birdie as they approached the edge of the camp.

"Probably," Birdie answered. "You know he wouldn't be able to stand it if he wasn't the first one out here."

Ev smiled slightly. "Yeah, that's for sure. Should we go look for him?"

"I'm sure you could just ask someone. I need to find Syrus."

Ev looked a tad hurt. "I'm sure he can wait a few more minutes. Jax would really like it if you checked in with him."

"I know he would, but I really need to talk to Syrus."

Now Ev looked at Birdie with concern. "This isn't about what Dezeroth said, is it? I thought we already settled that."

"I have to deliver the degradation as soon as possible," Birdie deflected. "I'll talk to Jax after that. I promise."

Birdie gave Ev a reassuring smile.

"Well, okay then. I guess I'll just tell him you said hi and are too busy to do it yourself."

"Please do," Birdie responded. She knew Ev wasn't happy with her, but this really couldn't wait, and she didn't want Ev worrying.

Inside the camp, Ev asked for Jax, then took Tallis, Helcant, and Umber to go find him. In the meantime, Birdie asked where Syrus was, and one of the Shadow Guard took her to a large tent on the outskirts of the camp.

Birdie stepped inside where Syrus sat behind a table — meditating? Birdie wasn't quite sure, but as soon as she said his name he opened his eyes and stood to greet her.

"Birdie! I'm glad you could make it here so quickly. Did Dezeroth give you any trouble?"

"Oh, I think you could say that. He's dead now."

Syrus froze, then blinked a few times. "I'm sorry. What?"

Birdie pulled over a stool and sat down. She then explained everything Dezeroth had said and everything that had happened in Greater Ascension.

Syrus mulled it all over, chin resting on the back of his hands. "I see. That is very unfortunate indeed. It's a good thing you have the respect of Zun-Roven. I may not know the extent of Lux Rosa's military assets, but I doubt we would be able to win this battle with the Shadow Guard alone. On a related note, did you bring the degradation?"

Birdie, annoyed at the sudden change in topic, removed the degradation from the pot at her hip and transferred it to Syrus.

"Excellent," he stated. "I've been researching a possible means of tracking Lux Rosa's reformation process should we split her. If it succeeds, I'll be able to identify her registration as a Divine and permanently remove her from the world. I've also been working on replicating her enhancements, and since this degradation came from Ars Summis, it should provide similar entry points to the ones I'm familiar with. With any luck, I can create a tool that we can distribute to our entire army."

"That's all well and good, but what good will any of that do if she turns off magic?" Birdie frowned. "We need a way to stop that. If we can't, we might as well not even fight. For that matter, what difference will fighting make, anyway? What's the difference between her taking over this world or you?"

Syrus stopped and stared at Birdie, then sighed and moved the degradation behind the desk where it was out of sight. He then clasped his hands together and placed them on the table.

"If I'm going to be honest, Birdie, I don't have an answer to that question for you."

"What do you mean, 'you don't have an answer'?" Birdie nearly slammed her hands on the table as she stood up. "We're risking thousand— no, millions of lives, and you can't even tell me what we're doing it for?"

Syrus tilted his head and raised an eyebrow. "You are the one who came to me saying we need to stop Lux Rosa. I merely agreed. So you tell me, what do you think the difference would be?"

"I don't know," Birdie answered, frustrated. "I don't know anything about her! I just know she's obsessed with banishing you from the world and will do anything to do it."

"Perhaps I can help you come up with an answer, then," Syrus stated calmly. "Mind you, this assumes that she truly does intend to hand this world over to higher authorities should she gain control of it, but I believe, given the evidence, that is a reasonable assumption.

"Should she triumph here today, be it through victory or our choosing not to oppose her, then she will have until she gains full control of the world to reshape Doxla as she sees fit. After that, she will have to hand the world over to said authorities or risk unwanted scrutiny when they see evidence of delay. Now, perhaps she truly wishes to simply hand over the world as soon as possible to be done with it, perhaps she wishes to leave her mark here because she has a touch of vanity, or perhaps she will warp the world to give the illusion that her work here had more value than it did. How she might approach that latter scenario depends on how much risk she is willing to take, but given that there is a very real threat that the Masters may return, I doubt she will take a slow and safe approach.

"You say you don't know anything about her, but you know more about her than I do. You have experienced her efforts first hand. So, tell me, what do you think Lux Rosa will do if we leave her to her own devices?"

Shaking her head, Birdie sat back down again. "I don't know. All I do know is that if she does have control over all magic, every undead and elemental will die if we fight against her."

Syrus looked at Birdie with sympathy. "It is not my place to make this decision. I am not part of this world. You are. I will not perish if magic is erased. You will. Even if she returns that magic, only other immortals will truly revive because you were never meant to serve the same role as them."

Birdie squeezed her fists on the table. That, too, had been on her mind since Dezeroth's revelation. There was something a side of her wanted to bring up in response, but she felt herself a coward for even considering the idea. Instead, she simply stood up and prepared to exit the tent.

"I'm sorry," she said. "I need more time to think."

Syrus nodded. "Take your time, but preferably not too much time. We march in three days. Until you say otherwise, I will continue to work on developing a means of defeating Lux Rosa. After your revelation about her control of magic, however, I do think a different approach might be in order."

Birdie gave a subtle nod, but that was all. She would leave Syrus to his own devices. Right now, she needed to face the thoughts she'd been avoiding.

Wandering further away from camp, Birdie found a secluded grove beside the lake where she was sure she wouldn't be bothered. There, she squeezed into a nice little vegetative alcove where she could sit and continue mulling over the concerns plaguing her for the past two weeks. The only difference was that this time, she wouldn't let herself be distracted by the possibility of capitulating to Lux Rosa. Perhaps Syrus was simply better at hiding his true character, but somehow Birdie doubted that. Lux Rosa, on the other hand, had committed atrocities even upon the very people serving her. Maybe in the end Lux's actions would be good for Doxla, but the path she was on to reach that point was paved in bloodshed and slavery. The thought of what more she might do to shape this world in preparation for "saving" it was not a pleasant one.

No, Birdie knew she had to be stopped, even if it meant sacrificing countless lives in the process. After all, those lives belonged to immortals who would return in a year, which made it not quite as bad. Right?

Birdie crossed her arms over her knees and buried her head in them. No matter how she thought about it, she couldn't bring herself to come to terms with destroying the lives of millions of people — the vast majority of whom had no knowledge of what was even happening in this corner of the world. Worse, the thought of using her privileged position to save herself from the same fate; but if she didn't, how could she help ensure it would all even make a difference?

Before she knew it, night had already fallen. Birdie was sure the others were probably worried about her, but she wasn't ready to see them again yet. No, there was only one person she needed to talk to — one person who might be able to give her the perspective that she needed.

Sneaking back into the camp, Birdie took on the form of a random soldier to avoid being accosted by anyone who might have been looking for her. Weaving her way around the tents, Birdie paused for only a second when she spotted a large, dark-skinned woman with a face she'd once thought she would never see again. As nice as it was to see her, old acquaintances were not what she was searching for, so she quickly resumed stride.

Finding where Ev and the others had set up camp, the sight of a tent already prepared for her was touching but, right now, only a distraction.

Passing by a small tent on the edge, Birdie spoke using illusory sound to its occupant so as not to alert anyone else that she was there.

"Meet me at the eastern edge of camp. I have to talk to you. Alone."

Her message sent, Birdie continued on her way.

About fifteen minutes later, the person she was waiting for appeared beside her.

"Thanks for coming, Umber."

Umber rose up out of the shadows, taking on the appearance of a young human male this time. "It is my privilege to assist you. What is the topic of this discussion?"

Birdie had trouble bringing her eyes to meet Umber's, but she forced herself to do so. "It's about what Dezeroth said. I think Lux Rosa can erase all magic, and I think she will if we attack her."

Umber tilted his head, mirroring Birdie's mannerism. "That would be most unfortunate. Do you have a counter for this scenario?"

Birdie shook her head. "I don't, at least not for most people."

"I am afraid I do not understand."

Birdie mimicked a sigh, and looked up at the sky. "When I was in Ars Summis, Syrus told me that I am a special kind of shade. He said Divine used us to create human vessels for themselves. I don't know how it works, but it might be possible for me to become human."

"Intriguing," remarked Umber, making a convincing show of a furrowed brow. "That would certainly protect you from any loss of magic."

"I know," Birdie frowned, "but it feels wrong. I'd be starting a fight that will result in countless people dying just to cheat my way out of the same fate as them." She shook her head. "I'm not sure I could live with myself if I did that."

"It seems to me the alternative is to 'start a fight' and let others do the fighting. Is that what you would prefer?"

"Of course not," Birdie replied, "but letting everyone else suffer because of my actions isn't much better! I don't know what I should do. That's why I was hoping you could tell me. Would you become human if you could?"

Umber contemplated that for a moment, remaining silent as he stared out into the distance. His brow shifting into a full-on frown, he finally answered.

"I would not desire this change unless necessitated. I do not believe I would enjoy a life as a human. I have only recently begun to truly experience it as what I already am." He then turned his head and looked Birdie in the eyes. "In your scenario, however, I believe the choice is obvious. You fear abandoning those who would perish if you flee from death, but you would abandon them even more so if you did not fight for them in their stead."

Birdie stared at Umber. She knew he was right. She'd known what she had to do before she even asked him. Perhaps it was more his permission that she sought than his advice, but now that she had it, she had no more excuses to put it off.

"Thank you," she told him, then she forced a smile. "You've been getting very good with your expressions by the way."

"I acquired a small mirror from Bailey Town. I have noticed that since its acquisition, my conversations with others have been more interesting. It appears we have both benefited from the other's advice."

Birdie smiled genuinely this time. "Indeed it does. Please tell Ev and the others that I will return soon. I just have a little more work I need to do with Syrus."

Umber gave her a nod. "I will deliver this message. Do you wish for me to inform them of your plan?"

Birdie shook her head. "No, thank you. I'm not sure I want anyone else to know what I'm doing just yet."

Umber gave a second nod, and in a flash, he was gone.

* * * *

Upon arriving back at Syrus's tent, Birdie pushed open the flap and stepped inside, reverting back to her preferred appearance.

Syrus immediately ceased his work with the shimmer. "Ah, there you are. Several visitors have come looking for you, you know."

"I needed some time alone," Birdie replied.

Syrus leaned back in his chair. "That's what I assumed. Have you come to a decision?"

Birdie approached Syrus's desk but this time remained standing. "I have. I'm not happy with it, but you were right. No matter how many will be hurt by us challenging Lux Rosa, I believe even more would suffer if she isn't stopped."

Syrus clasped his hands together in front of him. "I don't believe I ever made that statement, but if that is what you believe, then we will move forward with our plans once the rest of our forces arrive."

"There's one more thing," Birdie said, shifting uncomfortably.

Syrus tilted his head.

"You said shades like me can be turned into humans," Birdie hesitated before finishing. "Is that something I could still do?"

Syrus closed his eyes for a moment before letting out a single "heh" as he smiled ever so slightly. Standing up, he grabbed his shimmer and walked around his desk over to Birdie.

"It is indeed very possible. However, I must warn you of making such a decision. The first warning should be obvious. You will lose your shade abilities and much of your potential strength. You will no longer be able to shapeshift or absorb magic, and your ability to sense magic will be dampened. You will still be able to sense the type of magic being used, but you won't be able to identify people from their magic alone. You will take injuries the way that a human does. You will also need to take care of your body's more varied needs."

"I'm well aware of all of that," Birdie nearly scowled. "I've lived with humans long enough to know all about how they work."

Syrus simply continued. "The second thing I must warn you about is that this is something I will not be able to reverse. Even if I were to gain complete control of the Masters' systems, I would have to create a new transformation from scratch. That is unfortunately well beyond my abilities. Perhaps the seitti who created my world would be able to do this, but there are many, many obstacles that might prevent that possibility from ever even arising.

"Finally, this transformation was never meant to be used on a body with a mind of its own, and I do not know the mechanisms behind it. There is a very real possibility you will lose connection to your othermind, or even yourself entirely."

Syrus looked Birdie dead in the eyes. "Are you sure this is what you want?"

"No," Birdie returned his gaze, "but I don't have a choice. Lux Rosa had control of air magic over a month ago. How could she not have control over all of it by now?"

Syrus looked almost sad as he answered. "Air magic is an augmenting system. The magic that keeps you alive is a fundamental one and would be much more difficult to manipulate. Nonetheless, considering the time frame, I concur with your conclusion. Before we commit to this, however, are you certain you don't wish to speak with Ev or Jax first? This may be your last chance to do so."

Birdie clenched her fists and looked at the ground. She closed her eyes for second, but she knew what she had to do.

"No," she said. "If I don't do this now, I might not ever do it. Besides, Ev would only try to stop me if she knew."

Syrus's pupils dilated as he shifted his gaze to behind Birdie.

A chill went down Birdie's back as she heard, "I'd stop you if I knew what?"

More slowly than she knew she should have, Birdie turned to face an irritated Ev standing in the tent's entrance.

"Ev, I—"

Syrus answered for her. "Birdie asked me to use her Divine status to convert her into a human in case Lux Rosa does have control over magic."

A look of bewilderment spread across Ev's face. "But, that's a great idea! Why would you ever think I wouldn't support that?"

"But, you told me you don't think Lux Rosa has that kind of power," Birdie answered.

"So?" Ev laughed incredulously. "That doesn't mean I'm right. This way you'll be safe no matter what happens."

Birdie forced a smile. "Thanks, Ev. I'm sorry I didn't tell you what I was thinking. I should have been more open."

"You're right, you should have," Ev scolded, but then she smiled. "Don't worry. Being human's not so bad. I'll help you out until you go back to being a shade."

"I'm afraid that won't be possible," Syrus interjected.

A look of concern crossed Ev's face, but Birdie reassured her. "I'll be fine. I know what I'm asking, and besides, I'll still be me, right?"

As Birdie said that, she projected her face on the back of her head to shoot Syrus a look warning him not to say another word.

Thankfully, he obliged.

Ev hesitated, but ultimately nodded. "If you're sure, then I've got your back."

"I'm glad to know that," Birdie answered, then she turned back to Syrus. "I'm ready."

Syrus grunted. "If you insist. I trust this is the form you desire?"

Birdie gave the affirmative.

Syrus's eyes briefly shifted to Ev before returning back to Birdie. "Then stay still. This will only take a second."

Birdie braced herself as Syrus lifted up his hand, his shimmer grasped firmly in the other. Gently, Syrus placed three of his fingers against Birdie's forehead, triggering a minor flash as the degradation disrupted her connection to her othermind. Even though she felt his fingers pressed against her, it almost felt as if they reached deep inside. There was a slight tingle, and her vision glazed over with an iridescent sheen before going dark.

Syrus removed his hand, and Birdie nearly panicked when the darkness remained.

"Something's wrong!" she said frantically, and she felt Ev's hands on her in an instant.

"You have to open your eyes," Syrus stated.

Oh, right. Eyelids were a thing. It only took a second for her to figure out how to use them; her body thankfully seemed to already know how.

Birdie felt a warmth in her cheeks as she opened her eyes for the first time.

Great. She'd also forgotten about all those involuntary signals humans gave off. Even worse, human eyes were different. Even with them open, the world was still darker than she remembered.

This was going to take some getting used to.

She sighed — for the first time in her life an actual sigh — surprising herself with the pressure building up in her chest. Well, she supposed it was a good thing her body already knew how to breath too, though the scents entering her nostrils were very different from the ones her magic sensing ever picked up.

"Does everything feel alright?" Ev asked, touching Birdie's face.

"Agh, yes!" Birdie flinched at the touch and stepped back. "At least, I think so."

She then stopped to examine herself. "Do I look the same?"

Syrus answered, a hint of displeasure still in his voice, though most of his disapproval had vanished. "I don't know. Are you still casting the illusion of your preferred appearance?"

Birdie nearly slapped herself as she realized she was. Ceasing her spellcasting, she held out her hand and watched as nothing changed.

"Not anymore," she replied. "Is my face…?" she pointed at herself.

"You look like you," Ev replied cheerfully. "That's incredible! I had no idea this kind of thing was possible."

"Yes, well," Syrus interrupted, "I'm just happy the transformation had no ill effects on you."

Ev turned toward Syrus. "Ill effects? What sort of ill effects?"

Birdie glared at Syrus while Ev faced away, but thankfully the answer he gave wasn't the one she wanted kept secret.

"I wasn't certain Birdie's abilities would be fully retained, but her statement confirms she can still use illusions, telling me they were. That said, with the work I've been doing, such a setback would have been inconsequential."

Syrus brought his shimmer back to his desk and sat once again. Both Birdie and Ev followed him, sitting as well.

"It's far from complete, mind you," he continued, "but it will act as a method of enhancement for our army regardless of whether they use magic or not. When touched, all learned skills, magical or otherwise, will be granted their highest proficiency bonus. It will also grant minor increases to physical strength, magic power, and durability, though minor is all I dare attempt on that front. Attempting to push it further could easily prove fatal if not done correctly."

"Amazing!" Ev exclaimed. "Does that mean we could use it to learn new spells more quickly?"

Syrus halfway shrugged. "In a sense. It will make your body maximally attuned to any spells you learn, so you will not have to practice with them to improve their power. That said, actually learning them will still take the normal amount of time. The exception to this is Birdie, however, as her othermind will already know how to use all spells. So, for her, I suppose the answer is completely yes, at least up to the maximum number of spells one can wield."

"Did you hear that?" Ev turned to Birdie. "If you combine that with the shimmer from Lux Rosa, you'll be unstoppable!"

"At least until magic gets turned off," Birdie stated cynically.

"Oh, come on. Her soldiers' greatest strengths are their spells. If she does turn off magic, it will only be the kinds immortals need to survive."

That was a very good point, even if it was a morbid one. "You're right. This could be useful."

Syrus spoke again. "That's what I'm hoping for, but not just for you. If I can get this, it will do a lot to shift the battle in our favor."

"That's great news," Ev replied. "If anyone can do it, we know you can."

Syrus smiled. "I appreciate the confidence. I'll do everything I can not to let you down."

Ev and Birdie got up to leave, but before Birdie exited the tent, she cast an illusory sound thanking Syrus for his help — not just for turning her human, but also for not telling Ev how the transformation could have changed her.

Back outside, the night was darker than Birdie had ever seen despite there being a full moon.

"Is this what night always looks like to you?" she asked.

Ev simply grabbed Birdie's arm and pulled her toward where their tents had been set up. "You'll get used to it. Come on. We should still have some soup left over. I think it's time you had your first meal as a human."

Chapter 20

Atop a hill on the outskirts of camp, Birdie surveyed the extent of her forces. Two days had passed since her transformation. More and more troops had joined up since that time — now totaling nearly six thousand in size. About a third of that number belonged to the Shadow Guard and associated militias. The rest were comprised of the rather diverse forces Zun-Roven had mustered. Nearly half of those were revenants, but the rest were comprised of all manner of beings, including gargoyles, harpies, onis, shades, brigands, and even a trio of dragons. How well they would fare against Lux Rosa was yet to be seen, but if Dezeroth's claims proved false, then even without knowing the extent of Lux's forces, Birdie felt confident victory was at hand. If his claims turned out to be true, however, she feared that hope was slim at best.

Before long, she spotted Ev climbing up the hill carrying a bowl of steaming white mush.

"I brought you breakfast," she chimed when she drew close.

Birdie grimaced. The required consumption of physical matter was rapidly moving up in contention for her least favorite part of the transformation.

"Thanks," she said, "I'll eat it later, I think."

Birdie received a look she'd only seen Ev's Gran give before, usually preceding a lengthy lecture. "I know it's not the best, but you still have to eat. I promise you human food is normally better than this. We just have to tough it out until we get back home. Then you can try a *real* meal."

Birdie begrudgingly accepted the bowl and sat down. Ev took a seat as well — close enough that Birdie could smell her scent. It hadn't taken her long after becoming human to understand Ev's remarks about bathing — the camp had plenty of individuals whose smells were less than pleasant. Ev's scent, though, didn't bother her. Birdie was sure it must have been some weird psychological thing, but Ev's scent seemed familiar, comforting, and she found that she quite liked it around.

Birdie scooted a tad closer to Ev. "You know it's not the flavor that's the problem right? How can you stand having stuff pass through you like this?"

Ev shrugged, but smiled. "It's not like you really notice it."

"You do when it's going in or out," Birdie grumbled.

Whether Ev didn't hear or chose to ignore that remark, the topic was quickly changed.

"Anyway," Ev started, "Syrus and Zun-Roven have called for an officers' meeting in half an hour. Jax wanted me to tell you since he's busy organizing the new arrivals. Oh! Speaking of which, Gare showed up last night."

"Oh, really?" that was a bit of pleasant news to sweeten the unpleasant meal. "I thought he wasn't supposed to arrive until this evening."

Ev shrugged again. "Apparently he left early after putting his dad in charge. I can't say I'm surprised. Gare's never been one for organization, but his dad's a natural."

"Yes, I am aware," Birdie stated, recalling her multiple encounters with the merchant.

"So, when do you think you'll make it public?" Ev asked, sipping on her canteen.

"Probably after I tell everyone at the meeting," Birdie answered. "When word gets out, I'd like the officers to have my back about my decision."

Ev nodded in understanding. "Well, you'd better finish eating soon. They're meeting in Jax's tent on the other side of camp. I don't want you to be late."

"Sure thing, Gran, you can count on me."

Ev gave Birdie a solid punch in the shoulder, prompting a brief smile on Birdie's lips before they had to meet once more with the gruel.

* * * *

When Birdie pushed aside the curtains to Jax's tent, she was met by the faces of a dozen officers, Syrus not included. The moment she entered, a large bearded man on her left spread his arms wide.

"Birdie!" the man shouted before giving her a great slap on the back.

The force of the gesture nearly caused her to stumble, but she merely smiled in response. "Hey, Gare. Long time, no see."

"I'll say it's been a long time! What's it been, like, four months? You should visit more often. Little Marin loves her shadow auntie."

Birdie felt that uncomfortable warmth she knew meant she was blushing but tried to take things in stride. "I've been really busy, but I'll be sure to stop by once all of this is over."

"You better," Gare grinned. "If you don't, you can bet I'll come and drag you over myself."

Jax shuffled his way around the other officers to get closer to the conversation. "Gare, now isn't really the time. We need to focus on the battle ahead."

"Nonsense," Gare puffed out his chest. "Syrus isn't here, right? How can we make a plan if we don't even know what he's got for us?"

A voice behind Birdie responded. "Allow me to remedy that lack of information."

Gare practically jumped, and Jax saluted as Syrus squeezed past Birdie and approached the center table with his shimmer.

"Allow me to begin with the bad news," Syrus stated. "Zun-Roven, I'm afraid I have been unable to find a way to circumvent the possibility that Lux Rosa may erase necromantic magic, nor do I think it feasible for such a discovery to be made before our assault, or honestly even within a month. The best I will be able to do is seize control of her own power if and when we defeat her, which would allow me to undo any harm she may cause."

Zun-Roven closed his eyes in a sigh, then pushed his glasses up as he reopened them. "That truly is unfortunate, but I appreciate the attempt. I only hope that we at least offer some contribution in the coming battle before darkness comes for us yet again."

Syrus leaned forward, placing one hand on the table and the other on the jewel of his rod. "Be assured of this: no matter what happens, your joining us here will not be in vain. For the first time in history, mortals and immortals stand together. None who are here this day will forget that, in the time of crisis, nepacs broke free from the shackles of division placed on them by the Masters. Even if magic-dependent immortals are denied the chance to fight, their bravery will be remembered, and when they rise again, mortals and immortals will continue to walk arm in arm as we rid ourselves of the Masters' control forever."

Zun-Roven gave a grunt and a wide grin. "Well said. I can see how you convinced so many to join you in your fight against Grandis."

Syrus removed his hand from the table and looked around at the other faces present. "The only other news I have that might be considered ill is that Birdie, who some of you may know as Eclipse, no longer possesses her former power as a Radiant."

None of the officers looked surprised. That was about what Birdie had expected. She knew word would have gotten around.

"Furthermore," Syrus continued, "she no longer has her abilities as a shade."

That got a few murmurs.

Syrus then gestured back to Birdie, stepping aside in an invitation to come forward.

Birdie obliged, and Syrus continued.

"The reason for this is that I used her Divine status to convert her body into that of a human."

Now the officers showed surprise.

"What are you talking about, 'you turned her into a human'?" Gare asked.

"I said what I said," Syrus replied plainly. "Even without the powers of a shade, she possesses abilities unique only to her, which, combined with something I've developed for everyone here, will in some ways compensate for the strength that she has lost."

Syrus gestured to his ball of degradation. "I have not yet developed a means of replicating the magic boon that Lux Rosa's soldiers have been given, but I have developed something similar."

He went on to explain what he had told Birdie he was working on the last time they had spoken.

"We are still four days' march from Lux Rosa. If I can replicate her magic enhancements in that time, we can level the playing field even more. That said, I do not expect that Lux Rosa has been idle in her efforts. She will have found ways to further the strength of her own warriors as well, so we will need every advantage we can get."

One of Zun-Roven's officers grunted. "So this fuzzy thing here is supposed to give us super powers, or something?"

"Not this exactly," Syrus corrected. He reached his hand into the shimmer and pulled out a smaller one. "This can. I will produce as many of these as necessary to distribute to everyone. If I am able to create a magic boon as well, I will do so again before we begin our assault. However, before I can begin work on that, there is one more thing that I must do."

"And what's that?" Jax asked.

Syrus looked Jax in the eye, then shifted his gaze to the others at the table. "Recall that when Grandis was defeated, both he and Escalor severed their connection with Doxla of their own accord. They knew that their misguided goal of ending the world had been thwarted. They had no recourse other than to attempt taking control of the world themselves. Given the fact they deemed the world impossible to save, I believe it is obvious they thought such a feat also impossible, or at least not worth pursuing.

"Lux Rosa, however, clearly does not believe this. Defeating her in battle will not stop her ambitions. The only way to permanently remove her from the world is for me to use the Masters' ability to banish Divine from the world. Unfortunately, I have yet to develop the tool that I need in order to do this, and it is a tool that must be used on her directly before she is split. As such, that is my priority for now."

Jax spoke up again. "We understand. Defeating her won't do much good if she'll just revive somewhere else, but what happens when she comes back? Not even the Masters could keep Divine out of Doxla forever."

Syrus looked at Jax once again. "The Masters chose not to permanently banish Divine from Doxla. I guarantee they had such power, and I guarantee that I will use it once I am able."

"In that case, I agree with your choice of priorities," announced Zun-Roven. "I cannot help but wonder, however, would it not be wise to postpone the assault until both of your projects are completed?"

The others nodded in agreement.

Syrus turned his attention to Zun-Roven. "I have every intention of completing both before we arrive at the Colosseum. Birdie's knowledge of the effects of Lux Rosa's boon gave me substantial direction in my initial efforts. There are but a few unknown variables that I have yet to account for. If I have not completed my work by the day of the assault, and it is the general consensus that we should wait, we shall."

Zun-Roven gave an approving nod. "That is good to hear. In that case, we should plan our assault with your success assumed."

"That still leaves us with two main scenarios to plan for," Jax added. "We need to be ready for both the possibility she will turn off magic and that she won't."

Birdie had an additional scenario to add. "And the possibility she only turns off certain magic."

Syrus turned back to Birdie once more. "Agreed. Birdie, you have seen Lux Rosa's abilities firsthand on multiple occasions. Tell us what we can expect, and we will go from there."

Birdie stepped up to the table and recounted every detail she could remember from her encounters with the Radiant and her subjects.

The rest of the day was devoted to going over different scenarios and how to approach them. Birdie's othermind proved useful in the planning, and though she felt at times she took over more than she perhaps should have, Syrus seemed to encourage this, and she received few objections to her ideas.

By the time Syrus called the session to a close, dusk had already returned once again. Before leaving, he produced a number of his augmenting shimmers to distribute around the camp. The other commanders sent for spellcasters to be taught how to carry the things, but most of them didn't bother waiting around for the carriers to actually arrive. Birdie didn't feel like staying either, so Syrus simply handed her a shimmer of her own to pass around.

Stepping out of the tent into the dimming light, Birdie still wasn't confident they would win, but she was at least confident they had the best plan possible given what they knew.

Making her way back to her tent, she told Ev and the others about what had transpired before presenting the shimmer to them.

Helcant gave the first wicked grin he'd made in a while. "At long last, we shall match their unfair tactics. It is time for their wicked blood to flow across the land!"

"Agreed," Tallis said, his expression sour. "Lux Rosa's going to pay for what she did to Roehelm and to Waylen."

Birdie and Ev exchanged glances. Neither of them had spoken much of Waylen since his passing, but Birdie knew Ev and she both felt the same way.

"Well, no point in putting it off," Birdie said. "Let's all get this over with. I need to help spread it around camp."

"You need not say so twice!" Helcant practically leapt forward, thrusting his hand into the shimmer.

His body flashed briefly before he backed away, grinning maniacally as he shot his hand into the air and unleashed a blast of flames halfway on par with what Lux's Rosa's soldiers had mustered. The searing heat was so intense it forced Birdie to cover her face with her arm.

"Fantastic!" he cackled.

"Yeah, really great," muttered Tallis. "Maybe *don't* try and burn the whole camp down, though?"

Helcant stepped further away from the shimmer, still grinning.

Ev stepped up next. "We should test the extent of our abilities after this, but I agree with Tallis. We probably shouldn't do that in camp."

She, too, touched the shimmer, also flashing briefly, then made room for

Tallis to do the same. Once done, they all looked to Birdie with anticipation — Ev with a touch of worry.

Birdie sighed. She knew she had to use the shimmer sooner or later. It might as well be now.

Reaching in, she felt a slight tingle, and that was all. No world-flashing-white or disconnection from her othermind.

"Huh," she remarked, but didn't bother elaborating. She guessed Syrus must have been right in his diagnosis of why previous brushes with degradation had caused her so much distress.

"Come," declared Helcant. "We must exercise our abilities to learn our full strength."

"Maybe later," Birdie replied. "I still have to help distribute this to the rest of the camp. I just thought I'd share it with you first."

"Well, we appreciate it," Ev said. "Besides, we still have five days before we attack the Colosseum. We can see how much that thing helped us along the way."

* * * *

Those five days came and went more quickly than Birdie would have liked. Before she knew it, they were practically on Lux Rosa's doorstep. The final camp they set up was just shy of a large hill covered in dead forest. From atop that hill, the Colosseum — still as pristine as Are Summis — could be seen only two miles away. Lux Rosa's forces would surely see them coming and prepare accordingly, but considering their plan there was no way around that.

Only a few hours before the assault, Jax joined Birdie and Ev up on the hilltop. "Syrus wants you to know he's finished that magic thing he was working on. We're spreading it around camp as we speak. You should probably go use it, too," he said to Ev.

"Right, I'll be right back," Ev answered, smiling at Birdie before heading back down the hill.

Jax walked further up and took Ev's place at Birdie's side. "You ready for this?"

"Not really," she answered.

"Yeah, me neither. I can't tell the troops, but I've never been this worried about a battle before. If this lady's anything at all like Grandis, she'll do anything she can to win."

"She's not like Grandis," Birdie replied, staring out at the Colosseum. "Say what you will about him, but my impression is that he at least treated his soldiers as more than disposable tools."

"Maybe," Jax responded, then joined her in staring out over the forest. "At least this time we'll all be fighting together from the beginning."

A small smile tugged at Birdie's lip. That was a comforting point, if only fleetingly so.

"You'll do what I asked, right?" she prompted.

"Hopefully, I won't need to," Jax answered, rubbing his head. "Ev might be stubborn, but she knows how to listen to reason… usually."

Birdie turned to look him in the eyes. "I'm serious. I don't care what happens. Do *not* let her face Lux Rosa with me. She knows I have a soft spot for Ev."

"Relax. I told you I've got your back. You think *I* want Ev going in there?"

Birdie shifted her gaze to the side.

"Look, don't worry about Ev. You focus on getting to Lux Rosa."

Birdie narrowed her eyes. "Oh, don't you worry about that. One way or another, I'm splitting Lux Rosa today. I'm done dealing with her puppets. Even if we lose this battle, I'm making sure her plans end here."

Jax nodded, looked as if he wanted to say something more, but ultimately decided against it, instead turning to head back down the hill. After a few steps, he stopped and turned back.

"Oh, yeah, and one more thing. Syrus said he wants us all to meet in an hour. The scouts have reported back and he wants to make final adjustments to the plan."

Birdie nodded in the affirmative and watched Jax as he walked the rest of the way down the hill. Once he was out of sight, she turned her attention back to the Colosseum once more.

Three more hours, and the final battle would commence. Three more hours, and she would face Lux Rosa.

Chapter 21

Dark clouds filled the skies, matching the lifeless gray plains surrounding the Colosseum. The forces of Lux Rosa had spread out all along the outer wall of the great structure, taking up positions in the windows of all twelve floors as well as at the gates and on the roof, though none ventured far from the safety of its halls. In the surrounding fields, Birdie's army had spread out to attack from all sides save for the east where the Hall of Champions was located. Though they had reason to believe the Hall was the most likely place for Lux Rosa to be, it could only be entered from within the Colosseum walls.

Birdie touched her hand to a small clay pot at her side as she waited on the southern side of the Colosseum. That pot was her secret weapon — that and the two new spells she'd added to her arsenal since becoming human.

Waiting with her were Ev, Tallis, Helcant, and Umber, along with one of the dragons and a force two-thousand strong. A third of those with her were revenants or other types of beings dependent on magic for their survival. Birdie had placed them on the front lines to give them their best chance of contributing before Lux Rosa went through with her threat, just in case she actually was that monstrous.

Birdie could see Zun-Roven and his contingent to the west, but Syrus's forces were hidden from her sight beyond the Colosseum to the north. Regardless, they would all be able to see one another's signals when the time came.

As Birdie surveyed the scene before her, she spotted Jax rapidly approaching her on horseback.

"Everyone's in place," he reported on his arrival.

Birdie gripped her horse's reigns tightly. "Is everyone aware of what might happen when we attack?"

"They are," Jax answered. "We're all ready for it. No matter what happens, we keep pressing forward. If the soldiers here are like the ones who attacked Roehelm, we just have to get through the walls and we can win."

"Something tells me they won't be so cocky this time around," Birdie stated, but then she gave him a reassuring smirk, "so let's make them slip up from panic instead. They think they're safe just because the walls of the Colosseum can't be damaged. Once we break through, we'll show them that hiding won't protect them."

Jax nodded. "That's the plan. Should I give the signal?"

Birdie surveyed her forces one final time. It was clear many of them were nervous, especially those dependent on magic, but many more appeared resolute. At her side, Ev gave Birdie a nod. Past Ev, both Tallis and Helcant — each on horseback — stared back at her with fire in their eyes. She stopped when her eyes landed on Umber, who stated confidently, "I am ready."

Birdie closed her eyes and took a deep breath, then turned her gaze back to Jax. "Do it."

Raising his sword high into the air, Jax fired two beams of light into the sky.

From the far side of the Colosseum, Birdie spotted another two beams pierce the gray clouds above, followed soon after by a red flare from Zun-Roven's regiment.

That was confirmation that everyone was ready.

Birdie raised a her enchantment breaker and thrust it forward. "Attack!"

A nearby soldier blasted his trumpet, and the battle began.

The lines of immortals led the charge, roaring and shrieking as they bolted on foot and through the air toward the Colosseum. Immediately behind them went the dragon. Birdie and her squad followed, with the Shadow Guard taking up the rear. Jax set off on horseback along with Tallis, Helcant, and a team of elemental magic users, charging ahead of everyone else.

Lux's forces attacked as soon as Jax's group drew close, raining all manner of powerful spells down onto the field. Tallis and the earth mages raised up great stone walls to block the attacks and provide cover while Jax fired a few beams from his sword at the wall. Once they were close enough, the ice and fire users combined their spells to stir up a great cloud of mist all along the edge of the Colosseum, giving the remaining forces the cover they'd need to get close and break through.

Wind users from the loyalist defenders worked to blow away the mist, but the action revealed their positions, leaving them exposed to Jax's beams and other attacks. In retaliation, the defenders lobbed poison spells down below, but Birdie's own wind users blasted the toxic gases back into the windows, stopping that tactic in its tracks. Soon, more mist was created obscuring the battlefield, and the loyalists gave up trying to thwart it.

Instead, they resorted to firing blindly, and Jax's group focused on raising up more earthen barriers. The barriers protected against attacks, but more importantly they also formed tunnels leading to the gates for the bulk of Birdie's forces to pass through.

"It's working!" Ev shouted to Birdie's left as the pair of them chased behind the dragon.

Birdie didn't respond. She'd expected the pegasus riders to have attacked by now, but they all remained above and around the Colosseum, flitting back and forth from a single spot at the top of the eastern wall. The only thing she could think of was that they were relaying information, most likely to Lux Rosa. If Lux did have power over magic, she would exercise it any moment now.

Birdie turned to Umber.

"You should go on ahead," she called to him. "You might not have much time."

Umber looked sideways at her and gave a nearly natural smile. "I have accompanied you this far. I will—"

Umber stopped and stumbled, his illusion fading.

Birdie froze as she watched him fall. He barely had time to even look back at her before he vanished in wisp of smoke, leaving behind only a small satchel with a mirror slipping from it.

Birdie could hardly breathe. She'd never put it past Lux Rosa to actually go through with her threat, but seeing Umber vanish before her...

She clenched her fists. Whatever doubts she'd had about the morality of her choice vanished with Umber. Anyone who would do something so unfathomably terrible had to be stopped. There was no room in this world or any for such absolute cruelty.

Ev grabbed Birdie's arm, looking at her with sympathy but speaking firmly. "We can't stop now. We have to finish this."

"I know," Birdie responded, and with one last look at Umber's mirror she charged ahead, doing her best to ignore the hundreds of now lifeless revenants littering the ground between her and the Colosseum.

She followed the dragon into the mist. The fog lit up orange as the beast let loose her flames on the Colosseum wall. Even from behind, Birdie could feel the heat; the dragon had also been augmented with Syrus's enhancements.

The spells and arrows from the loyalists ceased until the dragon stopped to recharge, but they then quickly renewed with increased vigor. Magical explosions of ice, lightning, and fire went off all around, some of them striking the dragon as she let out a pained roar.

The dragon hobbled behind one of the stone barriers as Birdie and Ev ran past with a small contingent of the shadow guard. The dragon peaked out to unleash another blast, which scorched the side of the Colosseum. Now in front of the source of the flames, Birdie felt the heat singe her hair, even though she was far from in its direct path. She was sure not even Lux's enchantments could protect her soldiers from such intensity.

The loyalists retaliated once again, though this time with a noticeable decrease in the number of attacks. Nonetheless, Birdie knew one of the attacks must have struck true, because in the midst of the explosions she heard a loud thud, and the dragon fire did not come again.

The dragon had done her job, however. The number of defenders on the wall seemed to have dropped and their preoccupation with bringing her down had given Birdie and the rest of her forces the chance to reach the wall.

The remaining immortals had broken past the gates, but they appeared to be having more trouble than Birdie had anticipated at pushing deeper into the Colosseum.

"What's wrong?" she asked a wounded demon near the entrance.

"They are too strong," the demon coughed. "They ignore damage and strike as ogres!"

Birdie cursed. Unless they could get everyone inside they wouldn't stand a chance.

Jax, Tallis, and Helcant rode up beside her and Ev. "What's the matter?" Jax asked.

"What we were worried about," she answered.

"Then we go the other way," Jax responded, dismounting from his horse. "The illusionists should be waiting."

Tallis and Helcant also dismounted, and the five of them ran out from under their protective stone cover and past the series of ramps the earth mages had made leading up to the second floor windows. Birdie couldn't see what was happening, but the sound of metal clashing was loud in her ears, telling her the battle for the second floor was well underway.

Jax grabbed about fifty soldiers on the way as they headed to the eastern side of the Colosseum. There, about ten soldiers well-versed in illusion magic were waiting for them in the fog near the Hall of Champions.

Birdie turned to Tallis. "Okay, Tallis, do your thing."

Tallis stretched his fingers before focusing all of his energy into making a massive ramp up to the third floor over the Hall.

Birdie channeled an illusion over herself and her companions, plus five of the soldiers following her, to give them similar armor to the loyalists. She also made certain to give Helcant a human appearance. The other illusionists did the same for the remaining soldiers, and the lot of them carefully made their way up the ramp.

Up at the window, Birdie took a quick look around to make sure no enemies were around and was pleased to see that was the case. She waved for the others to follow her in.

Once inside, twenty-five of the soldiers headed for the stairs to flank the blockade at the gates while twenty headed along the southern wall to clear the floor as they made their way to assist Zun-Roven's forces to the west. The remaining five soldiers stayed with Birdie.

"Which way to the Hall of Champions?" Jax asked.

"We aren't going to the Hall of Champions," Birdie responded, pointing with her finger to the ceiling above her. "We're going up."

Jax protested. "The plan was to—"

"Birdie said we're going up," Ev interrupted. "I'm sure she has a good reason."

Birdie appreciated Ev's assistance. "The pegasus riders are acting as messengers to someone at the top. I don't know if it's Lux Rosa or not, but whoever it is, they're coordinating the loyalists' defenses. We can't take the chance that it *isn't* her. Even if it's not, taking out whoever's giving orders will give us a significant advantage."

"Alright, let's do it," Jax responded. "Lead the way."

Birdie did, though after charging up ten flights of stairs in her armor one of the disadvantages of her human body reared it's ugly head.

"Th… there," Birdie panted out, barely maintaining her illusion as she tried to catch her breath.

About two hundred yards away at the top of another flight of stairs stood an old man in white robes with gold trim. The man barked out orders to pegasus riders as they flitted about and was guarded by a slew of foot soldiers.

"That can't be Lux Rosa, can it?" asked Tallis, equally winded.

"Not likely," Birdie answered, placing a hand on one of her daggers, "but as long as we're here—"

"We shall make him burn!" Helcant exclaimed.

"You leave him to me," Birdie ordered, still out of breath but with renewed vigor inside her. "Watch my back and keep the others away. Ev? Stay close enough to heal anyone who needs it."

Without another word, Birdie took off along the top of the wall, thankfully devoid of sentries on this side. Her companions followed closely behind. The old man in charge noticed her not too far into her sprint, but it wasn't until she was within fifty yards that he responded. With a point of his finger, he sent the three ground troops and five riders nearest him to intercept.

Before they had a chance to attack, Birdie whipped out her bow and fired at the riders, taking down one of the two flying out from the wall on the right.

Tallis and the accompanying soldiers joined her in the barrage, their spells and arrows knocking two of the other riders down onto the Colosseum seating to the left and dropping one yet another to the ground below on the right.

The fifth rider unleashed a wave of flame directly at Birdie, but Helcant jumped forward and countered the attack with his own, pushing it back.

The rider flew out over the seating to try again, but Ev was ready for him with her bow and brought down his pegasus. He and the other two who'd fallen in the seating area would be a problem again soon enough, but Birdie's immediate concern was the three other soldiers between her and Mr. Fancy Robes.

Deciding now was a good time to try out one of the new spells she'd added to her arsenal, she launched a disorientation spell at the first soldier in her path.

The soldier lifted up her great sword at Birdie's approach but toppled over before she ever had the chance to swing.

Birdie continued on past to where the next two soldiers blocked her path, but a spell from Tallis covered the both of them in a thick sheet of ice, allowing her to easily slip by.

At this point Birdie was within throwing distance of the robed man. Reaching for her magic drainer, she stopped when she sensed a familiar enchantment from her target, opting instead for the enchantment breaker.

Absolute fury etched onto his face, the man prepared a spell Birdie hoped she'd never encounter again and fired it at her.

Birdie made a spinning leap over the weakness spell as it flew right on by. Her enchantment breaker gripped tightly in her hand, she lobbed it straight towards the robed man's gut.

At this distance, he had no time to dodge, and Birdie felt Lux's enchantment fade just in time for her to turn and face another pair of soldiers running up the stairs toward her. She'd have to deal with them before the robed man, and most likely the dozen or so more pegasus riders now heading her way as well.

Birdie stretched out her hand for another disorientation spell and—nothing!

She barely had time to ponder what went wrong when she noticed the entirety of the pegasi forces careening out of the sky.

Horror set in as Birdie realized what had happened. The magic she'd been sensing all around her had completely vanished almost as soon as she'd severed Lux's connection to her commander. Lux Rosa was sacrificing her own soldiers by turning off magic! But... why?

That answer was soon apparent when the first soldier reached her from the stairs. The man swung an oversized morning star as if it were a twig, its enormous spikes grazing Birdie's nose as she just barely had time to shift backwards out of the way.

Whatever strength Lux Rosa may have given to her soldiers did nothing to reduce the weight of their weapons, however, and the soldier lost his balance in his overzealous attempt to land a blow. That meant an opportunity for Birdie.

Waiting for the man to strike again, Birdie used her othermind to predict the arc of his swing, ducked around it, and pivoting hard used the soldier's own momentum against him as she tossed her assailant over the side.

The second stairway soldier lunged forward while Birdie's back was turned, but she expected that, and with a nimble twirl she tripped the woman up and sent her down to the same fate.

"Ev! Healing!" Birdie called as she pointed to the robed man on the ground, but then she realized Ev couldn't help with magic gone.

Ev ran up anyway, looking dubious about the command, but she nonetheless attempted to heal the stranger who'd already removed Birdie's dagger, his robes now soaked a deep red. Jax and Helcant accompanied her and both pointed their swords at the man.

"I can't," Ev said shortly after her failed attempt.

"I know," Birdie answered. "Looks like Lux Rosa's turned off all magic now."

Tallis cursed. "Damn it! Why can't she just fight fair?"

Birdie ignored them and pulled the old man up by his robes. "Alright, who are you and why was Lux Rosa using you as a puppet to command these soldiers?"

The old man slapped Birdie's hands away with surprising ferocity as he glared at her. "I am Grand Curate Vellic Undom. Lady Rosa stole my authority just as you stole the same from Lord Grandis."

Tallis erupted. "Grandis was a liar and a traitor, you stupid—"

Birdie held up her hand to silence him. She leaned close to Vellic.

"Where is Lux Rosa?"

Vellic glanced down into the central arena of the Colosseum where a handful of Birdie's forces had manged to break through, now battling amongst the small makeshift town Lux's army had constructed within.

"She is in the Hall of Champions. The door to it is on the second floor against the outer wall. Her throne is surrounded with what she calls degradation. It is the source of most of her power. As long as she is in contact with it, none can defeat her."

"We already expected as much," replied Birdie. "We have a plan for dealing with that."

Vellic glared at Birdie once more, one hand over his wound. "Do not underestimate her. Not even I know what kind of enchantments she has, but I do know she has control of all magic. She will turn it on and off to attack while you will be helpless."

"Don't underestimate me, either," Birdie shot back. "If she turns it back on for even a moment, that will be all that I need."

Ev piped up. "I don't understand, why are you telling us this?"

Vellic turned his attention to Ev. "Don't misunderstand me. You and I are far from allies, but I will not stand to see my people used as fodder for that witch's ambitions. I do not do this for you; I do this for them."

"If you really care about them," Birdie said, "tell them to stand down and let my army through."

Vellic almost smirked. "Against immortals? When we have the advantage? They would rather perish. There is no stopping this battle now."

"Why you—" Jax started, but Birdie grabbed him by the arm.

"Leave him," she said, picking up her dagger. "We need to move."

Jax growled but followed her down the stairs. The rest followed right behind.

Halfway down the eleventh floor, Birdie spotted movement to her left in the stands and lifted her arm just in time to block an arrow from one of the fallen pegasus riders. She was very glad her little suit was crafted from unnaturally strong materials, as her othermind recognized the arrow as being made from dragon bone.

The other two riders fired as well, one missing but the other landing true.

Ev cried out as she fell down the stairs, an arrow having punched clean through the mail at her hip.

"Ev!" Jax yelled as he grabbed his sister and pulled her behind the cover of the stairway.

Birdie returned fire while the rest joined Jax out of sight. Only one of the soldiers with them possessed a bow, and as soon as he was behind cover he assisted Birdie in returning fire.

The loyalist soldiers ducked behind the stone seating, but it wasn't enough to protect them from the aim of Birdie's othermind. The enchantments on her arrows may have been suppressed now that magic was gone, but she could still damage their exposed faces. Unfortunately, whatever Lux had done to her soldiers was impressive — if somewhat horrifying — as despite multiple arrows lodged into their sinuses the enemy riders refused to go down.

Eventually, however, the damage did add up, and the riders decided it wasn't worth it to continue the fight, retreating instead.

Once they were gone, Birdie dropped down to where the others were. "Ev, are you okay?"

"I'll live," Ev responded. "You go on without me. I'll be okay here."

Birdie turned to Jax. "Get Ev to safety. The rest of us will deal with Lux Rosa."

"What? No!" Ev protested. "You'll need all the help you can get!"

"If what Vellic said is true, I'm the only one who can face her. The only help I need is with getting to her and making sure no one else interrupts our fight."

"Don't worry about us," Jax reassured her. "You go. I'll take care of Ev."

"I should stay, too," Tallis added, though clearly not happy about it. "Without magic, I'd just slow you down."

Birdie nodded in agreement, then got up to leave.

"Jax, you can't do this!" Ev almost shouted, but Birdie didn't stick around any longer to listen to the argument.

She motioned for the other soldiers to follow her, and they and Helcant obliged.

Once on the second floor and back inside, the path to the Hall of Champions was a simple one. With all fronts of the battle taking place far from this side of the Colosseum, the halls were all but empty. The only opposition was a quartet of guards stationed outside the great stone doors of the Hall of Champions, behind which waited the woman— no, the monster responsible for all of this.

The four guards formed a barricade across the hall the moment they spotted Birdie. Helcant, now fully exposed as a demon, rushed forward to place himself between Birdie and the guards, sword at the ready. He looked back at her with a grin.

"Leave the fools to us. Banish the wicked one back to whence she came!"

The five other soldiers accompanying Birdie took up positions alongside Helcant and, moving as one, they charged the guards.

The guards easily withstood the assault, but with six against four they had their hands full, giving Birdie the opportunity she needed to slip past them and push against the stone doors.

One of the guards attempted to stop her, but said guard was jumped by one of Birdie's allies, giving her just enough time to slip through.

No sooner had she entered the chamber than the sensation of magic abruptly returned as an unprecedented wall of energy blasted towards her. Diving to the ground, the wall of light struck so hard it cracked her armor and slammed the indestructible stone doors closed, leaving them glowing like the sun from the heat of the attack. The sensation of magic vanished as quickly as it had come, but fortunately, the self-repairing properties of Birdie's armor didn't seem to require magic to work — the damage to it mending almost immediately.

The moment having at last arrived, Birdie jumped back up to her feet and faced her attacker.

There, atop an ornate throne and surrounded by obscene amounts of iridescent shimmering light, sat Lux Rosa. She kept one hand thrust within the degradation and the other pointed at Birdie, her expression an odd mixture of smug confidence and absolute fury. In the brief flash of magic being active, Birdie had sensed several enchantments on her, the most problematic of which would be one of regeneration.

"So," Lux began, surprising Birdie by speaking to her, "we actually meet face to face. I must admit, you truly are impressive. Look at you, abandoning your fellow elementals all for the sake of victory."

"I didn't abandon anyone," Birdie countered. "I did what I had to do, so I could fight for them no matter what horrible things you did. You're a monster. You ended millions of lives without even a thought!"

"Spare me," Lux replied. "I did warn Dezeroth what would happen if he opposed me. Besides, it's not as if they won't get better. That's what immortals do, sweetie."

"That's beside the point!" Birdie erupted, not sure why she was even engaging in this conversation. "They had lives, too, and you took that away from them."

"So what?" Lux stood, her face now contorted. "Do you even realize what you are fighting for? It's beyond clear to me that your Syrus is completely inexperienced at breaking into the systems of other worlds. If he tries to take control away from the Masters and fails, they will know, and they will erase *everything!* Do you think this is the first time I've done this? I have succeeded in liberating nearly a dozen abandoned worlds, and I have profited *greatly* from it. I'll be the first to admit I've never encountered one quite like this one before, but if I have difficulty navigating its systems, your darling Syrus has all the hope of a moth in a forest fire!"

Birdie actually chuckled at that, and the look Lux gave appeared as if she was about to snap.

"You know," said Birdie, grinning, "you try so hard to get under my skin, but the one who's really insecure is you. It makes sense, really. After all, you're a seitti, right?'

Birdie cocked her head. "You're a seitti, yet the Syrus you're so threatened by and just can't seem to beat, he's just a prifae… and he's winning."

Lux exploded with more fury than all of Helcant's outbursts combined. The sensation of magic returned once more as Birdie felt Lux prepare the same attack as last time.

Lux roared as she unleashed another wall of light, but Birdie was ready with the second spell she'd learned for this battle.

Raising her own hand, Birdie cast a reflection spell in front of her. It unfortunately wouldn't be enough to fully bounce back an attack of that magnitude, so she also covered her exposed face with her other arm to protect herself.

Lux's spell collided with Birdie's, and with a deafening shatter the wall of reflection exploded as the bulk of Lux's attack bounced back at her and the rest scorched Birdie's armor, searing every inch of her face not protected by her arm.

When the light cleared, Birdie looked upon Lux Rosa to see her seething, her throne incinerated and the cloth of her outfit burned away to reveal white armor underneath. The blast had charred her skin black, but to Birdie's dismay Lux's wounds healed almost as quickly as they'd formed.

Lux thrust her arm back into the degradation, her eyes staring daggers at Birdie.

"Right, then," she almost whispered. "How about we try that again."

Lux raised her other arm and pointed two fingers at Birdie. Her magic spiked with a sensation Birdie's othermind didn't recognize, but Birdie knew she needed to dodge.

Casting the reflect spell just in case it would work, Birdie dove to the side as a rosy pink beam lanced across the room, piercing clean through the reflect and even through her armor.

Birdie winced in pain, the beam nicking her side deep enough to pierce her ribs but just missing her left lung.

Lux adjusted her aim and fired again, Birdie reacting in time to only receive a strike to her right shoulder.

Lux again shifted her aim.

Her chance of victory rapidly falling, Birdie had but one option remaining to her. She gave herself over to her othermind completely.

Lux fired.

In a single motion, Birdie twisted to take another hit to her left side while raising her right hand, ignoring the pain and casting her disorientation spell.

Lux reacted by shutting off magic again, Birdie's spell disappearing before it reached her.

Birdie bolted towards the stairs up to Lux's throne.

Lux turned magic back on and took aim once more.

Her arm already outstretched, Birdie fired another spell as soon as the magic was ready.

This time her spell hit, but so did Lux's, piercing straight through Birdie's right lung.

Her othermind ignored the pain and continued it's charge. Lux tried to fire again, but she couldn't aim properly, leaving her open for Birdie to land a full-forced tackle.

Taking back control from her othermind, Birdie smashed the clay pot against Lux and forced Syrus's creation into her as they both fell through the wall of degradation around the throne.

The world flashed white and Birdie felt her body spasm as the degradation washed over her. She crashed hard onto the floor. Laying on the ground,

Birdie suddenly found it very difficult to breath. Her othermind was gone —
vanished completely — leaving her to push through her injuries on her own.

Birdie coughed up blood as both she and Lux pushed themselves shakily to
their feet, one struggling from her injuries and the other from Birdie's spell.

Lux glared at Birdie from behind disheveled strands of blond hair, looking
like a feral animal as she launched and thankfully missed with her weakness
spell.

Pain or not, othermind or not, Birdie knew she had to finish this now.
Grabbing her enchantment breaker, she threw herself at Lux Rosa, aiming for
her throat.

Lux countered with a wild swing that cost her her balance but sent Birdie
once more to the ground.

Birdie found herself again choking on the blood in her lungs, her body
screaming for more oxygen.

Unable to get her body to do what she wanted, Birdie lay huddled over
helplessly as she felt her helmet ripped off of her. The next thing she knew,
powerful hands had wrapped themselves around her head, draining her of her
magic before bashing her skull against the ground.

"What's the matter?" she heard Lux practically foaming. "Having trouble
breathing? Maybe turning human wasn't such a good idea *after all!*"

Lux slammed Birdie's head to the ground again, then pressed her fingers
against Birdie's bleeding temple. Birdie closed her eyes as she felt Lux's magic
spike, only to be replaced with the sensation of her weakness spell?

Lux's vice-like grip loosened as her magic faded away.

Birdie opened her eyes to see Lux's face covered with shock and horror —
Grand Curate Vellic standing behind her.

Seizing on the opportunity, Birdie summoned the last of her strength to
push the weakened Lux Rosa off of her and to the ground. Birdie lunged
forward and, raising her enchantment breaker high over her head, plunged it
into Lux's neck.

All of the enchantments Lux had placed on herself vanished in an instant,
leaving the would-be tyrant bleeding out at the foot of her own throne.

"It's over…" Birdie barely panted out, "Syrus's tool — you won't be coming
back."

Lux's face twisted from shock to fury to a maniacal grin.

"So… be it." she somehow choked out. "You will see—"

Whatever she was going to say, Birdie didn't get to hear it. A beam of energy finished Lux off, the Radiant vanishing in a flash of light. Only a single shining orb remained.

The sound of armored footsteps made Birdie look up. Vellic, flanked by two heavily wounded soldiers, towered over her with a sword in his hand. His eyes told her she should have felt fear, but she had succeeded in her mission. It didn't matter what happened next.

She'd won.

Vellic pointed his sword at her. "I must thank you for ridding us of that deceiver, but I'm afraid the world you wish to bring about is not one I can stand for. We will yet find a way to rid Doxla of immortals, and with you out of the way—"

Vellic stopped and looked down at his chest, the head of a bloody arrow having burst out right through his heart.

The two soldiers accompanying him spun around, one to be greeted with an explosive blast of light to the face and the other a spear of ice. The soldiers fell to the ground, and Vellic right after, landing right at Birdie's feet.

Beyond them, Ev, Jax, and Tallis had just burst through the door, the sight of them bringing a smile to Birdie's lips. Ev rushed over, her augmented healing magic making short work of Birdie's would-be fatal wounds.

"I thought I told you to get to safety," Birdie said after spitting out the last of the blood.

"Yeah, right, did you really think we'd just leave you?" Ev asked. "Besides, we saw Vellic follow you after breaking his soldiers out of Tallis's ice."

"We would have gotten here sooner," Jax added, "but we wanted to keep our distance to see what he was up to. Ev couldn't move fast anyway. It wasn't until we heard that explosion that we realized magic was working again."

"What happened to Helcant?" Birdie asked.

Ev's eyes opened wide and she quickly bolted back out of the room.

Jax gave Birdie her answer. "Your demon friend was pretty hurt, but he told us you needed help first. I'm glad he did."

"Yeah, me too," Birdie said as Jax and Tallis helped her back up.

Standing once more, she waited for Ev, Helcant, and one of the other soldiers to join them. Once they'd arrived, they all looked down at the orb that was Lux Rosa's Heart.

Ev spoke first. "I guess this means it's finally over."

"Not unless Syrus's little device works, it isn't," Birdie responded tiredly, "and even if it does, we still have to get out of here. There are still a thousand soldiers out there wanting to kill us."

"Oh, I believe that won't be a problem," a deep voice from the hallway called in.

Birdie was relieved to see Syrus appear, his outfit in tatters but he in good health, a small squad of soldiers at his heels.

"How is it not a problem?" Jax asked. "Birdie's right. Most of Lux's soldiers are still fighting."

"My boy," Syrus stated, using his rod as a cane as he climbed the stairs to Lux's collection of degradation, "you might be surprised by how much a broken morale can do to turn a battle."

Syrus stopped and pointed his rod at Vellic. "Speaking of which, who is that? He looks rather important."

Jax answered. "He called himself the Grand Curate. I'm pretty sure he was in charge before Lux Rosa came along. Said his name was Vellic."

Syrus smiled. "Perfect."

He then placed his hand into the swirling shimmers and entered into that vacant stare, feeling around for a while.

"Ah, there it is," he said at last. "I'd have been surprised if Lux Rosa hadn't created such a tool. How nice of her to even configure it to only work around the Colosseum for me."

The next time he opened his mouth, his voice seemed to come from everywhere and nowhere at once.

"Attention, soldiers of Vellic and Lux Rosa. Both of your leaders are dead. Lux Rosa's power has been turned against her, and she will not revive. Your walls have been breached, your forces overwhelmed. The Colosseum now belongs to Lady Eclipse. Surrender now, and you will be spared. Refuse and be slaughtered. The choice is yours."

Syrus removed his hand from the degradation and smiled down at the others. "That should take care of that problem. As for the other one…" he said, jumping down from the throne and landing next to Lux's Heart.

He pulled out a small bit of degradation he'd kept hidden beneath his cloak, interacted with it for a moment, then simply said, "Ah, there we are. Goodbye, Máõk-Tréé."

As soon as the words left his mouth, Lux's Heart vanished, and Birdie breathed a sigh of relief.

Finally, it really was over.

Chapter 22

Three days after the defeat of Lux Rosa, the skies had cleared, inviting warm sunlight to shine down on the still barren land surrounding the Colosseum. Most of Lux's soldiers had surrendered after Syrus's announcement. Those who did so had been captured and imprisoned in the Colosseum's own cells as they waited to have their power stripped from them once Syrus could figure out Lux's weakness spell. No longer needed, Zun-Roven had withdrawn the bulk of his forces, leaving the Shadow Guard in charge of cleanup. Jax had more or less taken charge on that front. Syrus was too busy digging through Lux's degradation, and Birdie — she didn't exactly feel up to taking on any more responsibilities at the moment.

On the far side of a small hill a few hundred yards from the Colosseum, Birdie sat next to one of the few patches of green in the area where she stared at a single fragrant flower listing gently in the breeze. As much of a mixed blessing as it was, the ability to smell was one of the few parts of her new human existence she overall enjoyed.

The sound of footsteps alerted her to Ev's approach. Birdie didn't bother looking up and instead simply waited for Ev to take a seat beside her.

"How are you holding up?" Ev asked Birdie. "You've been really down ever since the battle ended. Did something happen when you were with Lux Rosa?"

Birdie sighed and crossed her arms over her knees. "When I pushed Lux Rosa away from her degradation, I ended up passing though it. I lost my othermind."

"Oh," Ev said, her tone unsure. "Um, can't Syrus get it back?"

Birdie shook her head. "I already asked him. The only reason he could connect it to me before was because I was an empty shell when he found me. If he tried it now, it would erase part of who I am."

Ev looked at Birdie. "Wow, I'm sorry Birdie. But, at least you don't have to worry about it taking over you anymore, right?"

Birdie shook her head again. "Lux Rosa lied about that. My othermind was never going to take over me. It made me who I am. It was always with me. I don't even know how I'm going to live without it."

Sympathy in her eyes, Ev placed a hand on Birdie's arm. "Hey, I know your othermind was amazing, but you can't tell me that everything you've ever done was because of it. Was it your othermind who decided to fight that squid to save me that one time I got sick?"

Birdie looked over at Ev, knowing full well what she was trying to do. "No, but it was my othermind that made it possible for me to do it."

"Your othermind may have made it easier, but Jax helped, too, didn't he? I guarantee he doesn't have any 'othermind.' If he can learn how to get dressed in the morning, let alone fight a giant squid, I'm sure you can learn how to get by without your othermind, too."

Birdie cracked a smile at that. "I guess you've got a point there."

"Of course I do," Ev smiled back. "Don't you worry. Whatever happens, I've got your back. We all do."

Ev rubbed Birdie's arm, and Birdie felt a warmth enter her cheeks. She placed one of her hands on Ev's and squeezed it gently. She may have sacrificed both her body and her othermind, but in the end, she'd protected what really mattered to her.

"Anyway," Ev said after a few moments, "Syrus says he finally found something. He wanted to share it with all of us."

Birdie perked up. "Really? Did he find out how to take control away from the Masters?"

Ev tilted her head. "Somehow, I don't think that's what this is, but he did want to keep it a surprise. Whatever it is, it sounds like a pretty big deal."

Birdie sighed and pushed herself to her feet.

"Alright," she said, cocking her head. "Where is he? Please say he's not back in the Hall of Champions."

"Actually, he's just over there," Ev pointed after climbing a few steps to the top of the hill.

Birdie walked over and followed Ev's finger to a small gathering not far away. Jax, Tallis, Helcant, and Gare stood around Syrus, all looking in Birdie's direction.

"I guess I don't have a choice, do I?"

"Sure you do," Ev shrugged. "You can come with me, or you can get stared at for the rest of the day."

Birdie rolled her eyes. "Wow. Such freedom. Maybe for supper I'll have the choice between bread and bricks."

"Oh, just come on," Ev said, grabbing Birdie by the arm.

The others all smiled at Birdie's approach.

"Finally," Helcant proclaimed. "Why do you keep us waiting? Do you not wish to know the Masters' secrets?"

"Secrets? What secrets?" Birdie asked.

Syrus smirked, his hands resting on his jeweled rod. "That's what we will soon find out together. Though neither Lux Rosa nor myself were able to make significant progress in cracking the Masters' most fundamental systems on our own, I have found something of hers that I can combine with my own work to sidestep one of the barriers separating Doxla from the reality that lies beyond it. It is a single wedge in a crack that may ultimately lead to salvation. More importantly, I will be able to bring in some of my own tools from beyond your world to share with you. No longer will I be the only one capable of interfacing with the Masters' systems. Anyone whom I grant this capability with will be able to as well."

Tallis put up his hands. "Wait, whoa, wait. Are you saying *nepacs* will be able to control the power of the *Masters?*"

Syrus turned his head halfway toward Tallis. "To an extent. It will be several years yet before we can truly wrest control of Doxla from its creators. With some assistance from capable minds, however, I believe it may be possible to succeed before the next awakening of Apollyon."

"Are we sure that's a good idea?" asked Jax. "That kind of power shouldn't be given to just anyone."

Syrus laughed. "Of course it shouldn't. That's the whole reason your world's in the shape it's in to begin with." He shook his head. "No. Though this will likely change in the future, I have but one candidate in mind at the moment."

Birdie tensed as all eyes shifted to her. She frowned and held up her hands.

"Oh, no. Don't you even think of putting this on me. I already have enough to deal with thanks to you."

"I know," responded Syrus. "I wasn't referring to you."

Birdie blinked. She hadn't expected that, and from the look of everyone's faces neither had anyone else. "You weren't? Then who—"

Without a word, Syrus looked directly at Ev.

Ev stepped back. "Wait, me?"

"Of course," Syrus responded. "Though you may not have worked with anther or degradation per se, you have aided me in my experiments for some time and understand the general ideas behind how your world's systems work.

I know you are trustworthy, and though you are young, you are far more responsible than most I have encountered. I can think of no one better to aid me, and certainly no one whom I can more trust."

"I-I…" Ev stammered.

"Now, hold on," Jax stepped forward. "I get that Ev likes studying, but—"

"Do *you* know what a modal schism is?" Syrus challenged.

"I, uh…" Jax fumbled.

"Ev, would you care to enlighten your brother?"

"It's…" Ev cleared her throat. "It's a location where the physics of a world change suddenly. It's an artificial boundary to make different regions behave differently."

"And they are the source of most degradation in a world." Syrus finished, smiling triumphantly at Jax.

"Okay, fine," Jax said, crossing his arms and glancing briefly at Ev. He sighed. "I guess you've got a point. We can't risk another Lux Rosa happening, and if Ev helping you means getting things done sooner, then I'm all for it — if she is, at least."

"I…" Ev looked over at Birdie.

Birdie gave her a half shrug and a smile. "I gotta say I'm with Jax. It's long past time that we fixed this mess the Masters left us. I say go for it."

"Hell, yeah," Gare crowed. "Then you can finally get rid of all those monsters you hate so much."

That lit up a fire in Ev's eyes.

"Yeah, good point." She turned to Syrus. "You can count on me."

Syrus smiled, tilting his rod forward. "I knew I could. It will take some getting used to, but with diligence and dedication, I have confidence that you will adapt and thrive."

Tallis rubbed the back of his head nervously, "Um, do you think there's room on your team for one more?"

Syrus turned his head toward Tallis once again. "Perhaps. Only time will tell."

"Yes!" Helcant shouted excitedly. "Soon we shall all take hold of the Masters' power!"

"I… don't know about that," Syrus stated. "The control I will give you will only last for a time. Once we have taken official ownership of the world away from the Masters, I will transfer it to those who I know can be trusted to care for it, even if they do so in a hands-off manner. When that happens," Syrus turned his attention back to Birdie, "I will also leave this world, and you may step down as Radiant. You will finally be able to live the carefree life you always wanted to."

Birdie took a brief look at the faces of her friends around her. So much had changed since her reincarnation ten years ago — so much of it for the worse, so much of it for the better, and so much just, different.

She turned her attention back to Syrus. "You know, I'm more than willing to give up being Radiant, but my life? I think I'm happy with it exactly as it is."

Coming Soon:

The Soul of the Radiant

Ev found herself on the rocky shore that circled Doxla's oceans. Looking around, she spotted portals as far as she could see, with countless people of all races pouring through them and out through the tears in the world's boundary. Before her sat one such tear — the landscape beyond it shrouded in darkness.

Ev recalled the various anther fields Syrus had taught her, then plunged on through to the other side. Immediately, she felt her magic and strength leave her as the air of her world billowed past into the cold darkness. She also felt the anther all around her, and she channeled her will to create a region of warmth as large as she could manage. She then tried her best to tell the surrounding space to produce breathable air.

Whether by her efforts or not, someone must have succeeded. Lights from other anthermancers sparked to life around her. Ev joined in, producing a giant bubble of light that followed her as she moved and revealing a twisted, roiling gray landscape.

She ran deeper into the darkness, her sense of time distorted in the chaos, until she felt it — a wave of heat crashing into her back. Looking back, Ev shielded her eyes against the blinding blaze erupting from each of the tears in Doxla's boundary.

Then, just as quickly as it had come, the blaze vanished, leaving only darkness in its place.

Doxla was gone.

Ev stood frozen in place — a still figure in a sea of statues all processing the loss that they had all known was coming, yet still a loss none of them were ready for.

After a few minutes of standing in silence, Ev felt Birdie place a hand on her arm. "We need to keep moving. It's up to us to keep these people safe now."

Ev swallowed, then nodded. They'd need to search to find a place to make shelter. To do that, she needed to figure out how to make portals out here. They were one of few things that were supposed to work similarly to how they did within Doxla, so with just a little bit of time….

A bright light bathed the entire area. Her thoughts vanished as a terrible fear gripped her. Heart pounding, she forced her head upwards to see the source of the light.

There, high above them all, floated a lone figure in pearly armor.

The Master, Sylvra, tilted his gaze downward.

Before Ev could even blink, the wasteland around her vanished. The people around her vanished. Birdie and Jax vanished.

Everything disappeared in a blinding flash of white.

For more information about upcoming books in this series and others, check out D. S. Kogler's website at

dskogler-books.com

While you're there, be sure to sign up for the mailing list as well!

www.ingramcontent.com/pod-product-compliance
Lightning Source LLC
Chambersburg PA
CBHW021122190726
48288CB00008B/2452